W9-BVS-583

By Lois McMaster Bujold

THE SHARING KNIFE: LEGACY
THE SHARING KNIFE: BEGUILEMENT
THE HALLOWED HUNT
PALADIN OF SOULS
THE CURSE OF CHALION
DIPLOMATIC IMMUNITY
A CIVIL CAMPAIGN
KOMARR
MEMORY
MIRROR DANCE
BROTHERS IN ARMS
BORDERS OF INFINITY
ETHAN OF ATHOS
CETAGANDA
THE VOR GAME
THE WARRIOR'S APPRENTICE
BARRAYAR
SHARDS OF HONOR
FALLING FREE
THE SPIRIT RING

Forthcoming

THE SHARING KNIFE: PASSAGE

LOIS McMASTER BUJOLD

THE
SHARING
KNIFE

∽ VOLUME TWO ∽
LEGACY

An Imprint of HarperCollinsPublishers

This book is a work of fiction. The characters, incidents, and dialogue are drawn from the author's imagination and are not to be construed as real. Any resemblance to actual events or persons, living or dead, is entirely coincidental.

EOS
An Imprint of HarperCollins*Publishers*
10 East 53rd Street
New York, New York 10022-5299

Copyright © 2007 by Lois McMaster Bujold
Excerpt from *The Sharing Knife: Passage* copyright © 2008 by Lois McMaster Bujold
Map by Lois McMaster Bujold
Cover art by Julie Bell
ISBN: 978-0-06-113906-2
www.eosbooks.com

First Eos paperback printing: May 2008
First Eos hardcover printing: July 2007

HarperCollins® and Eos® are registered trademarks of HarperCollins Publishers.

Printed in the U.S.A.

10 9 8 7 6 5 4 3 2 1

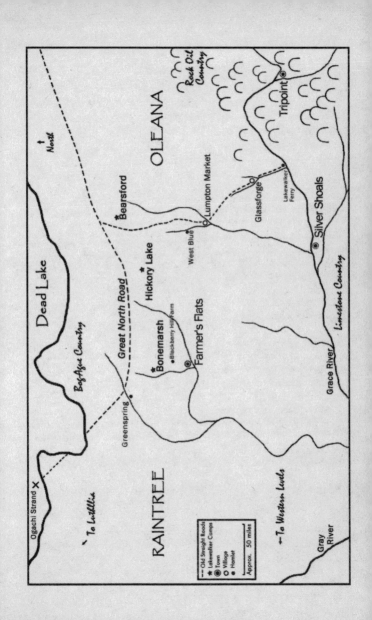

THE
SHARING
KNIFE
LEGACY

1

Dag had been married for a whole two hours, and was still light-headed with wonder. The weighted ends of the wedding cord coiling around his upper arm danced in time with the lazy trot of his horse. Riding by his side, Fawn—*my new bride,* now there was a phrase to set a man's mind melting—met his smile with happy eyes.

My farmer bride. It should have been impossible. There would be trouble about that, later.

Trouble yesterday, trouble tomorrow. But no trouble now. Now, in the light of the loveliest summer afternoon he ever did see, was only a boundless contentment.

Once the first half dozen miles were behind them, Dag found both his and Fawn's urgency to be gone from the wedding party easing. They passed through the last village on the northern river road, after which the wagon way became more of a two-rut track, and the remaining farms grew farther apart, with more woods between them. He let a few more miles pass, till he was sure they were out of range of any potential retribution or practical jokers, then began keeping an eye out for a spot to make camp. If a Lakewalker patroller with this much woods to choose from couldn't hide from farmers, something was wrong. *Secluded,* he decided, was a better watchword still.

At length, he led Fawn down to the river at a rocky ford, then upstream for a time till they came to where a clear creek, gurgling down from the eastern ridge, joined the flow. He turned Copperhead up it for a good quarter mile till he found a pretty glade, all mossy by the stream and surrounded by tall trees and plenty of them; and, his groundsense guaranteed, no other person for a mile in any direction. Of necessity, he had to let Fawn unsaddle the horses and set up the site. It was a simple enough task, merely laying out their bedrolls and making just enough of a fire to boil water for tea. Still, she cast an observant eye at him as he lay with his back against a broad beech bole and plucked irritably at the sling supporting his right arm with the hook replacing his left hand.

"You have a job," she encouraged him. "You're on guard against the mosquitoes, ticks, chiggers, and blackflies."

"And squirrels," he added hopefully.

"We'll get to them."

Food did not have to be caught or skinned or cooked, just unwrapped and eaten till they couldn't hold any more, although Fawn tried his limits. Dag wondered if this new mania for feeding him was a Bluefield custom no one had mentioned, or just a lingering effect of the excitement of the day, as she tried to find her way into her farmwifely tasks without, actually, a farm in which to set them. But when he compared this to many a cold, wet, hungry, lonely, exhausted night on some of the more dire patrols in his memory, he thought perhaps he'd wandered by strange accident into some paradise out of a song, and bears would come out tonight to dance around their fire in celebration.

He looked up to find Fawn inching nearer, without, for a change, provender in her hands. "It's not dark yet," she sighed.

He cast her a slow blink, to tease. "And dark is needed for what?"

"Bedtime!"

"Well, I admit it's a help for sleeping. Are you that sleepy? It's been a tiring day. We could just roll over and . . ."

She caught on, and poked him in reproof. "Ha! Are you sleepy?"

"No chance." Despite the sling he managed a pounce that drew her into his lap. The prey did not precisely struggle, though it did wriggle enchantingly. Once she was within kissing range, they found occupation for a little. But then she grew grave and sat up to touch the cord wrapping her left wrist.

"How odd that this all should feel harder, now."

He kissed her hair beneath his chin. "There's a weight of expectation that wasn't there before, I suppose. I didn't . . ." He hesitated.

"Hm?"

"I rode into West Blue, onto your family's farm, last week thinking . . . I don't know. That I would be a clever Lake-walker persuader and get my way. I expected to change their lives. I didn't expect them to change my life right back. I didn't used to be *Fawn's patroller,* still less *Fawn's husband,* but now I am. That's a ground transformation, in case you didn't realize. It doesn't just happen in the cords. It happens in our deep selves." He gave a nod toward his left sleeve hiding the loop binding his own arm. "Maybe the hard feeling is just shyness for the two new people we've become."

"Hm." She settled down, briefly reassured. But then sat up again, biting her lip the way she did when about to tackle some difficult subject, usually head-on. "Dag. About my ground."

"I love your ground."

Her lips twitched in a smile, but then returned to serious-ness. "It's been over four weeks since . . . since the malice. I'm healing up pretty good inside, I think."

"I think so, too."

"Do you suppose we could . . . I mean, tonight because . . . we haven't ever yet . . . not that I'm *complaining,* mind you. Erm. That pattern in their ground you said women get when they can have babies. Do I have it tonight?"

"Not yet. I don't think it'll be much longer till your body's back to its usual phases, though."

"So we could. I mean. Do it in the usual way. Tonight."

"Tonight, Spark, we can do it any way you want. Within the range of the physically possible, that is," he added prudently.

She snickered. "I do wonder how you *learned* all those tricks."

"Well, not all at once, absent gods forfend. You pick up this and that over the years. I suspect people everywhere keep reinventing all the basics. There's only so much you can do with a body. Successfully and comfortably, that is. Leaving aside stunts."

"Stunts?" she said curiously.

"We're leaving them aside," he said definitely. "One broken arm is enough."

"One too many, I think." Her brows drew down in new worry. "Um. I was envisioning you up on your elbows, but really, I think maybe not. It doesn't exactly sound comfortable, and I wouldn't want you to hurt your arm and have to start healing all over, and besides, if you slipped, you really would squash me like a bug."

It took him a moment to puzzle out her concern. "Ah, not a problem. We just switch sides, top to bottom. If you can ride a horse, which I note you do quite well, you can ride me. And you can squash me all you want."

She thought this through. "I'm not sure I can do this right."

"If you do something really wrong, I promise I'll scream in pain and let you know."

She grinned, if with a slight tinge of dismay.

Kissing blended into undressing, and again, to his mixed regret and entertainment, Fawn had to do most of the work. He thought she was much too brisk and businesslike in getting her own clothes off, although the view when she finished was splendid. The setting sun reached fingers of golden light into the glade that caressed her body as she flickered in and out of the leaf shadows; she might well have been one of those legendary female spirits who were supposed to step out of trees and beguile the unwary traveler. The way her sweet breasts moved not *quite* in time with the rest of her was fair riveting to his eye, too. She folded up his astonishing wedding shirt with fully the care he would have wished, tucking it away. He lay back on his bedroll and let her pull off his trousers and drawers with all her considerable determination. She folded them up too, and came and sat, no, plunked, again beside him. The after-wobble was delightful.

"Arm harness. On or off?"

"Hm. Off, I think. Don't want to risk jabbing you in a distracted moment." The disquieting memory of her bleeding fingers weaving her wedding cord flitted through his mind, and he became conscious again of it wound around his upper arm, and the tiny hum of its live ground. *Her* live ground.

With practiced hands, she whisked the hook harness away onto the top of the clothes pile, and he marveled anew at how easy it was all becoming with her.

Except for, blight it all again, having no working hand. The sling had gone west just before the shirt, and he shifted his right arm and attempted to wriggle his fingers. *Ouch.* No. Not enough useful motion there yet. Inside his splints and wrappings, his skin, damp from the sweat of the warm day, was itching. He couldn't *touch*. All right, there was a certain amount he could do with his tongue— especially right now, as she returned and nuzzled up to him—but getting it to the right place at the right time was going to be an insurmountable challenge, in this position.

She withdrew her lips from his and began working her way down his body. It was lovely but almost redundant; it had been well over a week, after all, and . . . *It used to be years, and I scarcely blinked.* He tried to relax and let himself be made love to. Relaxation wasn't exactly what was happening. His hips twitched as Fawn's full attention arrived at his nether regions. She swung her leg over, turned to face him, reached down, and began to try to position herself. Stopped.

"Urk?" he inquired politely. Some such noise, anyway.

Her face was a little pinched. "This should be working better."

"Oil?" he croaked.

"I shouldn't need oil for *this*, should I?"

Not if I had a hand to ready you nicely. "Hang *should,* do what works. You shouldn't have that uncomfortable look on your face, either."

"Hm." She extracted herself, padded over to his saddle-bags, and rummaged within. Good view from the back, too, as she bent over . . . A mutter of mild triumph, "Ah." She padded back, pausing to frown and rub the sole of one bare foot on her other shin after stepping on a pebble. *Was* this a time to stop for pebbles . . . ?

Back she came, sliding over him. Small hands slicked him, which made him jolt. He did not allow himself to plunge upward. Let her find her way in her own time. She attempted to do so.

She was getting a very determined look again. "Maiden-heads don't *regrow,* do they . . . ?"

"Shouldn't think so."

"I didn't think it was supposed to hurt the second time."

"Probably just unaccustomed muscles. Not in condition. Need more exercise." It was driving him just short of mad to have no hands to grasp her hips and guide her home.

She blinked, taking in this thought. "Is that true, or more of your slick patroller persuasion?"

"Can't it be both?"

She grinned, shifted her angle, then looked brighter, and said, "Ah! There we go."

Indeed, we do. He gasped, as she slid slowly and very, very tightly down upon him. "Yes . . . that's . . . very . . . nice."

She muttered, "They get whole babies through these parts. Surely it's supposed to stretch more."

"Time. Give it." Blight it, at this point in the usual proceedings, *she* would be the one who couldn't form words anymore. They were out of rhythm tonight. He was losing his wits, and she was getting chatty. "Fine now."

Her brows drew down in puzzlement. "Should this be like taking turns, or not?"

"Uhthink . . ." He swallowed to find speech. "Hope it's good for you. Suspect it's better for me. 'S *exquisite* for me right now."

"Oh, that's all right, then." She sat for a moment, adjusting. It would likely not be a good idea at this point to screech and convulse and beg for motion; that would just alarm her. He didn't want her alarmed. She might jump up and run off, which would be tragic. He wanted her relaxed and confident and . . . there, she was starting to smile again. She observed, "You have a funny look on your face."

"I'll bet."

Her smile widened. Too gently and tentatively, she at last began to move. *Absent gods be praised.* "After all," she said, continuing a line of thought of which he had long lost track, "Mama had *twins,* and she isn't that much taller than me. Though Aunt Nattie said she was pretty alarmin' toward the end."

"What?" said Dag, confused.

"Twins. Run in Mama's side of the family. Which made it really unfair of her to blame Papa, Aunt Nattie said, but I guess she wasn't too reasonable by then."

Which remark, of course, immediately made his reeling mind jump to the previously unimagined idea of Spark bearing twins, *his,* which made his eyes cross. Further. He really hadn't even wrapped his mind around the notion of their having one child, yet. *Considering just what you're doing right now, perhaps you should, old patroller.*

Whatever this peculiar digression did to him—his spine

felt like an overdrawn bow with its string about to snap—it seemed to relax Fawn. Her eyes darkening, she commenced to rock with more assurance. Her ground, blocked earlier by the discomfort and uncertainty, began to flow again. *Finally.* But he wasn't going to last much longer at this rate. He let his hips start to keep time with hers.

"If I only had a working hand to get down there, we *would* share this turn . . ." His fingers twitched in frustration.

"Another good reason to leave it be to heal faster," she gasped. "Put that poor busted arm back on the blanket."

"Ngh!" He wanted to touch her *so much.* Groundwork? A mosquito's worth was not likely to be enough. *Left-handed groundwork?* He remembered the glass bowl, sliding and swirling back together. That had been no mere mosquito. Would she find it perverse, frightening, horrifying, to be touched so? Could he even . . . ? This was her *wedding night.* She must not recall it with disappointment. He laid his left arm down across his belly, pointed at their juncture. *Consider it a strengthening exercise for the ghost hand. Beats scraping hides all hollow, doesn't it? Just . . . there.*

"Oh!" Her eyes shot wide, and she leaned forward to stare into his face. "What did you just *do*?"

"Experiment," he gritted out. Surely his eyes were as wide and wild as hers. "Think the broken right has been doing something to stir up my left ground. Like, not like?"

"Not sure. More . . . ?"

"Oh, *yeah* . . ."

"Oh. *Yeah.* That's . . ."

"Good?"

Her only reply was a wordless huff. And a rocking that grew frantic, then froze. Which was fine because now he did drive up, as that bowstring snapped at last, and everything unwound in white fire.

He didn't think he'd passed out, but he seemed to come

to with her draped across his chest wheezing and laughing wildly. "Dag! That was, that was . . . could you do that all along? Were you just saving it for a wedding present, or what?"

"I have no idea," he confessed. "Never done anything like that before. I'm not even sure what I *did* do."

"Well, it was quite . . . quite nice." She sat up and pushed back her hair to deliver this in a judicious tone, but then dissolved into helpless laughter again.

"I'm dizzy. Feel like I'm about to fall down."

"You *are* lying down."

"Very fortunate."

She tumbled down into the cradle of his left arm and snuggled in for a wordless time. Dag didn't quite nap, but he wouldn't have called it being awake, either. Bludgeoned, perhaps. Eventually, she roused herself enough to get them cleaned up and dressed in clothes to sleep in, because the blue twilight shadows were cooling as night slid in, seeping through the woods from the east. By the time she cuddled down again beside him, under the blanket this time, he was fully awake, staring up through the leaves at the first stars.

Her slim little fingers traced the furrows above his brows. "Are you all right? *I'm* all right."

He managed a smile and kissed the fingers in passing. "I admit, I've unsettled myself a bit. You know how shaken I was after that episode with the glass bowl."

"Oh, you haven't made yourself sick again with this, have you?"

"No, in fact. Although this wasn't near such a draining effort. Pretty, um, stimulating, actually. Thing is . . . that night I mended the bowl, that was the first time I experienced that, that, call it a ghost hand. I tried several times after, secretly, to make it emerge again, but nothing happened. Couldn't figure it out. In the parlor, you were upset, I was upset, I wanted to, I don't know. Fix things. I wasn't upset just now, but I sure was in, um, a heightened mood. *Flying,* your aunt Nattie called it. Except now I've fallen back down, and the ghost hand's gone again."

He glanced over to find her up on one elbow, looking at him with the same interested expression as ever. Happy eyes. Not shocked or scared or repelled. He said, "You don't mind that it's, well, strange? You think this is just the same as all the other things I do, don't you?"

Her brows rose in consideration. "Well, you summon horses and bounce mosquitoes and make firefly lamps and kill malices and you know where everyone is for a country mile all around, and I don't know what you did to Reed and Rush last night, but the effect was sure magical today. And what you do for me I can't hardly begin to describe, not decently anyhow. How do you know it isn't?"

He opened his mouth, then closed it, squinting at his question turned upside down.

She cocked her head, and continued, "You said Lake-walker folks' groundsense doesn't come in all at once, and not at all when they're younger. Maybe this is just something you should have had all along, that got delayed. Or maybe it's something you should have now, growing right on time."

"There's a new thought." He lay back, frowning at the blameless evening sky. His life was full of new things, lately. Some of them were new problems, but he had to admit, a lot of the tired, dreary, old problems had been thoroughly shaken out. He began to suspect that it wasn't only the breaking of his right arm that was triggering this bizarre development. The farmer girl was plowing his ground, it seemed. What was that phrase? *Breaking new land.* A very literal form of ground transformation. He blinked to chase away these twisting notions before his head started to ache.

"So, that's twice," said Fawn, pursuing the thought. "So it can happen, um, more than once, anyhow. And it seems you don't have to be unhappy for it to work. That's real promising."

"I'm not sure I can do it again."

"That'd be a shame," she said in a meditative tone. But her eyes were merry. "So, try it again next time and we'll see, eh? And if not, as it seems you have no end of ingenuity in a bedroll, we'll just do something else, and that'll be good, too." She gave a short, decisive nod.

"Well," he said in a bemused voice. "That's settled."

She flopped down again, nestling in close, hugging him tight. "You'd best believe it."

To Fawn's gladness they lingered late in the glade the next morning, attempting to repeat some of last night's trials; some were successful, some not. Dag couldn't seem to induce his ghost hand again—maybe he was too relaxed?—which appeared to leave him someplace between disappointment and relief. As Fawn had guessed, he found other ways to please her, although she thought he was trying a bit too hard, which made her worry for him, which didn't help *her* relax.

She fed him a right fine breakfast, though, and they mounted up and found their way back to the river road by noon. In the late afternoon, they at last left the valley, Dag taking an unmarked track off to the west. They passed through a wide stretch of wooded country, sometimes in single file on twisty trails, sometimes side by side on broader tracks. Fawn was soon lost—well, if she struck east, she'd be sure to find the river again sometime, so she supposed she was only out of her reckoning for going forward, not back—but Dag seemed not to be.

For two days they pushed through similar woodland. *Pushed* might be too strong a term, with their early stops and late starts. Twice Dag persuaded his ghost hand to return, to her startled delight, twice he didn't, for no obvious reason either way, which plainly puzzled him deeply. She wondered at his spooky choice of name for this ground ability. He worried over it equally afterwards whether or not he succeeded, and Fawn finally decided that it had been so long since he hadn't known exactly what he was doing all the time, he'd forgotten what it felt like to be blundering around in the dark, which made her sniff with a certain lack of sympathy.

She gradually became aware that he was dragging his feet on this journey, despite his worries about beating his patrol back to Hickory Lake, and not only for the obvious reason of extending their bedroll time together. Fawn herself was growing intensely curious about what lay ahead, and inclined to move along more briskly, but it wasn't till the third morning that they did so, and that only because of a threatened change in the weather. The high wispy clouds that both farmers and Lakewalkers called horsefeathers had moved in from the west last night, making fabulous pink streaks in the sunset indigo, and the air today was close and hazy, both signs of a broad storm brewing. When it blew through, it would bring a sparkling day in its wake, but was like to be violent before then. Dag said they might beat it to the lake by late afternoon.

Around noon the woods opened out in some flat meadowlands bordering a creek, with a dual track, and Fawn found herself riding alongside Dag again. "You once said you'd tell me the tale of Utau and Razi if you were either more drunk or more sober. You look pretty sober now."

He smiled briefly. "Do I? Well, then."

"Whenever I can get you to talk about your people, it helps me form up some better idea what I'm heading into."

"I'm not sure Utau's tale will help much, that way."

"Maybe not, but at least I won't say something stupid through not knowing any better."

He shrugged, though he amended, "Unknowing, maybe. Never stupid."

"Either way, I'd still end up red-faced."

"You blush prettily, but I give you the point. Well. Utau was string-bound for a good ten years to Sarri Otter, but they had no children. It happens that way, sometimes, and even Lakewalker groundsense can't tell why. Both his family and hers were pressuring them to cut their strings and try again with different mates—"

"Wait, what? People can cut their marriage strings? What does that mean, and how does it work?" Fawn wrapped a protective right hand around her left wrist, then put her palm hastily back on her thigh, kicking Grace's plump sides to encourage her to step along and keep up with Copperhead's longer legs.

"What leads up to a string-cutting varies pretty wildly with the couple, but lack of children after a good long time trying is considered a reason to part without dishonor to either side. More difficult if only one partner assents to the cutting; then the argument can spread out to both their families' tents and get very divisive. Or tedious, if you have to listen to them all go on. But if both partners agree to it, the ceremony is much like string-binding, in reverse. The wedding cords are taken off and rewrapped around both partners' arms, only with the opposite twist, and knotted, but then the string-blesser takes a knife and cuts the knot apart, and each takes back the pieces of their own."

Fawn wondered if that knife was carved of bone.

"The grounds drain out back to their sources, and, well, it's done. People usually burn the dead strings, after." He glanced aside at her deepening frown. "Don't farmer marriages ever come apart?"

"I think sometimes, but not often. The land and the families hold them together. And there's considered to be a shame in the failure. People do up and leave, sometimes, men or women, but it's more like chewing off your leg to escape a trap. You have to leave so much behind, so much work. So much hope, too, I suppose." She added, "Though

I heard tell of one marriage down south of the village that came apart again in two weeks. The bride and all her things just got carted right back to her family, being hardly settled in yet, and the entry was scratched out in the family book. Nobody would ever explain to me why, although the twins and Fletch were snickering over it, so I suppose it might have had to do with bed problems, though she wasn't pregnant by someone else or anything. It was all undone right quick with no argument, though, so someone must have had something pretty big to apologize for, I'd guess."

"Sounds like." His brows rose as he considered this in curiosity, possibly of the more idle sort. "Anyway. Utau and Sarri loved each other despite their sorrow, and didn't want to part. And they were both good friends with Utau's cousin Razi. I'm not just sure who persuaded who to what, but one day Razi up and moved all his things into Sarri's tent with the pair of them. And a few months later Sarri was pregnant. And, to top the matter, not only did Razi get string-bound with Sarri, Razi and Utau got string-bound with each other, so the circle went all the way around and each ended up wearing the strings of both the others. All Otters now. And everyone's families went around for a while looking like their heads ached, but then there came this beautiful girl baby, and a while after, this bright little boy, that all three just dote on, and everyone else pretty much gave up the worrying. Although not the lewd speculation, naturally."

Fawn laughed. "Naturally." Her mind started to drift off in a little lewd speculating of its own, abruptly jerked back to attention when Dag continued in his thoughtful-voice.

"I've never made a child, myself. I was always very careful, if not always for the same reasons. There's not a few who have trouble when they switch over from trying to miss that target to trying to hit it. All their prior care seeming a great waste of a sudden. The sort of useless thing you wonder about late at night."

Had Dag been doing so, staring up at the stars? Fawn said, "You'd think, with that pattern showing in women's grounds, it would be easier rather than harder to get a baby just when you wanted." She was still appalled at how easy it had been for her.

"So you would. Yet so often people miss, and no one knows why. Kauneo and I—" His voice jerked to a halt in that now-familiar way.

She held her peace, and her breath.

"Here's one I never told anyone ever—"

"You need not," she said quietly. "Some people are in favor of spitting out hurts, but poking at them too much doesn't let them heal, either."

"This one's ridden in my memory for a long, long time. Maybe it would look a different size if I got it outside my head rather than in it, for once."

"Then I'm listenin'." Was he about to uncork another horror-tale?

"Indeed." He stared ahead between Copperhead's ears. "We'd been string-bound upwards of a year, and I felt I was getting astride my duties as a company captain, and we decided it was time to start a child. This was in the months just before the wolf war broke. We tried two months running, and missed. Third month, I was away on my duties at the vital time; for the life of me I can't now remember what seemed so important about them. I can't even remember what they *were*. Riding out and checking on something or other. And in the fourth month, the wolf war was starting up, and we were both caught up in the rush." He drew a long, long breath. "But if I could have made Kauneo pregnant by then, she would have stayed in camp, and not led out her patrol to Wolf Ridge. And whatever else had happened, she and the child would both have lived. If not for that lost month."

Fawn's heart felt hot and strange, as if his old wound were being shared through the very ground of his words. *Not a good secret to lug around, that one.* She tried the obvious patch. "You can't know that."

"I know I can't. I don't think there's a second thought I can have about this that I haven't worn out by now. Maybe Kauneo's leadership, down at the anchor end of the line, was what held the ridge that extra time after I went down. Maybe . . . A patroller friend of mine, his first wife died in childbed. I know he harbors regrets just as ferocious for the exact opposite cause. There is no knowing. You just have to grow used to the not knowing, I guess."

He fell quiet for a time, and Fawn, daunted, said nothing. Though maybe the listening had been all he'd needed. She wondered, suddenly, if Dag was doubting whether he could sire children. Fifty-five years was a long time to go without doing so, for a man, although she had the impression that it wasn't that he'd been with so many women, before or after Kauneo, as that he'd paid really good attention when he had. In the light of her own history, if no child appeared when finally wanted, it would seem clear who was responsible. Did he fear to disappoint?

But his mind had turned down another path now, apparently, for he said, "My immediate family's not so large as yours. Just my mother, my brother, and his wife at present. All my brother's children are out of the tent, on patrol or apprenticed to makers. One son's string-bound, so far."

Dag's nephews and nieces were just about the same age range as Fawn and her brothers, from his descriptions. She nodded.

He went on, "I hope to slip into camp quietly. I'm of two minds whether to report to Fairbolt or my family first. It's likely rumors have trickled back about the Glassforge malice kill ahead of Mari's return, in which case Fairbolt will want the news in full. And I have to tell him about the knife. But I'd like to introduce you to my brother and mother in my own way, before they hear anything from anyone else."

"Well, which one would be less offended to be put second?" asked Fawn.

"Hard to say." He smiled dryly. "Mama can hold a grudge longer, but Fairbolt has a keen memory for lapses as well."

"I should not like to begin by offending my new mama-in-law."

"Spark, I'm afraid some people are going to be offended no matter what you and I do. What we've done . . . isn't done, though it was done in all honor."

"Well," she said, trying for optimism, "some people are like that among farmers, too. No pleasing them. You just try, or at least try not to be the first to break." She considered the problem. "Makes sense to put the worst one first. Then, if you have to, you can get away by saying you need to go off and see the second."

He laughed. "Good thinking. Perhaps I will."

But he didn't say which he believed was which.

They rode on through the afternoon without stopping. Fawn thought she could tell when they were nearing the lake by a certain lightness growing in the sky and a certain darkness growing in Dag. At any rate, he got quieter and quieter, though his gaze ahead seemed to sharpen. Finally, his head came up, and he murmured, "The bridge guard and I just bumped grounds. Only another mile."

They came off the lesser track they'd been following onto a wider road, which ran in a sweeping curve. The land here was very flat; the woods, mixed beech and oak and hickory, gave way to another broad meadow. On the far side, someone lying on the back of what looked to be a grazing cart horse, his legs dangling down over the horse's barrel, sat up and waved. He kicked the horse into a canter and approached.

The horse wore neither saddle nor bridle, and the young man aboard it was scarcely more dressed. He wore boots, some rather damp-looking linen drawers, a leather belt with a scabbard for a knife, and his sun-darkened skin. As he approached, he yanked the grass stem he'd been chewing from his mouth and threw it aside. "Dag! You're alive!" He pulled up his horse and stared at the sling, and at Fawn trailing shyly behind. "Aren't you a sight, now! Nobody said anything about a broken bone! Your right arm, too, absent gods, how have you been managing anything at all?"

Dag returned an uninformative nod of greeting, although he smiled faintly. "I've had a little help."

"Is *that* your farmer girl?" The guard stared at Fawn as though farmer girls were a novelty out of song, like dancing bears. "Mari Redwing thought you'd been gelded by a mob of furious farmers. Fairbolt's fuming, your mama thinks you're dead and blames Mari, and your brother's complaining he can't work in the din."

"Ah," said Dag in a hollow voice. "Mari's patrol get back early, did it?"

"Yesterday afternoon."

"Lots of time for everyone to get home and gossip, I see."

"You're the talk of the lake. Again." The guard squinted and urged his horse closer, which made Copperhead squeal in warning, or at least in ill manners. The man was trying to get a clear look at Fawn's left wrist, she realized. "All day, people have been giving me urgent messages to pass on the instant I saw you. Fairbolt, Mari, your mama—despite the fact she insists you're dead, mind—and your brother all want to see you first thing." He grinned, delivering this impossible demand.

Dag came very close, Fawn thought, to just laying his head down on his horse's mane and not moving. "Welcome home, Dag," he muttered. But he straightened up instead and kicked Copperhead around head to tail beside Grace. He leaned over leftward to Fawn, and said, "Roll up my sleeve, Spark. Looks like it's going to be a hot afternoon."

2

The bridge the young man guarded was crudely cut timber, long and low, wide enough for two horses to cross abreast. Fawn craned her neck eagerly as she and Dag passed over. The murky water beneath was obscured with lily pads and drifting pond weed; farther along, a few green-headed ducks paddled desultorily in and out of the cattails bordering the banks. "Is this a river or an arm of the lake?"

"A bit of both," said Dag. "One of the tributary creeks comes in just up the way. But the water widens out around both curves. Welcome to Two Bridge Island."

"Are there two bridges?"

"Really three, but the third goes to Mare Island. The other bridge to the mainland is on the western end, about two miles thataway. This is the narrowest separation."

"Like a moat?"

"In summer, very like a moat. All of the island chain backing up behind could be defended right here, if it wanted defending. After the hard freeze, this is more like an ice causeway, but the most of us will be gone to winter camp at Bearsford by then. Which, while it does have a ford, is mostly lacking in bears. Camp's set on some low hills, as much as we have hills in these parts. People who haven't walked out of this hinterland think they're hills."

"Were you born here, or there?"

"Here. Very late in the season. We should have been gone to winter camp, but my arrival made delays. The first of my many offenses." His smile at this was faint.

Flat land and thin woods gave little to view at first as the road wound inward, although around a curve Copperhead snorted and pretended to shy as a flock of a dozen or so wild turkeys crossed in front of them. The turkeys returned apparent disdain and wandered away into the undergrowth. Around the next curve Dag twitched his horse aside into the verge, and Fawn paused with him, as a caravan passed. A gray-headed man rode ahead; following him, on no lead, were a dozen horses loaded with heavy basket panniers piled high with dark, round, lumpy objects covered in turn with crude rope nets to keep the loads from tumbling out. A boy brought up the rear.

Fawn stared. "I don't suppose that's a load of severed heads going somewhere, but it sure looks like it at a distance. No wonder folks think you're cannibals."

Dag laughed, turning to look after the retreating string. "You know, you're right! That, my love, is a load of plunkins, on their way to winter store. This is their season. In late summer, it is every Lakewalker's duty to eat up his or her share of fresh plunkins. You are going to learn *all about* plunkins."

From his tone Fawn wasn't sure if that was a threat or a promise, but she liked the wry grin that went along-with. "I hope to learn all about everything."

He gave her a warmly encouraging nod and led off once more. Fawn wondered when she was going to at last see tents, and especially Dag's tent.

A shimmering light through the screen of trees, mostly hickory, marked the shoreline to the right. Fawn stood up in her stirrups, trying for a glimpse of the water. She said in surprise, "Cabins!"

"Tents," Dag corrected.

"Cabins with awnings." She gazed avidly as the road swung nearer. Half a dozen log buildings in a cluster hugged the shore. Most seemed to have single central fireplaces, probably double-sided, judging from the fieldstone chimneys she saw jutting from the roof ridgelines. Windows were few and doors nonexistent, for most of the log houses were open on one side, sheltered by deerhide canopies raised on poles seeming almost like long porches. She glimpsed a few shadowy people moving within, and, crossing the yard, a Lakewalker woman wearing a skirt and shepherding a toddler. So did only patrolling women wear trousers?

"If it's missing one full side, it's still a tent, not a permanent structure, and therefore does not have to be burned down every ten years." Dag sounded as if he was reciting.

Fawn's nose wrinkled in bafflement. "What?"

"You could call it a religious belief, although usually it's more of a religious argument. In theory, Lakewalkers are not supposed to build permanent structures. Towns are targets. So are farms, for that matter. So is anything so big and heavy or that you've invested so much in you can't drop it and run if you have to. Farmers would defend to the death. Lakewalkers would retreat and regroup. If we all lived in theory instead of on Two Bridge Island, that is. The only buildings that seem to get burned in the Ten-year Rededication these days are ones the termites have got to. Certain stodgy parties predict dire retribution for our lapses. In my experience, retribution turns up all on its own regardless, so I don't worry about it much."

Fawn shook her head. *I may have more to learn than I thought.*

They passed a couple more such clusters of near buildings. Each seemed to have a dock leading out into the water, or perhaps that was a raft tied to the shore; one had a strange boat tied to it in turn, long and narrow. Smoke rose from chimneys, and Fawn could see homely washing strung on lines to dry. Kitchen gardens occupied sunny patches, and small groves of fruit trees bordered the clearings, with a few beehives set amongst them. "How many Lakewalkers are there on this island?"

"Here, about three thousand in high summer. There are two more island chains around the lake too separated to connect to us by bridge, with maybe another four thousand folks total. If we want to visit, we can either paddle across two miles or ride around for twenty. Probably another thousand or so still back maintaining Bearsford, same as about a thousand folks stay here all winter. Hickory Lake Camp is one of the largest in Oleana. With the biggest territory to patrol, as a penalty for our success. We still send out twice as many exchange patrollers as we ever get in return." A hint of pride tinged his voice, even though his last remarks ought to have sounded more complaint than brag. He nodded ahead toward something Fawn did not yet see, and at a jingle of harness and thud of many hooves gestured her into the weeds to make way, turning Copperhead alongside.

It was a patrol, trotting in double file, very much as Fawn had first seen Mari and Dag's troop ride into the well-house farm what was beginning to seem a lifetime ago. This bunch looked fresh and rested and unusually tidy, however, so she guessed they were outward bound, on their way to whatever patch of hinterland they were assigned to search for their nightmare prey. Most of them seemed to recognize Dag and cried surprised greetings; with his reins wrapped around his hook and his other arm in a sling, he could not return their waves, but he did nod and smile. They didn't pause, but not a few of them turned in their saddles to stare back at the pair.

"Barie's lot," said Dag, looking after them. "Twenty-two."

He'd counted them? "Is that good or bad, twenty-two?"

"Not too bad, for this time of year. It's a busy season." He chirped to Copperhead, and they took to the road once more.

Fawn wondered anew what the shape of her life was going to be, tucked in around Dag's. On a farm, a couple might work together or apart, long hours and hard, but they would still meet for meals three times a day and sleep together every night. Dag would not, presumably, take her patrolling. Therefore, she must stay here, in long, scary separations punctuated by brief reunions, at least till Dag grew too old to patrol. Or too injured, *or didn't come back one day,* but her mind shied from thinking too hard about that one. If she was to be left here with these people and no Dag, she'd best try to fit in. Hardworking hands were needed everywhere all the time; surely hers could win her a place.

Dag pulled up Copperhead and hesitated at a fork in the road. The rightward, eastern branch followed the shoreline, and Fawn eyed it with interest; she could hear voices echoing over the water farther along it, a few cheery shouts and calls and some singing too distant to make out the words. Dag straightened his shoulders, grimaced, and led left instead. Half a mile on, the woods thinned again, and the distinctive silvery light reflecting from the water glimmered between the shaggy boles. The road ended at another that ran along the northern shore, unless it was just rejoining the same one circling the perimeter of the island. Dag led left again.

A brief ride brought them to a broad cleared section with several long log buildings, many of which had walls all the way around, with wooden porches and lots of rails for tying horses. No kitchen gardens or washing, although a few fruit trees were dotted here and there, broad apple and tall, grace-ful pear. On the woodland side of the road was an actual barn, if built rather low, the first Fawn had seen here, and a couple of split-rail paddocks for horses, though only a few horses idled in them at the moment. A trio of small, lean, black pigs rooted among the trees for fallen fruit or nuts. On the lakeside a larger dock jutted out into the water.

Dag edged Copperhead up to one of the hitching rails outside a log building, dropped his reins, and stretched his back. He cast Fawn an afterthought of a smile. "Well, here we are."

Fawn thought this a bit too close-mouthed, even for Dag in a mood. "This isn't your house, is it?"

"Ah. No. Patroller headquarters."

"So we're seeing Fairbolt Crow first?"

"If he's in. If I'm lucky, he will have gone off somewhere." Dag dismounted, and Fawn followed, tying both horses to the rail. She trailed him up onto the porch and through a plank door.

They entered a long room lined with shelves stuffed with piles of papers, rolled parchments, and thick books, and Fawn was reminded at once of Shep Sower's crammed house. At a table at one end, a woman with her hair in iron-gray braids, but wearing a skirt, sat writing in a large ledger book. She was quite as tall as Mari, but more heavily built, almost stout. She was looking up and setting aside her quill even as their steps sounded. Her face lit with pleasure.

"Woo-ee! Look what just dragged in!"

Dag gave her a wry nod. "How de', Massape. Is, um . . . Fairbolt here?"

"Oh, aye."

"Is he busy?" Dag asked, in a most unpressing tone.

"He's in there talking with Mari. About you, I expect, judging from the yelps. Fairbolt's been telling her not to panic. She says she prefers to start panicking as soon as you're out of her sight, just to get beforehand on things. Looks like they're both in the right. What in the world have you done to yourself this time?" She nodded at his sling, then sat up, her eyes narrowing as they fell on the braid circling his left arm. She said again, in an entirely altered tone, "Dag, what in the wide green world have you *done*?"

Fawn, awash in this conversation, gave Dag a poke and a look of desperate inquiry.

"Ah," he said. "Fawn, meet Massape Crow, who is captain to Third Company—Barie's patrol that we passed going out is in her charge, among others. She's also Fairbolt's wife. Massape, this is Missus Fawn Bluefield. My wife." His chin did not so much rise in challenge as set in stubbornness.

Fawn smiled brightly, clutched her hands together making sure her left wrist showed, and gave a polite dip of her knees. "How de', ma'am."

Massape just stared, her lower lip drawn in over her teeth. "You . . ." She held up a finger for a long, uncertain moment, drawling out the word, then swung and pointed past the room's fireplace, central to the inner wall, to a door beyond. "See Fairbolt."

Dag returned her a dry nod and shepherded Fawn to the door, opening it for her. From the room beyond, Fawn heard Mari's voice saying, "If he's stuck to his route, he should be somewhere along the line here."

A man's rumbling tones answered: "If he'd stuck to his route, would he be three weeks overdue? You haven't got a line, there, you've got a huge circle, and the edges run off the blighted map."

"If you've no one else to spare, I'll go."

"You just got back. Cattagus would have words with me till he ran out of breath and turned blue, and then *you'd* be mad. Look, we'll put out the call to every patroller who leaves camp to keep groundsense and both eyes peeled . . ."

Both patrollers, Fawn realized, must have their ground-senses locked down tight in the heat of their argument not to be flying to the door by now. No—she glanced at Dag's stony face—all three. She grabbed Dag by the belt and pushed him through ahead of her, peeking cautiously around him.

This room was a mirror to the first, at least as far as the shelving packed to the ceiling went. A plank table in the middle, its several chairs kicked back to the wall, seemed to be spread with maps. A thickset man was standing with his arms crossed, a frown on his furrowed face. Iron-colored hair was drawn back from his retreating hairline into a single plait down his back; he wore patroller-style trousers and shirt but no leather vest. Only one knife hung from his belt, but Fawn noticed a long, unstrung bow propped against the cold fireplace, together with a quiver of arrows.

Mari, similarly clad, had her back to the door and was leaning over the table pointing at something. The man glanced up, and his gray brows climbed toward what was left of his hairline. His leathery lips twisted in a half grin. "Got that coin, Mari?"

She looked up at him, exasperation in the set of her neck. "What coin?"

"The one you said we'd flip to see who got to skin him first."

Mari, taking in his expression, wheeled. "Dag! You . . . ! Finally! *Where have you been?*" Her eyes, raking him up and down, caught as usual first on the sling. "Ye gods."

Dag offered a short, apologetic nod, seemingly split between both officers. "I was a bit delayed." He motioned with his sling by way of indicating reasonable causes. "Sorry for the worry."

"I left you in Glassforge pretty near four weeks ago!" said Mari. "You were supposed to go straight home! Shouldn't have taken you more than a week at most!"

"No," Dag said in a tone of judicious correction, "I told you we'd be stopping off at the Bluefield farm on the way, to put them at ease about Fawn, here. I admit that took longer than I'd planned. Though once the arm was busted there seemed no rush, as I figured I wouldn't be able to patrol again for nigh on six weeks anyway."

Fairbolt scowled at this dodgy argument. "Mari said that if your luck was good, you'd come to your senses and dump the farmer girl back on her family, but if it ran to your usual form, they'd beat you to death and hide the body. Did her kin bust your bone?"

"If I'd been her kin, I'd have broken *more* of them," Mari muttered. "You still got all your parts, boy?"

Dag's smile thinned. "I had a run-in with a sneak thief in Lumpton Market, actually. Got our gear back, for the price of the arm. My visit to West Blue went very pleasantly."

Fawn decided not to offer any adjustment to this bald-faced assertion. She didn't quite like the way the patrollers—all three of them—kept looking right at her and talking right over her, but they were on Dag's land here; she waited for guidance, or at least a hint. Though she thought he could stand to speed up, in that regard. Conscious of the officers' eyes upon her—Fairbolt was leaning sideways slightly to get a view around Dag—she crept out from behind her husband. She gave Mari a friendly little wave, and the camp captain a respectful knee-dip. "Hello again, Mari. How de' do, sir?"

Dag drew breath and repeated his blunt introduction: "Fairbolt, meet Missus Fawn Bluefield. My wife."

Fairbolt squinted and rubbed the back of his neck, his face screwed up. The silence stretched as he and Mari looked over the wedding cords with, Fawn felt, more than just their eyes. Both officers had their sleeves rolled up in the heat of the day, and both had similar cords winding around their left wrists, worn thin and frayed and faded. Her own cord and Dag's looked bright and bold and thick by comparison, the gold beads anchoring the ends seeming very solid.

Fairbolt glanced aside at Mari, his eyes narrowing still further. "Did you suspect this?"

"This? No! This isn't—how could—but I told you he'd likely done some fool thing no one could anticipate."

"You did," Fairbolt conceded. "And I didn't. I thought he was just . . ." He focused his gaze on Dag, and Fawn shrank even though she was not at its center. "I won't say *that's impossible* because it's plain you found a way. I will ask, what Lakewalker maker helped you to this?"

"None, sir," said Dag steadily. "None but me, Fawn's aunt Nattie, who is a spinner and natural maker, and Fawn. Together."

Though not so tall as Dag, Fairbolt was still a formidably big man. He frowned down at Fawn; she had to force her spine straight. "Lakewalkers do not recognize marriages to farmers. Did Dag tell you that?"

She held out her wrist. "That's why this, I understood." She gripped the cord tight, for courage. If they couldn't be bothered to be polite to her, she needn't return any better. "Now, I guess you could look at this with your fancy ground-sense and say we weren't married if you wanted. But you'd be lying. Wouldn't you."

Fairbolt rocked back. Dag didn't flinch. If anything, he looked satisfied, if a bit fey. Mari rubbed her forehead.

Dag said quietly, "Did Mari tell you about my other knife?"

Fairbolt turned to him, not quite in relief, but tacitly accepting the shift of subject. Backing off for the moment; Fawn was not sure why. Fairbolt said, "As much as you told her, I suppose. Congratulations on your malice kill, by the way. What number was that? And don't tell me you don't keep count."

Dag gave a little conceding nod. "It would have been twenty-seven, if it had been my kill. It was Fawn's."

"It was both ours," Fawn put in. "Dag had the knife, I had the chance to use it. Either of us would have been lost without the other."

"Huh." Fairbolt walked slowly around Fawn, as if looking, *really* looking, at her for the first time. "Excuse me," he said, and reached out to tilt her head and study the deep red scars on her neck. He stepped back and sighed. "Let's see this other knife, then."

Fawn fished in her shirt. After the scare at Lumpton Market she had fashioned a new sheath for the blade, single and of softer leather, with a cord for her neck to carry it the way Lakewalkers did. It was undecorated, but she'd sewn it with care. Hesitantly, she pulled the cord over her curls, glanced at Dag, who gave her a nod of reassurance, and handed it over to the camp captain.

Fairbolt took it and sat down in one of the chairs near a window, drawing the bone blade out. He examined it much the way Dag and Mari had, even to touching it to his lips. He sat frowning a moment, cradling it in his thick hands. "Who made this for you, Dag? Not Dar?"

"No. A maker up in Luthlia, a few months after Wolf Ridge."

"Kauneo's bone, yes?"

"Yes."

"Did you ever have reason before to think the making might be defective?"

"No. I don't think it was."

"But if the making was sound, no one but you should have been able to prime it."

"I am very aware of that. And if the making was unsound, no one should have been able to prime it at all. But there it sits."

"That it does. So tell me exactly what happened in that cave, again . . . ?"

First Dag, and then Fawn, had to repeat the tale for Fairbolt, each in their own words. They touched but lightly on how Dag had come upon Fawn, kidnapped off the road by bandits in the thrall of the malice. How he'd tracked her to the malice's cave. And come—Dag bit his lip—just too late to stop the monster from ripping the ground of her two-months-child from her womb. Fawn did not volunteer, nor did Fairbolt ask, how she came to be alone, pregnant—and unwed—on the road in the first place; perhaps Mari, who'd had the tale from Fawn back in Glassforge, had given him the gist.

Fairbolt's attention and questions grew keener when they described the mix-up with Dag's malice-killing sharing knives. How Dag, going down under the malice's guard of mud-men, had tossed the knife pouch to Fawn, how she'd stuck the monster first with the wrong, unprimed knife, then with the right one, shattering it in its use. How the terrifying creature had dissolved, leaving the first knife so strangely charged with the mortality of Fawn's unborn daughter.

By the time they were half-through, Mari had pulled up a chair, and Dag leaned against the table. Fawn found she preferred to stand, though she had to lock her knees against an unwelcome trembling. Fairbolt did not, to Fawn's relief, inquire into the messy aftermath of that fight; his interest seemed to end with the mortal knives.

"You are planning to show this to Dar," Fairbolt said when they'd finished, nodding to the knife still in his lap; from his tone Fawn wasn't sure if this was query or command.

"Yes."

"Let me know what he says." He hesitated. "Assuming the other matter doesn't affect his judgment?" He jerked his head toward Dag's left arm.

"I have no idea what Dar will think of my marriage"— Dag's tone seemed to add, *nor do I care,* but he didn't say it aloud—"but I would expect him to speak straight on his craft, regardless. If I have doubts after, I can always seek another opinion. There are half a dozen knife makers around this lake."

"Of lesser skill," said Fairbolt, watching him closely.

"That's why I'm going to Dar first. Or at all."

Fairbolt started to hand the knife back to Dag but, at Dag's gesture, returned it to Fawn. She put the cord back over her head and hid the sheath away again between her breasts.

Fairbolt, almost eye to eye with her, watched this coolly. "That knife doesn't make you some sort of honorary Lakewalker, you know, girl."

Dag frowned. But before he could say anything, Fawn, despite the heat flushing through her, replied calmly, "I know that, sir." She leaned in toward him, and deepened her voice. "I'm a farmer girl and proud of it, and if that's good enough for Dag, the rest of you can go jump in your lake. Just so *you* know this thing I have slung around my neck wasn't an *honorary* death." She nodded curtly and stood straight.

A little to her surprise, he did not grow offended, merely thoughtful, if that was what rubbing his lips that way signified. He stood up with a grunt that reminded her of a tired Dag, and strode across the room to the far side of the fireplace.

Covering the whole surface between the chimney stone and the outer wall and nearly floor to ceiling was a panel made of some very soft wood. It was painted with a large grid pattern, each marked with a place name. Fawn realized, looking at the names she recognized, that it was a sort of map, if lines on a map could be pulled about and squared off, of parts of the hinterland—all the parts, she suspected. To the left-hand side was a separate column of squares, labeled *Two Bridge Island, Heron Island, Beaver Sigh, Bearsford,* and *Sick List.* And, above them all, a smaller circle in red paint labeled *Missing.*

About a third of the squares had hard wooden pegs stuck in them. Most of them were in groups of sixteen to twenty-five, and Fawn realized she was looking at patrols—some squares were full of little holes as though they might have been lately emptied. Each peg had a name inked onto the side in tiny, meticulous writing, and a number on its end. Some of the pegs had wooden buttons, like coins with holes bored in the middle, hung on them by twisted wires, one or two or sometimes more threaded in a stack. The buttons, too, were numbered.

"Oh!" she said in surprise. "These are all your patrollers!" There must have been five or six hundred pegs in all. She leaned closer to search for names she recognized.

Fairbolt raised his brows. "That's right. A patrol leader can keep a patrol in mind, but once you get to be a company or camp captain, well, one head can't hold them all. Or at least, mine can't."

"That's clever! You can see everything all at once, pretty nearly." She realized she needed to look more closely at Two Bridge Island for names. "Ah, there's Mari. And Razi and Utau, they're home with Sarri, oh good. Where's Dirla?"

"Beaver Sigh," said Dag, watching her pore over the display. "That's another island."

"Mm? Oh, yes, there she is, too. I hope she's happy. Does she have a regular sweetheart? Or sweethearts? What are the little buttons for?"

Mari answered. "For the patrollers who are carrying sharing knives. Not everyone has one, but every patrol that goes out needs to have two or more."

"Oh. Yes, that makes sense. Because it wouldn't do a bit of good to find a malice and have no knife on hand. And you might find another malice, after. Or have an accident." Dag had spoken with a shudder of the ignominy of accidentally breaking a sharing knife, and now she understood. She hesitated, thinking of her own spectacular, if peculiar, sharing knife accident. "Why are they numbered?"

Dag said, "The camp captain keeps a book with records of the owners and donors, for if a knife is used. To send the acknowledgments to the kinfolk, or know where to send the pieces if they chance to be recovered."

Fawn frowned. "Is that why the patrollers are numbered, too?"

"Very like. There's another set of books with all the names and next of kin, and other details someone might want to know about any particular patroller in an emergency. Or when the emergency is over."

"Mm," said Fawn, her frown deepening as she pictured this. She set her hands on her hips and peered at the board, imagining all those lives—and deaths—moving over the landscape. "Do you connect the pegs to people's grounds, like marriage cords? Could you?"

"No," said Dag.

"Does she always go on like this?" asked Fairbolt. She glanced up to find him staring at her rather as she'd been staring at the patroller board.

"More or less, yes," said Dag.

"I'm sorry!" Fawn clapped her hand to her mouth in apology. "Did I ask too many questions?"

Fairbolt gave her a funny look. "No." He reached up and took a peg out of the *Missing* circle, one of two jutting there. He held it out at arm's length, squinting briefly at the fine print on the side, and grunted satisfaction. "I suppose this comes off, now." With surprising delicacy, his thick fingers unwound its wire and teased off one numbered button. The second he frowned at, but twisted back into place. "I never met the Luthlia folks; never got up that way. You be taking care of the honors on this one, Dag?"

"Yes."

"Good. Thanks." He held the peg in his palm as if weighing it.

Dag reached up and touched the remaining peg in the red circle. "Still no word of Thel." It didn't sound like a question.

"No," sighed Fairbolt.

"It's been near two years, Fairbolt," Mari observed dispassionately. "You could likely take it down."

"It's not like the board's out of room up there, now is it?" Fairbolt sniffed, stared unreadably at Dag, gave the peg in his hand a toss, and bent down and thrust it decisively into the square marked *Sick List*.

He straightened up and turned back to Dag. "Stop in at the medicine tent. Let me know what they say about the arm. Come see me after you have that talk with Dar." He made a vague gesture of dismissal, but then added, "Where are you going next?"

"Dar." Dag added more reluctantly, "Mother."

Mari snorted. "What are you going to say to Cumbia about that?" She nodded at his arm cord.

Dag shrugged. "What's to say? I'm not ashamed, I'm not sorry, and I'm not backing down."

"She'll spit."

"Likely." He smiled grimly. "Want to come watch?"

Mari rolled her eyes. "I think I want to go back out on patrol. Fairbolt, you need volunteers?"

"Always, but not you today. Go along home to Cattagus. Your stray has turned up; you've no more excuse to loiter here harassing me."

"Eh," she said, whether in agreement or disagreement Fawn could not tell. She cast a vague sort of salute at Fairbolt and Dag, murmured, "Good luck, child," at Fawn, in a rather-too-ironical voice, and took herself out.

Dag made to follow, but stopped with a look of inquiry when Fairbolt said, "Dag."

"Sir?"

"Eighteen years ago," said Fairbolt, "you persuaded me to take a chance on you. I never had cause to regret it."

Till now? Fawn wondered if he meant to imply.

"I don't care to defend this in the camp council. See that it doesn't boil up that high, eh?"

"I'll try not," said Dag.

Fairbolt returned a provisional sort of nod, and Fawn followed Dag out.

Missus Captain Crow was gone from the outer room. Outside, the sky had turned a flat gray, the water of the lake a pewter color, and the humidity had become oppressive. As they made their way down the porch steps to where the horses were tied, Dag sighed. "Well. That could have gone worse."

Fawn recognized her own words tossed back to her, and remembered Dag's. "Really?"

His lips twitched; it wasn't much of a smile, but at least it was a real one, and not one of those grimaces with the emphasis on the *grim* he'd mostly had inside. "Really. Fairbolt could have pulled my peg and chucked it in the fire. Then all my problems would have been not his problems anymore."

"What, he could have made you not a patroller?"

"That's right."

Fawn gasped. "Oh, no! And I said all those mouthy things to him! You should have warned me! But he made me mad, talking over the top of my head." She added after a moment's reflection, "You all three did."

"Mm," said Dag. He pulled her into his left arm and rested his chin on her curls for a moment. "I imagine so. Things were moving pretty fast there for a while."

She wondered if the patrollers had all been saying things to one another through their groundsenses that she hadn't caught. For sure, she felt there was a good deal back there she hadn't caught.

"As for Fairbolt, you won't offend him by standing up to him, even if you're wrong, but especially if you're right. His back's broad enough to bear correction. He doesn't much care for folks who go belly-up to him to his face then whine about it behind his back, though."

"Well . . . stands to reason, that."

"Indeed. You didn't make a bad impression on him, Spark. In fact, judging from the results, you made a pretty good impression."

"Well, that's a relief." She paused in puzzlement. "What results?"

"He put my peg in the sick box. Still a patroller. The camp council deals with any arguments the families can't solve, or arguments that come up between clan heads. But any active patroller, the council has to go through the camp captain to deal with. It's like he's clan head to all of us. I won't say Fairbolt will or even can protect me from any consequences of this" —he shrugged his left arm to indicate his marriage cord—"but leastways he's keeping that possibility open for now."

Fawn turned to untie the horses, considering this. The tailpiece seemed to be that it was Dag's job—and hers?—to keep the consequences from getting too out of hand. As she scrambled up on Grace, she saw under some pear trees at a little distance Mari sitting on a trestle table swinging

her legs, and Massape Crow on the bench beside her. Mari
seemed to be talking heatedly, by the way she was waving
her arms, and Massape had her head cocked in apparent
fascination. Fawn didn't think she needed groundsense to
guess the subject under discussion, even without the curious
glances the pair cast their way.

Dag had wrapped Copperhead's reins around his hook.
Now he led the horse beside the porch and used the steps for
a mounting block, settling into the saddle with a tired grunt.
He jerked his chin by way of a *come-along* gesture and led
them onto the shore road, heading back east.

3

Fawn turned in her saddle to look as they passed the woodland road they'd come in on, and turned again as the shore road bent out toward a wooden bridge spanning a channel about sixty feet across. The next island spread west, bounding the arm of the lake across from the patroller headquarters. Past the bridge, its farther shoreline curved north and the lake beyond opened out for a square mile. In the distance she could see a few narrow boats being paddled, and another with a small triangular sail. The island reached by the bridge had only a scattering of trees; between them horses and goats and a few sheep grazed, and beneath them more black pigs dozed.

"Mare Island?" Fawn guessed.

"Yep. It and Foal Island, which you can't see beyond the far end over there"—Dag waved vaguely northwest—"are our main pastures. No need to build fences, you see."

"I do. Clever. Is there a Stallion Island?"

Dag smiled. "More or less. Most of the studs are kept over on Walnut Island"—he pointed to a low green bump across the open lake patch—"which works fine until one of the fellows gets excited and ambitious and tries to swim across in the night. Then there's some sorting out to do."

The shore road swung back into the trees, passing behind the clusters of log buildings along the lake bank. After a scant quarter mile, Dag pulled up Copperhead and frowned at a clearing enclosing just two buildings. The lake glimmered dully beyond in the hot afternoon's flat light. "Tent Redwing," Dag said.

"Well" —Fawn took a breath—"this is it, I guess."

"Not quite. Everyone seems to be out. But leastways we can drop off our saddles and bags and take the horses back to pasture."

They rode into the clearing. The two buildings were set facing each other at an angle opening toward the lake, both with long sides gaping under deerhide awnings. Other deer-hide rolls along the eaves looked as though they could be dropped down to provide more wall at need. Houses and porches seemed to be floored with planks, not dirt, at least. Fawn tried to think *simple,* not *squalid.* A stone-lined fire pit lay in the clearing between the two structures—Fawn still could not make herself think of them as tents—in addition to the central fireplaces that could apparently heat both the outer and the enclosed inner chambers. Seats of stumps or sawn-off logs were dotted about; in summer, no doubt almost all work was done outdoors.

She hopped down and helped unsaddle, dealing with the straps and buckles; Dag with his hook hauled the gear from the horses' backs and dumped it on the plank porch of the house on the right. He scratched the back of his head gently.

"Not sure where Mama's got off to. Dar's likely at the bone shack. And if Omba's not out on Mare Island, it'll be a first. Dig down in the bottom of my saddlebags, Spark, and find those strings of horseshoes."

Fawn did so, discovering two bunches of new horseshoes tied together, a dozen each. "My word, no wonder your bags were so heavy! How long have you been carting these around in there?"

"Since we left Glassforge. Present for Omba. Hickory Lake's a rich camp in some ways, but we have few metals in these parts, except for a little copper-working near Bearsford. All our iron has to be traded for from other

camps, mostly around Tripoint. Though we've been getting
more from farmer sources in the hills beyond Glassforge,
lately." He grinned briefly. "When a certain young
exchange patroller from Tripoint walking the hinterlands
arrived at Massape Crow and said, *That's far enough,* it's
told his bride-gift string of horses came in from back home
staggering under loads of iron. It made the Crows rich and
Fairbolt famous, back in the day."

Fawn led Grace to a log seat and climbed up bareback,
and Dag hooked her up the horseshoe bundles, which she
twisted about each other and laid over her lap. He climbed
up on Copperhead in turn, and they went back out to the
road and returned to the bridge.

At the far end of the span he dismounted again to unhook
a rope loop from the board gate, open it for Fawn, and shut
it again behind them. He did not bother remounting, but led
them instead toward a long shed that lay a hundred paces
or so away. Fawn slid off Grace, managing not to drop the
horseshoes, and Dag hooked off both bridles, flopping them
over his shoulder. Copperhead scooted away at once, and
after a moment's doubt, Grace followed, soon putting her
head down to crop grass.

Of all of his relatives, Dag had talked most freely about
his brother's wife, the Waterstrider sister who'd changed her
name for her mother-in-law's sake. In order of increasing
reticence came his grandfather, remembered with nostalgia
from scenes of Dag's youth; Dar, of whom Dag spoke with
cool respect; his father, tinged with distance and regret;
and, in a pool of silence at the center, his mother. Every
conversation Fawn had tried to lead toward her, Dag had led
away. About Omba—horse trainer, mare midwife, maker of
harness, and, it appeared, farrier—there had been no such
problem.

As they rounded the corner of the shed and stepped
under its wooden overhang, Fawn had no trouble recog-
nizing Omba, for she came striding out of a door crying,

"Dag! Finally!" She was not so thin as Mari, and quite a bit shorter, though still as tall as any man in Fawn's family; Fawn would have guessed her age at fifty or so, which meant she was likely fifteen years older than that. She was dressed much like a patroller woman, and Fawn finally decided that the trousers were just Lakewalker riding garb, period. Her skin, though tanned and weathered, was paler than Dag's, and her eyes a pretty silvery blue. Her dark hair, shot with a few white streaks, ran down her back in a single swift plait, without ornament. She caught sight of the sling, planted her hands on her hips, and said, "Absent gods, brother, what have you done to your right arm!" And then, after a momentary pause, "Absent gods, Dag, what have you done to your *left* arm?"

Dag gave her a nod of greeting, his smile lopsided. "Hello, Omba. Brought you something." He gestured Fawn forward; she held out the horseshoes.

Omba's face lit, and she pounced on the prize. "Do I need those!" She came to a dead halt again at the sight of the cord on Fawn's wrist, and made a choked noise down in her throat. Her gaze rose to Fawn's face, her eyes widening in something between disbelief and dismay. "You're a farmer! You're *that* farmer!"

For an instant, Fawn wondered if there was some Lakewalker significance to Dag's tricking Omba into accepting this gift from Fawn's hands, but she had no time or way to ask. She dipped her knees, and said breathlessly, "Hello, Omba. I'm Fawn. Dag's wife." She wasn't about to make some broader claim such as, *I'm your new sister*; that would be for Omba to decide.

Omba wheeled toward Dag, her eyebrows climbing. "And what does that make you, Dag Redwing Hickory? Besides head down in the slit trench."

"Fawn's husband. Dag Bluefield . . . To-Be-Determined, at this point."

Or would the effect instead be to make Dag not Omba's

brother anymore? Lakewalker tent customs continued to confuse Fawn.

"You seen Fairbolt yet?" asked Omba.

"Just came from there. Saw Mari there, too."

"You told him about this?" She jerked her head toward Fawn.

"Certainly."

"What did he do to you?"

"Put me on sick list." Dag wriggled his sling. "That was the To-Be-Determined part, or so I took it."

Omba blew out her breath in unflattering wonder. But not, Fawn thought, in hostility; she hung on tight to that realization. It did not seem as though Dag had taken her advice to start with the hardest ones first. By later today, *not hostile* might yet look pretty good.

"What did Mari say to you all, last night?" asked Dag.

"Oh, *there* was a scene. She came in asking if we'd heard from you, which was a jolt to start, since you were supposed to be with her. Then she said she'd sent you home from Glassforge weeks ago, and everyone was worried you'd been injured, but she said not. Is that right?" She stared at the sling.

"Was at the time. I collected this on the way. Go on."

"Then she had this wild tale about some cutie farmer girl being mixed up in your latest malice kill" —her eyes went curiously to Fawn—"which I barely believed, but now, hm. And that you'd jumped the cliff with her, which your mama hotly denied the possibility of, while simultaneously yelling at Mari for letting it happen. I kept my mouth shut during that part. Though I did wish you well of it."

"Thank you," said Dag blandly.

"Ha. Though I never imagined . . . anyway. Mari said that you'd gone off with the farmer girl, supposed to deliver her home or something. She was afraid you'd met some mishap at the hands of her kin—she said she was picturing gelding.

That must have been some cliff. When Mari and your mama got down to arguing over lapses from twenty-five years back, I slipped out. But Mari took Dar down to the dock after, to talk private. He wouldn't say what she'd added, except that it was about bone craft, which even your mama knows by now is the sign she'll get no more from him."

It seemed Mari was still keeping the tale of the accident to the second sharing knife close. Nor had the term *pregnant* turned up in relation to Fawn, at least in front of Dag's mama. Fawn felt suddenly more charitable to Mari.

"Oh, Dag," sighed Omba. "This is going to top anything you've done ever."

"Look on the bright side. Nothing you can do ever after will top this. The effect might even be retroactive."

She gave a bemused nod. "I'll grant you that." She slung the horseshoes onto some pegs on the nearest post, and held up her hands palm out in a warding gesture. "I think I'll just stay out of this one altogether if you don't mind."

"You're welcome to try," said Dag amiably. "We were just over to the tent to drop our things, but it was empty. Where is everyone?"

"Dar went to the shack to work, or hide out. Mari was worried sick for you, and that shook him more than he was willing to let on, I think. She actually said *I'm sorry* to your mother at one point last night."

"And Mama?" said Dag.

"Out on raft duty. Rationing plunkins."

Dag snorted. "I'll bet."

"They tried to convince her to stay ashore with her bad back, but she denied the back and went. There will be no vile plunkin ear chucking today."

Now Fawn was lost. "Rationing plunkins? Is there a shortage?"

"No," said Dag. "This time of year, they're worse than in season—they're in glut."

Omba grinned. "Dar still waxes bitter about how she'd nurse her supply through the Bearsford camp, like there was some sort of prize for arriving at spring with the most winter store still in hand. And then make you all eat up the old ones before allowing any fresh ones."

Dag's lips quirked. "Oh, yeah."

"Did she ever go through a famine?" Fawn asked. "That makes people funny about food, I hear tell."

"Not as far as I know," said Omba.

She's speaking to me, oh good! Though people wishful to vent about their in-laws would bend the ear of anyone who'd listen, so it might not signify much.

"Not that the choices don't get a bit narrow for everyone by late winter," Omba continued. "She's just like that. Always has been. I still remember the first summer Dar and I were courting, when you grew so tall, Dag. We thought you were going to starve. Half the camp conspired to slip you food on the sly."

Dag laughed. "I was about ready to wrestle the goats for the splits and the mishaps. Those are feed plunkins," he added to Fawn aside. "Can't think why I didn't. I wouldn't be so shy nowadays."

"It is a known fact that patrollers will eat anything." Omba twitched a speculative eyebrow at Fawn that made her wonder if she ought to blush.

To quell that thought, Fawn asked instead, "Plunkin ear chucking?"

Dag explained, "When the plunkin heads are dredged up out of the lake bottom, they have two to six little cloves growing up the sides, about half the size of my hand. These are broken off and put back down in the mud to become next year's crop. Plunked in, hence the name. There are always more ears than needed, so the excess gets fed to the goats and pigs. And there are always a lot of youngsters swimming and splashing around the harvesting rafts, and, well, excess plunkin ears make good projectiles, in a reasonably nonlethal sort of way. Especially if you have a good slingshot," he added in a suddenly warmly reminiscent tone. He paused and cleared his throat. "The grown-ups disapprove of the waste, of course."

"Well, some do," said Omba. "Some remember their slingshots. Someone should have given one to your mother when she was a girl, maybe."

"At her age, she's not going to change."

"You've made a change."

Dag shrugged, and asked instead, "How're Swallow and Darkling?"

Omba's face brightened. "Wonderful well. That black colt's going to be fit to go for a stud when he's grown, I think. He'll fetch you a good price. Or if you finally want to trade in Snakebrain over there for dog meat, you could ride him yourself. I'd train him up for you. You two'd look mighty fine, patrolling."

"Mm, thanks, but no. Sometime tomorrow or the next day, soon as I have a chance, I want to pull them out of the herd. I'll get a packsaddle for Swallow, and Darkling can trot at her heels. Send them down to West Blue with my bride-gifts to Fawn's mama, which I am fearsome late presenting."

"Your best horses!" said Omba in dismay.

Dag smiled a slow smile. "Why not? They gave me their best daughter."

"But I'm their only daughter," said Fawn.

"Saves argument there, eh?" said Dag.

Omba caught up her braid and rubbed the end. "To farmers! What do they know about Lakewalker horses? What if they try to make Swallow pull a plow? Or cut Darkling? Or . . ." Her face screwed up, as she evidently pictured even worse farmer misuse of the precious horses.

"My family takes good care of our horses," said Fawn stiffly. "Of all our animals."

"They won't *understand*," said Omba.

"I will," said Dag. He gave her a nod. "See you at dinner. Who's cookin'?"

"Cumbia. You might want to grab a plunkin off the goats on the way, to fortify yourselves."

"Thanks, but I guess we'll survive." He gestured Fawn away. She gave Omba another knee-dip and smile by way of farewell; the Lakewalker woman just shook her head and returned a sardonic wave. *But not hostile,* Fawn reminded herself.

As they reached the bridge again, Dag held the gate aside for a girl leading a couple of horses with pannier baskets piled high with plunkins; she gave him a nod of thanks. These plunkins did indeed seem to be mostly broken or weirdly misshapen or with odd discolorations. Fawn glanced back to see her walking along chirping and tossing out plunkins along her path, and a general movement among the goats and pigs toward this feast.

"Lakewalker animals eat plunkins too, do they?"

"Horses and cows and sheep can't. The pigs and goats chomp them down. So will dogs."

"I haven't seen many dogs. I'd think you'd have more, for hunting and such. For hunting malices, even."

"We don't keep many. Dogs are more hazard than help on patrol. The malices snap them right up, and they have no defense. Except us, and if you're trying to bring down a malice, it'd be no use to be distracted trying to protect a dog, especially if it's turning on you itself."

As they strolled back along the shore road, Fawn asked curiously, "Was your mother ever a patroller?"

"I think she had the training, way back when. All the youngsters at least get taken out on short trips around the camps. Patrollers are chosen for two things, mainly. General health and strength, and groundsense range. Not everyone can project their groundsense out far enough to be useful on patrol. The lack's not considered a defect, necessarily;

many's the quite competent maker who can't reach out much beyond his arm's length."

"Is Dar like that?"

"No, his range is almost as long as mine. He's just even better at what he does with bones. What my mother always wanted, now . . ." He trailed off.

Volunteering useful information at last? No, evidently not. Fawn sighed and prompted, "Was what?"

"More children. Just didn't work out that way for her, whether because Father was out on patrol too much, or they were just unlucky, or what, I don't know. I should have been a girl. That was my immediate next lapse after arriving late. Or been eight other children. Or had eight other children, in a pinch, and not off in Luthlia or someplace, but here at Hickory Camp. My mother had a second chance with Dar and Omba's children. She kind of commandeered them from Omba to raise; which I gather caused some friction at first, till Omba gave up and went to concentrate on her horses. They'd worked it all out by the time I got back from Luthlia minus the hand, anyway. There's still just a little . . . I won't call it bad feeling, but feeling, there over that."

Mother-in-law versus daughter-in-law friction was common coin in Fawn's world; she had no trouble following this. She wondered if Cumbia's thwarted thirst for daughters would extend itself to a little farmer girl, dragged in off patrol like some awkward souvenir. She had taken in one daughter-in-law, quite against custom, after all. Some hope there?

"Dag," she said suddenly, "where am I going to live?"

He looked over and raised his eyebrows at her. "With me."

"Yes, but when you're gone on patrol?"

Silence. It stretched rather too long.

"Dag?"

He sighed. "We'll just have to see, Spark."

They were nearly back to his family tent-cabins when Dag

paused at a path leading into the woods. If he was checking anything with his groundsense, Fawn could not tell, but he jerked his chin in a come-along gesture and led right. The high straight boles, mostly hickory, gave a pale green shade in the shadowless light, as though they were walking into some underwater domain. The scrub was scant and low on the flat terrain. Fawn eyed the poison ivy and stuck to the center of the well-trodden path, lined here and there with whitewashed rocks.

About a hundred paces in, they came to a clearing. In the center was a small cabin, a real one with four sides, and, to Fawn's surprise, glass windows. Even the patrol headquarters had only had parchment stretched on window frames. More disturbingly, human thighbones hung from the eaves, singly or in pairs, swaying gently in the air that soughed in the papery hickory leaves overhead. She tried not to imagine ghostly whispering voices in the branches.

Dag followed her wide gaze. "Those are curing."

"Those folks look well beyond cure to me," she muttered, which at least made his lips twitch.

"If Dar's busy with something, don't speak till he speaks to us," Dag warned in a quiet voice. "Actually, the same applies even if it looks like he's doing nothing."

Fawn nodded vigorously. Putting the picture together from Dag's oblique descriptions, she figured Dar was the closest thing to a real Lakewalker necromancer that existed. She could not picture being foolish enough to interrupt him in the midst of some sorcery.

A hickory husk, falling from above, made a *clack* and a *clatter* as it hit the shingle roof and rolled off, and Fawn jumped and grabbed Dag's left arm tightly. He smiled reassuringly and led her around the building. On the narrower south side was a porch shading a wedged-open door. But the man they sought was outside, at the edge of the clearing. Working a simple sapling lathe, so ordinary and unsorcerous-looking as to make Fawn blink.

Dar was shorter and stockier than Dag, a solid middle-aged build, with a more rectangular face and broader jaw. He had his shirt off as he labored; his skin was coppery like Dag's but not so varied in its sun-burnishing. His dark hair was drawn back in a Lakewalker-style mourning knot, which made Fawn wonder who for, since his wife Omba's hadn't been. If there was gray in it, she wasn't close enough to see. One leg worked the lathe; the rope to the sapling turned a clamp holding a greenwood blank. Both hands held a curved knife and bore it inward, and pale yellow shavings peeled away to join a kicked-about pile below. Two finished bowls sat on a nearby stump. In the shavings pile lay discarded a partially carved, cracked blank, and another finished bowl that looked to Fawn perfectly fine.

His hands most drew her eye: strong and long-fingered like Dag's, quick and careful. And what a very odd thing it was that it should *feel* so odd to see them in a pair, working together that way.

He glanced up from his carving. His eyes were a clear bronze-brown. He looked back down, evidently trying to keep working, but after another spin muttered something short under his breath and straightened up with a scowl, allowing the blank to wind down, then unclamped it and dropped it into the shavings pile. He tossed the knife in the general direction of the stump and turned to Dag.

"Sorry to interrupt," said Dag, nodding to the half bowl. "I was told you wanted to see me immediately."

"Yes! Dag, where have you been?"

"Been getting here. I had a few delays." He made the sling-gesture.

For once, it did not divert his interrogator's eye. Dar's voice sharpened as his gaze locked on his brother's left arm. "What fool thing have you gone and done? Or have you finally done something right?" He let his breath out in a hiss as his eyes raked over Fawn. "No. Too much to hope for."

His brow wrinkled as he frowned at her left wrist. "*How* did you do that?"

"Very well," said Dag, earning an exasperated look.

Dar walked closer, staring down at Fawn in consternation. "So there really was a farmer-piglet."

"Actually"—Dag's voice suddenly went bone dry—"that would be my wife. Missus Fawn Bluefield. Fawn, meet Dar Redwing."

Fawn attempted a tremulous smile. Her knees felt too weak to dip.

Dar stepped half a pace back. "Ye gods, you're serious about this!"

Dag's voice dropped still further. "Deadly."

They locked eyes for a moment, and Fawn had the maddening sense that some exchange had passed or was passing that, once again, she hadn't caught, although it had seemed to spin off the rather insulting term *piglet*. Or, from the heated look in Dag's eye, very insulting term, although she couldn't see exactly why; *chickie* and *filly* and *piglet* and all such baby-animal terms being used interchangeably for little endearments, in Fawn's experience. Perhaps it was the tone of voice that made the difference. Whatever it was, it was Dar who backed down, not apologizing but changing tack: "Fairbolt will explode."

"I've seen Fairbolt. I left him in one piece. Mari, too."

"You can't tell me he's happy about this!"

"I don't. But neither was he stupid." Another hint of warning, that? Perhaps, for Dar ceased his protests, although with a frustrated gesture. Dag continued, "Omba says Mari spoke to you alone last night, after the others."

"Oh, and wasn't that an uproar. Mama always pictures you dead in a ditch, not that she hasn't been close to right now and then just by chance, but I don't expect that of Mari."

"Did she tell you what happened to my sharing knife?"

"Yes. I didn't believe half of it."

"Which half?"

"Well, that would be the problem to decide, now, wouldn't it?" Dar glanced up. "Did you bring it along?"

"That's why we came here."

To Dar's work shack? Or to Hickory Lake Camp generally? The meaning seemed open.

"You seen Mama yet?"

"That will be next."

"I suppose," Dar sighed, "I'd best see it here, then. Before the real din starts."

"That's what I was thinking, too."

Dar gestured them toward the cabin steps. Fawn sat beside Dag, scrunching up to him for solace, and Dar took a seat near the steps on a broad stump.

"Give Dar the knife," said Dag. At her troubled look, he dropped a reassuring kiss atop her head, which made Dar's face screw up as though he was smelling something rank. Fawn frowned but fished the sheath out of her shirt once more. She would have preferred to give it to Dag to hand to his brother, but that wasn't possible. Reluctantly, she extended it across to Dar, who almost as reluctantly took it.

Dar did not unsheathe it immediately, but sat with it in his lap a moment. He took in a long breath, as though centering himself somehow; half the expression seemed to drop from his face. Since it was mostly the sour, disapproving half, Fawn didn't altogether mind. What was left seemed distant and emotionless.

Dar's examination seemed much like that of the other Lakewalkers: cradling the knife, holding it to his lips, but also cheek and forehead, eyes open and closed in turn. He took rather longer about it.

He looked up at last, and in a colorless voice asked Dag to explain, once again, the exact sequence of events in the malice's cave, with close guesses as to the time each movement had taken. He did not ask anything of Fawn. He sat a little more, then the distant expression went away, and he looked up again.

"So what do you make of it?" asked Dag. "What happened?"

"Dag, you can't expect me to discuss the inner workings of my craft in front of some farmer."

"No, I expect you to discuss them—fully—in front of that donor's mother."

Dar grimaced, but counterattacked, unexpectedly speaking to Fawn directly for the very first time: "Yes, and how *did* you get pregnant?"

Did she have to confess the whole stupid episode with Stupid Sunny? She looked up beseechingly at Dag, who shook his head slightly. She gathered her courage and replied coolly, "In the usual way, I believe."

Dar growled, but did not pursue the matter. Instead, he protested to Dag, "She won't understand."

"Then you won't actually be giving away any secrets, will you? Begin at the beginning. She knows what ground is, for starters."

"I doubt that," said Dar sourly.

Dag shifted his splinted hand to touch his marriage cord. "Dar, she made this. The other as well."

"She couldn't . . ." Dar went quiet for a time, brow furrowing. "All right. Flukes happen. But I still think she won't understand."

"Try. She might surprise you." Dag smiled faintly. "You might be a better teacher than you think."

"All right, all right! All right." Dar turned his glower on Fawn. "A knife . . . that is, a dying body that . . . agh. Go all the way back. Ground is in everything, you understand that?"

Fawn nodded anxiously.

"Living things build up ground and alter its essence. Concentrate it. They are always making, but they are making themselves. Man eats food, the food's ground doesn't vanish, it goes into the man and is transformed. When a man—or any living thing—dies, that ground is released. The ground associated with material parts dissipates slowly with the decaying body, but the nonmaterial part, the most complex inner essence, it goes all at once. Are you following this?" he demanded abruptly.

Fawn nodded.

His look said, *I don't think so,* but he went on. "Anyway. That's how living things help a blight recover, by building up ground slowly around the edges and constantly releasing it again. That's how blight kills, by draining ground away too fast from anything caught away from the edge too long. A malice consumes ground directly, ripping it out of the living like a wolf disemboweling its prey."

Dag did not wince at this comparison, although he went a little stony. Actually, that was a brief nod of agreement, Fawn decided. She shivered and concentrated on Dar, because she didn't think he'd respond well to being stopped for questions, at least not by her.

"Sharing knives . . ." He touched the curve of hers. "The inner surface of a thighbone has a natural affinity for blood, which can be persuaded to grow stronger by the maker shaping the knife. That's what I do, in addition to . . . to encouraging it to dwell on its fate. I meet with the pledged heart's-death donor, and he or she shares their blood into the knife in the making. Because their live blood bears their ground."

"Oh!" said Fawn in a voice of surprise, then closed her mouth abruptly.

"Oh what?" said Dar in aggravation.

She looked at Dag; he raised an unhelpful eyebrow. "Should I say?" she asked.

"Certainly."

She glanced sideways at the frowning and—even shirtless—thoroughly intimidating maker. "Maybe you'd better explain, Dag."

Dag smiled a trifle too ironically at his brother. "Fawn reinvented the technique herself, to persuade her ground into my marriage cord. Took me by surprise. In fact, when I recognized it, I nearly fell off the bench. So I'd say she understands it intimately."

"You used a *knife-making* technique on a *marriage* cord?" Dar sounded aghast.

Dag hitched up his left shoulder. "Worked. The only clue I gave her was to mention—days earlier, in another conversation altogether—that blood held a person's ground for a while after leaving the body."

"Fluke," muttered Dar, though more faintly. Craning anew at the cord.

"Yeah, that's life with Spark. Just one fluke after another. Seems no end to them. You were halfway through explaining a making. Go on."

Dag, Fawn realized, had been through the process from the donor's side at least once, if with some maker up in Luthlia and not with Dar. In addition to whatever he had learned from being around his brother, however intermittently.

Dar took a breath and went on. "So at the end of the knife-making, we have a little of the pledged donor's ground in the knife, and that ground is . . . well, you could say it's hungry for the rest. It wants to be reunited with its source. And the other way around. So then we come to the priming itself." His face was stern, contemplating this, for reasons that had nothing to do with her, Fawn thought.

"When the knife is"—he hesitated, then chose the plain word—"driven into the donor's heart, killing him, his essential ground begins to break up. At this very point of dissolution, the ground is drawn into the knife. And held there."

"Why doesn't it just all dissolve then?" Fawn couldn't help asking, then mentally kicked herself for interrupting.

"That's another aspect of my making. If you can fluke it

out, good luck to you. I'm not just a bone-carver, you know."
His smile was astringent. "When someone—like Dag, for
example—then manages to bring the primed knife up to a
malice and plunge it in, the malice, which eats ground and
cannot stop doing so, draws in the dissolving ground released by the breaking of the knife. You could say the mortal
ground acts as a poison to the malice's ground, or as a stroke
of lightning to a tree, or . . . well, there are a number of ways
to say it, all slightly wrong. But the malice's ground shares
in the dissolution of the mortal ground, and since a malice
is made of nothing *but* ground, all the material elements it is
holding in place fall with it."

Fawn touched the scars on her neck. "That, I've seen."

Dar's brows drew down. "How close were you, really?"

Fawn held out her arm and squinted. "About half my arm's
length, maybe." And her arms weren't all that long.

"Dar," said Dag gently, "if you haven't grasped this, I'll
say it again; she drove my primed knife into the Glassforge
malice. And I speak from repeated personal experience
when I tell you, that's way, way closer than any sane person
would ever want to be to one of those things."

Dar cleared his throat uncomfortably, staring down at the
knife in his lap.

It popped out before she could help herself: "Why can't
you just use dying animals' grounds to poison malices?"

Dag smiled a little, but Dar scowled in deep offense. Dar
said stiffly, "They haven't the power. Only the ground of a
Lakewalker donor will kill a malice."

"Couldn't you use a lot of animals?"

"No."

"Has it been tried?"

Dar frowned harder. "Animals don't work. Farmers don't
work either." His lips drew back unkindly. "I'll leave you to
make the connection."

Fawn set her teeth, beginning to have an inkling about the
piglet insult.

Dag gave his brother a grim warning look, but put in, "It's not just a question of power, although that's part of it. It's also a question of affinity."

"Affinity?" Fawn wrinkled her nose. "Never mind. What happened to my—to Dag's other knife?" She nodded to it.

Dar sighed, as if he was not quite sure of what he was about to say. "You have to understand, a malice is a mage. It comes out of the ground, sessile and still in its first molt, a more powerful mage than any of us alone will ever be, and just gets stronger after. So. First, this malice snatched the ground of your unborn child."

Fawn's spirits darkened in memory. "Yes. Mari said no one had known malices could do that separately. Is that important?" It would be consoling if that horror had at least bought some key bit of knowledge that might help someone later.

Dar shrugged. "It's not immediately clear to me that it makes any practical difference."

"Why do malices want babies?"

He held out his hand and turned it over. "It's the inverse of what the sharing knives share. Children unborn, and to a lesser extent, young, are in the most intense possible period of self-making of the most complex of grounds. Malices building up to a molt—to a major self-making, or self-remaking—seem to crave that food."

"Couldn't it steal from pregnant animals?"

Dar raised a brow. "If it wanted to molt into an animal body instead of a human one, perhaps."

"They can and do," Dag put in. "The Wolf Ridge malice couldn't get enough humans, so it partly used wolves as well. I was told by patrollers who were in on the knifing of it that its form was pretty . . . pretty strange, at the end, and it was well past its first molt."

Fawn made a disturbed face. So, she noticed, did Dar.

Dar continued, "Anyway. Secondly, you drove Dag's unprimed knife into the thing."

Fawn nodded. "Its thigh. He said, anywhere. I didn't know."

"Then—leaving that knife in place, right . . . ?"

"Yes. That was when the bogle—the malice—picked me up the second time, by the neck. I thought it was going to shake me apart like a chicken."

Dar glanced at her scars, and away. "Then you drove in the actual primed knife."

"I figured I'd better be quick. It broke." Fawn shivered in the remembered terror, and Dag's left arm tightened around her. "I thought I'd ruined it. But then the malice dropped me and . . . and sort of melted. It stank."

"Simplest explanation," said Dar crisply. "A person carrying something very valuable to them who trips and falls, tries to fall so as to protect their treasure, even at the cost of hurting themselves. Malice snatches rich ground. Seconds later, before the malice has assimilated or stored that ground, it's hit with a dose of mortality. In its fall, it blindly tries to shove that ground into a safe spot for it: the unprimed knife. A malice certainly has the power to do so by force and not persuasion. End result, one dissolved malice, one knife with an unintended ground jammed into it." Dar sucked his lip. "More complicated explanations might be possible, but I haven't heard anything in your testimony that would require them."

"Hm," said Dag. "So will it still work as a sharing knife, or not?"

"The ground in it is . . . strange. It was caught and bound at a point of most intense self-making *and* most absolute self-dissolution, simultaneously. But still, only a farmer's ground after all." He glanced up sharply. "Unless there's something about the child no one is telling me. Mixed blood, for example?" His look at his brother was coolly inquiring and not especially respectful.

"It was a farmer child," Fawn said quietly, looking at the soil. It was bare at the base of the steps, with a few broken hickory husks flattened into the old mud. Dag's arm tightened silently around her again.

"Then it will have no affinity, and is useless. An unprimed knife that gets contaminated can be boiled clean and rededicated, sometimes, but not this. My recommendation is that you break it to release that worthless farmer ground, burn it—or send the pieces back to Kauneo's kin with whatever explanation you can concoct that won't embarrass you—and start over with a new knife." His voice softened. "I'm sorry, Dag. I know you didn't carry this for twenty years for such a futile end. But, you know, it happens that way sometimes."

Fawn looked up at Dar. "I'll have that back, now," she said sturdily. She held out her hand.

Dar gave Dag an inquiring look, found no support, and reluctantly handed the sheathed knife back to Fawn.

"A lot of knives never get used," said Dag, in a would-be casual tone. "I see no special need of rushing to dispose of this one. If it serves no purpose intact, it serves no more destroyed."

Dar grimaced. "What will you keep it for, then? A wall decoration? A gruesome memento of your little adventure?"

Dag smiled down at Fawn; she wondered what her own face looked like just now. It felt cold. He said, "It had one use, leastways. It brought us together."

"All the more reason to break it," said Dar grimly.

Fawn thought back on Dag's offer of the same act, way back at the Horsefords' farmhouse. *We could have saved a lot of steps.* How could two such apparently identical suggestions feel like utter opposites? *Trust and untrust.* She hoped she could get Dag alone soon, and ask him whether he accepted his brother's judgment, or only some part of it, or none, or if they should seek another maker. There was no clue in his face. She hid the knife away again in her shirt.

Dag stood and stretched, rolling his shoulders. "It's about dinnertime, I expect. You want to come watch, Dar, or hide out here?"

Fawn began to wish she and Dag could hide out here. Well—she eyed the bones hung from the eaves swinging in the freshening breeze—maybe not just here. But somewhere.

"Oh, I'll come," said Dar, rising to collect his carving knife and the finished bowls and take them inside. "Might as well get it over with."

"Optimist," said Dag, stepping aside for him as he trod up the steps.

Fawn caught a glimpse of a tidy workroom, a very orderly bench with carving tools hung above it, and a small fieldstone fireplace in the wall opposite the door. Dar came back out fastening his shirt, entirely insensible of the ease with which his buttons cooperated with his fingers, latched the door, and passed efficiently around the shack closing the shutters.

The green light of the woods was growing somber as scudding dark clouds from the northwest filled the sky above. The staccato pop of falling nuts sounded like Dag's joints on a bad morning. Fawn clung to Dag's left arm as they started back up the path. His muscles were tight. She lengthened her steps to match his, and was surprised to find she didn't have to lengthen them very much.

4

$\mathcal{B}$eyond the clearing with the two tent-cabins, the gray of the lake was darkening, waves starting to spin off white tails of spume. Fawn could hear them slapping the shore beneath the nearby bank, where a stand of cattails bent and hissed in the rising wind. Only a single narrow boat was still in view, with two men paddling like mad for a farther shore. In the slate-colored air to the north, dazzling forks of lightning snaked from sky to earth, their thunder still laggard in arriving. The pearl of the sun, sinking toward Mare Island, disappeared behind a darker cloud even as she watched, turning the light gloomy.

Under the awning of the cabin on the right, a thin, straight, rigid figure in a skirt stood beside their piles of saddles and gear, watching anxiously up the path they were descending. Omba in her riding trousers lurked in the shadows behind, leaning against a support post with her arms crossed.

"What are you going to say?" Fawn whispered urgently to Dag.

"Depends."

"On what?"

"On what she says. If the rumors have run ahead of me, she'll have had time to get over being happy I'm alive and move on to other concerns. Depending on who all 'sides Omba got to her with the rumors, she could be pretty well stirred up."

"You left our gear in plain sight—she'd have to know you're back even without Omba."

"There is that."

Did he even have a plan? Fawn was beginning to wonder.

As they neared, the woman in the skirt stood bolt up-right. Her hands twitched out once, then she planted them firmly on her hips. Cumbia Redwing wore her silvery-gray hair pulled back in the simple mourning knot. Her skin had less of the burnished copper in it than Dag's—darker, more leathery, more worn—if striking in contrast with the hair. Fawn might have guessed her age as a healthy seventy, though she knew she was two decades beyond that. Her eyes were the clear tea color, narrowing under pinched-in streaks of silver brows as they swept over Fawn; in a better light, Fawn suspected they would be bright gold like Dag's.

As they came up to the edge of the awning, Cumbia thrust out her chin, and snapped, "Dag Redwing Hickory, I'm speechless!"

Behind them, Dar muttered, "Bet not." Dag's brows barely twitched acknowledgment of this.

Proving Dar right, she went on, "Whatever you patrollers do out on the road, the rule is, you don't bring it home. You can't be bringing your farmer whore into my tent."

As if he hadn't heard her, Dag pulled the shrinking Fawn forward, and said, "Mama, this is my wife, Fawn Blue-field."

"How de' do, ma'am." Fawn dipped her knees, frantically searching amongst the hundred rehearsed speeches in her mind for something to follow. She hadn't imagined doing this in a thunderstorm. She hadn't imagined most of this.

Dag forestalled her. Now standing behind her, he slid his hook, carefully turned downward, under her left wrist and elevated it. "See? Wife." He shrugged his left shoulder to display his own marriage cord.

Cumbia's eyes widened in horror. "You can't have—" With a hiccough of breath, she choked out, "Cut those things."

"No, ma'am," said Dag in a weirdly affable tone. *Flying*, Fawn thought. Off in that other place he went to when things turned deadly sour, when action moved too fast for thought, and he turned it all over to some other part of himself that could keep up. Or not . . .

"Dag, if you do not burn those abominations and take that girl right back where you found her, you are never entering my tent again." Had Cumbia been rehearsing too? Coached by excited rumormongers? There seemed something deeply awkward about her, as if her mouth and eyes were trying to say two different things. Dag might know with his ground-sense, if he hadn't obviously closed it down as hard as a hickory shell.

Dag smiled, or at any rate, his mouth curved sunnily, though his eyes stayed tight, making him look, for a moment, oddly like his mother. "Very good, ma'am." He turned to his stunned listeners. "Omba, Dar, good to see you again. Fawn, get your bags and bedroll. We'll send someone back for the saddles tomorrow. Omba, if she throws them out in the rain, could you put them under cover for me?"

Omba, staring wide-eyed, nodded.

Wait, what? "But Dag—"

He bent and hooked up Fawn's saddlebags and handed them to her, then hooked his own over his shoulder. She clutched the heavy load awkwardly to her chest as he put his arm around her back and turned her toward the clearing. The first big raindrops spattered down, batting the hickory leaves and hitting the dirt with audible plops.

"But Dag, no one—she hasn't—I haven't—"

Reversing herself abruptly, Cumbia said, "Dag, you can't go out there now, it's coming on to storm!"

"Come along, Spark." He hustled her out.

A few fat drops plunked onto the top of her head like hard finger-taps, soaking cold down to her scalp. "But Dag, she's not hardly—I didn't even get a chance to—" Fawn turned back to dip her knees again and call a desperate, "Nice to meet you, ma'am!" over her shoulder.

"Where are you going?" cried Cumbia, echoing Fawn's thoughts exactly. "Come back out of the rain, you fool!"

"Keep walking," Dag muttered out of the corner of his mouth. "Don't look back, or it'll be all to do over again." As they passed a big basket leaning against a stump, piled high with dark round shapes, he thunked his hook into one, snatching it up in passing. His stride lengthened. Fawn scurried to keep up.

As they reached the road, Dag hesitated, and Fawn panted, "Where *are* we going?"

He glanced over his shoulder. Through the trees, the far shore of the lake had disappeared behind a thick gray curtain of rain; Fawn could hear the oncoming hiss of it. "I have some folks who owe me favors, but that'll best be for tomorrow, I think. Right now we just need shelter. This way."

To Fawn's considerable dismay, he turned down the path leading to the bone shack. She grappled her saddlebags around over her shoulder and trotted after. The fat raindrops gave way, in a cold gust, to little hailstones, slicing down through the leaves and bouncing off the path, and, more painfully, off her. The pebble-sized ice triggered a heavier and even more alarming hail of hickory husks as the trees creaked in the wind, and Fawn pictured heavy branches coming down on them like huge hammers. Both she and Dag ducked and ran through the ominous shadows.

She was gasping and even Dag was out of breath when they arrived back at Dar's work-cabin. Along the eaves, the bones spun and knocked against one another in the gusts like dreadful wind chimes. Hail and hickory husks rattled off the roof shingles, sometimes sailing up again in high arcs before plopping to earth that was rapidly turning to mud. She and Dag thumped up the steps and huddled under the little porch roof.

With his wet hair plastered to his forehead and his jaw set, Dag attempted to free his hook from the plunkin by grasping the round root under his sling-arm, which made his saddle-bags in turn slide off his shoulder and land on his feet. He cursed.

"Here," said Fawn in exasperation. "Let me."

She dumped her own bags, wriggled the plunkin free of his hook, set it down, then turned to pluck the latchstring out of its slot and pull the door open. The shuttered cabin was dark, and she peered in doubtfully.

Dag bent down to hook futilely at his bootlaces. "Undo these for me, would you, Spark?" he muttered. "Dar doesn't like his floor dirtied."

She knocked the hook aside before he could snarl the laces into inextricable wet knots, undid first his, then hers, and set both pairs beside the door. She wiped her hands in aggra-vation on her riding trousers and followed him inside. He bent over a workbench; a welcome light flared from a good beeswax candle in a clay holder. He lit a second from the first, and with that and the faint gray light leaking through the shutters and from the door, she was finally able to see clearly.

The space was a bare dozen feet long by ten or so wide, lined with shelves and a couple of scarred but cleared-off workbenches. Stools of various heights made from upended logs, cut away beneath for legs and above for short backrests, were thrust under the benches. The space smelled of old wood and fresh wood, herbs and solvents, the honeyed warmth of the candles, oil, leather, and time. And under it all, something undefinable; she tried not to think, *death*.

Dag dragged their bags just inside the door, rolling the plunkin along after with his foot. He closed the door against the gusts. Minus the rattling of bones and clatter of ice and nuts on the roof, the threatening creak of the trees in the wind, the howling storm, the interminable day, the harrowing scene, or half scene, they'd just been through, and both their moods, it might have been almost cozy. As it was, Fawn would have burst into tears if she hadn't been so close to just bursting.

"So," she said tightly, "what happened to all your smooth Lakewalker persuadin', back there?"

Dag sighed and stretched his back. "There were only two ways it could go, Spark. Slow and excruciating, or fast and excruciating. Like yanking a tooth, I prefer my pain to go fast."

"You didn't even give her a chance to say her piece!"

He cocked an eyebrow at her. "Fewest unforgivable things we had the time to say to each other the better, I'd say."

"I didn't get a chance to say *my* piece! I didn't even get to try with her! I'm not saying I would have got anywhere either, but at least I'd have known I tried!"

"I know that trying. Spark, it would've near broke my heart to watch you turning yourself inside out with it. I couldn't have stood it."

He turned to attempt to undo their bedroll strings with his hook; after watching him for a frustrated moment, Fawn reached past and plucked the knots apart, helping him unroll their blankets across the floor. He sat down on his with a weary grunt. She sat down opposite, cross-legged, frowning up at him, and raked her hands through her damp distracted curls.

"Sometimes, once folks have a chance to vent, they'll calm down and talk more reasonable." Cumbia had already advanced as far as promoting Fawn from *farmer whore* to *that girl* just in the short time she'd been given, scarcely worse than the *that fellow* that was Dag's common name in West Blue. Who knew where they might have ended up if they'd just kept at it a bit?

He shrugged. "She won. It's done."

"If she won, what was her prize?" Fawn demanded. "I don't see how anyone won anything much, back there."

"Look—I didn't leave, she threw me out. Either she means it, and she'll never speak to me again, or else it'll be up to her to apologize."

"So what you're actually saying is, you won. Some tactics, Dag!"

He grimaced. "Learned 'em at my mother's knee."

"*What* has got into you? I've seen you in some moods, but I never saw you in a mood like this one! Can't say as I much like it."

He lay back and stared up at the peeled-log ridgepole. None of the support timbers for the roof were squared off or dressed, being just slim bare trunks of the right length fitted into triangles. "I don't much like the way I get here, either. It's like I lose myself when I get mixed up with my closest kin. Dar and Mama mostly—my father when he was alive less so, but some. Mari I can stand. It's part of why I touch down here lightly, or not at all if I can help it. A mile away, or better yet a hundred, I can go back to being me."

"Huh," said Fawn, mulling this over. She didn't find it nearly as inexplicable as she might once have, remembering how vast new possibilities had seemed to open for her in Glassforge, and close down chokingly when she returned to West Blue. It was just that at Dag's age she figured folks ought to be long over that sort of thing. Or maybe they'd just had more time to work down into a rut. Deep, deep rut. "Funny sort of exile."

"Indeed it is." But he wasn't laughing.

The air was chilling fast as the storm rumbled through. The small stone fireplace was clearly there more for warming pots of work supplies than for heating the far from tight building, presumably not used in winter, but Dag bestirred them to lay a fire. "Have to replace that in the morning," he muttered at the neat pile of deadfall standing ready on the porch just outside the door. But once the flames caught—Dag did seem to have a peculiar lucky knack for getting fires going—the yellow light, the scent of woodsmoke, and the occasional orange spark popping out onto the slate hearth lent some much-needed cheer to the room. Their hair and clothes began to dry, and Fawn's skin lost its clamminess.

Fawn set a pot of rain-barrel water on an iron hook to boil for tea, swung it over the fire, and poked at the new coals with a stick, pushing more underneath her pot. "So," she said, in what she hoped did not sound too desperate a tone, "where do we go tomorrow?"

"I figure to draw our own tent from Stores."

They owned a tent? "Where will we set it up?"

"I have an idea or two. If they don't work out, I'll find a third."

Which seemed to be all she was going to get right now. Was this clash with his family over, or not? It wasn't that she thought Dag was lying to her, so much as that she was beginning to suspect his idea of a comfortable outcome did not match hers. If Lakewalkers didn't marry farmers—or at least, didn't do so and then take the farmers home—she wouldn't expect the feeling here against her to be trifling or easily set aside. If this was something no one had successfully done before, her faith that *Dag will know what to do* was . . . if not misplaced, more hope than certainty. She wasn't afraid of hard, but when did *hard* shade over into *insurmountable*?

Her stomach growled. If Dag was half as fatigued as she was, it was no wonder nobody seemed able to think straight. Food would help everything. She rolled the mysterious plunkin across in front of the hearth and stared at it. It still looked disconcertingly like a severed head. "What do we do with this?"

Dag sat cross-legged and smiled—not much of a smile, but a start. "Lots of choices. They all come down to plunkin. You can eat it raw in slices, peel it and cut it up and cook it alone or in a stew, boil it whole, wrap it in leaves and cook it in campfire coals, stick a sword through it and turn it on a spit, or, very popular, feed it to the pigs and eat the pigs. It's very sustaining. Some say you could live forever on plunkin and rainwater. Others say it would just seem like forever." He gestured to her belt knife, one of his spares that he'd insisted she wear since they'd left West Blue. "Try a slice."

Dubiously, she captured the rolling globe between her knees and stabbed it. The brown rind was rather hard, but once opened revealed a dense, pale yellow fruit, solid all the way through, without a core or pit or seeds. She nibbled out a bite as if from a melon slice.

It was crunchy, not as sweet as an apple, not as starchy as a raw potato . . . "A bit parsnippy. Actually, quite a bit nicer than parsnip. Huh." It seemed the problem was not in the quality, but in the quantity.

For simplicity, and because she really didn't feel comfortable cooking over Dar's fireplace, used for who knew what sorcerous processes, they ate it raw in slices. Although Fawn did draw the line at Dag's attempt simply to stab his portion with his hook and gnaw around the edges; she peeled his piece and made him get out his fork-spoon. The plunkin was surprisingly satisfying. Hungry as they both were, they only disposed of half a head, or root, or whatever it was.

"Why don't farmers have this?" Fawn wondered. "Food gets around. Flowers, too. Animals, too, really. We could grow it in ponds."

Dag gestured with his slice, stuck on his fork-spoon. All right, so the official eating tool hadn't made that much difference; it still made it all seem more like a real meal. "The ears need a little tickle in their grounds to germinate. If farmers planted them, they'd just go down in the mud and rot. It's a trick most every Lakewalker here learns. I hated raft duty when I was young, thought it was the dullest thing possible. Now I understand why the old patroller didn't mind taking their turns, and laughed at me. Soothing, y'know."

Fawn crunched valiantly and tried to picture a young, impatient Dag sitting out on a raft, mostly undressed, coppery skin gleaming in the sun, grouchily tickling plunkin ears, one after another after another. She had to smile. With two hands, scarless and unmarred. Her smile faded.

"They say the old high lords of the lake league made wonderful magical plants, and animals too," Dag said thoughtfully. "Not many seemed to have survived the disasters. Plunkins have tricky growing conditions. Not too deep, not too shallow, mud bottoms. They won't take in those deep, clear, rocky-bottomed lakes east or north. Makes them a regional, er, delicacy. And, of course, they need Lakewalkers, year after year after year. Makes me wonder how far back this camp goes, really."

Fawn considered the continuity of plunkins. When all their world was falling apart around them, some Lakewalker ancestors must have kept the crop going. For hope? For habit? For sheer stubbornness? Eyeing Dag, she was inclined to bet on stubbornness.

They burned the rinds on the fire, and Fawn set the spare half aside for breakfast. Outside, the green dark of the storm had given way to the blue dark of night, and the rain had slowed to a steady drizzle. Dag hooked their bedrolls closer together.

Fawn felt her knife sheath shift between her breasts as she crawled across to sit again on her blanket, and reached up to touch it. "Do you think Dar was telling the truth about the knife?"

Dag leaned back against his saddlebags, damp bare feet to the fire, and frowned thoughtfully. "I think everything Dar said was truth. As far as it went."

"So . . . what does that mean? Do you think he was holding something back?"

"Not sure. It's not that . . . I'd say, the knife is a problem he wants to have go away, not explore."

"If he's as good a knife maker as you say, I'd think he'd be more curious."

Dag shrugged. "Folks are at first. Like Saun the Sheep, or me at Saun's age—it's all new and exciting. But then it becomes the same task over and over, and the new becomes rare. Whether you then find novelty to be exciting or something to resent . . . Thing, is, Dar has spent thirty and more years, all day most every day, making weapons for his relatives and best friends to go kill themselves with. Whatever Dar is doing that lets him go on, I'm not inclined to fool with it."

"Maybe we should ask after a younger knife maker, then." Fawn shoved her own saddlebags around, trying for a more comfortable prop, and lay down next to Dag. "So . . . what did he—and you—mean when you said the ground had to have affinity? You used that word two or three times, like it meant something special."

"Ah. Hm." Dag rubbed his nose with his hook. His features were outlined in the orange glow from the fire, lapped by the light with the rest of him falling into shadow. The walls of the shack seemed to recede into a fathomless darkness. "Well, simply that malice ground takes up Lakewalker mortality readily, as the ground of bone takes up that of blood."

Fawn frowned. "You have to figure, bones take up blood because they were once both together."

"That's right."

"So . . ." She suddenly wasn't sure she liked where this was going. "So . . . ?"

"Legend would have it—*legend* is just like *they say*, only more dried up, you know?"

She nodded cautiously.

"In fact, no one alive now knows for sure. Those who knew died in the knowing, one, two thousand years ago. Chronicles were lost, time was lost—was it two centuries or five or ten that dropped out, how many generations disappeared in the dark?"

"They kept the plunkins going, anyhow."

His lips curved briefly. "There is that."

"So what is this thing that's known or not known?"

"Well, there is more than one version of how malices came into the world. We know they didn't used to be here."

"You've seen, what, twenty-seven of them? Up close? I don't want to know what other people say. What do you believe?"

He sighed. "*They say* is all I have to go on, for most of it. They say the old lords of the lake league worked great magics in great groups. They combined up under the mastery of the high king. One king, the last king, greater and more cunning than any before, at the apex of the greatest array of mages ever assembled, reached beyond the bounds of the world for . . . something. Some say immortality. Some say power. The king stories mostly assume evil intent because of evil results—if there is punishment, there must have been a crime. They blame pride and selfishness, or whatever vice they're especially miffed with. I'm not so sure. Maybe he was attempting to capture some imagined good to share, and it all went horribly wrong.

"You know I said the old lords used their magic to alter plants, animals, and themselves. And their children." He tapped his temple with the backside of his hook, and Fawn realized he thought his eye color was a relic of those efforts. "Extended life, improved groundsense and ability to move the world through its ground." He glanced, briefly and uneasily, at his left arm held up, and she knew he was thinking about his ghost hand again. He let it drop again to his side. "We Lakewalkers, we think, are the descendants of lesser hinterland lords—what must the great ones have been like?

"Anyway. In their attempt to enhance themselves, the high lords drew in *something* from outside the world. God, demon, other. If they'd kidnapped a god, it would explain why the gods shun us. And the king *combined* with it, or it with him. And became something that was neither. Vast, distorted, powerful, insane, and consuming ground instead of . . . of whatever they'd intended."

"Wait, are you saying your own *king* became the first malice?" Fawn rolled up on her elbow to stare in astonishment.

Dag tilted his head in doubt. "He became something. Some lords fell under his power—legend says—and some broke away. A war of matter and magic followed, which sank the lakes and left the Dead Lake and the Western Levels. Whether the malice-king's enemies discovered how to destroy him, or it was another accident, any who knew died in the finding out. *Someone* back then must have discovered how to share mortality. It must have been a great sharing, is all I can say. *Our* malices came from some cataclysmic ground transformation when he, or it, was at last destroyed, and blew up into those ten thousand—or however many—shards or seeds or eggs. But that's what we think the malices are all trying to do, clumsily, when they come out of the ground. Become kings again.

"Hence—to return roundabout to your original question—affinity. Malices take up Lakewalker mortality because they are, or were, partly us."

Along the eaves, bones clanked in a breath of night wind. Fawn found herself trying to shrink under her blankets, which had crept, during this reciting, from her feet to her waist to her nose. This was worse than any tall tale her brothers had ever tormented her with. "Are you saying all those malices are your *relatives*?"

He lay back and, infuriatingly, laughed. "Don't you just hate those family squabbles? Absent gods." The chuckles died down before she got up the nerve to poke him in reproof. "Collateral ancestors at most, Spark. But I suggest you not share that insight around. Some folks are like to be offended."

What have I married into, really? The revelations dismayed her. She thought back to her malice's tormented, merciless eyes. They might have been tea-brown, with a certain now-familiar iridescence.

He let out the last of his black humor in a sigh. "If not relatives, they are certainly our legacy. Our joint inheritance. Not sure what my share is." His hook drifted up to touch his heart. "One, I reckon."

A chill shook Fawn at this vision of his mortal fate. "And you all so proud. Riding by us like lords." And yet Lakewalkers lived, at home, in worse poverty than most farmers, unless the Bearsford camp was any more elaborate than this. She was beginning to suspect not. Noble grandeur was sadly lacking all around. *Squalid scramble* seemed a more apt description.

Dag shrugged. "We have to tell ourselves some flattering stories to keep ourselves going. Day after year after decade. What else? Lie down and die for the endless despair of it all?"

She lay back and followed his stare up into the dim rafters. "Is there an end?"

"Perhaps. If we just keep on. We think there were not an infinite number of malices planted. They don't come up under water or ice or above the tree line, or on old blight. Our maps of the lairs we've destroyed show them thicker toward the Dead Lake, but fewer and farther apart going out. And we say they are immortal, but in fact all that have hatched have been slain. So maybe they wouldn't live forever, but what they destroy betimes is more than enough. Maybe they'll stop hatching out someday just for sheer age, but that'd be a bad hope to count on or dwell on. Like to make a man impatient, and this is no war for the impatient. Yet if all things end, even despair must, too. Not in my lifetime. But sometime." He blinked up into the shadows. "I don't believe in much, but I'll believe that."

That despair must end? Or, not in his lifetime? Both, likely.

He sat up and stretched his back, wincing, and, after a desultory futile prod at his arm-harness buckles with his splinted hand, extended it to Fawn to free him for the night. She unbuckled it and set it aside as usual, decided they weren't going to do better than to sleep in their clothes, and, after a brief hesitation, cuddled down in her accustomed spot under his left arm, where she could press her ear to his heart. She pulled the blanket up over them both. Dag did not, by word or gesture, suggest lovemaking here tonight, and, relieved, neither did she. The fire died to embers before either of them slept.

5

Dag left on a mumbled errand soon after it was light, leaving Fawn to pack up. She had the bags and bedrolls stacked tidily on the porch, the cabin swept out, and even the fireplace ashes hauled away and scattered in the wet woods, with no sign of his return. She collected from the abundant new deadfall to replace the pile they'd burned last night, and then some, and finally sat on the porch steps with her chin in her hand, waiting. The flock of wild turkeys—or another flock, as there seemed to be a lot more of them this morning, upwards of forty—stalked through the clearing, and Fawn and they eyed each other gloomily.

A figure appeared on the path, and the turkeys ambled off. Fawn sat up eagerly, only to slump in disappointment. It was Dar, not Dag.

He glowered at her without approval but without surprise; likely his groundsense had told him where she and Dag had gone to hole up last night.

"Morning," she tried cautiously.

She received a grunt and a grudging nod in return. "Where's Dag?" he asked.

"He went off." She added warily, "He told me to wait here for him till he got back."

Another grunt. Dar inspected his lathe, wet but undamaged by the storm, and went around the cabin fastening open the shutters. He trod up the steps, stared down at her, slipped off his muddy shoes, and went inside; he came back out in a few minutes looking faintly frustrated, perhaps because she'd left nothing to complain of.

He asked abruptly, "You didn't couple in there last night, did you?"

Fawn stared up in offense. "No, but what business is that of yours?"

"I'd have to do a ground cleansing if you did." He stared at the firewood stack. "Did you collect that, or Dag?"

"I did, of course."

He looked as though he was reaching for a reason to reject it, but couldn't come up with one. Fortunately, at that point Dag came striding up the path. He looked reasonably cheerful; perhaps his errand had prospered?

"Ah." He paused when he saw his brother; they exchanged equally laconic nods.

Dar waited a moment as if for Dag to speak, then when nothing was forthcoming, said, "That was a clever retreat last night. *You* didn't have to listen to the complaints."

"You could've gone for a walk."

"In the rain? Anyway, I thought that was your trick—patroller."

Dag lowered his eyelids. "As you say." He nodded to Fawn and hooked his saddlebags and hers up over his shoulder. "Come along, Spark. G'day, Dar."

Fawn found herself trotting at his heels, casting a farewell nod over her shoulder at Dar, who by the opening and tight closing of his mouth clearly had wanted to say more.

"Were you all right?" Dag asked, as soon as they were out of earshot. "With Dar, I mean."

"I guess. Except that he asked one really rude question."

"Which was?"

Fawn flushed. "He asked if we'd made love in his cabin."

"Ah. Well, he actually does have a legitimate reason for wanting to know that, but he should have asked me. If he really couldn't trust me to know better."

"I hadn't worked round yet to asking him if your mama had softened any overnight. Didn't you want to ask?"

"If she had," Dag said distantly, "I'm sure Dar was able to stiffen her up again."

Fawn asked more quietly, looking down at her feet pacing along the muddy, leaf-and-stick-strewn path, "Did this—marrying me—mess things up any between you and your brother?"

"No."

"Because he seems pretty angry at you. At us."

"He's always annoyed at me for something. It's a habit. Don't worry about it, Spark."

They reached the road and turned right. Dag barely glanced aside as they passed his family's clearing. He made no move to turn in there. The road followed the shoreline around the island and curved south, running between the woods and more groups of cabins hugging the bank. The dripping trees sparkled in the morning light, and the sun, now well up above the farther shore, sent golden beams between the boles through the cool, moist air, which smelled of rain and moss.

Not a quarter mile along, Dag turned left into a clearing featuring three tent-cabins and a dock much like all the others. It was set a little apart from its neighbors by a stand of tall black walnut trees to its north and an orchard of stubbier fruit trees to its south; Fawn could see a few beehives tucked away among the latter. On a stump in front of one of the cabins sat an aging man dressed only in trousers cut off above the knees and held up by a rope belt, and leather sandals. His gray hair was knotted at his nape. He was carving away with long strokes on what looked to be some sort of oar or paddle in the making, but when he saw them he waved the knife in amiable greeting.

Dag dumped their saddlebags atop another stump and led Fawn over to the fellow. By his gnarly feet, she suspected he was an old patroller. He'd clearly been a big man once, now going a little stringy with age, except around his—for a Lakewalker—ample middle. He eyed Fawn as curiously as she eyed him.

Dag said, "Fawn, this is Cattagus Redwing, Mari's husband."

Making him Dag's uncle, then. So, this marriage hadn't estranged Dag from quite all his family. Fawn dipped her knees and smiled anxiously, looking around covertly for Mari. It would be wonderful to see a familiar face. She saw no one else, but heard cheery voices coming from down over the bank.

Cattagus tilted his head in dry greeting. "So, this is what all the fuss is about. Cute as a kitten, I'll grant you that." His voice was wheezy, with a sharp whistling running through it. He looked her up and down, a little smile playing around his lips, shook his head wryly, drew breath again, and added, "Absent gods, boy. I'd never have got away with something like this. Not even when I was thirty years younger."

Dag snorted, sounding more amused than offended. " 'Course not. Aunt Mari would've have had your hide for a tent flap."

Cattagus chuckled and coughed. "That's a fact." He waved aside with his knife. "The girls from Stores brought your tent by."

"Already?" said Dag. "That was quick."

Fawn tracked their gazes to a large handcart set at the side of one cabin, piled high with what appeared to be old hides, with a stack of long poles sticking out the back.

"They said, bring back their cart soon as you get it empty."

"That I can do. Where do Mari and Sarri want me to set up?"

"Better go ask 'em." Cattagus gestured toward the shore.

Fawn followed Dag to peek over the bank. To the left of the dock, at which two narrow boats were tied, a sort

of wooden cradle lay in the water, perhaps ten feet long
and six feet wide. A woman wearing long black hair to
her hips and nothing else, and a black-haired girl-child,
were tromping vigorously up and down in it. Marching
with them, Razi, equally nude, was clapping his hands
and calling to the little girl, who looked to be about four,
"Jump, Tesy! Jump!" She squealed with laughter and
hopped like a frog, splashing the woman, who ducked and
grinned. The cradle was apparently for retting some sort
of long-stemmed plant, and the treaders were engaged in
kicking off the rotting matter to clean the fibers. Beyond
them, Utau, standing in water to his waist, was supporting
the clutching fists of a small boy of perhaps two, whose
fat little legs kicked up a fountain of foam. Mari, dressed
in only a simple sleeveless shift hemmed at the calf and
sandals like her husband's, stood on the dock with her
hands on her hips watching them, smiling. She seemed to
be halfway through either loading or unloading a couple
dozen coils of rough-looking rope from one of the boats,
much like the rope netting Fawn had seen on the plunkin
panniers.

Dag called down over the bank, "Hey, Mari! We're
back."

Indicating that he'd been here once already this morning,
likely to arrange this. Fawn wondered if this had been his
first idea, or his third, and just how he had gone about explaining his needs. His ability to persuade had not entirely
deserted him, it seemed.

Mari waved back. "Be right with you!"

Steps laid from flat stones made a stairway down the
steep bank to the dock. In a few moments, Fawn was treated
to the somewhat startling sight of a whole family of nude,
wet Lakewalkers climbing up from the shore. They seemed
quite unconscious of their undress. Fawn, who had never
done more than wade in the shallows of the river with her
skirts rolled up, supposed it made sense, given that these

people were likely in and out of the water a dozen times a day for various purposes. She was nonetheless relieved when they streamed past her with only the briefest greetings and emerged a few minutes later from the cabin on the north of the clearing dressed, if simply: Razi and Utau in truncated trousers like Cattagus's, and Sarri and her daughter in shifts. The little boy, escaping, streaked past still in his skin in a beeline for the water, only to be scooped up and tickled into distraction from his purpose by Utau.

Mari followed up the steps and stopped by Dag. "Morning, Fawn." Her expression today was ironic but not unsympathetic. "Dag, Sarri thought you could set up under the apple tree over there. There's a bit of rising ground there, though you can hardly see it. It'll be the driest spot."

Utau, with the boy now riding atop his shoulders, small hands pulling his hair from its knot, came up with the long-haired woman. To Fawn's eyes, she looked to be about thirty; Fawn added the accustomed fifteen years to her guess. "Hello, Fawn," Utau greeted her, without surprise. Clearly, he'd been given the whole tale by now. "This is our wife, Sarri Otter." A nod at Razi, who had been inspecting the cart and now strode over to join them, confirmed the other part of that *our.*

Fawn had twigged that they were on Sarri's territory, and maybe Mari's; she gave her knee-dip, and said to the women, "Thank you for having us here."

Sarri folded her arms and nodded shortly, face not un-friendly, eyes curious. "Dag . . . well, Dag," she said, as if that explained something.

Dag, Razi, Utau, and Mari, with Cattagus following along and supplying wheezing commentary, then turned their attention to the alleged tent. The men hauled the cart to the orchard and swiftly unloaded it. The bewildering mess of poles and ropes was transformed with startling speed into a square frame with hides over its arching top and hanging down for walls, neatly staked to the earth. It had a sort of miniature porch, more hides raised up on poles, for an awning in front, which they arranged facing the lakeshore, canted so that the rising sun would not shine in directly. They rolled up and tied the front walls beneath the awning, leaving the little room open to the air much like the more solid structures.

"There!" said Dag in a satisfied voice, standing back and regarding the results. "Tent Bluefield!"

Fawn thought it looked more like Pup-Tent Bluefield; it made the other cabins seem positively palatial. She ventured near and peered in dubiously. *It's all right, I'm just temporary,* the tent seemed to say of itself. But temporary on the way to what?

Dag followed, looking down at her a shade anxiously. "Many's the young couple who starts with no more," he said.

Likely, but you aren't young. "Mm," said Fawn, and nodded to show willing. There was space inside for a double bedroll and a few possessions, but little else. At least the stubby apple tree was not likely to drop lethal branches atop.

"Don't lay anything out in it yet—let the ground dry a while more," said Dag. "We'll get reeds for bedding, rocks for a fire pit, maybe do something for flooring." He strode back to the clearing and collected a pair of short logs, hooking up the smaller and rolling the larger along with his foot, and set them upright beneath the awning for seats. "There."

Excited by this novelty, the little girl Tesy went inside and pranced and danced about, singing to herself. Truly, the tent seemed more playhouse-sized than Dag-sized, though the curved roof would allow him to stand upright, barely. Sarri made to call her daughter back out, but Fawn said, "No—let her. It's a sort of house blessing, I guess," which earned her a grateful and suddenly shrewd look from Sarri.

"If I might borrow your husbands once more," said Dag to Sarri, "I thought we'd go get my things before I take the cart back."

"Sure thing, Dag."

"Mari"—his gaze seemed to test his patrol-leader-and-relative's willingness—"maybe you could show Fawn around while we're gone?"

Implying, among other things, that Fawn was not invited on this expedition. But Mari nodded readily enough. It seemed Fawn was to be accepted by this branch of Dag's family, at least. If temporarily, like the tent. The three men went off with the cart, not altogether unloaded, as both children immediately scrambled atop for the ride. Or rather, Tesy scrambled up, and her little brother wailed in dismay till Razi popped him aboard with her.

"It's normally a bit livelier than this," Mari told Fawn, who was gazing around the clearing. "But as soon as I got back from patrol and could take charge of Cattagus, my daughter took her family across to Heron Island to visit with her husband's folks. They're building a new boat for her." A wave of her hand indicated the third cabin as belonging to this absent family. Was the daughter Mari's name-heiress? What else did Lakewalkers inherit, if they did not own land? Besides their fair share of malices. Was this site apportioned out like tents and horses from some camp pool?

Mari, with Sarri trailing in silent curiosity, took Fawn out back and showed her where the privy was hidden among the trees: not a shed but a slit trench with a hide blind, very tentlike. Water was drawn from the lake, and kettles kept permanently on the hob to boil that intended for drinking. Inside Mari's cabin, Fawn saw that the fireplace had a real oven, which she eyed enviously. Lakewalker women were not limited to pan bread cooked over an open fire, evidently. Though it seemed futile to ask to borrow the oven when Fawn owned no flour, baking pans, lard, butter, eggs, milk, or yeast.

Against the wall in Sarri's cabin stood a simple vertical loom loaded with work in progress, some tough-looking tight-woven fabric Fawn recognized from Lakewalker riding trousers. Fawn wondered at the thread; Sarri explained it was from the ever-useful plunkin, the stems of which, when retted, yielded up a long, strong, durable fiber, which accounted for the retting cradle in the lake. Fawn didn't see a spinning wheel. Little furniture met her eye, apart from some trestle tables and the common upended-log seats. There were no bed frames inside at all; by the bundles of bedding stacked along a wall, it seemed Lakewalkers slept in bedrolls even at home, and Fawn realized why Dag had taken so happily to the floor of Aunt Nattie's weaving room.

They went outside again to find that Dag and the cart had returned. Besides their saddles and bridles, a sword in a worn leather sheath, and a spear, it held only one trunk.

"Is this all you have?" Fawn asked him, as he set it all in a pile beside the tent for later stowage. The trunk hardly seemed large enough to contain, for example, surprise kitchen tackle. It barely seemed large enough for spare boots.

Dag stretched his back and grimaced. "My winter gear's in storage at Bearsford."

Fawn suspected it amounted to little more.

He added, "I also have my camp credit. You'll see tomorrow how that works."

And he was off again, dragging the emptied cart with his hook.

"What shall I do?" Fawn asked rather desperately after him.

"Take a rest!" he called unhelpfully over his shoulder, and turned onto the road.

Rest? She'd been resting, or at least, traveling, which while not restful was certainly not useful work. Her hand traced her wrist cord, and she looked up at the two Lakewalker women, looking down—dubiously?—at her. Sarri's cord, she saw, was two cords wrapped around each other.

"I aim to be a good wife to Dag," Fawn said resolutely, then her voice wavered. "But I don't know what that *means* here. Mama trained me up. If this were a farm, I could run it. I could make soap and candles, but I have no tallow or anything to make lye in. I can cook and preserve, but there's no jars and no storage cellars. If I had a cow, I could milk her, and make cheese and butter, if I had a churn. Aunt Nattie gave me spindles and knitting needles and scissors and needles and pins. Never saw a man more in need of socks than Dag, and I could make good ones, but I have no *fiber*. I can keep accounts, and make a fair ink, but there's no paper nor anything to record." Although those turkeys, she considered, could be forced to yield up quills. "I have knowing hands, but no *tools*. There must be more for me to do here than sit and eat plunkin!"

Mari smiled. "Let me tell you, farmer child, when you come back from weeks out on patrol, you're right glad to sit and eat plunkin for a time. Even Dag is." She added after a moment's reflection, "For about three days, then he's back badgering Fairbolt for a place in the next patrol going out. Fairbolt figures that the reason he has three times the malice kills of anyone else is that he spends twice the time looking for 'em."

Sarri said curiously, "What accounts for the rest?"

"Fairbolt wishes he knew." Mari scratched her head and regarded Fawn in bemusement. "Yeah, Dag said you'd get resty-testy if anyone tried to make you sit still. You two may have more in common than you look."

Fawn said plaintively, "Can you show me how to go on? Please, I'll do anything. I'll even crack nuts." One of her most hated tedious chores back home.

"We're a bit between on that one," said Sarri, with a lopsided smile. "The old falls are rotten and the new ones are too green. We leave 'em for the pigs to clean up, just this season. In a month, now, when the elderberries and the fruit trees come on, we'll all be busy. Cattagus and his wine-making, and nuts in plenty. Rope and baskets, now, that's for doing."

"I know how to make baskets," said Fawn eagerly, "if I had something to make them of."

"When that next batch of retting's done, I'll be glad for help with the spinning," said Sarri judiciously.

"Good! When?"

"Next week."

Fawn sighed. Razi and Utau were just finishing digging a fire pit in front of their tent, and Tesy and her brother were being kept usefully busy hauling stones to line it. Maybe Fawn could at least go gather more deadfall for their future fire. While her back was turned, she noticed, a split-wood basket with three fresh plunkins in it had appeared under her awning.

"Go along, fire-eater," said Mari, sounding amused. "Take a rest till Dag gets back from the medicine tent. Go for a swim."

Fawn hesitated. "In that big lake?" *Naked?*

Mari and Sarri stared at each other. "Where else?" said Sarri. "It's safe to dive off the end of the dock; the water's well over your head there."

This sounded the opposite of safe to Fawn.

Mari added, "Don't dive off the sides, though, or we'll have to pull your head out of the mud like a plunkin."

"I, um . . ." Fawn swallowed, and continued in a much smaller voice, "don't know how to swim."

Mari's brows shot up; Sarri pursed her lips. Both of them gazed at Fawn as though she were a freak of nature like a two-headed calf. That is, even more than most Lakewalkers looked at her that way. Fawn reddened.

"Does Dag know this?" demanded Sarri.

"I . . . I don't know." Would being so readily drownable disqualify one from being a Lakewalker's spouse? When she'd said she wanted to be taught how to go on here, she hadn't imagined swimming lessons being at the top of anyone's list.

"Dag," said Mari in a definite voice, "needs to know this." And added, to Fawn's increasing alarm, "Right away!"

The Two Bridge Island medicine tent was in fact three cabins with its own dock a few hundred paces past patroller headquarters. It seemed not very busy this morning, Dag saw as he neared after dropping the cart at Stores. Only a couple of horses were hitched to the rails out front. Good. No pestilence this week, no patrols dragging home too many smashed-up comrades.

As he mounted the porch to the main building, he met Saun coming out. Ah, one smashed-up comrade, then—if clearly on the path to recovery. The boy looked well, standing up straight and moving only a little stiffly, although he was looking down and touching his chest gingerly. Saun's face lit with delight as he glanced up and saw Dag, which turned to the usual consternation as he took in the sling.

"Dag, man! They said you were missing, then there was a crazy rumor going around you'd come back with the little farmer girl—married, if you can believe! Some people!" His voice trailed off in an *oh* as he took in the cord wrapping Dag's left arm, just visible below his rolled-up sleeve and above his arm-harness strap.

"We got back yesterday afternoon," said Dag, letting the last remark pass. "And you? Last I saw, you were bundled up in a wagon heading south from Glassforge."

"When I could ride again, one of the Log Hollow fellows brought me up to rendezvous with Mari's patrol, and they brought me home. Medicine maker says I can go out again when the patrol does if I rest up good the next couple of weeks. I'm still a little ouchy, but nothing too bad." His stare returned to Dag's left arm. "How did you . . . I mean, Fawn was cute and all, and she sure cheered you up, but . . . all right, there was the malice, maybe she . . . Dag, is your family going to accept this?"

"No."

"Oh." Saun fell silent in dismay. "If . . . what . . . where will you go?"

"That's to be seen. We've set up our tent at Mari's place for the moment."

"I suppose that makes sense. Mari's bound to defend her own . . . um." Saun shook his head, looking wary and confused. "I never heard tell of anything like this. Well, there was a fellow they told me about down at Log Hollow. He got into big trouble a few years back for secretly passing goods and coin along to his farmer lover and her half-blood child, or children—I guess it had been going on for some time when they caught up with him. He argued the goods were his, but the camp council maintained they were the camp's, and it was theft. He wouldn't back down, and they banished him."

Dag tilted his head.

"It was no joke, Dag," Saun said earnestly. "They stripped him to his skin before they turned him out. In the middle of winter. Nobody seemed to know what had happened to him after that, if he made it back to her, or . . . or what."

He was staring at Dag in deep alarm, as if picturing his mentor so used. Was Saun's hero worship of Dag finally to be called into question? Dag thought it a good thing if so, but not for this reason.

"Hardly the same situation, Saun." *For one thing, it's summer.* "In any case, I'll handle it."

Taking this heavy hint—anything lighter would not have penetrated, Dag thought—Saun managed an embarrassed laugh. "Yeah, I suppose you will." After a moment he added in a more chipper tone, turning the subject, "I'm something in the same line myself. Well, of course not with a . . . I'm thinking of asking Fairbolt for a transfer to Log Hollow this fall. Reela"—Saun's voice went suddenly shy—"said she'd wait for me."

Dag recognized that sappy look; he'd seen it in his own shaving mirror. "Congratulations."

"Nothing is *fixed* yet, you understand," Saun said hastily. "Some people think I'm too young to be, well. Thinking about anything permanent. But how can you not, when . . . you know?"

Dag nodded sympathetically. Because either snickering or pity would be a tad hypocritical, coming from him just now. *Was I ever that feckless?* Dag was very much afraid the answer was *yes*. Possibly even without the rider *at his age*.

Saun brightened still further. "Well. Looks like you need the makers more than I did. I won't hold you up. Maybe I'll stop by and say hi to Fawn, later on."

"I expect she'd be glad for a familiar face," Dag allowed. "She's had a rough welcome, I'm afraid."

Saun gave a short nod and took himself off. When in camp, Saun stayed with a family farther down the shore who had a couple of their own children out on exchange patrol at present; Dag gathered that the boy, away from home for the first time, did not lack for mothering.

Dag pushed open the door and made his way into the anteroom. The familiar smell of herbs—sharp, musty, deep, pungent—was strong today, and he glanced through the open door to the next room on this side to see two apprentices processing medicines. Pots bubbled on the fire, piles of dried greenery were laid out on the big table in the room's center, and one girl busied herself with a mortar.

They were making up packets: for patrols, or to be sold to farmers for coin or trade goods. Dag didn't doubt that some of what he smelled would end up in that shop at Lumpton Market, at double the price the Lakewalkers received for them.

Another apprentice looked up from the table crammed up to the anteroom's window, where he was writing. He smiled at the patroller, regarding Dag's sling with professional interest. But before he could speak, the door to the other chamber opened and a slight, middle-aged woman stepped out, her summer shift cinched at the waist by a belt holding half a dozen tools of her trade. She was rubbing her chest and frowning.

The medicine maker looked up. "Ah! Dag! I've been expecting you."

"Hello, Hoharie. I saw Saun coming out just now. Is he going to be all right?"

"Yes, he's coming along nicely. Thanks to you, he says. I understand you did some impressive emergency ground-work on him." She eyed Dag in speculation, but at least she refrained from comment on his marriage cord.

"Nothing special. In and out for a quick match at a moment he needed it, was all."

Her brows twitched, but she didn't pursue the point further. "Well, come on in, let's have a look at this." She gestured at his sling. "How in the world have you managed?"

"I've had help."

Dag followed her into her workroom, closing the door behind them. A tall bed, onto which he'd helped lift more than one hurt comrade over the years, stood out in the room's center, but Hoharie gestured him to a chair beside a table, taking another around the corner from it. He slipped his arm out of its sling and laid it out, and she pulled a pair of sharp scissors from her belt and began undoing the wrappings. Upon inquiry, he favored her with a much-shortened tale of how he'd come by the injury back in Lumpton Market. She ran her hands up and down the bared forearm, and he could feel the press of her ground on his own, more invasive than the long probing fingers.

"Well, this is a clean break and a straight setting," she reported. "Doing well, for what, two weeks?"

"Nearer three." It seemed a lot more than that.

"If not for that"—she nodded at his hook—"I'd send you home to heal on your own, but you'd like these splints off sooner, I'd imagine."

"Oh, yes."

She smiled at his heartfelt drawl. "I've done all the groundwork I can for today on your young friend Saun, but my apprentice will be pleased to try."

Dag gave this the grimace it deserved; she grinned back unrepentantly. "Come, Dag, they have to practice on someone. Youth to experience, experience to youth." She tapped his arm cuff. "How's the stump? Giving you any trouble?"

"No. Well . . . no."

She sat back, eyeing him shrewdly. "In other words, yes. Off with the harness, let me see."

"Not the stump itself," he said, but let her unbuckle the harness and lay it aside, and run her experienced hands down his arm and over its callused end. "Well, it's sometimes a little sore, but it's not bad today."

"I've seen it worse. So, go on . . . ?"

He said cautiously, "Have you ever heard of a missing limb still having . . . ground?"

She rubbed her bony nose. "Phantom limbs?"

"Yes, just like that," he said eagerly.

"Itching, pain, sensations? I've heard of it. It's apparently very maddening, to have an itch that can't be scratched."

"No, not that. I knew about that. Met a man up in Luthlia once, must be twenty-five years back, who'd lost most of both feet to frostbite. Poor fellow used to complain bitterly about the itching, and his toes that he didn't have anymore cramping. A little groundwork on the nerves of his legs usually cleared it right up. I mean the *ground* of missing limbs."

"If something doesn't exist, it can't *have* a ground. I don't know if someone could have an illusion of ground, like the illusion of an itch; folks have hallucinations about all sorts of bizarre things, though, so I don't see why not."

"A hallucination shouldn't be able to do real ground-work."

"Of course not."

"Well, mine did. I did."

"What's this tale?" She sat back, staring.

He took a breath and described the incident with the glass bowl in the Bluefield parlor, leaving out the ruckus that had led up to it and concentrating on the mending itself. "The most of it was done, I swear, with the ground of my left hand." He thumped his left arm on the table. "Which isn't there. I was deathly sick after, though, and cold all through for an hour."

She scowled in thought. "It sounds as though you drew ground from your whole body. Which would be reasonable. Why it should take that form to project itself, well, your theory about your right arm being lost to use forcing a, um"—she waved her hands—"some sort of compensation seems like a fair one. Sounds like a pretty spectacular one, I admit. Has it happened again?"

"Couple of times." Dag wasn't about to explain the circumstances. "But I can't make it happen at will. It's not even reliably driven by my own tension. It's just random, or so it seems to me."

"Can you do it now?"

Dag tried, concentrating so hard his brow furrowed. Nothing. He shook his head.

Hoharie bit her lip. "A funny form of ground projection, yes, maybe. Ground without matter, no."

Dag finally said what he hadn't wanted to say, even to himself. "Malices are pure ground. Ground without matter."

The medicine maker stared at him. "You'd know more about that than I would. I've never seen a malice."

"All a malice's material appearance is pure theft. They snatch ground itself, and matter through its ground, to shape at will. Or misshape."

"I don't know, Dag." She shook her head. "I'll have to think about this one."

"I wish you would. I'm"—he cut off the word *afraid*—"very puzzled."

She nodded shortly and rose to fetch her apprentice from the anteroom, introducing him as Othan. The lad looked thrilled, whether at being allowed to do a ground treatment upon the very interesting patroller, or simply at being allowed to do one at all, Dag couldn't quite tell. Hoharie gave up her seat and stood observing with her arms folded. The apprentice sat down and determinedly began tracing his hands up and down Dag's right arm.

"Hoharie," he said after a moment, "I can't get through the patroller's ground veil."

"Ease up, Dag," Hoharie advised.

Dag had held himself close and tight ever since he'd crossed the bridge to the island yesterday. He really, really didn't want to open himself up here. But it was going to be necessary. He tried.

Othan shook his head. "Still can't get in." The lad was starting to look distressed, as though he imagined the failure was his fault. He looked up. "Maybe you'd better try, ma'am?"

"I'm spent. Won't be able to do a thing till tomorrow at the earliest. Ease up, Dag!"

"I can't . . ."

"You *are* in a mood today." She circled the table and frowned at them both; the apprentice cringed. "All right, try swapping it around. You reach, Dag. That should force you open."

He nodded, and tried to reach into the lad's ground. The strain of his own distaste for the task warred with his frantic desire, now that the opportunity was so provokingly close, of getting the blighted splints off for good. The apprentice was looking at him with the air of a whipped puppy, bewildered but still eager to please. He held his arm lightly atop Dag's, face earnest, ground open as any gate.

On impulse, Dag shifted his stump across and slammed it down beside both their arms. Something flashed in his groundsense, strong and sharp. Othan cried out and re-coiled.

"Oh!" said Hoharie.

"A ghost hand," said Dag grimly. "A ground hand. Like *that*." His whole forearm was hot with new ground, snatched from the boy. His ghost hand, so briefly perceptible, was gone again. He was shaking, but if he put his arms out of sight below the table, it would only draw more attention to his trembling. He forced himself to sit still.

The apprentice was holding his own right arm to his chest, rubbing it and looking wide-eyed. "*Ow*," he said simply. "What was that? I mean—I didn't do—did I do anything?"

"Sorry. I'm sorry," mumbled Dag. "I shouldn't have done that." *That was new.* New and disturbing, and far too much like malice magic for Dag's comfort. Although perhaps there was only one kind of groundwork, after all. Was it theft, to take something someone was trying with all his heart to press upon you?

"My arm is cold," complained Othan. "But—did it help? Did I actually do any healing, Hoharie?"

Hoharie ran her hands over both her apprentice's arm and Dag's, her frown replaced by an oddly expressionless look. "Yes. There's an extremely dense ground reinforcement here."

Othan looked heartened, although he was still chafing his own forearm.

Dag wriggled his fingers; his arm barely ached. "I can feel the heat of it."

Hoharie, watching them both with equal attention, talked her apprentice through a light resplinting of Dag's arm. Othan gave the flaking, smelly skin a wash first, to Dag's intense gratitude. The boy's own right arm was decidedly weak; he fumbled the wrappings twice, and Hoharie had to help him tie off the knots.

"Is he going to be all right?" Dag asked cautiously, nodding at Othan.

"In a few days, I expect," said Hoharie. "That was a much stronger ground reinforcement than I normally let my apprentices attempt."

Othan smiled proudly, although his eyes were still a trifle confused. Hoharie dismissed him with thanks, closed the door behind him, and slid back into the seat across from Dag. She eyed him narrowly.

"Hoharie," said Dag plaintively, "what's happening to me?"

"Not sure." She hesitated. "Have you ever been tested for a maker?"

"Yes, ages ago. I'd no knack nor patience for it, but my groundsense range was a mile, so they let me go for a patroller. Which was what I'd desperately wanted anyway."

"What was that, nigh on forty years ago? Have you been tested lately?"

"No interest, no point. Such talents don't change after youth . . . do they?"

"Nothing alive is unchanging." Her eyes had gone silvery with interest—or was that covetousness? "I will say, that was no ghost, Dag. That was one of the live-est things I've ever seen. Could it do shaped reinforcements, I wonder?"

Did she think of training him as a medicine maker, in the sort of subtle groundwork that she herself did? Dag was taken aback. "*Dar's* the maker in my family."

"So?" Her shrewd look that went with this made him shift uncomfortably.

"I don't control this. It's more like it works me."

"What, you can't remember how wobbly you were when your groundsense first came in? Some days, my apprentices are all over the map. Some days I still am, for that matter."

"Fifty-five's a bit old for an apprentice, don't you think?" Hoharie herself was younger than Dag by a decade. He could remember when *she'd* been an apprentice. "And any road—a maker needs two good hands." He waved his left, by way of a reminder.

She started to speak, but then sat back, frowning over this last.

"Patrolling's what I do. Always have. I'm good at it." A shiver of fear troubled him at the thought of stopping, which was odd, since hunting malices should be the scariest task there was. But he remembered his own words from Glass-forge: *None of us could do the job without all of us, so all of us are owed.* Makers and patrollers alike, all were essential. *All essential, all expendable.*

Hoharie shrugged surrender, and said, "In any case, come back and see me tomorrow. I want to look at that arm again." She added after a moment, "Both of them."

"I'd take it kindly." He gestured with his sling. "Do I really still need this splint, now?"

"Yes, to remind you not to try anything foolish. Speaking of experience. You patrollers are all alike, in some ways. Give that ground reinforcement some time to work, and we'll see."

Dag nodded, rose, and let himself out, conscious of Hoharie's curious gaze following him.

6

Dag returned from the medicine tent reluctant to speak of the unsettling incident with the maker's apprentice, but in any case, no one asked; instead, five persons took the chance to tell him that he needed to teach his wife to swim. Dag thought the idea fine, but Fawn seemed to find the fact that he still wore splints and a sling to be a great relief to her mind.

"Well, you certainly can't go swimming with that rig on," she said firmly. "When will you have it off, did they say?"

"Soon."

She relaxed, and he did not clarify that *soon* could well mean *tomorrow*.

Sarri's little boy, having been coaxed earlier into hauling rocks for their fire pit and warmly praised for his efforts by his fathers, had crept back to the task, toddling across the clearing with stones as big as his little fingers could clutch and flinging them in with great determination. It set off a small crisis when his excess offerings were removed. His outraged tears were diverted by a treat from Fawn's dwindling store of farm fare, and Dag, grinning, hauled him back to his assorted parents. That evening, Dag and Fawn boiled tea water on their first home fire, even if supper was cold plunkin again. Fawn looked as though she was finally beginning to understand all the plunkin jokes.

They burned the rinds and sat together by the crackling

flames, watching through the trees as the sunset light faded on the farther shore. For all his weary unease, Dag still found it a pleasure just to look at the play of light and shadow across Fawn's features, the shine and spring of her hair, the gleam of her dark eyes. He wondered if gazing upon her face through time would be like watching sunsets, never quite the same twice yet unfailing in joy.

As the shadows deepened, the tree frogs in the woods piped a raucous descant to the deep croaking of bullfrogs hidden in the rushes. At last it was time to wave good night across the campsite at the others turning in, and drop the tent flap. By the light of a good beeswax candle, a gift from Sarri, they undressed and lay down in their bedroll. A few hours in Fawn's company had soothed Dag's strained nerves, but he must still have looked tense and absent, for she ran her hand along his face, and said, "You look tired. Do you . . . want to . . . ?"

"I could grow less tired." He kissed her curls away from her face and let his ground ease open a trifle. "Hm."

"Hm?"

"Your ground is very pretty tonight. Glittery. I think your days of fertility are starting up."

"Oh!" She sat up on one elbow. "Am I getting better, then?"

"Yes, but . . ." He sat half-up as well. "From what Mari said, you should be healing up inside at about the same rate as outside. Ground and flesh are still deep-damaged, and will recover slowly. From these"—he touched his lips to the carmine dimples in her neck—"my guess is your womb's not ready to risk a child yet, nor will be for some months."

"No. Nor is the rest of me, really." She rolled back and stared up at their hide roof. "I never thought to have a baby in a tent, though I suppose Lakewalker ladies do. We're not prepared for winter or anything, really. Not enough"—her hands waved uncertainly—"things."

"We travel lighter than farmers."

"I saw the inside of Sarri's cabin. Tent. She doesn't travel all that light. Not with children."

"Well, that's so. When all of Dar and Omba's children were home, shifting camp in season was a major undertaking. I usually tried to be out on patrol," he admitted ruefully.

Fawn sighed in uncertainty, and continued, "It's past midsummer. Time to be making and saving. Getting ready for the cold and the dark."

"Believe me, there is a steady stream of plunkins on their way to winter stores in Bearsford even as we speak. I used to ride that route as a horse boy in the summers, before I was old enough to go for patroller. Though in this season, it's easier to move the folks to the food than the food to the folks."

"Only plunkin?"

"The fruit and nuts will be coming on soon. A lot of the pigs we eat here. One per tent per season, so with four tents on this site, that makes four pig-roasts. Fish. Turkey, of course, and the hunters bring in venison from the woods on the mainland. I used to do that as a boy, too, and sometimes I go out with them between patrols. I'll show you how Stores works tomorrow."

She glanced up at him, catching her lower lip with her white teeth. "Dag—what's our plan, here?" One small hand reached out to trace over his splinted arm. "What happens to me when you go back out on patrol? Because Mari and Razi and Utau—everyone I know—will all be gone then, too."

He hardly needed groundsense to feel the apprehension in her. "By then, I figure, you'll be better acquainted with Sarri and Cattagus and Mari's daughter and her family. Cattagus is Sarri's uncle, by the way—he's an Otter by birth, as if you couldn't tell. My plan is to lie up quiet, get folks used to the idea of you. They will in time, I figure, like they grew used to Sarri's having two husbands."

And yet . . . normally, when patrollers went out, they could be sure their spouses would be looked after in their absences, first by their families, then by their patrol comrades, then by the whole community. It was a trust Dag had always taken for granted, as solid as rock under his feet. It was deeply disturbing to imagine that trust instead cracking like misjudged ice.

He went on in a casual voice, "I think I might skip the next patrol going out and take some of my unused camp time. Plenty to do here. Sometimes, between patrols, I help Omba train her young horses, get them used to a big man up. She mostly has a flock of girls for apprentices, see."

Fawn looked unconvinced. "Do you suppose Dar and your mama will be speaking to you again by then?"

Dag shrugged. "The next move is up to them. It's plain Dar doesn't like this marriage, but he detests rows. He'll let it pass unless he's pressed to act. Mama . . . had her warning. She has ways of making me crazy, and I suppose the reverse is true, but she's not stupid. And she'd be the last person on the lake to invite the camp council to tell her what to do. She'll keep it in the family. All we need do is let time go by and not borrow trouble."

She eased back in reassurance, but there remained a dark streak in her spirit, interlaced with the fresh brightness from her recovering body. Dag suspected the strangeness of it all was beginning to accumulate. He'd seen homesickness devastate young patrollers far less dislocated than Fawn, and he resolved to find familiar tasks for her hands tomorrow. Yes, let her be as busy as she was used to being, till her balance grew steadier.

Meanwhile—here inside Tent Bluefield—the task to hand was surely growing less frantic and more familiar, but no less enchanting for all of that. *Back to taking turns.* He sought her tender lips in a kiss, opening his heart to all the intricacy of her ground, dark and light together.

Dag vanished for a couple of hours the next morning, but returned for lunch—plunkin *again*, but he didn't seem to mind. Then, as promised, he took Fawn to the mysterious Stores. This proved to be a set of long sheds tucked into the woods, down the road past the patroller headquarters. Inside one, they found what appeared to be a woman clerk; at any rate, she sat at a table scratching in a ledger with a quill, surrounded by shelves crammed with more ledgers. A toddler lay asleep in a sort of wooden pen next to her. More sets of shelves, ceiling-high, marched back in rows the length of the building. The dim air smelled of leather and herbs and less-identifiable things.

While Fawn walked up and down the rows of shelves, staring at the goods with which they were crammed, Dag engaged the woman in a low-voiced consultation, which involved dragging out several more ledgers and marking off and initialing lists therein. At one point Dag said, "You still have those?" in a voice of surprise, laughed, and dipped the quill to mark some more. His splints, Fawn noticed, hardly seemed to slow him down today, and he was constantly taking his arm out of the sling.

Dag then led Fawn up and down the rows and had her help him collect furs and other leather goods according to some scheme of his own. A half dozen beautiful dark brown pelts looking like the coats of some extraordinary ferret-shaped creature he explained as coming from mink, small woodland predators from north of the Dead Lake; an exquisite white pelt, soft as whipped cream, was from a winter fox, but it was like no fox fur Fawn had ever seen or touched. These, he said, could be bride-gifts for Mama and Aunt Nattie, and Fawn had to agree they were marvelously better than the local hides they'd rejected back at Lumpton Market.

"Every patrol usually brings back something," Dag explained. "It varies with where they've been and what opportunities they've found. Whatever part of his or her share a patroller doesn't want or can't use is turned over to Stores, and the patroller gets a credit for them, either to draw the equivalent item out later or trade for something of use. Excess accumulations are taken down to farmer country to trade for other things we need. After all my years of patrolling, I have a long credit at Stores. You be thinking about what you want, Spark, and chances are we can find something like."

"Cooking ware?" she said hopefully.

"Next building over," he promised.

One at a time, he pulled three more folded hides from dusty back shelves, and Fawn staggered under the weight of each as they took them to the clerk's table to be signed out. He also, after judicious study, selected a sturdy pack-saddle in good condition from a rack of such horse gear. They hauled it all out through the double doors onto the end porch.

Dag prodded the three big bundles with his toe. "Now these," he said, "are actually my own. Bit surprised to still find them here. Two were sent down from Luthlia after I came home, and the other I picked up about three years back during a winter season I spent patrolling in the far south. This one, I figure for your papa. Go ahead and unroll it."

Fawn picked apart the stiff, dry rawhide cords and unfolded what appeared to be an enormous wolf skin. "My word, Dag! This thing must have been as big as a horse!"

"Very nearly."

She frowned. "You can't tell me that was a natural beast."

"No. Mud wolf. The very one they found me under at Wolf Ridge, I'm told. My surviving tent-brothers—you'd say brothers-in-law—skinned and tanned it for me. Never had the heart to tell them I didn't want it. I put it in Stores thinking someone would take it off, but there it's sat ever since."

She wondered if this same beast had savaged his left hand. "It would make a rug for our whole parlor, back in West Blue. But it would be rather horrible, knowing how you came by it."

"I admit I've no desire to look at it. Depending on how your papa feels about me by now, he might wish it hadn't stopped gnawing on me so soon, but on the whole I think I won't explain its history. The other two are worth a look as well."

Fawn unfolded the second big pelt, and recoiled. Heavy black leather in a shape altogether too human was scantily covered with long, ratty gray hair; the mask of the thing, which had a manlike look, still had the fanged jaw attached.

"Another mud wolf. Different version. Fast and vicious, and they moved like shadows in the dark. That one for Reed and Rush, I think," said Dag.

"Dag, that's evil." Fawn thought it through. "Good choice."

Dag chuckled. "Give them something to wonder about, I figure."

"It'll give them nightmares, I should imagine!" Or was that, *I hope*? "Did you kill it?" *And for pity's sake, how?*

Dag squinted at the mummified horror. "Probably. If not that one, plenty like it."

Fawn refolded and bound up both old hides, and undid the third. It was thinner and more supple, and hairless. She unrolled and kept unrolling, her brows rising in astonishment, until fully nine feet of . . . of whatever it was lay out on the porch floor. The fine leather had a beautiful pattern, almost like snakeskin magnified, and gleamed smoothly under her hand, bronze green shading to rich red-brown. For all that the animal was as long as a horse, it seemed to have had short, stubby legs; wicked black claws still dangled from their ends. The jaws of this one, too, had been set back in place after tanning, and were frankly unbelievable, like a stretched-out bear trap made of teeth.

"What kind of malice made *that*? And what poor creature was it made from?"

"Not a mud-man at all. It's an alligator—a southern swamp lizard. A real, natural animal. We think. Unless one of our ancestor-mages got really drunk. Malices do not, thank all the absent gods, emerge too often so far south of the Dead Lake, but what happens when they do get hold of these fellows is scarcely to be imagined. The southern wetlands are one of the places you want to do your patrolling in winter, because cold makes the alligators, and the alligator-men, sluggish. That one we just caught on an ordinary hunting and trapping run, though."

"Ordinary? It looks as if it could eat a man in two bites!"

"They're a danger along the shores of the channels. They lie in the water like logs, but they can move fast when they want. They clamp onto their prey and drag it down into the water to drown, and rip it up later, after it rots a bit." He bent and ran his fingers along the shiny hide. "I should think your papa and Whit could both get a pair of boots out of this one, and belts and something for your mama as well."

"Dag," said Fawn curiously, "have you ever seen the sea?"

"Oh, yeah, couple of times. The south shore, that is, around the mouth of the Gray River. I've not seen the eastern sea."

"What's it like?"

He sat back, squatting, fingers still caressing the swamp-lizard skin, and a meditative look came over his face. "First time was almost thirty years ago. Never forget it. West of the Gray, between the river and the Levels, the land is flat and mostly treeless. All mounted patrols in that wide-sky country. Our company commander had us all spread out, half a mile or more apart, in one long line—that sweep must have been fifty miles across. We rode straight south, day after day. Spring it was, the air all soft and blue, and new green coming up all around, and flowers everywhere. Best patrolling I ever did in my life. We even found one sessile, and did for it without hardly pausing. The rest was just riding along in the sunshine, dangling our feet out of the stirrups, scanning the ground, just barely keeping touch with the patrollers to the right and left. End of the week, the color of the sky changed, got all silvery and light, and we came up over these sand dunes, and there it was . . ." His voice trailed off. He swallowed. "The rollers were foaming in over the sand, grumbling and grumbling, never stopping. I never knew there were so many shades of blue and gray and green. The sea was as wide and flat as the Levels, but *alive.* You could feel with your groundsense how alive it was, as if it was the mother of the whole wide green world. I sat and stared . . . We all dismounted and took off our boots, and got silly for a while, running in and out of that salty water, warm as milk."

"And then what happened?" Fawn asked, almost holding her breath.

Dag shrugged. "Camped for the night on the beach, turned the line around and shifted it fifty miles, and rode back north. It turned cold and rained on the way back, though, and we found nothing for our pains." He added after a moment, "Wood washed up on the beach burns with the most beautiful strange colors. Never saw anything like."

His words were simple and plain, as his words usually were; Fawn scarcely knew why she felt as though she were eavesdropping on a man at prayers, or why water blurred her eyes.

"Dag . . ." she said. "What's beyond the sea?"

His brows twitched up. "No one's sure."

"Could there be other lands?"

"Oh, that. Yes. Or there were, once. The oldest maps show other continents, three of them. The original charts are long gone, so it's anyone's guess how accurate the copies are. But if any ships have gone to see what's still there, they haven't come back that I ever heard. People have different theories. Some say the gods have interdicted us, and that anyone who ventures out too far is destroyed by holy curses. Some guess the other lands got blighted, and are now all dead from shore to shore, and no one's there anymore. I'm not too fond of that picture. But you'd think, if there were other folks across the seas, and they had ships, some might have got blown off course sometime in the last thousand years, and I've never heard tell of any such. Maybe the *people* over there have interdicted us, till our task is done and all's safe again. That would be sensible."

He paused, gazing into some time or distance Fawn could not see, and continued, "Legend has it there is, or once was, another enclave of survivors on our continent, to the west of the Levels and the great mountains that were supposed to be beyond them. Maybe we'll find out if that's true someday, if anyone, us or them, ever tries to sail all around the shore of this land. Wouldn't need such grand ships for hugging the coast."

"With silver sails," Fawn put in.

He smiled. "I think that's got to happen sometime. Don't know if I'll live to see it. If . . ."

"If?"

"If we can keep the malices down long enough for folks to get ahead. The river men are bold enough to try, but it would risk a lot of resources, as well as lives. You'd need a rich man, a prince or a great lord, to fund such a voyage, and they're extinct."

"Or a bunch of well-off men," Fawn suggested. "Or a whole big bunch of quite ordinary men."

"And one fast-talking lunatic to coax the money out of their pockets. Well, maybe." He smiled thoughtfully, considering this vision, but then shook his head and rose. Fawn carefully rerolled the astonishing swamp-lizard skin.

Dag went back inside to cadge paper, ink, and quills from the clerk, then they both sat at the nearest trestle table in the dappled shade to write their letters to West Blue. Fawn didn't miss West Blue—she'd longed to get away, and she hadn't changed her mind on that—but she couldn't say her feet were planted in their new soil yet. Given the way Lakewalkers kept moving around, maybe home would never be a place. It would be Dag. She watched him across the table, scribbling with his quill clutched in his right fingers and holding down the paper, lifting in the warm breeze, with his hook. She bent her head to her own task.

Dear Mama, Papa, and Aunt Nattie. We got here day before yesterday. Had it only been two days? *I am fine. The lake is very . . .* She brushed the quill over her chin, and decided she really ought to say more than *wet.* She wrote *large,* instead. *We met up with Dag's aunt Mari again. She has a nice . . .* Fawn scratched out the start of *cabin* and wrote *tent. Dag's arm is getting better.* And onward in that vein, till she'd filled half the page with unexceptionable remarks. Too much blank space left. She decided to describe Sarri's children, and their campsite, which filled the rest with enough cheery word pictures to grow cramped toward the end. There.

So much left out. Patroller headquarters, and Fairbolt Crow's pegboard. Dar, the unnerving bone shack, Dag's angry mama, the futility of the sharing knife after all this journey. Dag's dark, nervy mood. The threat of swimming lessons. Naked swimming lessons, at that. Some things were *best* left out.

Dag, finishing, handed his letter across for her to read. It was very polite and plain, almost like an inventory, making clear which gifts were for which family members. Both horses and the packsaddle were to be Mama's, as well as some of the fine furs. The mud-man skin for the twins was blandly described, entirely without comment. Fawn grinned as she pictured the three alarming hides being unpacked at West Blue.

Dag stepped inside and returned the quills and ink to the clerk, coming out with the letters folded and sealed just in time to greet a girl who rode up, bareback, on a tall, elegant, dappled gray mare. A dark foal about four months old pranced after, flicking his fuzzy ears; he had the most beautifully shaped head and deepest liquid eyes Fawn had ever seen on a colt, and she spent the time while Dag and the girl organized the packsaddle trying to make up to him. He flirted with her in turn, yielding at last to ear scratching just *there*. Fawn couldn't imagine her mother riding that mare, nor any of her family; maybe the dappled beauty could be broken to harness and pull the light cart to the village, though. *That* would turn a few heads.

A man dressed as a patroller came riding from the direction of the headquarters building. He turned out to be a courier on his way south, apparently a trusted comrade; exactly what old favor Dag was calling in was not clear to Fawn, but however dubiously he greeted the farmer bride or raised his brows at Dag, he had undertaken to deliver the bride-gifts. He stopped with them long enough to get a clear description of the Bluefield farm and how to find it, and then he was off, with the silvery mare following meekly on a lead and the colt capering and scampering. The horse girl, trudging back to Mare Island, looked after them with a downright heart-broken expression.

Dag then led Fawn off to the next storehouse, where they found some lightly used cooking gear—not a proper kitchen's worth, but at least a few things to permit more elaborate meals over an open fire than sliced raw plunkin and tea.

And, to Fawn's joy, several pounds of cotton from south of the Grace River, cleaned and combed, an equally generous bag of washed wool, and three hanks of good flax. The tools Aunt Nattie had given Fawn for a wedding present would find their proper use. Despite her burdens her steps were lighter turning back toward their campsite, and she made plans for getting Dag to hold still long enough to measure his gnarly feet for socks.

The following day Dag returned from the medicine tent with no sling or splints, but with a smile on his face that would hardly go away. He flexed and stretched his hand gratefully. He reported he'd been instructed to take it easy for another week, which he interpreted liberally as *no weapons practice yet.* Everything else he embraced immediately, including Fawn.

To her muffled alarm, the next thing he did that afternoon was make her put down her spindle and go with him for her first swimming lesson. She was distracted from her fear of the water only by her embarrassment at their lack of clothes, but somehow Dag made both better. They picked their way past the bending cattails into water to his waist and her chest. At least the lake's murkiness gave them a more decent cloak, its greeny-gold translucence turning opaque just a short way down. The top foot of the water was as warm in the sun as a bath; beneath that it grew cooler. The soft mud squelched between Fawn's curling toes. They were accompanied by a dizzy escort of water bugs, flocks of little black ovals that whirled merrily like beads on a string, and agile water striders, their thin legs making dimples in the brown surface as they skated along. Dag promptly made the bead-shaped bugs an example to Fawn, inviting her to spin them down in little whirlpools with her hands and watch them bob right back to the surface.

Dag insisted she was naturally more buoyant than he, taking the opportunity to pat her most buoyant parts. Fawn thought his assertion that *It doesn't matter how deep the water is, Spark, you're only going to use the top two feet* overly optimistic, but under the influence of his confidence and unfailing good cheer, she gradually began to relax in the water. By the second day, to her own astonishment, she floated for the first time in her life; on the third afternoon, she achieved a dog paddle of several yards.

Even Dag had to admit that the lake's muddiness made Hickory Lake residents all tend to smell a bit green by the end of the summer—*sooner than that*, Fawn did not say aloud—but Sarri took Fawn into the woods and showed her where a clear spring ran that not only allowed her to give lake-scrubbed clothes a final rinse, but also to draw water that didn't need to be boiled before drinking. Fawn managed her first laundry day, and sniffed their clothes, drying on a line strung between two trees, with satisfaction at a job well done.

That afternoon, Dag came in with a small turkey to pluck. Fawn happily started a bag to save feathers, looking ahead to pillows and ticks. They roasted the bird over their fire and invited Mari and Cattagus to help eat it up. Fawn ended the evening casting on her first cotton yarn to her double-ended needle set for Dag's socks, and feeling that this place might become home after all.

Two days later, instead of a swimming lesson, Dag took her out in one of the narrow boats. He had a specially shaped hook for his wrist cuff that allowed him to manage his paddle. Fawn, after a brief lesson on the dock, was placed in the front with a paddle of her own. She felt nervous and clumsy at first, looking over all that expanse of water with Dag out of sight behind her, but she soon fell into the rhythm of the task. Around behind Walnut Island, winking water gave way to a surface that was downright glassy, and Fawn relaxed still more. They paused to admire a dead tree reflected in the water, its bare white branches startling against the green of the woods. It was a roosting place for broad-winged hawks, a few circling gracefully overhead or perching on the branches, and Fawn smiled to remember the day they'd been startled by that big red-tail near Glassforge. Any larger predators, Fawn had gathered, were kept off the islands by Lakewalker magic.

Up the back channel, the air grew still and hot, and the water clear. Huge elderberry bushes leaned over the banks, their branches heavy with thick clusters of green fruit slowly acquiring a promising rosy blush; in another month the berries would be black and ripe, and Fawn could easily see how a boy might gather them from a boat like this one. A shiny sunfish jumped right into their boat at Dag's feet; Dag, laughing at Fawn's startled squeal, scooped the flopping creature gently back into the water and denied that he had enticed it by Lakewalker persuasion. "Much too small, Spark!"

Rounding a tangle of wrack and cattails where red-winged blackbirds traded barking chirps and hoarse whistles, they came at last upon a broad open space crowded with flat lily pads, their white flowers wide to the sun. Thin, iridescent blue dragonflies, and thicker scarlet ones, stitched the air above the marsh, and rows of turtles sunned themselves on logs, yellow-striped necks stretched out, brown backs gleaming like polished stones. A blue heron stalked slowly along the farther shore; it froze briefly, then darted its long yellow beak into the water. A silvery minnow flashed as the heron twisted its neck around, gulped, then stood folded for a moment looking smug. Fawn hardly knew whether it made her happier to watch the flowers or the contented look on Dag's face. Dag sighed in satisfaction, but then frowned.

"I thought this was the same place, but it seems smaller. This water is a lot shallower, too. I remember it as being well over my head. Did I take a wrong turn somewhere?"

"It looks plenty deep to me. Um . . . how old were you, again, first time you found this place?"

"Eight."

"And how tall?"

Dag began to open his mouth, then grinned sheepishly. "Shorter than you, Spark."

"Well, then."

"Well, indeed." He laid his paddle across his lap and just gazed around.

The water lilies, though beautiful, were the same common variety Fawn had sometimes seen in quiet backwaters around West Blue, she decided. She had seen cattails, dragonflies, turtles, blackbirds, and herons before. There was nothing new here, and yet . . . *this place is magical.* The silence in the warm, moist air, broken only by the little noises of the marsh, seemed holy in her ears, as if she were hearing a sound beneath all sound. *This is what having groundsense must be like, all the time.* The thought awed her.

They sat quietly in the narrow boat, beyond all need of words, until the heat of the sun began to grow uncomfortable; with a sigh, Dag took up his paddle once more and turned them around. His stroke left a glossy whirlpool spiraling down into the clear water, and Fawn's eye followed it. *This is where his heart is anchored. I can see why.*

They had almost rounded the corner into the main arm of the lake when Dag paused again. Fawn twisted around; he held his finger to his lips and grinned at her. His eyes half-lidded, he sat there with an absentminded, sleepy look on his face that didn't reassure her a bit. So she didn't *quite* fall out of the boat when a sudden splash and movement resolved into a huge black bass, twisting in the air and trailing sparkling drops. It fell into the bottom of the narrow boat with a resounding thud, flopped and flapped like mad, then at last lay still, bright gills flexing.

"There's a better size for dinner," said Dag in satisfaction, and thrust his paddle into the water once more.

"Now, *that's* persuasion. Is that how you folks fish all the time?" asked Fawn in amazement. "I wondered why I didn't see any poles or lines lying around."

"Something like that. Actually, we usually use hand-nets. You ever see old Cattagus lying on the dock looking as if he's dozing, with one hand trailing over the side, that's what he's likely doing."

"It seems almost like cheating. Why are there any fish left in this lake?"

"Well, not everyone has the knack."

As they pulled into the dock, sunburned and happy, Fawn made plans for begging some herbs from Sarri's garden and grilling Dag's catch worthily. She managed to clamber onto the weathered gray planks from the wobbly boat without taking an inadvertent swimming lesson, and let Dag hand her up his prize before he tied off the boat's lines. Clutching the bass, she turned her face up to Dag for a quick kiss and hug, and they climbed the stone steps up the steep bank.

His arm around her waist gave her an abrupt squeeze, then fell away. She looked up to follow his glance.

Dar waited in the shade at the top of the bank, frowning like a bit of rainy dark detached from winter and walking around. As they crested the rise, he said to Dag, "I need to talk to you."

"Do you? Why?" Dag inquired, but he gestured toward their tent and the log seats around their fire pit.

"Alone, if you please," Dar said stiffly.

"Mm," said Dag, without enthusiasm, but he gave his brother a short nod. He saw Fawn back to the tent and left her to deal with the fish. Fawn watched uneasily as the pair strolled away out of the campsite and turned onto the road, leaning a little away from each other.

7

They turned left onto the shady road between the shore campsites and the woods. Dag was tired enough not to need to shorten his steps to match his brother's, and not yet annoyed enough to lengthen them to his full patroller's stride and make Dar hurry to keep up. On the whole, he wouldn't bet on that remaining the case. *What is he about?* It didn't take groundsense to see that although Dar had come to Dag, conciliation and apology were not strong in his mood.

"And so?" Dag prodded, although it would have been better tactics to wait Dar out, make him start. *This isn't supposed to be a war.*

"You're the talk of the lake, you know," Dar said curtly.

"Talk passes. There will be some other novelty along soon enough." Dag set his jaw to keep himself from asking, *What are they saying?* He was glumly sure Dar was about to tell him anyway.

"It's a pretty unsavory match. Not only is that girl you dragged home a farmer, she's scarcely more than an infant!"

Dag shrugged. "In some ways Fawn's a child; in others not. In grief and guilt, she's fully grown." *And I am surely qualified to judge.* "In knowing how to go on, I'd call her an apprentice adult. Basic tasks aren't yet routine for her, but when all that energy and attention get freed up at last, watch out! She's ferociously bright, and learns fast. Main thing about the age difference, I reckon, is that it hands me a special burden not to betray her trust." His eyebrows pinched. "Except that the same is true of anyone at any age, so maybe it's not so special after all."

"Betrayal? You've shamed our tent! Mama's become a laughingstock to the ill willed over this, and she hates it. You know how she values her dignity."

Dag tilted his head. "Huh. Well, I'm sorry to hear it, but I suspect she brought that on herself. I'm afraid what she calls dignity others see as conceit." On the other hand, perhaps it was the accident of Cumbia's having so few children that made her insist on their particular value, to hold her head up against women friends who could parade a more numerous get. Although it was plain fact that Dar's skills were rare and extraordinary. Remembering to placate, Dag added, "Some of it is pride in you, to be fair."

"It could have been in you, too, if you'd bestirred yourself," Dar grumbled. "Still just a patroller, after forty years? You should have been a commander by now. Anything that Mama and Mari agree on must be true, or the sky's like to fall."

Dag gritted his teeth and did not reply. His family's ambition had been a plague to him since he'd returned from Luthlia and recovered enough to begin patrolling again. His own fault, perhaps, for letting them learn he'd turned down patrol leadership despite, or perhaps because of, the broad hint that it could soon lead to wider duties. Repeatedly, till Fairbolt had stopped asking. Or had that leaked out through Massape, reflecting her husband's plaints? At this range, he could no longer remember.

Dar's lips compressed, then he said, "It's been suggested—I won't say who by—that if we just wait a year, the problem will solve itself. The farmer girl's too small to birth a Lakewalker child and will die trying. Have you realized that?"

Dag flinched. "Fawn's mama is short, too, and she did just fine." *But her papa wasn't a big man, either.* He fought the shiver that ran through him by the reflection that the size of the infant and the size of the grown person had little relation; Cattagus and Mari's eldest son, who was a bear of a fellow now, was famous in the family for having been born little and sickly.

"That's more or less what I said—don't count on it. Farmers are fecund. But have you even thought it through, Dag? If a child or children survived, let alone their mother, what's the fate of half-bloods here? They couldn't make, they couldn't patrol. All they could do would be eat and breed. They'd be despised."

Dag's jaw set. "There are plenty of other necessary jobs to do in camp, as I recall being told more than once. Ten folks in camp keep one patroller in the field, Fairbolt says. They could be among that ten. Or do you secretly despise everyone else here, and I never knew?"

Dar batted this dart away with a swipe of his hand. "So you're saying your children could grow up to be servants of mine? And you'd be content with that?"

"We would find our way."

"We?" Dar scowled. "So already you put your farmer get ahead of the needs of the whole?"

"If that happens, it won't be by my choosing." Would Dar hear the warning in that? Dag continued, "We actually don't know that all cross-bloods lack groundsense. If anything, the opposite; I've met a couple who have little less than some of us. I've been out in the world a good bit more than you. I've seen raw talent here and there amongst farmers, too, and I don't think it's just the result of some passing Lakewalker in a prior generation leaving a present." Dag frowned. "By rights, we should be sifting the farmers for hidden groundsense. Just like the mages of old must have done."

"And while we're diverting ourselves in that, who fights the malices?" Dar shot back. "*Nearly* good enough to patrol isn't going to do the job. We need the concentration of bloodlines to reach the threshold of function. We're stretched to the breaking point, and everyone knows it. Let me tell you, it's not just Mama who is maddened to see you wasting the talent in your blood."

Dag grimaced. "Yeah, I've heard that song from Aunt Mari, too." He remembered his own reply. "And yet I might have been killed anytime these past four decades, and my blood would have been no less wasted. Pretend I'm dead, if it'll make you feel better."

Dar snorted, declining to rise to that bait. They had reached the point where the road from the bridge split to cut through the woods to the island's north shore. At Dar's gesture, they turned onto it. The earth was dappled golden-green in the late sun, leaf shadows barely flickering in the breathing summer air. Their pacing sandals kicked up little spurts of dirt in the stretches between drying puddles.

Dar gathered himself, and continued, "It's not just your own family you put to shame. This stunt of yours creates disruption and a bad example in the patrol, as well. You've a reputation there, I don't deny. Youngsters like Saun look up to you. How much harder will this make it for patrol leaders to prevent the next ill-fated farmer romance? I swear, you're thinking only of yourself."

"Yes," said Dag, and added meditatively, "it's a new experience." A slow smile turned his lips. "I kind of like it."

"Don't make stupid jokes," snapped Dar.

I wasn't. Absent gods help me. In fact, it grew less funny the longer he thought about it. Dag took a long breath. "What are you after, Dar? I married Fawn for true—mind, body, and ground. That isn't going to change. Sooner or later, you'll have to deal with it."

"Dealing with it is just what I'm trying to avoid." Dar's scowl deepened. "The camp council could force a change. They've ruled on string-cuttings before."

"Only when the couple was divided and their families couldn't negotiate an agreement. No one can force a string-cutting against the will of *both* partners. And no one of sense would tolerate the precedent if the council tried. It would put everyone's marriage at risk—it would fly against the whole meaning of string-binding!"

Dar's voice hardened. "Then you'll just have to be forced to will it, eh?"

Dag let ten steps pass in silence before he replied. "I'm stubborn. My wife is determined. You'll break your knife on that rock, Dar."

"Have you grasped what you risk? Shunning—banishment? No more patrolling?"

"I've a lot of patrol years left in me. We're stretched, you say—and yet you'd throw those years away into a ditch? For mere conceit?"

"I'm *trying* for exactly the reverse." Dar swiped an angry hand across his brow. "You're the one who seems to be galloping blindly for the ditch."

"Not by my will. Nor Fairbolt's. He'll stand up for me." Actually, Fairbolt had said only that he didn't care to defend this before the camp council—not whether he would overcome his understandable distaste if he had to. But Dag was disinclined to confide his doubts to Dar at this point.

"What," scoffed Dar, "with all the trouble this will make for patrol discipline? Think again."

Had Dar and Fairbolt been talking? Dag began to be sorry he had held himself aloof from camp gossip these past days, even though it had seemed wiser not to present his head for drumming on or let himself be drawn into arguments. He countered, "Fawn's a special case anyway. She's not just any farmer, she's the farmer girl who slew a malice. As contrasted with, for example, your malice count. What was it, again? Oh, yes—none?"

Dar's lips thinned in an unfelt smile. "If you like,

brother. Or maybe the count is, every malice that any knife of my making slew. Without a sharing knife no patroller is a malice killer. You're just malice food walking around."

Dag drew breath through his nostrils and tried to get a better grip on his temper. "True. And without hands to wield them, your knives are just—what did you call them?—wall decorations. I think we need to cry truce on this one."

Dar nodded shortly. They paced beside each other for a time.

When he could trust himself to speak again, Dag went on, "Without Fawn's hand, I would be dead now, and maybe a good part of my patrol with me. And you'd have spent the past weeks having memorial rites and making tender speeches about what a fine fellow I was."

Dar sighed. "Almost better, that would be. Simpler, at least."

"I appreciate that *almost*. Almost." Dag gathered his wits, or attempted to. "In any case, your bird won't fly. Fairbolt's made it clear he'll tolerate this for the sake of need and won't take it to the council. And neither will Mama. Get used to us, Dar." He let his voice soften to persuasion, almost plea. "Fawn is her own sort of worthy. You'd see it if you'd let yourself look at her straight. Give her a chance, and you won't be sorry."

"You're besotted."

Dag shrugged. "And the sun rises in the east. You're not going to change either fact. Give up the gloom and set your mind to some more open view."

"Aunt Mari was a feckless fool to let this get by."

"She made all the same arguments that you just did." Rather better phrased, but Dar had never been a diplomat. "Dar, let it ride. It'll work out in time. Folks will get used to it. Fawn and I may always be an oddity, but we won't start a stampede any more than Sarri did with her two husbands. Hickory Lake will survive us. Life will go on."

Dar inhaled, staring straight ahead. "I will go to the camp council."

Dag covered the chill in his belly with a slow blink. "Will you, now. What will Mama say? I thought you hated rows."

"I do. But it's come down to me. Someone has to act. Mama cries, you know. It has to be done, and it has to be done soon." Dar grimaced. "Omba says if we wait till you get your farmer girl pregnant, you'll never be shifted."

"She's right," said Dag, far more coolly than he felt.

Dar bore the look of a man determined to do his duty, however repugnant. Yes, Dar would stiffen Cumbia, even against her better judgment. Did both imagine Dag would cave in to these threats—or did they both realize he wouldn't? Or was it one of each?

"So," said Dag, "I'm a sacrifice you're willing to make, am I? Is Mama so willing?"

"Mama knows—we all know—your passion for patrolling. How hard you fought to get back in after you lost your hand. Is dipping your wick in this farmer girl worth casting away your whole life?"

Dar was remembering the brother from eighteen years back, Dag thought. Agonized, exhausted, seeking only to deal death in turn to that which had made him the walking corpse he'd felt himself to be. And then, with luck, to be reunited in death with all that he'd lost, because no other course seemed possible or even imaginable. Something strange and new had happened to that Dag in the malice cave near Glassforge. Or—something that had been happening below the surface had finally been brought to light. *I'm not who you think I am anymore, Dar. You look at me yet don't see me.* Dar seemed curiously like Fawn's kin, in that way. *So who am I?* For the first time in a long time, Dag wasn't sure he knew the answer, and that was a lot more disturbing than Dar's old assumptions.

Dar misinterpreted Dag's uneasy look. "Yeah, that's got

you thinking! About time. I'm not going to back off on this. This is your warning."

Dag touched the cord below his rolled-up left sleeve. "Neither am I. That's yours."

They both maintained a stony silence as they reached the shore road again and turned right. Dar managed a nod when he turned off at the Redwing campsite, but he spoke no word of farewell, of further meetings, or of any other indication of his intent. Dag, fuming, returned an equally silent nod and walked on.

On the mere physical level, Dag thought he need have no fear for either Fawn or himself. It wasn't Dar's style to gather a bunch of hotheads like Sunny and his friends to deliver violent rebuke. A formal charge before the camp council was precisely what Dar would do, no question there. His was no idle threat. Dag felt a curious blankness within himself at the thought, in a way like the familiar empty moment before falling into attack on a malice lair.

He considered the current makeup of the camp council. There were normally a representative and an alternate from each island, chosen yearly by rotation from the heads of the various clans and other elders, plus the camp captain as a permanent member on behalf of the patrol and its needs. Cumbia had been on the council herself once, and Dag's grandfather, before he'd grown too fragile, had been an alternate twice. Dag had scarcely paid attention to who was in the barrel on council this year, or to tell the truth any other year, and suddenly it mattered.

The council resolved most conflicts by open discussion and binding mediation. Only in matters involving banishment or a death sentence did they make their votes secret, and then the quorum was not the usual five, but the full seven. There had only been two murders in Hickory Lake Camp in Dag's lifetime, and the council had settled the more ambiguous by ordering a payment between the families; only one had led to an execution. Dag had never

yet witnessed a banishment like the one at Log Hollow that
Saun had gossiped about. Dag couldn't help feeling that
there must have been a more unholy mess backing up behind
that incident than Saun's short description suggested. *Like
mine?* Maybe not.

Dag had deliberately steered clear of camp gossip in the
past days if only to avoid the aggravation, keeping to himself
with Fawn—and healing, don't forget that—but in any case
he doubted very many of his friends would repeat the most
critical remarks to his face. He could think of only one man
he could trust to do so without bias in either direction. He
made plans to seek Fairbolt after supper.

Fawn glanced up from the perfect coals in the fire pit to
see Dag stride back into the clearing, his scowl black. She
had never seen so much quiet joy in Dag as this afternoon
out in the lily marsh, and she set her teeth in a moment of
fury for whatever his brother had done to wreck his happi-
ness. She also bade silent good-bye to her hope, however
faint, that Dar had come as a family peacemaker, dismissing
the little fantasy she had started to build up about maybe a
dinner invitation from Dag's mama, and what Fawn could
bring and how she could act to show her worth to that branch
of the Redwings.

At her eyebrows raised in question, Dag shook his head,
adding an unfelt smile to show his scowl was not for her. He
sat on the ground, picked up a stick, and dug it into the dirt,
his face drawn in thought.

"So what did Dar want?" Fawn asked. "Is he coming
around to us?" She busied herself with the bass, gutted,
cleaned, stuffed with herbs begged from Sarri's garden, and
ready to grill. It sizzled gently as she laid it on the rack above
her coals, and she stirred the pot of mashed plunkin with
onions she'd fixed to go with. Dag looked up at the enticing

smells pretty soon, his eyes growing less pinched, although he was still a long time answering.

"Not yet, anyway," Dag said at last.

Fawn pursed her lips. "If there's some trouble, don't you think I need to know?"

"Yes," he sighed. "But I need to talk to Fairbolt first. Then I can say more certainly."

Say what? "Sounds a little ominous."

"Maybe not, Spark." Attracted by his supper, he got up and sat again by her, giving her neck a distracting nuzzle as she tried to turn the fish.

She smiled back, to show willing, but thought, *Maybe so, Dag.* If something wasn't a problem, he usually said so, with direct vigor. If it was a problem with a solution, he'd cheerfully explain it, at whatever length necessary. This sort of silence, she had gradually learned, betokened unusual uncertainty. Her vague conviction that Dag knew everything about everything—well, possibly not about farms—did not stand up to sober reflection.

As she'd hoped, feeding him did brighten him up considerably. His mood lightened still further, to a genuine grin, when she came out from their tent after supper with her hands behind her back, and then, with a flourish, presented his new cotton socks.

"You finished them already!"

"I used to have to help make socks for my brothers. I got fast. Try them under your boots," she said eagerly. "See if they help."

He did so at once, walking experimentally around the dying fire, looking pleased, if a little mismatched in the boots with the truncated trousers that Lakewalker men seemed to wear here in hot weather, when they weren't called on to ride.

"These should be better in summer than those awful lumpy old wool things you were wearing—more darns than yarn, I swear. They'll keep your feet dryer. Help those calluses."

"So fine! Such little, smooth stitches. I'll bet my feet won't bleed with these."

"Your feet bleed?" she said, appalled. "Eew!"

"Not often. Just in the worst of summer or the worst of winter."

"I'll spin up some of that wool for winter later. But I thought you could use these first."

"Indeed." He sat again and removed his boots, drawing the socks off carefully, and kissed her hands in thanks. Fawn glowed.

"I'm going to help Sarri start to spin her plunkin stem flax tomorrow, now the retting's all done," she said. "These women need a wheel to speed things up, they really do. Surely a little one wouldn't be so hard to cart back and forth, and we could all share it around the camp. I could teach them how to use it, give something back for all the help Sarri and Mari have been giving me. Do you think you could bring one back next time you patrol around Lumpton or Glassforge—or West Blue, for that matter? Mama and Nattie could make sure you got a good one," she added in a burst of prudence.

"I could sure try, Spark." And won her heart anew by not protesting a bit about the sight he would present hauling such an unwieldy object atop Copperhead.

She drew him into a promissory sort of cuddle for a time, but at length he recalled whatever Dar had brought to trouble him, and stood up with a sigh.

"Will you be gone long?" she asked.

"Depends on where Fairbolt's got off to."

She nodded, struggling to be content with the vague answer and what all it left out. The dark mood seemed to settle over his shoulders again like a cloak as he strode out to the road and vanished beyond the trees.

⁂

Dag tracked Fairbolt down at last at the end of a string of several campsites devoted to the extensive Crow clan on the western side of the island. Fairbolt took one look at his face and led him away from the noisy group of tents, crowded with his and Massape's children and grandchildren, and down to the dock. They sat cross-legged on the boards. Fairbolt's leathery skin was turned to blood-copper by the sunset light, which painted the silky wavelets lapping the shore purple and gleaming orange; his eyes were dark and unrevealing.

Dag drummed his fingers on the wood, and began, "I spoke with Dar a bit ago. Or rather, he spoke to me. He's threatening to go to the camp council. What he thinks they can do, I can't imagine. They can't force a string-cutting." He faltered. "He speaks of banishment."

Fairbolt scarcely reacted. Dag continued, "You're on the council. Has he talked to you?"

"Yes, some. I told him that was a bad plan. Though I suppose there could be worse ones."

Dag braced himself. "What are folks saying, behind my back?"

Fairbolt hesitated, whether embarrassed to repeat the gossip or just organizing his speech Dag wasn't sure. Perhaps the latter, for when he did begin, it was blunt enough. "Massape says some are cruelly amused to see Cumbia's pride crack."

"Idle talk," said Dag.

"Maybe. I'd discount that whole line, except the more they make your mother squirm, the more she leans on Dar."

"Ah. And are there other lines? Naming no names."

"Several." Fairbolt shrugged in a *what-would-you?* gesture. "You want a list? Naming no names."

"Yes. Well, no, but . . . yes."

Fairbolt drew breath. "To start, anyone who's ever been part of a patrol that came to grief relying on farmer aid.

Or who endured ingratitude rescuing farmers whose panic resulted in unnecessary patroller injuries or deaths."

Dag tilted his head, half-conceding, half-resisting. "Farmers are untrained. The answer is to train them, not to scorn them."

Fairbolt passed on this with a quirk of his lips and continued, ticking off his fingers, "Anyone who has ever had a relative or friend harassed or ambushed and beaten or killed by farmers over misguided fears about Lakewalker sorcery."

"If we kept less to ourselves, there wouldn't be such misunderstandings. Folks would know better."

Fairbolt ignored this, too. "More closely still, any patroller or ex-patroller who has ever been made to give up a farmer lover themselves. Some pretty bitter anger, there. A few wish you well, but more wonder how you're getting away with it. Those who have had the ugly job of enforcing the rules aren't best pleased with you, either. These people have made real sacrifices, and feel justifiably betrayed."

Dag rubbed his fingers gently back and forth along the wood grain, polished smooth by the passage of many feet. "Fawn slew a malice. She shared a death. She's . . . different."

"I know you think so. Thing is, everyone thinks their own situation was special, too. Which it was, to them. If the rules aren't for everyone, a system for finishing arguments turns into a morass of argument that never ends. And we don't have the time."

Dag looked away from Fairbolt's stern gaze and into the orange disk of the sun, now being gnawed by the black-silhouetted trees across the lake. "I don't know what Dar imagines he can make me do. I made an oath in my ground."

"Aye," said Fairbolt dryly, "in conflict with your prior duty and known responsibilities. You sure did. I swear you look like a man trying to stunt-ride two horses, standing with one foot on the back of each. Fine if he can keep 'em together, but if they gallop up two separate paths, he has to choose, fall, or be torn apart."

"I meant—mean—to keep my duties yoked. If I can."

"And if you can't? Where will you fall?"

Dag shook his head.

Fairbolt frowned at the shimmering water, gone luminous in the twilight to match the sky. A few last swallows swooped and wheeled, then made away for their nests. "The rules issue cuts another way. If it's seen that even so notable a patroller as Dag Redwing can't evade discipline, it makes it that much easier to block the next besotted idiot."

"Am I notable?"

Fairbolt cast him a peculiar look. "Yes."

"Dag Bluefield," Dag corrected belatedly.

"Mm."

Dag sighed and shifted to another tack. "You know the council. Will they cooperate with Dar? How much has he put to them privately already? Was his talk today a first probing threat, or my final chance?"

Fairbolt shrugged. "I know he's been talking to folks. How fast would you think he'll move?"

Dag shook his head once more. "He hates disputes. Hates getting his knife-work interrupted. It takes all his concentration, I know. By choice, I don't think he'd involve himself at all, but if he has to, he'll try to get it all over with as quickly as possible. So he can get back to work. He'll be furious—not so much with me, but about that. He'll push."

"I read him that way as well."

"Has he spoken to you? Fairbolt, don't let me get blind-sided, here."

This won another fishy look. "And would you have me repeat my confidential talks with you to him?"

"Um." Dag trusted the fading light concealed his flush. He leaned his back, which was beginning to ache, against a dock post. "Another question, then. Is anyone but Dar like to try to bring this to a head?"

"Formally, with the council? I can think of a few. They'll leave it to your family if they can, but if the Redwing clan fails in its task, they might be moved to step forward."

"So even if I smooth down Dar, it won't be over. Another challenge and another will pop up. Like malices."

Fairbolt raised his eyebrows at this comparison, but said nothing.

Dag continued slowly, "That suggests the road to go down is to settle it, publicly and soon. Once the council has ruled, the same charge can't be brought again. Stop 'em all." *One way or another.* He grimaced in distaste.

"You and your brother are more alike than you seem," said Fairbolt, turning wry.

"Dar doesn't think so," Dag said shortly. He added after a thoughtful pause, "He hasn't been out in the world as much as I have. I wonder if banishment seems a more frightening fate to him?"

Fairbolt rubbed his lips. "How's the arm?"

"Much better." Dag flexed his hand. "Splints have been off near a week. Hoharie says I can start weapons practice again."

Fairbolt leaned back. "I'm planning to send Mari's patrol back out soon. A lot of time lost at Glassforge to make up, plus her patrol isn't the only one that's run late this season. When will you be ready to ride again?"

Dag shifted, unfolding his legs to disguise his unease. "Actually, I was thinking of taking some of my unused camp time, till Fawn's more settled in."

"So when will that be? Leaving aside the matter of the council."

Dag shrugged. "For her part alone, not long. I don't think there's a camp task she can't do, if she's properly taught. I have no doubt in her." His hesitation this time stretched out uncomfortably. "I have doubt in us."

"Oh?"

He said quietly, "Betrayal cuts two ways as well, Fairbolt. Sure, when you go out on patrol you worry for your family in camp—sickness, the accidents of daily life, maybe even a malice attack—there's a residue of danger, but not, not . . . *untrust.* But once you start to wonder, it spreads like a stain. Who can I trust to stand by my wife in her need, and who will fold and leave her to take the brunt alone? My mother, my brother? Clearly not. Cattagus, Sarri? Cattagus is weak and ill, and Sarri has her own troubles. You?" He stared hard at Fairbolt.

To Fairbolt's credit, he did not drop his gaze. "I suppose the only way you'll find out is to test it."

"Yeah, but it won't exactly be a test of Fawn, now, will it."

"You'll have to sooner or later. Unless you mean to quit the patrol." The look that went with this remark reminded Dag of Hoharie's surgical knives.

Dag sighed. "There's soon and there's too soon. You can cripple a young horse, which would have done fine with another year to let its bones grow into themselves, by loading it too soon. Young patrollers, too." *And young wives?*

Fairbolt, after a long pause, gave a nod at this. "So when is not-too-soon, Dag? I need to know where I can put your peg. And when."

"You do," Dag conceded. "Can you give me a bit more time to answer? Because I don't think I can leave the council aside."

Fairbolt nodded again.

"Mind, I can only answer for myself and Fawn. I don't control the acts of anyone else."

"You can persuade," said Fairbolt. "You can shape. You can, dare I suggest, not be a stubborn fool."

Too late for that. This man, Dag was reminded, had six hundred other patrollers to track. Enough for tonight. The frogs were starting their serenade, the mosquitoes were out in companies, and the fat double-winged dragonflies darting over the lake were giving way to the night patrol of flitting bats. He levered himself to his feet, bade Fairbolt a polite good evening, and walked into the gathering dark.

8

They were making ready to lie down in their bedroll before Dag reported his conversations with his brother and Fairbolt to Fawn. From the brevity of his descriptions, compared to the time he'd been gone, Fawn suspected he was leaving a good bit out; more than these clipped essentials had cast him into his dark mood. *Brothers can do that.* But his explanation of the camp council was frightening enough.

In the light of their candle stub atop Dag's trunk, which did for their bedside table, Fawn sat cross-legged, and said, "Seven people can just vote you—us—to be banished? Just like that?"

"Not quite. They have to sit and hear arguments from both sides. And they'll each speak with other folks around their islands, gather opinions, before delivering a ruling of this . . . this gravity."

"Huh." She frowned. "Somehow I thought your people not liking me being here would take the form of . . . I don't know. Leaving dead rotten animals outside our door to step on in the morning, nasty tricks like that. Fellows in masks setting fire to our tent, or sneaking from the bushes and beating you up, or shaving my head, or something."

Dag raised quizzical brows. "Is that the form it would take in farmer country?"

"Sometimes." Sometimes worse, from tales she'd heard.

"A mask won't hide who you are from groundsense. Anyone wants to do something that ugly around here, they sure can't do it in secret."

"That would slow 'em up some, I guess," allowed Fawn.

"Yes, and . . . this isn't a matter for boys' tricks. Our marriage cords, if nothing else, draw it up to another level altogether. Serious dilemmas take serious thought from serious folks."

"Shouldn't we be making a push to talk to those serious folks, too? Dar shouldn't have it all his own way, seems to me."

"Yes—no . . . *blight* Dar," he added, in a burst of aggravation. "This shoves me into exactly the worst actions to ease you in here smoothly. Drawing attention, forcing folks to choose sides. I wanted to lie low, and while everyone was waiting for someone else to do something, let the time for choosing just slip on by. I figured a year would do it."

Fawn blinked in astonishment at his timetable. Perhaps a year didn't seem like such a long time to him? "This isn't exactly your favorite sort of arguin', is it?"

He snorted. "Not hardly. It's the wrong thing at the wrong time, and . . . and I'm not very smooth at it, anyway. Fairbolt is. Twenty minutes talking with him, and your head's turned around. Good camp captain. But he's made it clear this is my own bed to lie in." He added in a lower voice, "And I hate begging for favors. Figured I used up a life's supply long before this." A slight thump of his left arm on the bedroll indicated what favors he was thinking of, which made Fawn huff in turn. Whatever special treatment had won him his arm harness and let him back on patrol must, it seemed to her, have been paid back in full a good long time ago.

Nevertheless, Dag began the next morning to show their presence more openly by taking Fawn out in the narrow boat for plunkin delivery duty. The first step was to paddle out to a gathering raft, which over the season had worked its way nearly to the end of their arm of the lake and would shortly start back up the other side. A dozen Lakewalkers of various ages, sexes, and states of undress manned the ten-foot-square lashing of tree trunks, which seemed to be munching its way down a long stretch of water lilies. This variety had big, almost leathery leaves that stuck up out of the water like curled fans, and small, simple, unappealing yellow flowers, which also stood up on stalks. The crew worked steadily to dig, then trim and separate the stems, roots, and ears, and then replant. Churned-up mud and plant bits left a messy trail in the raft's inching wake.

Dag saluted an older woman who seemed to be in charge. A couple of naked boys rolled a load of plunkins into the narrow boat that made it ride alarmingly low in the water, and after polite farewells, Dag and Fawn paddled off again, a good bit more sluggishly. Fawn was intensely conscious of the stares following them.

Delivery consisted of coasting along the lakeshore, pulling up to each campsite in turn, and tossing plunkins into big baskets affixed to the ends of their docks, which at least showed Fawn where their daily plunkins had been coming from all this time. She hated the way the boat wobbled as she scrambled around at this task, and was terrified of dropping a plunkin overboard and having to go after it, especially in water over her head, but at length they'd emptied their boat out again. And then went back for another load and did it all over again, twice.

Dag waved or called a *how de'* to folks in other boats or along the shore, seemingly the custom here, and exchanged short greetings with anyone working on the docks as their boat pulled up, introducing Fawn to enough new folks that she quickly lost track of the names. No one was spiteful, though some looked bemused; but few of the return stares or greetings seemed really warm to her. After a while she thought she would have preferred rude, or at least blunt, questions to this silent appraisal. But the little ordeal came to an end at noon, when they climbed wearily back up the bank to Tent Bluefield. Where lunch, Fawn reflected glumly, would be plunkin.

They repeated the exercise on the next four mornings, until the raft-folk and dock-folk stopped looking at them in surprise. In the afternoons, Fawn began to help Sarri with the task of spinning up her new plunkin flax, and, for more novelty, aid Cattagus with his rope-braiding, one of his several sitting-down camp chores that did not strain his laboring lungs. His breathing, he explained between wheezes, was permanent damage left from a bad bout of lung fever a few years back that had nearly led him to share, and had forced him finally to give up patrolling and grow, he claimed, fat.

Fawn found she liked working with Cattagus more than with any other of the campsite's denizens. Sarri was stiff and wary, or distracted by her children, and Mari wryly dubious, but Cattagus seemed to regard *Dag's farmer girl* with grim amusement. It was daunting to reflect that his detachment might stem from how close he stood to death—Mari, for one, was very worried about leaving him come bad weather—but Fawn finally decided that he'd likely always had a rude sense of humor. Further, though not as patient a teacher as Dag, he was nearly as willing, introducing her to the mysteries of arrow-making. He produced arrows not only for his patroller wife, but for Razi and Utau as well. It was very much a two-handed chore; Dar, it seemed, had used to make Dag's for him, in his spare time. It didn't need, nor did Cattagus make, any comment that Dag now needed a new source. Fawn found in herself a knack for balance and a sure and steady hand at fletching, and shortly grew conversant with the advantages and disadvantages of turkey, hawk, and crow quills.

Dag trudged off several times to, as he said, *scout the territory*, returning looking variously worried, pleased, or head-down furious. Fawn and Cattagus were sitting beneath a walnut tree having a fletching session when he stalked back from one of the latter sort, ducked into the tent without a word, returned with his bow and quiver, grabbed a plunkin from the basket by the tent flap, and set it up on a stump in the walnut grove. Within fifteen minutes he had reduced the plunkin to something resembling a porcupine smashed by a boulder and was breathing almost steadily again as he tried to unwedge his deeply buried near-misses from the tree behind the stump. There were no wider misses to retrieve from the grove beyond.

"That one sure ain't gettin' away," Cattagus observed, with a nod at the remains of the plunkin. "Anybody I know?"

Dag, treading over to them, smiled a bit sheepishly. "Doesn't matter now." He sat down with a sigh, unlatched and set aside his short bow, then picked up one of the new arrows and examined it with a judicious eye. "Better and better, Spark."

She decided this was deliberate diversion. "You know, you keep saying I shouldn't come with you so's folks'll talk frank and free, but it seems to me you might get further with some if they were to talk a little less frank and free."

"That's a point," he conceded. "Maybe tomorrow."

But the next morning ended up being dedicated to some overdue weapons practice, with an eye to the fact that Mari's patrol would be going out again soon. Saun turned up, invited by Razi and Utau, and Fawn grew conscious for the first time of how few visitors had come to the campsite. If she and Dag were indeed a wonder of the lake, she would have thought curiosity, if not friendliness, should have brought a steady stream of neighbors making excuses to get a peek at her. She wasn't sure how to interpret their absence: politeness, or shunning? But Saun was as nice to her as ever.

The session began with archery, and Fawn, fascinated, made herself useful trotting into the walnut grove after misses, or tossing plunkin rinds up into the air for moving targets. Her arrows seemed to work as well as her mentor's, she saw with satisfaction. Cattagus sat on a stump and appraised the archers' skills as freely as his breathlessness would allow. Saun was inclined to be daunted by him, but Mari gave him back as good as she got; Dag just smiled. The five patrollers moved on to blade practice with wooden knives and swords. Mari was clever and fast, but outmatched in strength and endurance, not a surprise in a woman of seventy-five, and soon promoted herself to a seat beside Cattagus to shrewdly critique the others.

The action grew hotter then, with what seemed to Fawn a great many very dirty moves, not to mention uncertainty of whether she was watching sword fighting or wrestling. The clunk and clatter of the wooden blades was laced with cries of *Ow!*, *Blight it!*, or, to Saun's occasional gratification, *Good one!* Dag pushed the others on far past breathlessness, on the gasped-out but convincing theory that the real thing didn't come with rest breaks, so's you'd better know how to move when you couldn't hardly move at all.

The sweat-soaked and filthy combatants then took a swim in the lake, emerging smelling no worse than usual, and assembled in the clearing to munch plunkin and try, without success, to persuade Cattagus to uncork one of his last carefully hoarded jugs of elderberry wine from the prior fall. Dag, slouched against a stump and smiling at the banter, suddenly frowned and sat up, his head turning toward the road.

"What is it?" Fawn, sitting beside him, asked quietly.

"Fairbolt. Not happy about something."

She lowered her voice further. "Think it's our summons from the camp council, finally?" She had lived in increasing dread of the threat.

"Could be . . . no. I'm not sure." Dag's eyes narrowed.

By the time Fairbolt's trotting horse swung into the clearing, all the patrollers had quieted and were sitting up watching him. He was riding bareback, and his face was as grim as Fawn had ever seen. She found her heart beating faster, even though she was sitting still.

Fairbolt pulled up his horse and gave them all a vague sort of salute. "Good, you're all here. I'm looking for Saun, first."

Saun, startled, stood up from his stump. "Me, sir?"

"Yep. Courier just rode in from Raintree."

Saun's home hinterland. Bad news from there? Saun's face drained, and Fawn could imagine his thoughts suddenly racing down a roster of family and friends.

"They've got themselves a bad malice outbreak north of Farmer's Flats, and are calling for help."

Everyone straightened in shock at this. Even Fawn knew by now that to call for aid outside one's own hinterland was a sign of things going very badly indeed.

"Seems the blighted thing came up practically under a farmer town, and grew like crazy before it was spotted," Fairbolt said.

Saun's gnawed plunkin rind fell from his hand. "I'll ride— I have to get home at once!" he said, and lurched forward. He caught himself, breathless, and looked beseechingly at Fairbolt. "Sir, may I have leave to go?"

"No."

Saun flushed, but before he could speak, Fairbolt went on, "I want you to ride with the rest tomorrow morning as pathfinder."

"Oh. Yes, of course." Saun subsided, but stayed on his flexing feet, like a dog straining on the end of a chain.

"Being the high season, almost three-quarters of our patrols are out right now," Fairbolt continued, his gaze sweeping over the suddenly grave patrollers in front of him. "For our first answer, I figure I can pull up the next three patrols due to go out. Which includes yours, Mari."

Mari nodded. Cattagus scowled unhappily, his right hand rubbing on his knee, but he said nothing.

"Being out of the hinterland, it's on a volunteer basis as usual—you folks all in?"

"Of course," murmured Mari. Razi and Utau, after a glance at each other, nodded as well. Fawn hardly dared move. Her breath felt constricted. Dag said nothing, his face oddly blank.

Saun wheeled to him. "You'll come, won't you, Dag? I know you meant to sit out our next patrol in camp, and you've earned some time off your feet, but, but—!"

"I want to speak to Dag private-like," said Fairbolt, watching him. "The rest of you can start to collect your gear. I figure to send the first company west at dawn."

"Couldn't we start tonight? If everyone pulled themselves together?" said Saun earnestly. "Time—you never know how much difference a little time could make."

Dag grimaced at that one, not, Fawn thought, in disagreement.

Fairbolt shook his head, although his glance was sympathetic. "Folks are spread all over the lake right now. It'll take all afternoon just to get the word out. You can't outpace the company you're leading, pathfinder."

Saun gulped and nodded.

Fairbolt gave a gesture of dismissal, and everyone scattered, Razi and Utau for their tent, where Sarri had come to the awning post with her little boy on her hip, staring hard at the scene, Mari and Cattagus to theirs. Saun waved and started jogging up the road back to his own campsite on the island's other end.

Fairbolt slid down from his horse and left it to trail its reins and browse. Dag motioned toward Tent Bluefield, sheltered in the orchard, and Fairbolt nodded. Fawn hurried after their matched patrollers' strides. Fairbolt eyed her, neither inviting nor excluding, so when each man took a seat on an upended log in the shade of her tent flap, she did, too. Dag gave her an acknowledging nod before turning his full attention on his commander.

"With three patrols sent out in a bunch, they're going to need an experienced company captain," Fairbolt began.

"Rig Crow. Or Iwassa Muskrat," said Dag, watching him warily.

"My first two choices exactly," Fairbolt said. "If they weren't both a hundred and fifty miles away right now."

"Ah." Dag hesitated. "Surely you're not looking to me for this."

"You've been a company captain. Further, you're the only patroller in camp right now who's been in on a real large-group action."

"And so successfully, too," murmured Dag sourly. "Just ask the survivors. Oh, that's right—there weren't any. That'll give folks lots of confidence in my leadership, sure enough."

Fairbolt made an impatient chopping motion. "Your habit of picking up extra duty means you've worked, at one time or another, with almost every other patroller in camp. No problem with unfamiliar grounds, or not knowing your people pretty much through and through. Weaknesses, strengths, who can be relied on for what."

Dag's slow blink didn't deny this.

Fairbolt lowered his voice. "Another angle. I shouldn't be saying this, but your summons to stand before the camp council is due out in a very few more days. But they can't set a hearing if you're not here to receive the order. You wanted delay? Here's your chance. Do a good job on this, and if you're still called to stand before the council, you'll do so with that much more clout."

"And if I do badly?" Dag inquired, his voice very dry.

Fairbolt scratched his nose and grinned without humor. "Then we are all going to be having much more pressing problems than one patroller's personal lapses."

"And if I'm killed in the field, the problem goes away, too," said Dag with false brightness.

"Now you're thinking like a captain," said Fairbolt affably. "Knew you could."

Dag huffed a very short laugh.

Patroller humor, Fawn realized. *Yeep.*

Fairbolt sat back more seriously. "Not my first pick of solutions, though. Dag, when it comes to malices you're known as about the most volunteerin' fellow in camp. This is your chance to show 'em all nothing's changed."

Dag shook his head. "I don't know what's changed. Changing. More than . . . I sometimes think." His hand touched his left arm, and while Fairbolt might take it to mean his marriage cord, Fawn wondered how much the gesture was for his ghost hand.

Fairbolt glanced at Fawn. "Aye, it's a hard thing to ask a patroller newly string-bound to go out in the field under any circumstances. But this one's bad, Dag. I didn't want to give more details in front of Saun right off, but word from the courier is that they've already lost hundreds of people, farmers and Lakewalkers both. The malice has shifted from its first lair under that poor farmer town to attack Bonemarsh Camp. Most everyone got away, but there's no question the malice captured some. Once our first company is dispatched, I'm going to start scraping up a second—absent gods know from where—because I have an ugly hunch they'll be wanted."

Dag rubbed his brow. "Raintree folks will be off-balance, then. Focusing on the wrong things, defense and refugees and the wounded. People will get frantic for each other, and lose sight of the main chance. Get a knife in the malice. Everything else is a distraction."

"An outsider might be better at keeping his head," said Fairbolt suggestively.

"Not necessarily. It's been thirty years since I patrolled in north Raintree, but I still remember friends."

"And the terrain?"

"Some," Dag admitted reluctantly.

"Exactly. Never been out that way, myself. I figured, by the by, that I'll pair Saun as pathfinder with the company captain."

Dag did not respond directly to this, but touched his throat. "I don't have a primed knife right now. First time I've walked bare in decades. I usually carried two, sometimes three. You wondered how I took out so many malices, besides the extra patrolling? Folks gave me more knives. It was that simple."

"Not the captain's job to place the knife. It's his job to place the knife-wielders."

"I know," Dag sighed.

"And I know you know. So." Fairbolt stood up. "I'm going to finish passing the word up this side of the island. I'll ride back this way. You can give me your answer then." He didn't say *Talk it over with each other,* but the invitation was plain. He stared a moment at Fawn, as if thinking of making some plea to her, but then just shook his head. His horse came wandering over in a way that she suspected was not by chance, and he stepped up on his log seat and swung his leg over. He was back on the road in moments, setting the animal into a lope.

Dag had risen when Fairbolt had; he stood staring after him, but his face was drawn and inward-looking, as if contemplating quite another view. Her own face feeling as stiff and congealed as cold dough, Fawn rose too, and went to him. They walked into each other's arms and held on tight.

"Too soon," whispered Dag. He set her a little from him, looking down in anxiety. Fawn wondered whatever was the use of putting on a brave face when he could see right through to whatever wild roil her ground was in right now. She stiffened her spine anyhow, fighting to keep her breathing even and her lips firm.

"Fairbolt's right about the experience, though," he continued, his voice finding its volume again. "This sort of thing is different from hunting sessiles, or even from that mess we had near Glassforge. I run down the patrol lists in my head and think, *They don't know.* Especially the youngsters. How far north of Farmer's Flats was that town, anyway? Farmer settlements aren't supposed to be allowed above the old cleared line . . ." He shook his head abruptly, and grasped her hands. His gold eyes glittered with an expression she'd never seen in them before; she thought it might be *frantic*.

She swallowed, and said, "You did this once. So the question isn't, Can you do it? but, Can you do it better than someone doing it for the first time ever?"

"No—yes—maybe . . . It's been a while. Still—if not me, who am I condemning to go in my place? Someone has to—"

She reached up and pressed her fingers to his lips, which stilled. She said simply, "Who are you arguin' with, Dag?"

He was silent for the space of several heartbeats, though at length a faint wry smile turned his mouth, just a little.

Fawn took a deeper breath. "When I married a patroller instead of a farmer, I figured I must be signing up for something like this. You for the leaving . . . me for the being left." His hand found her shoulder, and tightened. "It's come on sooner than we thought, but . . . there has to be a first time." She raised her arms to catch his beloved cheekbones between her hands, pressing hard, and gave his head a stern little shake. "Just you make sure it's not the last, you hear?"

He gathered her in. She could feel his heartbeat slow. The scent of him, as she turned and buried her face in his shirt, overwhelmed her: sweat and summer and sun and just plain Dag. She opened her mouth and widened her nostrils as though she could breathe him in and store him up. *Forever. And a day.* Well, there wasn't any forever. *Then I'll take the day.*

"You're not afraid to be left alone here?" he murmured into her curls.

"On the list of things I'm afraid of, that one's just dropped down. Quite a ways."

She could feel his smile. "You have to grant, I've always come back so far."

"Yeah, the other patrollers in Glassforge said you were like a cat, that way." *But they all went out looking for you anyhow.* "Papa used to say to me, when I got all upset about one of our barn cats that had got its fool self in a fix and was crying all woeful, *Lovie, you ever seen a cat skeleton in a tree?*"

That deep chuckle she so loved, too seldom felt lately, rumbled through his chest. They stood there wrapped in each other until the unwelcome sound of trotting hoofbeats echoed from the road. "Right, then," muttered Fawn. She backed off and stared up.

He was looking down with a curious smile. He returned her nod. Squeezed and released her, all but her hand. Turned to face Fairbolt, looking down from his horse.

Fairbolt didn't speak, merely raising his brows in question.

"I'll want to talk to that courier," said Dag. "And have a fresh look at whatever large-scale maps we have of the northern Raintree region."

Fairbolt accepted this with no more comment than a short jerk of his chin. "Get up behind me, then. I'll give you a lift to headquarters." He kneed his horse around, and Dag stepped up on a stump and slid aboard. The burdened beast took to the road again at a rapid walk.

Fawn's eyes were hot but dry. Mostly. Blinking, she ducked inside her tent flap to see what she could do to help get Dag's saddlebags in order.

9

It was midnight before Dag returned to Tent
Bluefield. Fawn raised her head at the sound of his steps,
falling slower than usual out of the dark, and poked up their
campfire coals with a stick, lighting their candle stub from
it. In the weak flare of golden light his lips gave her a smile,
but his eyes seemed abstracted.

"I was wonderin' if you were going to get any chance to
sleep," she said quietly, rising.

"Some. Not much. We'll be saddling the horses just before
dawn."

"That's no way to start out, all tired. Should I stay awake
to get you up?" It wouldn't be that many more hours at this
point.

"No. Someone will come for me. I'll try to go out quiet."

"Don't you dare go sneaking off without waking me," she
said, a little fiercely, and led him inside, where the contents
of his saddlebags were laid out in neat stacks. His bow lay
next to them, its quiver stuffed with arrows. "I was going
to pack up your gear, but then I thought I'd better have you
check first, see if I got everything right."

He nodded, knelt, and began handing her stacks, briefly
inspected; she tucked them into the bags as tidily as she
could. The only thing he set aside was his tambourine in
its leather case. Fawn wanted to ask *Won't you need that to
celebrate the kill?* but then thought perhaps he wanted to
protect it, this riding-out being out of the routine. The other
possibilities she refused to contemplate. She closed the flaps,

buckled them, and turned to pick up the last item, laid out on the trunk beside the flickering stub.

"You've got no sharing knife. You want to take this one?" She held her—their—knife out to him, tentatively.

His face grew grave. Still kneeling, he took it from her and drew it from its sheath, frowning at the faded writing on the bone blade. "Dar thinks it won't work," he said at last.

"I wasn't thinking of it for your first pick. Only to keep by you just . . . just in case. If there were no other choices."

"There will be a dozen and more other knives among my company."

"How many patrollers are going?"

"Seventy."

"Will it be enough?"

"Who knows? One is enough, but it can take all the rest to get that one to the right place at the right time. Fairbolt will hold all the regular patrols going out, and fold in the ones coming home, but he has to think not only of sending help, but of defense."

"I'd think sending help would *be* the best defense."

"To a point. Things might go badly in Raintree, but also another malice could pop up here in Oleana. Since this commotion will put everyone behind schedule—again— it's just that more likely. That's the problem with malices emerging so randomly. Nice when we go months and months at a time without one, but when they come up in a bunch, we can get overwhelmed." His brows drew in; slowly, he resheathed the knife, handing it back to her with a somewhat apologetic grimace. "Better not. I have an old bad habit of jumping into things feetfirst, and that's not my job this time."

She accepted his words, and the knife, with a little nod, although her heart ached.

"I have some ideas," he went on, his mind clearly elsewhere. Or perhaps several elsewheres. "But I'm going to need more recent news than what that courier brought. She near rode her horse to death, but she was still two days getting here. Part of what went wrong at Wolf Ridge was due to, hm, not so much bad, as old information. Though for whatever consolation, I'm not sure but what we'd have done just the same if we had known what was coming down on us. If we'd spared a few more to the ridge, it would just have been that many more dead. And a few was all we had." His mouth set in irony. "The help from out of the hinterland not having arrived yet."

Fawn didn't think Dag's company would be dawdling on their road tomorrow.

There seemed so little she could do for him. Socks. Arrows. Packing. It all felt so trivial. All things he had accomplished perfectly well for himself for years before she'd come along to so disrupt his life. She might help by putting him to bed and sitting on him, maybe; it was clear his body needed its rest, and equally clear his mind would scarcely allow it. She raised her hands and began tenderly unbuttoning his shirt. As her wrist moved, her eye was caught by the gold beads of her marriage cord. *He needs to be thinking about his task, not about me.* But time was growing desperately short.

"Dag . . ."

"Mm, Spark?" His fingers in turn gently twisted themselves in the curls of her hair, letting the locks flow over and between them.

"You can feel me through your wedding cord, right? And all the other married Lakewalkers, Mari and Cattagus and all, they can do the same for each other?"

He nodded. She drew his shirt off that long, strappy-muscled torso, folding it up atop his clean and mended riding trousers for morning. Later in the night. Whatever that grim predawn hour was.

She went on, "Well, I can't. I've taken your word that our cords work the same as everyone else's, but I can't feel it for myself."

"Others can tell. And tell you."

"Yeah, well, except I can't be all the time asking, twenty times a day. Cattagus for one doesn't take to being pestered. And besides, he'll have his own worries about Mari."

"True," he conceded, eyeing her.

She slipped out of her own shirt, his hand helping not so much for need, as to trail over her skin in passing. The light touch made her shiver. "I want to know in my own heart. Isn't there anything at all you can do to, to *make* me feel you? The way all the others can?"

He said after a moment, "Not the way the others can, no. You're no Lakewalker."

Nor ever would be, but his wording caught her attention. "Some other way?"

"Let me . . . think about that for a little, Spark. It would take some unusual groundwork."

Stripped for sleep, he was altogether unaroused. If he felt half as distracted as she did right now, that was no surprise. She felt obscurely that she ought to send him off having been thoroughly made love to, but for the first time ever, such intimacy felt forced and unhappy. That was no good either.

"You're all tense. How if you lie down and I give you a back rub? Might help you sleep."

"Spark, you don't have to—"

"And a real good foot rub," she added prudently.

He rolled over into their bedroll with a muffled noise indicating abject surrender, and she smiled a little. She started at his neck. His muscles there were plenty hard and tense, though this seemed poor compensation for the limpness elsewhere. The corded unease gave itself up but slowly as her hands pressed, slid, caressed. Unhurriedly, she worked her way from tousled top to gnarly toe, not making love, just loving.

Perhaps the lack of expectation paid off; in any case, when he at length rolled over again a more alert interest had clearly returned to him. There might yet be sleep for him tonight, if the long way around. She slid down against him

to capture his mouth in a deep kiss; his own hand snaked
around her shoulder and began tracing lazily over her. She
tried to soak up every sensation, hold them like painted patterns on her skin, but racing time washed them constantly
beyond her reach.

He arched above her like a clouded night sky, lowering,
entering her; if not easily, far more easily than their first
urgent fumbles on their wedding night. *Exercise, indeed*
she thought, and smiled in memory. She felt a pang of
regret that tonight was bound to be futile for trying to catch
a child, both too late for this month and too soon for her
healing. In these hurried, frightening circumstances, she
might have been tempted to take a chance on the healing.
Still . . . surely it would be ill omened to conceive their first
child out of fear and despair. *Dag'll come back. He must
come back.*

He slipped his left arm behind her back, clutched her, and
heaved them both over. She adjusted herself with a wriggle
and sat up, looking down at him curiously. His face held a
different abstraction, and she feared for a moment that they
would again lose their intimate impetus to the creeping chill
of tomorrow's worries.

No, evidently not. But he watched her though half-lidded
eyes as his left arm began a peculiar circuit, briefly touching
the cord bound on her left wrist, then her forehead, heart,
belly, groin, and wrist again.

"What are you doing?"

"Not sure. Something by feel. A little left-handed groundwork, maybe."

What he'd called his left-handed groundwork hadn't appeared in their lovemaking since he'd recovered the use of
his right hand. She had missed his eerie caresses, though she
supposed it wasn't to her credit that they'd made her feel so
downright smug for marrying a black sorcerer instead of a
mere farmer. But that seemed not to be what he was about,
this time.

"I'm trying to patch a bit of ground reinforcement into you that will dance with my ground in your cord. Shaped inside your own ground—pretty ground! If you—as you—grow open to me, I think I can coax it in through natural channels. Not sure exactly what the effect will be. Just . . ."

She opened eyes, heart, and body to him, wide and vulnerable. "Need blood?" she asked breathlessly.

She wasn't sure if his huff was a laugh or a sob. "Don't think so. Just . . . just love me . . ."

She found their rhythm again, taking over the lovemaking, abandoning the magic-making to him. His eyes were as wide and black as she'd ever seen them, pools of night with liquid stars in their depths. His left arm continued its rounds, more slowly but somehow more intensely. It ended laid diagonally across his belly just as his back began to arch. Her eyes squeezed shut as the wonderful, increasingly familiar wave of sensation coursed up from her heated loins, stopping her breath. A stranger, sharper wave of sweet warmth wound with it, rising up through her heart and down her arm in time with the pulse of her blood.

Oh. Oh!

Then, as he sank beneath her, the ecstatic shudders in his own body damping out, she said "Oh!" in quite another voice of surprise. She clapped her right hand to the cord encircling her left wrist. "It—it *tingles*. It feels like winter sparks."

"Too much? Does it hurt?" he wheezed anxiously, opening his eyes again.

"No, not at all. Strange . . . oh! It's fading a bit. Am I losing . . . ?"

"You should be able to call it up to you when you wish. Try."

She bit her lip and concentrated. The warm sensation faded. "No . . . no, oh dear. Am I not doing it right?"

"Instead of concentrating, try relaxing. Make yourself open."

"That," she said after a minute, "is a lot harder than concentrating."

"Yes. Not force, but persuasion. Enticement."

She sat astride him with her eyes closed, right hand wrapping her wrist, and tried again. She imagined herself smiling wordlessly, trying to attract Dag over to her for a kiss and a cuddle. *I love you so much . . .*

A prickling heat around, no, inside her wrist seemed like an answering whisper, *Yes, I'm here.* "That's you? In the cord?"

"That's a bit of me that's been in the cord since that night in your aunt Nattie's weaving room," said Dag, smiling up at her.

"And you can feel a bit of me in your cord like this, too?"

"Yep." He added in caution, "It may not last more than a few weeks, as you absorb the ground reinforcement."

"It'll do fine." She vented a long, elated sigh, and slumped down across his chest. But since he couldn't kiss any more of her than the top of her head in this position, she roused herself and reluctantly parted from him. They cleaned up briefly and lay back down just as the candle guttered out. Dag was asleep before she was.

She woke in the dark and rolled over to clutch an empty bedroll. Her heart lurched in panic. Feeling around frantically, she found Dag's dented pillow still warm. She gripped her cord, calmed her breathing, and tried to sense him. *Alive*, of course, the reassuring prickle told her; just over . . . thataway.

He's just gone out to the slit trench, you fool girl, she scolded herself in relief. She rolled on her side, bringing her hands up to her breasts, and bent her head to kiss the heavy, twice-blessed braid.

The tent flap lifted in a few minutes. The shadows outside were nearly as inky as in here. Dag slipped his bare, chilled body into their bedroll again; they wound their arms around each other, and Fawn did her best to share heat through her skin so that he might ease swiftly into whatever space of sleep was left to him this night. But before his breathing slowed, a slap sounded on the leather of their tent flap, and a low voice called, "Dag?" *Utau*, Fawn thought.

"I'm awake," Dag groaned.

"Omba's girls just brought our horses around."

"Right. Be right with you."

From the middle distance sounded a muffled equine snort, and Copperhead's familiar, irritable squeal. Fawn slipped her shift on in the dark and went out to coax a bit of flame from the gray ashes of their fire, trying to get a last few minutes of light from the melted candle stub in the bottom of its clay cup. Back inside, she found Dag dressed already, running his hand over his gear as if in final inventory. There would be no turning back for forgotten items this trip. His face looked tired and strained, but not, she thought, from fear. At least . . . not physical fear. They shared slices of plunkin, gnawed down quickly and without ceremony. Or, in Fawn's case, appetite.

"Now what?" said Fawn.

"The company will assemble at the headquarters tent. Most folks say good-bye at home."

"Right, then."

He hooked up his saddle, Fawn tottered after with the saddlebags, and they went out to where the horses were tied. Razi, Utau, and Mari were saddling theirs, in the light of a torch held aloft by Cattagus. Sarri stood ready to hand things up. In the east, across this arm of the lake, the black shapes of the trees were just growing distinguishable from the graying sky. Mist shrouded the water, and the grass and weeds underfoot were damp with dew.

Cattagus handed the torch to Sarri long enough to hug Mari, muttering into her knotted gray hair, "Mind your steps, you fool old woman." To which she returned, "You just mind yourself, you fool old man." Despite his wheezing, he gave her a leg up, his hand lingering a moment on her thigh as she settled into her saddle.

Dag gave Copperhead a knee to the belly, ducked the return snap of yellow teeth, and tightened his girth for a second time. He turned to grip Fawn's hands, then embraced her as she flung her arms around him and held hard. He put her from him with a kiss, not on her lips, but on her forehead: not farewell, but blessing. The tenderness and terror of it wrenched her heart as nothing else had this anxious morning.

And then he was heaving himself up on Copperhead. The gelding, clearly refreshed by his holiday in pasture, signified his displeasure at being put back to work so early in the morning by sidling and some halfhearted bucking, firmly checked by his rider. The four patrollers angled onto the road and vanished in the shadows; Fawn saw a few more mounted shapes trotting to catch up. Those left behind turned back silently to their tents, though Cattagus gave his niece Sarri a hug around the shoulders before he went in.

Fawn was entirely unable to contemplate falling back to sleep. She went into her tent and straightened her few belongings—housekeeping was a short task with so little house to keep—and tried to set her mind to the work of the day. Spinning was endless, of course. She was helping Sarri with her weaving in return for share of the tough cloth she was presently making and for teaching Fawn how to sew a pair of Lakewalker riding trousers, but it was too early to go over there. She wasn't hungry enough yet to eat more plunkin.

Instead, she traded her shift for a shirt and skirt, put on her shoes, and walked down the shore road toward the split to the bridge. The gray light was growing, with the faintest tinge of blue; only a few pricking stars still shone down through the leaves. She was not, she discovered, the only person with this notion. A dozen or more Lakewalkers, men and women, old and young, had collected along the main road in small groups, scarcely talking. She tried nodding to some neighbors she recognized from the plunkin delivery chore; at least some nodded back, though none smiled. But nobody was smiling much.

Patience was rewarded in a few minutes by the sound of hoofbeats coming from the woodland road. The cavalcade had already broken into the ground-eating trot of the long-legged patrol horses. Dag was in the lead, riding alongside Saun, listening with a thoughtful frown as the young man spoke; but he swiveled his head and flashed a smile at Fawn in passing, and Saun looked back and managed a surprised salute. Others along the road craned their necks for a glimpse of their own, exchanging a few last waves. One woman ran alongside a young patroller and handed up something folded in a cloth that Fawn thought might be a forgotten medicine kit; in any case, the girl grinned gratefully and twisted in her saddle to thrust it away in her bags.

Fawn wasn't sure how seventy patrollers could seem at once so many and so few. But every one had been well kitted-up: good sturdy gear, fine weapons, good horses. *Good wishes.* And what she'd just seen was only a tenth of Fairbolt's patrollers. It wasn't hard to see where the wealth of this straitened island community was being spent.

As the tail of the company vanished around the bend, the onlookers broke up and began walking back to their tents. Almost at the last, an angular figure emerged from the cover of some straggling, sun-starved honeysuckle bushes across the road. Fawn, startled, recognized Cumbia at the same moment the Lakewalker woman saw her. She gave a nod and a polite knee-dip to her mother-in-law, wondering for a moment if this was a good chance to begin speaking with her again. It occurred to Fawn that this task might actually be easier without Dag and his nervy . . . well, *prick-*

liness seemed an inadequate word for it. *Pigheadedness* came closer. She mustered up a smile to follow, but Cumbia abruptly turned her head and began walking rapidly down the woodland road, back stiff.

It dawned on Fawn that the preparations for such dark morning departures had for long been Cumbia's task. And Cumbia had once had a husband who hadn't returned from patrol, or only in the form of a deathly bone blade. Was this the first time her son had ridden out without bidding her farewell? Fawn wasn't sure if Cumbia had tried to show herself or hide herself, over there on the other side of the road, but she knew Dag hadn't glanced that way. Dar, Fawn noted, had not come with his mother, and she wondered what it meant.

Face pinched, Fawn turned back onto the shore road. She held her hand over her marriage cord, trying for that reassuring tingle. *Come on, girl, he's not even over the bridge yet.* But *there*, the little prickling answered her silent query nonetheless. *Thataway.* She took a deep breath and walked on.

In the inadequate light of their half dozen campfires flickering across this roadside clearing, Dag walked down the horse lines inspecting, but not with his eyes alone. *Three horses lame.* Not bad for three days of hard pushing. The company had traveled with several packhorses carrying food and precious grain. Patrol horses were normally grassfed, except now and then in farmer country where grain was easier to come by, but grazing took time and grain gave better strength. The loads of provender were rapidly dwindling; tomorrow morning, they could cache three emptied packsaddles and trade out animals, and leave no one slowing the rest by going double-mounted. *Yet.*

Dag had led his company miles north from Hickory Lake to pick up the straight road west, despite Saun's pleas that he could guide them, once they'd passed the borders of Oleana into Raintree, on a shorter, swifter route. They were now, by Dag's reckoning, a half day's ride due north of Bonemarsh Camp. Not a direction from which relief—or, from the malice's point of view, attack—might be expected. According to the shaken party of Lakewalker refugees, mostly women with children, that they had encountered and questioned late this afternoon, the malice had holed up at Bonemarsh. *Temporarily.* Dag had been waiting for such intelligence. Now he had it, it was time to commit his company to his plan. *No excuses, no delays.*

He sighed and began a roundabout stroll through the settling camp, touching this patroller or that on the shoulder. "Meet by my campfire in a few minutes." Razi and Utau were both among them, and to Dag's deeper regret, Mari and Dirla. Others from other patrols, all with skills known to him; not of bow or sword or spear, though all were proficient enough, but of groundsense control. A few were partnered, but most would be leaving their usual partners behind. *They won't like that.* He wished that might prove the worst of their worries.

The night sky was misty, only a few stars showing through, and the ground was sodden. The company had ridden through miserable rain all day yesterday, blowing east into their faces as they pressed west. The next few days should prove fair, though Dag wondered if that would be more to their advantage or to their quarry's. Hauling logs to keep their haunches out of the damp, the patrollers he'd tapped collected quietly around the dwindling fire, watching attentively as Dag came up. In all, sixteen: his twelve chosen, the other two patrol leaders, Saun, and himself.

"All right"—he drew breath—"this is what we're going to do tomorrow. We're facing a malice not only at its full strength, and mobile, but who now certainly knows what sharing knives are. Getting close enough to kill it will be a lot trickier."

Saun stirred and subsided on his log, and Dag gave him an acknowledging nod. "I know you weren't too happy about not sending word ahead, Saun, but a courier could barely have outpaced us, and I wasn't keen to send a rider alone into woods maybe full of mud-men. We are several days ahead of any other possible reinforcements from the east, and also well ahead of any return messengers. No one knows we're coming, no one knows we're here—including the malice."

Dag controlled an urge to pace, grasping his hook behind his back and rocking slightly instead. "I have—one time— seen a malice this advanced taken down, at Wolf Ridge in Luthlia." The younger patrollers around the fire blinked and sat up; a few older ones nodded knowingly, gazes growing more intent. "The strategy had two pieces, though the way it played out was partly accidental. While the most of us held the malice's mud-men and slaves—and attention—in open battle up on the ridge, by way of diversion, a small group of patrollers good at veiling their grounds slipped up on the lair. There were eight pairs in that group, and each pair carried a sharing knife. Orders were, if anyone went down, their partner didn't stay by them, but was to take the knife and go on. If any pairs went down, the same with their linking pairs." The reverse, Dag and everyone listening to him was aware, of the usual patrol procedure to leave no one behind. "When enough patrollers got close enough to the malice to risk a rush, they did." It had been down to four survivors by then, Dag had been told later. "And that was the end of that malice." But not of the cleanup, which had gone on for months thereafter.

"With a malice that strong, didn't they risk getting their grounds ripped?" asked Dirla. And if it was in fear, none could tell, for her voice did not quaver, and she had her groundsense well locked down.

"Some did," said Dag. Bluntly, without apology. "But I think we can try a similar strike. Whatever resistance is forming up right now south of Bonemarsh Camp, trying to protect Farmer's Flats, gets to play the part of the company on the ridge, overwhelming the malice's concentration. We here"—Dag unlocked his hand and gestured around the campfire—"will be for the sneak attack. You were all picked for your groundsense control."

"Not Saun!" complained Dirla. Saun flushed and glowered at her.

"No, he's our walking map. And someone's going to have to stay with the horses." Dag cast Saun an apologetic look; the boy grimaced but subsided.

"And the rest of the company?" asked Obio Grayheron, one of the remaining patrol leaders.

Dag gave him a short nod. "You'll give us a half-day start. At which point it will either be over—or command will pass to you and you'll be free to try again, try something else, or circle to join forces however you can with the Raintree Lakewalkers."

Obio settled back, digesting this unhappily. "And you're going with . . . well. Yes, of course."

Going with the veiled patrol, Dag finished for him. Because Dag was well-known to be one of the cleverest at that trick in camp. Which begged the question, in his own mind if not theirs, whether he had chosen this strategy because it was the best they could do, or because it played to his personal quirks. Well, if the gamble paid off, the subtle self-doubt would be moot. *And also if it doesn't. You can't lose, old patroller. In a sense.*

Saun was shoving shallow furrows in the drying mud with his boot heel. He looked up. "A little cruel on the folks fighting the retreat toward Farmer's Flats. They don't even get to know they're the bait."

"Neither did most of the folks up on Wolf Ridge," said Dag dryly. And, before Saun could ask *How do you know?* continued, "Saun, Codo, Varleen, you're all familiar with Bonemarsh. Stand up and give us a terrain tutorial."

A customary task; Dag stepped back, the local knowledge stepped forth, and the other patrollers began pelting them with variously shrewd questions as the precious parchment maps were passed around, and annotations scribbled in the dirt with sticks, rubbed out, and redrawn. Dag listened as hard or harder than anyone else, casting and recasting tactical approaches in his head, glumly aware that nine-tenths of the planning would prove useless in the event.

There was enough brains and experience in this bunch that Dag scarcely needed to guide the detailed discussion from here; two bad ideas were knocked down, by Utau and Obio respectively, before Dag could open his mouth, and three better ones that Dag wouldn't even have thought of were spat forth, to be chewed over, altered, and approved with only the barest shaping murmurs on his part. Mari, bless her, took over the problem of coaxing sharing knives from a couple of patrollers who were not going with the veiled patrol, as there were six pairs but only four knives among those here assembled. They even sorted themselves out in new partner-pairs before the group, growing quiet and thoughtful, broke up to seek their bedrolls. Dag hoped they would all sleep better than he seemed likely to.

He rolled on his back in his own bedroll, thin on the cold, damp ground, and searched the hazy sky for stars, trying to quiet the busy noise in his head. There was no point in running over the plans for tomorrow yet again, for the tenth, or was that the twentieth, time. He'd done all he could for tonight, except sleep. But when he forced the roiling concerns for his company out, the ache of missing Fawn crept back in.

He'd grown so accustomed to her companionship in so few weeks, as if she'd always been there, or had slotted into some hollow place within him just her shape that had been waiting for years. He'd come to delight not only in her sweet body, awakening appetites he'd imagined dulled by time, age, and exhaustion, but in the way her shining eyes opened wide in her endless questions, that determined set to her mouth when she faced a new problem, her seemingly boundless world-wonder. And if her hunger for life was a joy to him, his own, renewed, was an astonishment.

He considered the dark side of that bright coin uneasily. Had this marriage also reawakened his fear of death? For long, his inevitable end had seemed neither enemy nor friend, just *there*, accepted, to be worked around like his missing hand. If a fellow had nothing to lose, no risk held much alarm, and fear scarcely clogged thought. If that indifference had given him his noted edge, was that edge becoming blunted?

His right hand crept across his chest to trace the heavy cord wrapping his left arm above the elbow, calling up the reassuring hum of Spark's live ground. Indeed, he had something to lose now. By the shadow of his fear, he began to see the shape of his desire, the stirrings of curiosity for a future not constrained and inevitable but suddenly containing a host of unknowns, places and people altogether unimagined, *unconceived* in all senses. *Blight it, I want to live.* Not the best time to make that discovery, eh? He snorted self-disdain.

Instead of letting his thoughts chase one another back around the circle, he folded his left arm in, rolled over around the absence of Spark, and resolutely closed his eyes. The summer night was short. They would head due south at dawn. *And make sure your body and your wits are riding the same horse, old patroller.*

10

Three days gone, Fawn thought. Today would begin the fourth. Was it over, was it even begun, was Dag's company there yet? Wherever *there* was. Somewhere to the west, yes, and he was still alive; so much her marriage cord now told her. Better than no news, but far, far from enough.

She watched across the campsite as Cattagus settled himself at a log table with knife, awl, and assorted deerhide scraps. His task of the morning was to make a new pair of slippers for his great-niece Tesy, judging by the fascinated way she danced around him, giggling when he tickled her feet after measuring them against his pieces. It might have been mere chance that his right hand rested for a moment on his left wrist before he leaned forward and began cutting.

Fawn stretched her back against the apple tree and forced herself to take up her knitting again. Without Sarri's two children, the campsite would have fallen all too quiet these past days. Although the distraction they'd provided by disappearing for several hours day before yesterday didn't exactly count as a help. They'd been found by a neighbor, pressed into aiding the search, in the woods nearly at the other end of the island—on a quest of their own, looking for their fathers. From their infant points of view, Fawn supposed, Razi and Utau were grand playmates who vanished as mysteriously as they arrived, and Sarri's strained, carefully repeated explanations about *gone on patrol* as baffling as if she'd announced they had gone off to the moon.

Fawn's monthly had begun the day after Dag had left, not a surprise, but an unpleasant reminder of too many regrets. Sarri had shown Fawn how Lakewalker women used cattail fluff as absorbent stuffing for their ragbags, which could be emptied into the slit trench instead of tediously washed out along with the bags, after. The consolation was slight. Fawn had spent two unhappy days sitting, spinning, and cramping, trying without success to decide if this was just a bad one, or some abnormal relic from the malice's mishandling, and wishing Mari were here to ask; but the grinding pain had passed off at last, and her fears eased with her bleeding. Today was much better.

Last row. Fawn cast off neatly and laid the new pair of cotton-yarn socks out on her skirted thigh. They had come out well; the few dropped stitches had been properly recaptured, the heels turned at a natural angle and not something that her brothers would have threatened to dress the rooster in. She grinned in memory of the irate bird stalking around with those misshapen wool bags tied to its feet, though at the time she'd been even madder than it had.

She slipped into her tent and combed her unruly hair, tying it up with a ribbon, then rummaged in her scrap bag for a bit of colored yarn. She folded the socks neatly and made a bow around the bundle with the yarn, to help them look more like a present. Then she straightened up, put her shoulders back, and walked down the road toward Cumbia Redwing's encampment.

Rain had blown through from the west last night, and the tall hickory trees shed sparkling drops as a fresh breeze stirred them. Dag's company must have ridden through the same broad storm, Fawn calculated, though whether it had caught them on the road or in shelter she could not guess. Despite the lingering damp, when Fawn came to the Redwing site she spotted Cumbia working outside, sitting on a leather cushion atop the inevitable upended log seat at one of the crude plank tables. She was wearing the sleeveless calf-length shift that seemed usual for women in summer here, this one a faded bluish-red that spoke of some berry dye. The lean, upright posture was slightly bent, the shining silver head turned down over her task. Skeins of the long-fibered plunkin flax yarn lay out on the table; with a four-pronged lucet, Cumbia was looping them into the strong, light cord Lakewalkers used. As Fawn had hoped, Dar and Omba were nowhere in sight—off to the bone shack and Mare Island, presumably.

Cumbia looked up and scowled as Fawn approached. Her hands, as gnarled with work and age as any farmwife's, went on expertly braiding.

Fawn dipped her knees, and said, "How de'. Nice morning."

Silence.

Unpromising, but Fawn hadn't expected this to be easy. "I knitted Dag a pair of socks to go under his riding boots, very fine. He seemed to like them a lot. So I made a pair for you, too." She thrust out her little bundle. Cumbia made no move to take it. If Fawn had been offering a dead squirrel found rotting in the woods, Cumbia's expression might have been much the same. Fawn set the socks down next to the skeins and stepped back just a little, schooling herself not to turn and flee. She had to hook up some response to build on besides that dead stare. "I was glad to see you come watch Dag ride out the other morning. I know you wanted him to become an officer."

The hands reached the end of some counting turn, stopped, and set the wooden tool on the table with a sharp clack. The scowl deepened. As if the words were jerked from her, Cumbia said, "Not like this."

"How else should it be? It seemed very like Dag."

"It came out all wrong." Cumbia blew out her breath. "It generally does, with that boy. The aggravation and sorrow he has brought me, first to last, can hardly be counted." Her gaze on Fawn left no doubt as to what she considered the latest entry in that tally.

At least she's started talking. "Well, folks we're close to most often do aggravate us. Because otherwise we wouldn't care. He's brought good things as well. Twenty-seven malice kills, to start. You have to be proud of that."

Cumbia grimaced. "Oh, he's proven himself on patrol, right enough, but he'd done that by the time he was twenty-five. It's in camp where he's ducked his duties, as if patrolling got him off responsibility for all else. If he'd married when he should have, years ago, we wouldn't be in this muddle now."

"He did, once," Fawn pointed out, in an attempt at a dignified reply. "Right on time for a Lakewalker man, I guess. It turned into a hurtful tragedy that still haunts him."

"He's not the first nor the last to suffer such. Plenty of others have lost folks in the maw of some malice." And Cumbia was one of them, Fawn was reminded. "He's had twenty years to put it behind him."

"Well, then"—Fawn took a breath—"it looks like he's not going to, doesn't it? You all had your chance with him, and a good long chance it was. Maybe it's someone else's turn now."

Cumbia snorted. "Yours?"

"Seems like. I'd say you haven't lost anything to me that you had in the first place. When I met him, he wasn't betrothed to anything but his own death, near as I could tell. And if he's lost *that* infatuation, well, good!"

Cumbia leaned back, her attention now fully engaged. Which wasn't exactly a comfortable feeling, but at least it was a shift from her attempt to pretend Fawn didn't exist at all.

Fawn went on, "You're both of you stiff-necked. I think Dag must get it from you, to tell the truth. *Somebody* has to bend before things break." *Hearts, for one.* "Can't you please stop Dar from going to the camp council? It's bound to end badly."

"Yes, for you," said Cumbia. More level than venomous, oddly.

Fawn raised her chin. "Do you really believe Dag'll choose to cut strings if he's forced to the edge? That he'd break his word? You have a strange idea of your son, for knowing him so long."

"I believe he'll be secretly relieved to be freed of that ill-chosen oath to you, girl. Embarrassed, sure, and obnoxious about it—men always are, when they're caught in the wrong. But in the long run, glad to be rescued from his own mistakes, and gladder still not to have to do it himself."

Fawn bit her lip. *So you think your son's a coward, as well as a liar?* She didn't say it. Or spit it. She was shaken by a faint undercurrent of plausibility in Cumbia's argument. *I've known him half a summer. She's known him all his life.* She gripped the cord around her left wrist, for solace and courage. "What if he chooses banishment?"

"He won't. No Lakewalker could. He'll remember what he owes, and who to."

In general, Dag tried to keep as much distance between himself and his family as he could, and Fawn was beginning to see why. People left their families all the time—it was as normal for a Lakewalker man as it was for a farmer woman. Sometimes it was the straight path for growing up, like Dag's marriage in Luthlia; he presumably had never intended to return from there once he'd wed Kauneo. Sometimes families were impossible in their own right, and could not be fixed, only fled from, and she was beginning to wonder if a little of that might have been behind Dag's first marriage, too. She chose at last, "Who's pushing this camp council showdown—you, or Dar?"

"The family is united in trying to rescue Dag from this—I grant, self-inflicted—disaster."

"Because I think Dar knows better. And if he's telling you something else, he's lying."

Cumbia looked faintly bemused. "Farmer girl, I'm a Lakewalker. I know when someone is lying."

"Fooling himself, then." Fawn tried another tack. "All this is hurting Dag. I can see the strain in him. It wasn't right to send him off to war with all this mess on his mind."

Cumbia's brows rose. "So whose fault was that? It takes two sides to tear a man apart. The solution is simple. Go back to your farm. You don't belong here. Absent gods, girl, you can't even veil your ground properly. It's as if you're walking around naked all the time, do you even know that? Or did Dag not tell you?"

Fawn flinched, and Cumbia looked briefly triumphant. In sudden panic, Fawn wondered if her mother-in-law was reading her ground the way Dag did. *If so, she'll know how to split me up the middle easy as splitting a log with a wedge and mallet.*

Cumbia's head cocked curiously; her eyes narrowed. As if in direct response to this thought, she said, "What use to him is a wife so stupid and ignorant? You'll always be doing the wrong thing here, a constant source of shame to him. He might be too stiff-necked to admit it, but inside, he'll writhe. You'd bear children with weak grounds, incapable of the simplest tasks. If your blighted womb can bear at all, that is. You're pretty now, I admit, but that won't last, either—you'll age fast, like the rest of your kind, growing as fat and distracted as any other fool of a farmwife, while he goes on, rigid with regret."

She's probing. Shooting not at any facts that could possibly be known to her, and certainly not blind, but at Fawn's fears. A vision of her mama and Aunt Nattie, both grown downright dumpy in their middle age, nonetheless assaulted Fawn's imagination. Half a dozen barbs, half a dozen direct hits—*no, not blind. Still . . . I must have hit her somewhere, too, for her to be counterattacking so cruelly.*

Fawn remembered a description she'd heard down in Glassforge of how the rougher keelboat men fought duels.

Their wrists were strapped together with rawhide thongs, and their free hands given knives. So they were forced to circle close, unable to disengage or get out of their enemy's stabbing range. This fight with Cumbia felt like that. Driven to her wits' end by her own family, Fawn had not believed Dag when he'd said his would be worse, but if her people fought to bruise and tumble, his aimed to slice to the bone. Maybe Dag was right about the best contact being none. *I didn't come here to fight this old woman, I came to try for some peace. Why am I letting her have her war?*

Fawn took a deep breath, and said, "Dag is the most truthful man I ever met. If we have a problem, he'll tell me, and we'll fix it."

"Huh." Cumbia sat back. Fawn could sense another shift in her mood, away from the sudden, sharp attack, but it did not reassure her. "Then let me tell you the truth about patrollers, girl. Because I was married to one. Sister, daughter, and mother to the breed—walked with them, too, when I was your age, 'bout a thousand years ago. Men, women, old, young, kind or mean-minded, in one thing they are all the same. Once they've seen their first malice, they don't ever give up patrol unless they're crippled or dead. And they don't ever put anyone else before it. Mari—by all right reason, she should be staying in camp taking care of Cattagus, but off she goes. And he sends her, being just as bad. Dag's father was another. All of 'em, the whole lot. Don't you be thinking I imagine Dag'll choose to cut strings because of any consideration for me, or Dar, or anyone else who has supported him his whole life.

"Here's the fork. If Dag doesn't love you enough, he'll choose the patrol. And if he loves you beyond all sense— he'll choose the patrol. Because you're standing in the center of that world he's sent to save, and if he doesn't save it, he doesn't save you, either. When Fairbolt called on him the other night with the news from Raintree, how long did it take your bridegroom to decide to go off and leave you? All alone, with no friends or kin?"

Not very long, Fawn did not say aloud. Her mouth had grown too dry for speech.

"And it wouldn't make a whit of difference if you were Lakewalker-born, or a hundred times prettier, or writhing in birth-bed, or crying at his child's deathbed, or in agony on your own. Patrollers turn and go all the same. You can't win this one." She sat back and favored Fawn with a slow blink, cold as any snake. "Neither could I. So take your foolish knitting and go away."

Fawn swallowed. "They're good socks. Maybe Omba would like to have them."

Cumbia set her jaw. "You're a touch hard of listening, aren't you, girl?" And then plucked up the little bundle and tossed it into the fire pit smoldering a few yards away.

Fawn almost screamed aloud. *Three days of work!* She dove after it. It had not yet caught, but the dry cotton smoked against the red coals, and a stray end of the jaunty woolen yarn winked in scarlet sparks, curling up and starting to blacken. She leaned in and snatched it back out, brushing off a smear of soot and glowing bits from the browning edge, drawing in her breath sharply at the burning bite of them. Her blue skirt had muddy patches from where her knees had thumped down, and she scrubbed at them as she rose, glaring uselessly at Cumbia.

It wasn't just the pain of the burn on her fingers that started tears in Fawn's eyes. She choked out, "Dag said it would be useless to try and talk to you."

"Should have listened to him, too, eh?" said Cumbia. Her face was nearly expressionless.

"I guess," returned Fawn shortly. Her bright theory that letting Cumbia vent might clear the air seemed singularly foolish now. She wanted to shoot some devastating last word over her shoulder as she stalked off, hurting as she'd been hurt, but she was far too shaken to think of any. She wanted only to escape.

"Go, then," said Cumbia, as if she could hear her.

Fawn clutched the knit bundle in her unburned hand and marched away. She didn't let her shoulders bow till she was out of sight on the road and having to pick her footfalls among the drying puddles. Her stomach shuddered, and this island seemed abruptly lonely and strange, hostile and pinched, despite the bright morning air. Oppressive, like a house turned prison. She sniffed angrily, feeling *stupid stupid stupid*, and smeared away the drops on her lashes with the back of her hand, then turned it to capture the cooling moisture on her throbbing fingers. A reddening line crossed three of them; she thought one might be starting to blister. Mama or Aunt Nattie would have dabbed the spots with butter, made soothing murmurs, and maybe kissed them. Fawn wasn't too sure about the butter—in any case, she had none in the tiny cache of food that passed for her larder—but the rest of the remedy she missed desperately. *Not to be had. Ever again.* The thought made her want to bawl far more than the little pain in her hand.

She'd gone to Cumbia to try to head off the clash with the camp council at its apparent root. To save Dag. She had not only failed, she might have made it even worse. Cumbia and Dar could have no doubt now of what an easy target Dag's farmer wife was. *Why did I think I could help him? Stupid . . .*

In her home campsite—in Mari's and Sarri's campsite, Fawn corrected this thought—Cattagus was still sitting over his leatherwork, now stitching a diminutive slipper held up nearly to his nose, poking rawhide cords in and out of the holes he'd made with his awl. Tesy had gone off somewhere, though Cattagus was apparently keeping an eye on her brother, presently penned in a little corral and diverted with a pair of alarmed turtles; he was tapping on a shell and calling the creature to come out. As Fawn crossed the clearing, Cattagus put down his work and looked at her shrewdly. She recalled Cumbia's shot about walking around naked and wondered if all her efforts to put on a brave face were useless; if any Lakewalker looking at her could see what a seething mess she really was. *Likely.*

To her surprise, Cattagus beckoned her over. She stopped by his table, and he leaned on one elbow, regarding her rather ironically, and wheezed, "So, where have you been, girlie?"

"Went to talk to Cumbia," Fawn admitted. "Tried, anyhow."

"Burn your fingers, did you?"

Fawn hastily pulled her hand from her licking tongue and hid it behind her back. "She threw the socks I'd brought her for a present in the fire. Should have just let them burn, I guess, but I couldn't stand the waste."

"That what you been crouching over all these past three days?"

"Pretty much."

"Huh. Let's see. No, girlie, the burn," he added impatiently as she thrust out her scorched bundle. She gave him her other hand; he held it in his dry, thick fingers, and his gray head bent slightly. He was dressed as usual in nothing but the short trousers and sandals that were his summer uniform, and she was conscious of the smell of him, a mix of old man and lake green, not unpleasant at this concentration, and very Cattagus. Would Dag smell like that when he grew as old? She thought she could learn to like it.

Fawn stared at her rejected knitting as Cattagus kneaded her palm. "Do you think Mari would like those socks? They're too big for me and too small for Dag, but they're good for under riding boots. If she's not too proud to take work from a stupid farmer," she added bitterly. "Or Cumbia's castoffs."

"That last might actually be a draw," said Cattagus, with his whistling chuckle.

He released her hand, which had stopped throbbing; Fawn peeked at the red marks, which had faded to pink instead of raising blisters as she'd thought they would. *He does healing groundwork like Dag.* "Thank you," she said gratefully. Cattagus nodded, picked up the socks, and set them beyond his leather scraps, signifying acceptance of the gift, and Fawn blinked back eye-fog again.

Fawn turned away, then turned back, blurting, "Cumbia said because I can't veil my ground it's just like walking around naked."

"Well," said Cattagus in a slow, judicious drawl, "Cumbia tends to be a bit on the tight side, herself. Full of things she doesn't want others to see. Most folks our age just give up and be what they are."

Fawn tilted her head, considering this. "Older farm folk can be like that, some of them. Well, not with their grounds, of course, but with clothes, and what they do and say."

"Cumbia's still tryin' to fix the world, I'm afraid. She'd have been a relentless patroller. Thank the absent gods she went for a maker." He appeared to lose himself in a vision of patrolling with a younger Cumbia, and shuddered.

"What does she make? Particularly?"

"Rope and cord that does not break. Very much in demand for folks' boats and sailboats, y'see. And other key uses."

"Oh. So . . . so she was making magic when I, um, interrupted her . . . ?"

"No great thing if you did, she's been doing it for so long. Wouldn't have slowed her a bit if you'd been someone she wanted to see."

"I was not that," Fawn sighed. She blinked, trying to recapture her thought. "So do Lakewalkers go about with their grounds open, too?"

"If they're relaxed, or wishful to take in the world around them at its fullest, aye. Too, lots of folks have short groundsense ranges. So you're out of their sight, so to speak, at any little distance, even if you're flaring."

But everyone in this campsite, the children excepted, had long groundsense ranges. She had a sudden horrible thought. "But when Dag and I, when Dag opens up to me . . . um."

Cutting off her words was no help; Cattagus was chuckling downright evilly. Leaving no doubt that he'd caught her meaning, he said, "Me, I cheer for Dag. Even though Mari hits me. Those Redwing women are a stern sisterhood, I can tell you." He added to her hot blush, "It's this breath-thing, y'see. Puts me out of the action myself, mostly. 'Bout all I can do these days is wave on the luckier ones."

Fawn's blush deepened, but she dimly recognized that he had handed her back this intimate revelation by way of turnabout: even-all. Cruelty and kindness, how could one morning hold so much of both? "Folks is folks, I guess," she said.

Cattagus nodded. "Always have been. Always will be. That's better."

She realized she had grown much calmer; her throat no longer ached. She touched the cord on her left wrist, and nodded to Cattagus's. "Is Mari all right this morning? Too?"

"So far." His eyes narrowed at her cord. "Dag did something to yours, didn't he? Or . . . to you."

Fawn nodded, though she flushed again to recall the exact circumstances. But Cattagus, while he could be shrewd or crude, was not mean-minded, and seemed unlikely to press her for private details. "I got my ground to go into Dag's cord all right, by a . . . a trick, I guess, when we wove them, but I couldn't sense his. So he did some extra groundwork on mine just before he left. It's good to know I could find him, if I had to. Or he me, I suppose."

Cattagus opened his mouth, stopped. Blinked. "Beg pardon?"

She held up her wrist, closed her eyes, and turned about. Opening them, she found herself facing west into the woods. "That way. It's pretty vague, but I reckon, if I got closer, the sense of just where he is would grow tighter. It did the other morning when he was nearby, anyhow." She turned and looked in surprise at Cattagus's climbing brows. "Don't everyone's cords do that?"

"No."

"Oh."

Cattagus rubbed his nose. "Wasn't exactly the cord he did the work on, I think. Best not to mention that trick to anyone else till he gets back."

"Why not?"

"Um. Well. Let's just say, if Dag wants to add any complications to his argument with the camp council, let him pick and choose them himself."

There was an undercurrent, but in what direction it flowed Fawn could scarcely guess. "All right," she said doubtfully. Wistful, she stared west again. "When do you think they'll come back?"

He shrugged. "No knowing." But his eyes seemed to know too much.

Fawn nodded, not so much in agreement as silent sympathy, and took herself off to her tent. She needed to think of a new project for her hands. Not knitting. The sun was climbing toward noon. She hoped it lit Dag's path, wherever it was now winding.

Dead silence, thought Dag, was never a truer phrase.

The high summer sun beat down on a winter landscape. The marshland open to his gaze looked as if it had suffered a week of killing frost. What should have been high green stands of reeds lay flattened and tangled, browning. The line of planted poplars along which his patrol was ghosting looked ghostly themselves, yellowing leaves spinning down one by one in the breezeless air. The air itself was hot, moist, close as only a Raintree summer could be, but devoid of the whine and whirr of insects, empty of birdcalls. It was a blight indeed when even the mosquitoes lay dead, floating with rafts of miscellaneous pond wrack in long, gray smears atop the blank water. The undersides of a couple of dead turtles made dim yellow patches in the murk. The blue sky reflected there in crooked strips, weird contrast to the scum.

The blighted soil nipped at his feet, yet without the deeper sucking drain on his ground that marked land long occupied by a malice. More; Dag could not feel that dry shock in his midsection, like the reverberation of some great blow to the body, that told him a malice lay near. Cautiously, he stood up for a better view of the ruined Lakewalker village that lay along the shore across a quarter mile of open water.

Crouched down in the dead and dying weeds behind Dag, Mari hissed nervous warning.

"It's not here," he breathed to her.

She frowned, nodded acceptance of this, but whispered back, "Its slaves might still be."

He dared to open his groundsense just a little, swallowing against the nausea induced by so much recent blight beating against him. When he was sure he wasn't going to vomit, he opened himself further. Nothing fluttered in his perception but a few distraught blackbirds, fled from the earlier disruption, returning to search futilely for mates or nests.

"There's nothing alive for a mile—wait." He hunkered down again. A few hundred paces beyond the village, in a boggy stretch along the shore, something swirled in his senses, a familiar concentration of distorted ground. Ground around the patch seemed to seep toward it, creeping through the soil like draining water. He narrowed his eyes, searched more carefully.

"I believe there's a mud-man nursery planted beyond the camp. It doesn't seem to have guards just now, though. But there's something else."

Mari's brows twitched up, and her frown deepened. "You'd think it would be watched. If anything was."

Dag considered the possibility of a cleverly baited trap. That would seem to credit this malice with an unlikely degree of foresight, however. He hand-signaled Mari, who passed the order silently, and the patrol took up its stealthy, painfully slow, veiled approach once more, skirting through the scant cover around the edge of this lakelike section of the larger marsh until it reached the abandoned village, or what was left of it.

Perhaps ninety or a hundred dwellings were strung along the lakeside or back from it in kin clusters, home till lately of a community of over a thousand Lakewalkers, with another thousand souls scattered more widely around Bonemarsh. A dozen tent-cabins were burned to the ground; the recent rain had extinguished all coals. Signs of hasty flight were all around, but aside from the burned tents there was only a little mindless destruction. Dag did not see or smell corpses, only partly reassuring, as ground-ripped bodies were sometimes very slow to rot. Still, he permitted himself the hope that most here had escaped, fleeing southward. Lakewalkers knew how to pick up and run. Then he wondered what that little farmer town the malice was supposed to have come up under looked like right now. *What would Spark have done if . . .* he cut off the wrenching thought.

He reached the log wall of the last tent standing and peered uncertainly toward the boggy patch a couple hundred paces off. Back from it, a thicket of scrubby trees—willow, slim green ash, vicious trithorned honey locust—shaded something dark about their boles that he could barely make out with his eye. He opened his groundsense again, flinched, then snapped it back.

"Mari. Codo. To me," he said over his shoulder.

Mari was at his side at once; Codo, the oldest patroller here but for Mari, slid forward in a moment and joined them.

"There's somebody under those trees," Dag murmured.

"Not mud-men, not farmer slaves. I think it's some of us. Something's very wrong."

"Alive?" asked Mari, peering too. The half dozen figures didn't move.

"Yes, but . . . extend your groundsenses. Carefully. Don't get caught up. See if it's anything you recognize." *Because I think I do.*

Codo gave him a dry glance from under gray brows, silent commentary on Dag's earlier repeated insistence that no one open their grounds without a direct order. Both he and Mari stared with eyes opened, then closed.

"Not seen anything like that before," muttered Mari. "Unconscious?"

"Groundlocked . . . ?" said Codo.

"Ah. Yes. That's it," said Mari. "But why are they . . ."

Dag re-counted—six with his eyes, five with his groundsense. Which suggested one was a corpse. "I think they're tied to those trees." He turned to Mari's partner Dirla, hovering anxiously. "The rest of you stay back. Codo, Mari, come with me."

There was no cover between here and the stand of scrub. Dag gave up the fraying pretense of stealth and walked openly forward, Codo and Mari right on his heels.

The Bonemarsh Lakewalkers were indeed bound to the thicker tree boles, slumped or half-hanging. They appeared unconscious. Three men and three women, older for the most part; they seemed makers, not patrollers, if Dag could guess from their look and the remains of their clothing. Some bore signs of physical struggle, bruises and cuts, others did not. One woman was dead, waxy and still; Dag hesitated to touch her to check for the stiffness, or lack of it, that would tell him how long. But not very long, he suspected. *Late again, old patroller.*

Codo hissed and drew his knife, starting for the ropes that bound the prisoners.

"Wait," said Dag.

"Eh?" Codo scowled at him.

"Dag, what *is* this?" asked Mari. "Do you know?"

"Aye, I think so. A new malice has to stay by its mud-man nursery to keep them growing, part of what keeps it tied to its lair even after it's no longer sessile. This malice has gotten strong enough to . . . to farm out the task. It's linked up these makers to make its mud-men for it, while it goes . . . off." Dag glanced southward uneasily.

Codo breathed a silent whistle through pursed lips.

"Can we break them out of their groundlock?" said Mari, eyes narrowing.

"Not sure, but wait. What I don't know is how much of a sense the malice has of them, at whatever distance it's gone now. If we fool with them, with this groundwork, might be an announcement that we're here, behind it."

"Dag, you can't be thinking of leaving them!" said Codo in a shocked voice. Mari looked not so much shocked as grim.

"Wait," Dag repeated, and turned to walk toward the boggy patch. The other two exchanged glances and followed.

Every few feet along he found a shallow pit in the wet soil, looking like a mud pot dug by playing children. At the center of each, a snout broke the surface, usually flexing frantically to draw air. He identified muskrat, raccoon, possum, beaver, even squirrel and slow, cold turtle. All were starting to lose their former shapes, like caterpillars in a chrysalis, but none had yet grown to human size. He counted perhaps fifty.

"Well, that's handy," said Codo, looking over his shoulder with fascinated revulsion. "We can kill them in their holes. Save a lot of grief."

"These aren't going to be ready to come out for days, yet," said Dag. "Maybe weeks. We take the malice down first, they'll die in place."

"What are you thinking, Dag?" said Mari.

I'm thinking of how much I didn't want to be in command of this jaunt. Because of decisions like this. He sighed. "I'm thinking that the rest of the company is half a day behind us. I'm thinking that if we can get some drinking water down those poor folks, they'll last till nightfall, and Obio can cut them loose, instead. And we won't have given away our position to the malice. In fact, the reverse—it'll think any pursuit is still back here."

"How far ahead of us do you think this malice is by now?" said Codo.

Dag shook his head. "We'll scout around for clues, but not more than a day, wouldn't you guess? It's plain the malice has gathered up everything it's got and pressed south. Which says to me it's on the attack. Which also says to me it won't be looking behind it much."

"You mean to follow. Fast as we can," said Mari.

"Anyone here got a better idea?"

They both shook their heads, if not happily.

They returned to the patrol, now gathered warily in the village. Dag dispatched a pair to go get Saun and bring up the horses, sending the rest to scout around the desolation the malice had left. About the time Saun arrived with their mounts, Varleen found the butchering place back in the scrub where the malice's forces had eaten their last meal, bones animal and human mixed, some burned, some gnawed raw. Dag counted perhaps a dozen human individuals in the remains for sure, but *not more*. He tried hard to hang on to that *not more* as a heartening thought, but failed. Fortunately, there was no way for the three patrollers most recently familiar with Bonemarsh Camp to recognize anyone among the disjointed carcasses. The burying, too, Dag left for Obio and the company following.

His veiled patrol had been keyed up for a desperate attack. Gearing back down for a quiet, hasty lunch instead, especially for the ones who'd seen the butchery, went ill, and Dag had no desire to linger, if only for the certainty that the fierce argument over whether to attempt to release the groundlocked makers would start up again. Saun was par-

ticularly unhappy about that one, as he recognized some of
them from the two years he'd patrolled out of Bonemarsh
before he'd exchanged to Hickory Lake.

"What if Obio chooses another route?" Saun protested.
"You left him free to."

"Soon as we take the malice down, tonight or tomorrow,
we'll send someone back," said Dag wearily. "Soon as we
take the malice down, they may well be able to free themselves."

This argument was, in Dag's view, even more dodgy,
but Saun accepted it, or at least shut up, which was all
Dag wanted at this point. His own greatest regret was for
the time they'd lost in their stealthy on-foot approach; they
might have ridden into the village at a canter for all the difference it would have made. Dag suspected they were now
going to come up on the malice well after dark, exhausted,
at the end of a much too long and disturbing day. Part of a
commander's task was to bring his people to the test at the
peak of their condition and will. He'd fumbled both time and
timing, here.

Tracking the malice south presented no difficulty, at least.
Starting just beyond the marsh, it had left a trail of blight a
hundred paces wide that a farmer could not have missed, let
alone anyone with the least tinge of groundsense. *At the end
of this, one malice, guaranteed.* Finding it would be dead
easy now.

The malice not finding us first will be the hard part. Dag
grimaced and kicked Copperhead forward at a trot, his troubled patrol strung out in his wake.

11

*A*nother night attack—without the aid of ground-sense this time. *Gods, I'm as blind in the dark as any farmer.* Dag had feared the flare of their grounds would alert the malice's outlying pickets to his patrol, but blundering bodily into sentries in the murk now seemed as likely a risk. A misshapen moon was well up. When they cleared these trees, he might get a better look at what lay ahead. He glanced right and left at the shadows that were his flankers, Mari and Dirla, and Codo and Hann, and was reassured; if his dark-adapted eyes could scarcely make them out, neither could an enemy's.

He dared another deerlike step forward, and another, trying not to think, *Blight it, we've done this once today already.* His patrol had come up on signs of the malice's massed forces soon after midnight, and again left their horses in favor of this stealthy approach. Through terrain for which, unlike Bonemarsh, they had no maps or plan or prior knowledge. If his own exhaustion was a measure of everyone else's, Dag distrusted his decision to strike at once, without allowing a breather; but it was impossible to rest here, and every delay risked discovery. They had come into a level country, with little farms carved out of the woods becoming more and more common, not unlike the region above West Blue. Little abandoned farms. Dag hoped all the people hereabouts had been warned by the refugees from Bonemarsh and fled to Farmer's Flats.

The open fields allowed a glimpse ahead but equally

denied cover. As they reached the scrubby edge of what had
been a broad stand of wheat, now flattened and dying, Dirla
stole over to him. "See that?" she breathed, pointing.

"Aye."

On the field's other side, wooded land rose—as much
as any land rose in these parts—angling up to a low ridge.
The red glimmer of a few bobbing torches shone through
the trees, then vanished again. Silvered by the sickly moon,
a narrow triangular structure crowned the crest. A crude
timber tower perhaps twenty feet high, built of logs hastily
felled and notched to lock across one another, was briefly
silhouetted against a distant milky cloud. Whatever shapes
crouched on the plank platform at its top were too far away
for Dag to make out with his eyes; but despite his tight closure, the threat of the malice beat in his belly with his every
pulse.

"Lookout post?" Dirla whispered.

Dag shook his head. "Worse." *Absent gods help us.* This
malice was advanced enough to start building *towers.* Even
the Wolf Ridge malice had not developed enough for that
compulsion. "Can you see how many on the platform . . . ?"
Dirla's younger eyes might be sharper than his own.

"Just one, I think."

"It's up there, then. That's where we're headed. Pass the
word."

She nodded and silently withdrew.

Now they had to get next to that tower without being
spotted. So near—across a trampled field and up a wooded
hillside—so far. Dag guessed that the bulk of the malice's
mud-men and mind-slaves were camped on the ridge's far
side, probably along a stream. Smoke from hidden campfires rose in thin gray wisps into a high haze, confirming
his speculation. There was almost no wind, and he regretted
the absence of covering rustles from the branches overhead,
but what faint breeze there was moved the haze toward him.
He hardly needed his eyes now; he could *smell* the enemy:

smoke, manure, piss, the cooking of he-dared-not-guess-what meats.

Dag pushed through clutching blackberry brambles, setting his teeth against the gouge and scrape of sturdy thorns, and crouched by a fieldstone wall lining the high side of the wheatfield. He half crawled forward along its shadowed western side until he reached brambles again, then risked a look back. The moon emerged from a cloud, but the tight shapes of the patrollers following him did not once edge into the thin light. *Good, you folks are so good.* Half the distance down. He slid through more dying brambles into the black shade of the woods at the base of the ridge, the patrol too spreading out to ease from shadow to shadow.

To his horror, a muffled grunt and some thumps sounded from his left. He made his way hastily toward the sound. Codo and Hann were crouching over something half-concealed in a crackling deadfall. Hann had drawn his war knife, but glanced up and froze when Dag's hand fell on his arm.

Codo squatted across the chest of a grizzled man—farmer-slave, guard?—both his hands tight around the struggling fellow's throat. "Hann, hurry!" Codo hissed.

Dag touched Codo's shoulder, eased in, and studied their threat-and-victim. Farmer-slave, yes, clothes ragged, eyes wild and mad. Maybe from this farm, or else picked up along the way to add to the malice's straggling, growing army. He wasn't a big man, or young; he reminded Dag uncomfortably of Sorrel Bluefield. Dag took aim and landed several hard blows to the man's head, until his eyes rolled back and he stopped bucking. The meaty thumps sounded as loud as drumbeats in Dag's ears.

"Blight it, throat slitting's quieter," muttered Codo, cautiously rising. "Surer."

Dag shook his head and pointed uphill. This was no place for an argument, and the pair did not give him one, but turned to continue the silent climb. Dag could roll the issues over in his head without need of words—Hann's glare, burning through the dark, was enough to make the point. A throat-slit guard couldn't claw his way back to consciousness in a few minutes and raise the alarm.

I hate fighting humans. Of all the vileness in this long struggle, the malices' mind-theft of people who should be the Lakewalkers' friends and allies was the worst. Even when the patrollers won, they lost, in clashes that left farmer corpses in their wake. *We all lose.* Dag shook out his throbbing hand. *That might have been Sorrel.* Somebody's husband, father, father-in-law, friend.

I hate fighting. Oh, Fawn, I'm so tired of this.

The farmer's mad eyes were sign enough of his enslaved state, with no need for Dag's groundsense to trace the malice's grip in his mind. Even though they hadn't slit his throat, his brief alarm could have given little warning, surely? Indeed, Dag decided, the malice would be more likely to notice the shock of a death in its growing web of slaves than what might be mistaken for a sort of sleep. Much depended on how many individuals this malice controlled, at what distance, attempting what tasks. *Please, let it be stretched to its limits.* Whatever it was now doing at the top of that tower, ground was flowing toward it in a great sucking drain; Dag could feel the mortal throb of it passing under his boot soles. He had a wild vision of gripping the streaming power with his ghost hand and just letting it tow him right up the slope.

The patrol reached the edge of the clearing, bristling with stumps from the trees felled to build the tower—within the last day, Dag guessed from the still-pungent smell of the sap. In the faint moonlight he could make out the hulking shapes of at least four mud-man guards at the tower's base. Maybe bear-men or even bull-men; big, lithe, stinking. Without need for orders, he could sense his pairs moving to the front. His stomach clenched, and he fought down a wave of nausea. Time to clear the path.

At some faint *clink* or whisper of a weapon drawn from a sheath, a guardian's head turned toward them; it lifted its snout, sniffing suspiciously.

Now.

Dag did not cry his command, just yanked out his war knife and plunged forward, weaving around stumps. His thoughts narrowed to his task: slay the mud-men, get his knife-wielders past them and up the tower as fast as death. *Faster.* Dag took on the nearest mud-man to hand, ducking as it brought up a rusted sword stolen from who-knew-where and swung violently at his head. Dag's return stroke tore out the creature's throat, and he didn't even bother dodging the spray of blood. Arrows from the patrol's archers whispered fiercely past his head to sink into the chest of a mud-man beyond, although the shafts didn't drop it; the mud-man staggered forward, roaring. Mari, her sharing knife clenched between her teeth, reached the tower and began to climb. Codo darted past her around the tower's corner and swung himself upward too. Another patroller reached the tower, and another, all in that same intent silence. The rest turned to protect their climbing comrades. Dag could hear them engaging new mud-men reaching the clearing, as yet more came crashing up the hill yowling in alarm.

The dark shape at the top of the tower moved, standing up against a cobalt sky scattered with stars and luminous with moon-washed cloud. The four climbers had almost reached the top. Suddenly the figure crouched, leaped—descended as if floating the full twenty feet to land upon its folding legs and spring again upright. As if it were light as a dancer, and not seven solid feet of corded muscle, sinew, and bone. It wheeled, coming face-to-face with Dag.

This malice was lean, almost graceful, and Dag was shocked by its beauty in the moonlight. Fair skin moved naturally over a face of sculpted bone; hair swept back from its high brow to flow like a river of night down its back. Its androgynous body was clothed in stolen oddments—trousers,

a shirt, boots, a Lakewalker leather vest—which it somehow endowed with the air of some ancient high lord's attire.
How many molts must it have gone through, how quickly, to
have achieved such a human—no, superhuman—form? Its
glamour wrenched Dag's gaze, and he could feel his ground
ripple—he snapped himself closed, tight and hard.

And open again as Utau, sharing knife out, staggered with
a sudden cry. Dag could sense the strain in Utau's ground
as the malice turned and gripped it, starting to rip it away.
Frantic, Dag extended his left arm and stretched out his
ghost hand to snatch at the malice's ground in turn. Out of
the corner of his eye, Dag saw Mari, clinging to the tower
side, drop her sharing knife down in a pale spinning arc to
Dirla, who had temporarily broken free of mud-men.

As a fragment of its ground came away in Dag's ghost
hand, the malice turned back to him with an astonished
scream. Dag recalled that moment in the medicine tent
when he'd snatched ground from Hoharie's apprentice, but
this time it felt like clutching a live coal. Pain and terror
reverberated up his left arm. He tried to cast the fragment
into the earth, but it clung to his ground like burning honey.
The malice reached two-handed toward Dag, its dark eyes
wide and furious. Dag tried again to close himself against it,
and failed. He could feel the malice's grip upon his ground
tighten, and his breath locked at the surge of astounding pain
that seemed to start from his marrow and strike outward to
his skin, as if all his bones were being shattered in place
simultaneously.

And Dirla lunged forward onto a stump and plunged
Mari's sharing knife into the malice's back.

Dag felt the dying enter his own shredding ground, cloudy
and turbulent as blood poured into roiling water. For a
moment, he shared the malice's full awareness. The world's
ground stretched away from their center for miles, glowing
like fire, with slaves and mud-men moving across it in
scattered, blazing ranks. The confusing din of their several

hundred, no, thousand anguished minds battered his failing consciousness. The malice's vast will seemed to drain from them as Dag watched, leaving blackness and dismay. The irrational intelligence of the great being snatched at his own mind, hungry above all for understanding of its plight, and Dag knew that if this malice took him in, it would have nearly all it needed, and yet still not be saved from its own cravings and desires. *It is quite mad. And the more intelligent it grows, the more agonizing its own madness becomes to it.* It seemed a curious but useless insight to gain, here at the end of breath and light.

The malice screamed again, its voice rising strangely like a song, wavering upward into unexpected purity. Its beautiful body ruptured, caught by its clothing, and it fell in a welter of blood and fluid.

The earth rose up and struck Dag cruelly in the back. Stars spun overhead, and went out.

Fawn shot awake in the dark and sat up in her lonely bed-roll with a gasp. Shock shuddered through her body, then a wash of fear. A noise, a nightmare? No echoes pulsed in her ears, no visions faded in her mind. Her heart pounding unaccountably, she slapped her right hand over her left wrist. This panic was surely the opposite of relaxed persuasion and openness, but beneath her marriage cord her whole arm was throbbing.

Something's happened to Dag. Hurt? Hurt *bad . . . ?*

She scrambled up and pushed through her tent flap into the milky light of a partial moon, seeming bright compared to the inky shadows inside. Not stopping to throw anything over her sleeping shift, she picked her way across the clearing, wincing at the twigs and stones that bit her bare feet. It was all that kept her from breaking into a run.

She hesitated outside Cattagus and Mari's tent. The night

was cool after the recent rains, and Cattagus had dropped the porch flap down. She slapped it as Utau had theirs on the dark morning he'd come to wake Dag. She tried to guess the time from the moon passing over the lake—two hours after midnight, maybe? There was no sound from within, and she pounded the leather again, then shifted from foot to foot, trying to gather the nerve to go inside and shake the old man by the shoulder.

Before she did, the flap moved on Sarri's tent, and the dark-haired woman emerged. She had paused for sandals, but no robe either, and her feet slapped quickly across the stretch between the two tent-cabins.

"Did you feel that?" Fawn asked her anxiously, keeping her voice low for fear of waking the children. And then felt utterly stupid, for of course Sarri would not feel anything from a marriage cord wrapped around someone else's wrist. "Did you feel anything just now?"

Sarri shook her head. "Something woke me. Whatever it was, was gone by the time I'd gathered my wits." Her right hand too gripped her left wrist, kneading.

"Razi and Utau . . . ?"

"Alive. Alive. At least that." She shot Fawn a curious look. "Did you feel something? Surely you couldn't have . . ."

She was interrupted by a grunt from the tent. Cattagus shouldered through the flap, tying up his shorts around his stout middle and scowling. "What's all this too-roo in the moonlight, girlies?"

"Fawn says she felt something in her cord. Woke her up." Sarri added, as if reluctant to endorse this, "I woke up too, but there wasn't . . . anything. Mari?"

The same gesture, right hand over left, although by putting on an expression of exasperation Cattagus tried, unsuccessfully, to make it not look anxious. He shook his head. "Mari's all right." He added after a moment of reflection, "Alive, at least. What in the wide green world can all those galloping fools be about over there at this time of night?"

He glanced west, as if his eyes could somehow penetrate a hundred and more miles and see the answer, but that feat was beyond even his Lakewalker powers, a fact his dry snort seemed to acknowledge.

The two women followed his stare uneasily.

"Look, now," he said, as if in persuasion, "if Utau, Razi, Mari, and Dag are all still alive, the company can't be in that much trouble. Because you know that bunch'd find the manure pile first."

Sarri blew out her breath in not quite a laugh, accepting the thin reassurance as much, Fawn guessed, for his sake as her own.

" 'Specially Dag," Cattagus added under his breath. "You wonder what Fairbolt thought he was about, to put . . ."

"Cattagus." Fawn took a deep breath and thrust out her arm. "My cord feels funny. Can you figure out anything from it?"

His gray brows rose. "Not likely." But he took her wrist gently in his hand anyway. His lips moved briefly as if in surprise, but then schooled away a scowl to some more guarded line. "Well, he's alive. There's that. Can't have got himself ground-ripped if he's alive."

More Lakewalker secrets no one had bothered to mention? "What's ground-ripped?"

Cattagus exchanged a look with Sarri, but before Fawn could grit her teeth in frustration, relented, and said, "Same as what that malice down in Glassforge did to your childie, I take it. 'Cept Lakewalkers-grown can resist, close their grounds against it. If the malice is a sessile, or is not too strong yet."

"What if it *is* strong?" Fawn asked in worry.

"Well . . . they say it's a quick death. No chance to share, though." Cattagus frowned sternly. "But, see here, girlie, don't you go imagining things all night. Your boy's alive, isn't he now, eh?"

Fawn had trouble thinking of Dag as a boy, but the *your*

part she clutched hard to her heart, her wrists crossed over her chest. *Dag's mine, yes. Not some blighting malice's.*

"Maybe it's over," said Sarri in a low voice. "I hope it's over."

"When would we know?" asked Fawn.

Cattagus shrugged his ropy shoulders. "From the middle of Raintree, good news could get here in three days. Bad news in two. Very bad news . . . well, we won't worry about that. Ah, go back to bed, girlies!" He shook his head and set the example by ducking back inside, wheezing. Pointedly, Fawn thought.

Sarri shook her head in unwitting echo of her testy uncle, sighed deeply, and made her way back to her tent and her sleeping children. Fawn picked her way slowly back to little Tent Bluefield.

She dutifully lay down, but returning to sleep was beyond futile. After tossing for a time, she rose again and took out her drop spindle and a bundle of plunkin flax, and went out in the moonlight to clamber up on her favorite tall spinning-stump. At least she might have something to show for her night-restlessness. The tap of the gold beads flicking on her wrist as she spun was normally cheerful and soothing, but tonight felt more like fingers drumming. Flick, spin, shape.

She wished she could put spells for protection into her trouser cloth, the way a Lakewalker wife likely could. She could spin her thread strong, weave it tight, sew it soundly, double-stitched and secure. She could make with all her heart, but it would only give the ordinary expected armoring of cloth on skin. *Not enough.* Flick, spin, shape.

Three days till any news, huh. *I don't like this waiting part. Not one bit.* The helpless anxiety was worse than she'd expected it to be, and she felt pushed off-balance. *No more do Sarri or Cattagus like it, either, that's plain enough, but you don't catch them carrying on about it, do you?* Her own unease wasn't special just for being new to her. She felt she suddenly had more insight into Lakewalker moodiness. Her assurances to Dag before he'd ridden off seemed in retrospect unduly blithe and—well, if not *stupid*, a word he'd tried to forbid her, certainly ignorant. *I'm learning now. Again.* Flick, spin, shape.

If Dag died on patrol—her eyes went to her wrist cord, *still alive*, yes, it was a safely theoretical thought. She could dare to think it. *If something happened to him out there, what would become of me?* Despite Hickory Lake's fascinations, without Dag she knew she had no roots here. While these Lakewalkers seemed unlikely to cast her out naked, she had no doubt Fairbolt would whisk her back to West Blue in two shakes of a lamb's tail, likely with a patroller to make sure she arrived. Seemed like his idea of responsible. But she had no roots in West Blue now either; she'd cut them off, if not without a pang, without compunction. Twice. Cutting them a third time wasn't a task she wished to face. If she couldn't stay here, and she wouldn't go back . . .

It was a measure, perhaps, of what this sometimes-horrendous year had done for her that she found this thought curiously undaunting. There was Glassforge. There was Silver Shoals, beyond on the Grace River, an even finer town by Dag's descriptions. There was a world of possibility for an un–grass widow with determination and her wits held close about her. She was practical. She knew how to walk down strange roads, now. She'd come this far. She didn't have to cling to Dag like a drowning woman clutching the only branch in the torrent.

Everybody, it seemed, wanted Dag for something. Fairbolt Crow wanted him for a patroller. His mother wanted him to demonstrate the high value of her bloodline, maybe, to prove her worth through his. His brother Dar wanted him to not make a fuss or be a distraction—to stay quiet, safe inside the rules, ignorable. Fawn wasn't sure but what she should add herself into that tally, because she certainly wanted Dag for the father of her children someday, except Dag seemed to be thinking along those lines himself, so maybe that one was mutual and didn't count. Didn't anyone want Dag just for *Dag*? Without justification, like a milkweed or a water lily or, or . . . a summer night with fireflies.

Because later, in some very dry places, the memory of that hour was enough for going on with.

She had to stop spinning then, because she couldn't see through the silver light blurring in her eyes. She dashed her hand against her hot eyelids to clear her vision. Twice. Then just let the tears run down, sitting bent to her knees with her wrist cord pressed to her forehead. It took a long time to make her breathing stop hitching.

My heart's prize my best friend my true consolation . . . what trouble have you gone and found this time?

Her arm was still throbbing, though more faintly. *Alive*, yes, but . . . she might be just a farmer girl, without a speck of groundsense in her body, she might be any one of a hundred kinds of fool. She might be ignorant of a thousand Lakewalkerish things, but of this she was increasingly certain. *This is not good. This is something very wrong.*

The insides of his eyelids were red. Not black. There was light out there somewhere, warm dawn or warm fire. His curiosity as to which was not enough to make him drag open the heavy weights his lids had become.

He remembered panicked voices, and thinking he should get up and fix the cause, whatever it was. He should. Someone had been shouting about Utau, and Razi—of course it would be Razi—trying to match grounds. Mari's voice, sharp and scared, *Try to get in! Blight it, I'm not losing our captain after all that!* Fairbolt was here? When had that happened? Someone else, *I can't! His ground's too tight!* and later, *Can't, oh gods that hurts!* And, *So if it does that to you, what do you figure it's doing to him?*—Mari's tart voice at its least sympathetic; Dag felt for her victim, whoever he was. More gasping, *I can't, I can't, I'm sorry* . . . The panicked voices had faded then, and Dag had been glad. Maybe they would all go away and leave him be. *I'm so tired* . . .

He breathed, twitched; his gluey eyes opened on their own. Half-dead tree branches laced the paling blue of a new dawn. On one side, orange flames crackled up from a roaring campfire, deliciously warm. Dawn and fire both, ah, that solved the mystery. On his other side, Mari's face wavered into view between him and the sky.

Her dry voice spoke: " 'Bout time you reported for duty again, patroller."

He tried to move his lips.

Her hand pressed his brow. "That was a joke, Dag. You just lie there." Her hand went to his, under blankets it seemed. "Finally warming up, too. Good."

He swallowed and found his lost voice. "How many?"

"Eh?"

"How many died? Last night?" Assuming the malice kill *was* last night. He had mislaid days before, under unpleasantly similar conditions.

"Now you've seen fit to grace us with your gloomy face again—none."

That couldn't be right. Saun, what of Saun, left with the horses? Dag pictured the youth attacked in the dark by mudmen, alone, bloodied, overwhelmed . . . "Saun!"

"Here, Captain." Saun's anxiously smiling face loomed over Mari's shoulder.

That must have been a dream or a hallucination. Or this was. Did he get to pick which? He drew breath enough to get out, "What's happened?"

"Dirla took the malice—" Mari began.

"I got that far. Saw you drop your knife to her." Mari's son's bone. He managed to moisten his lips. "Didn't think you'd ever let that out of your hand."

"Aye, well, I remembered your tale of how you and the

little farmer girl got the Glassforge malice. Dirla was closer, and the malice was intent on Utau. I saw the chance and took it."

"Utau?" he repeated urgently. Yes, the malice had been about to rip the ground from his body . . .

Mari gripped his shoulder through the blankets. "Malice grazed him, no question, but Razi brought him home. You, now—that's the closest I've ever heard tell of anyone getting his ground ripped without actually dying. Never seen a man look more like a corpse and still breathe."

"Drink?" said Saun, putting an arm under Dag's shoulders to lift him a bit.

Oh, good idea. It was only stale water from a skin, but it was wonderfully *wet* water. Wettest he'd ever drunk, Dag decided. "Thankee'." And after a moment, "How many of us lost . . . ?"

"None, Dag," said Saun eagerly. Mari frowned.

"Go on."

"Eh, after that, it was all over but the shoutin', of which there was the usual," said Mari. "Sent two pairs to retrieve Saun and the horses, and kept the rest close to guard our camp from hazard. Let four off to sleep a bit ago." She nodded across the fire toward some sodden unmoving bundles stretched on bedrolls. Dag raised his head to look. Beside one of them, Razi sat cross-legged; he smiled tiredly at Dag and sent him a vague salute.

"What of the farmer-slaves?"

"There weren't as many right by here as we'd thought. Seems the malice had sent most of its slaves and mud-men marching off through the woods for some dawn attack on a town just northwest of Farmer's Flats. I imagine they're having a right mess down there this morning. Gods know what those poor farmers thought when the malice fog lifted from their minds and their mud-men scampered. I haven't much tried to herd the folks we found here, though we did check out their camp, and suggest no one try to travel home alone. Most of 'em have gone off by now to try and find friends and family."

Understandable; welcome, even. It might be cowardice, but Dag didn't want to try to deal with distraught farmers this morning, atop everything else. Let the Raintree Lakewalkers take care of their own.

Dag's brow wrinkled. "*How* many did we lose last night?"

Mari drew a long breath and leaned forward to peer into his face. "Dag, are you tracking me at all?"

" 'Course I'm tracking you." Dag unwound his left arm from his blankets and waved his hook at her. "How many fingers am I holding up?" Except it occurred to him that, on some very disturbing level, he did not know the answer.

Mari rolled her eyes in exasperation. Saun, bless him, looked adorably confused.

"Well, we still don't know about those makers we left at Bonemarsh," Saun offered hesitantly.

Mari turned to glare at him. "Saun, don't you dare start that up again with him now."

Yes, *that* was his missing piece, the thing he'd been trying so desperately to remember. Dag sighed, if not exactly in satisfaction.

"We haven't heard from Obio and the company yet," said Mari, "but there's scarcely been time. They might have reached there hours ago."

"They might have taken some other route," said Saun stubbornly.

It looked to turn into a bright day. People tied up outdoors in such heat without drink or food could die of exposure in a surprisingly short time, even without the added stress of whatever the malice's groundlock—or ground link—had done to them. If even one prisoner could release himself, he'd surely free the rest, but suppose none could . . . ? The throbbing headache of nightmare crept back up the base of Dag's skull. "We have to go back to Bonemarsh."

Saun nodded in eagerness. "I'll ride ahead."

"Not alone you won't!" said Mari sharply.

Dag got out, "I left them . . . yesterday. Because I could count. But today I can go back." Yes, as quickly as might be. "There was something wrong, and I knew it, but there was no time, and I knew that too. I have to get back there." *Enough human sacrifice for one malice, enough.*

Mari sat back, dubious. "Make you a deal, Dag. If you can get your fool self up on your fool horse all by yourself, I'll let you ride it. If not, you're staying right here."

Dag grinned wanly. "You'll lose that bet. Saun, help me sit up."

The boy slid an arm under his shoulders again. Dag's head drained nearly to blackness as he came upright, but he kept his blinking eyes open somehow. "See, Mari? I wager there's not a mark on me."

"Your ground's so tight it's cramping. You can't tell me you didn't take hurt under there."

"What does it feel like?" asked Saun diffidently. "A ground rip, that is?"

Dag squinted, deciding Saun was due an honest answer. "Right now, a lot like blood loss, truth to tell. It doesn't hurt anywhere in particular"—*just everywhere generally*—"but I admit I'm not my best."

Mari snorted.

If he ate, perhaps he would gain strength enough to . . . eat. Hm.

Mari went off to deal with less intractable people, and Saun, as anxious for the Bonemarsh makers as Dag, made it his business to get Dag ready to ride. While Saun fed him, Dag took counsel with Mari and Codo to split the patrol, sending six south to find the Raintree Lakewalkers and report on the malice kill, and the rest north with him to, with luck, rendezvous with the rest of the company at Bonemarsh.

In the event, Dag half cheated and used a stump to mount Copperhead. Mari, mounting from another stump, eyed him narrowly but let it pass. The horse was too tired to fight him, which was fortunate, because he was way too tired to fight back. He let Saun take the lead in the ride back north, swifter for the daylight, the lack of need for stealth, and the knowing where they were going, but slower for everyone's exhaustion. Dag sat his horse and wavered in and out of awareness, pretending to be dozing while riding like any good old patroller. Utau, slumping in his saddle and closely shepherded by Razi, looked almost as laid waste as Dag felt.

Dag let his groundsense stay shut, as it seemed to want; it reminded him of the way a man might walk tilted to guard a wound. Maybe, as for blood loss, time and rest would provide the remedy. He tried once to sneak out his ghost hand, but nothing occurred.

The thought of the tree-bound makers he had so ruthlessly abandoned yesterday haunted his hazy thoughts. He searched the memory of his glimpse of the malice's mind for a hint of them, but could recover only a sense of overwhelming confusion. The makers' fate seemed to hang in the air like some absent god's cruel revenge upon his wild hope, scarcely admitted even to himself. If only . . .

If only I could get through this *captaincy without losing anyone, I could stop.*

If only he could balance the long weight of Wolf Ridge? Would it? Dag was dubious of his mortal arithmetic. *In the long run no one gets out alive, you know that.*

They passed into, and out of, a slate-lined ravine, letting the horses drink as they crossed the creek. He could swear they'd passed this same ford not twelve hours ago, pointed the other way. Dizzied, he pressed Copperhead forward into the hot summer morning.

12

Dag knew they were approaching Bonemarsh again by the growing dampness of the soil and air, and a brightening in the corner of his eye as the flat woods opened out into flatter water meadows. He had been staring at nothing but the coarse rusty hairs of Copperhead's mane for the past hour, but looked up as Saun muffled an oath and kicked his tired horse into a canter. Above the Bonemarsh shore, life of a sort had returned: a flock of turkey vultures, the fingerlike fringes of their wing tips unmistakable on their black silhouettes as they wheeled. His impulse to canter after Saun was easily resisted, as neither he nor Copperhead was capable of more than a trot right now, the jolting of which would have tormented his sagging back. And . . . he didn't want to look. He let his horse walk on.

As they neared the south margin of the marsh, Dag straightened, squinting in guarded hope. The vultures were circling over the woods back behind the village, not over the boggy patch along the shore. Maybe they'd merely found the unburied carcasses from the mud-men's feast. Maybe . . .

The rest of his veiled patrol turned onto the shore track, and Dag craned his neck, heart thumping. There were several horses tethered around the scrubby trees, Saun's now among them. The rest of the company had made it, good! Some of them, at least. Enough. Dag could see figures moving in the shade, then his heart clenched again at the glimpse of several long lumps on the ground. He couldn't tell if the faces were covered or not. *Bedrolls, please, let it be bedrolls and not shrouds . . .* Had the company only just arrived? Because surely the next task would be to move the rescued makers off this half-blighted ground to some healthier campsite. But Obio was here, thank all the absent gods, striding out to wave greeting as they rode up.

"Dag!" Obio cried. "You're here—absent gods be praised!" His voice seemed to hold more than just relief to see Dag alive. It had the shaken timbre of a man with a crisis desperately seeking someone else to hand it to. *One of us is thanking the absent gods too soon, I think.*

Dag tried to get both eyes open at once and brace his spine. At least enough to dismount, after which he was determined not to climb back into that saddle again for a long, long time. He slid down and clung to his stirrup leather for a moment, partly for support as he woozily adjusted to standing again, partly because he could barely remember what he was trying to do.

Saun's anxious voice brought him back to the moment. "You have to see this, Captain!"

He turned, moistened his lips. Got out, "How many? Did we lose." He felt too close to weeping, and he feared frightening Saun with his fragility. He wanted to explain, reassure: *Fellows get like this after, sometimes. You'll see it, if you're around long enough.*

But Saun was babbling on: "Everyone's alive that was yesterday. Except now there's a new problem."

In a dim effort to fend it all off for just a moment longer, like a man pulling his blanket over his head when called from his bedroll by raucous comrades, Dag blinked at Obio, and asked in a voice raspy with fatigue, "When did you get here?"

"Last night."

"Where is everyone?"

"We've set up a camp about a mile east, just off the blight." Obio waved toward a distant, greener tree line. "I rested the company yesterday morning, then sent scouts out after you.

I started us all toward here at midafternoon, closing up the
distance in case, you know. We were getting pretty worried
toward dusk, when my scouts hadn't come back and my
flankers ran into a couple of mud-men. They did for them
pretty quick, but it was plain you hadn't got the malice when
you'd planned."

"No. Later. Couple hours after midnight, about twenty
miles south."

"So Saun just said. But if—well, here's Griff, my scout
who found this. Let him tell."

A worried-looking fellow of about Dirla's age came up and
gave Dag a nod. Griff had been walking for ten years, and in
Dag's experience was levelheaded and reliable. Which made
his current rumpled, wild-eyed appearance just that much
more disturbing.

"Gods, Dag, I'm so glad you're here!"

Dag controlled a wince, leaning his arm along Copperhead's back for secret support. "What happened?" And
added prudently, as Griff's distraught look deepened, "From
the beginning."

Griff gulped and nodded. "The two pairs of us scouts
came down here to Bonemarsh late yesterday afternoon. We
could track where your veiled patrol had passed through,
right enough. We figured—well, hoped—that the malice
had moved off and you all had moved after it. Then we
found these makers tied to the trees"—he glanced over his
shoulder—"and then we thought maybe you must have been
captured, instead."

*Because good patrollers don't abandon their own?
Charitable, Griff.* "No. We left them tied, passed them by,"
Dag admitted.

Griff straightened; to Dag's surprise, the look on his face
was not horror or contempt, but respect. He asked earnestly,
"How did you know it was a trap?"

Trap? What? Dag shook his head. "I didn't. They were
a sacrifice to pure tactics. I didn't want to chance warning

the malice there were patrollers coming up this close behind it."

"You said there was something really wrong," Saun corrected this, frowning. "And to keep our grounds shut tight when we were touching them."

"That wasn't exactly a stretch of my wits by that point, Saun. Go on, Griff."

"We could see they were groundlocked. Seemed to be. So Mallora did what you do to someone groundlocked, reached in and bumped grounds to break them out of the trance. Except—instead of her waking them up, the groundlock just seemed to, to reach out and suck her in. Her eyes rolled back, and she crumpled up in a heap. The mud-puppies all out in their pots over there"—Griff waved toward the bog—"made these strange bubbling noises and flopped around when it happened. Made us jump, in the dusk. I didn't notice how silent it all really was, till then. Mallora's partner Bryn panicked, I think—she reached out for her, tried to drag her back. And she got sucked in after. I grabbed my partner Ornig before he could reach for Bryn."

Dag nodded, provisionally, but Griff's face was tightening in something like despair. Dag murmured, "It used to happen up in Luthlia sometimes in the winter, someone would fall through rotten ice. And their friends or their kin would try to pull them out, and instead be pulled in after. One after another. Instead of running for help or a rope— though the smart patrollers there always wore a length of rope wrapped around their waists in the cold season. Except if someone's slipped under the ice—well, never mind. The hardest thing . . . the hardest thing in such a string of tragedy was to be the one who stopped. But you bet the older folks understood."

Griff blinked back tears, ducking his head in thanks. He swallowed for control of his voice, and went on, "Ornig and I agreed he would stay, and I would go for help. And I rode hard! But I think I should have stayed, because when we

made it back"—he swallowed again—"the makers were all
cut down from the trees, as if Ornig had tried to make them
more comfortable, but Ornig was all in a heap. He must
have . . . tried something." He added after a moment, "He's
sweet on Bryn, see."

Dag nodded understanding, and stepped away from
Copperhead to get a closer look at what was going on in the
grove. If only he could find a tree to lean against—not that
honey locust, bole and branches bristling with clusters of nasty
triple-headed spines—his hand found a low branch from a
young wild cherry, and he gripped it and peered. Three or
four patrollers, at least one of whom Dag recognized as one
of the company's better medicine makers, moved among bedrolls laid out where space permitted. He counted eight. *More
and more at risk.* Someone had a campfire going, though,
and something heating in pots—drinking water, medicine?

All good, but there was something deeply wrong with
the picture . . . oh. "Why haven't you moved them off this
blighted ground?"

Mari, Dirla, and Razi had dismounted during Griff's reci-
tation, moving closer to listen. Razi still held the reins of
Utau's horse; Utau drooped over his saddlebow, squinting.
Dag wasn't sure how much of this he was taking in.

"We tried," said Obio. "Soon as you carry someone more
than about a hundred paces away, they stop breathing."

"Must have been a thrill finding *that* out," Mari said.

"Oh, aye," agreed Obio, fervent. "In the middle of the
night last night."

"And if you kill one of the mud-men in their mudholes,"
Griff added morosely, "the people scream in their sleep. It's
pretty blighted unnerving. So we stopped that, too."

"I figured," said Obio, "that if—when—someone caught
up with the malice, the groundlock would break on its own.
I intended to detail a few folks to look after them and take
the company on, as soon as enough scouts came back to give
me a guess what we ought to try next. Except . . . you say

you all did for the malice, but that ugly groundlock's still holding tight."

"Dirla did," said Dag. "With Mari's sharing knife. Your first personal kill, I believe, Dirla?" It was a shame that the congratulations and celebration that should have been hers were being overwhelmed in this new crisis.

Dirla nodded absently. She frowned past Dag at the unmoving figures in the shaded bedrolls. "Could there be more than one malice? And that's why this link didn't break last night?"

Dag tried to think this utterly horrible idea through logically, but his brains seemed to be slowly turning to porridge. His gut said *no*, right enough, but he couldn't for the life of him say why, not in words.

Mari came to his rescue: "No. Because our malice would have turned all it had toward fighting the second, instead of chasing after farmers and Lakewalkers. Malices don't team up—they eat each other."

Well, that was true, too. *But that's not it.*

"That's what I thought," said Dirla. "But then why didn't this stop when the malice died, like what it does to the farmers and the mud-men?"

Maddening question. Lakewalkers, it must have to do with Lakewalkers . . . "All right," sighed Dag. "I'm thinking . . . we got water down those folks yesterday. If we can get more water and some sort of food—gruel, soup, I don't know—down them again, we can buy a little time, maybe."

"Been doing that," said Obio.

Bless your wits. Dag nodded. "Buy time to think. Keep a close eye, wait for the scouts—then decide. Depending, I'm thinking we might split the company—send some volunteers to help the Raintree folks with the cleanup, and the rest home maybe as early as tomorrow morning." So that Oleana might not, due to Fairbolt's robbed pegboard, find itself facing a similar runaway malice war next season.

The creeping alarm of this unnatural groundlock upon a
bunch of already-nervy patrollers was clearly contagious.
At this point, Dag could scarcely tell if his own sick unease
was from the makers or their distraught caretakers. "Blight
it, I wish I had Hoharie here. She works with people's
grounds all the time. Maybe she'd have an idea." He might
as well wish for that flock of turkey vultures to spiral
down, grab him, and fly him away home, while he was at
it. He sighed and cast an eye over his exhausted, bleary
comrades. "Everyone who was with my veiled patrol is
now off duty. Ride on over to the camp—get food, sleep,
a wash, whatever you want. Utau, you're on the sick list
till I say otherwise." Speaking of reasons to wish for the
medicine maker.

Utau roused himself enough to growl, "I like that! If that
malice scored me, it scored you a lot worse. I know what I
feel like. Why are you still walking around?"

A question Dag didn't care to probe just now, even if his
wits had been working. Utau, it occurred to him, had been
the only other patroller with his groundsense open, if in-
voluntarily, in those moments of confused terror last night
when Dag and the malice had closed on each other. What
had he perceived? Evidently not Dag's disastrous attempt to
rip the malice in return. Dag temporized, "Until Razi says
otherwise, then." Razi grinned and cast him an appreciative
half salute; Utau snorted. Dag added, "I'm going to lay me a
bedroll down here, shortly."

"On this blight?" said Saun doubtfully.

"I don't want to be a mile away if something changes suddenly."

Mari tugged Saun's sleeve, and murmured, "If that one's
actually volunteerin' for a bedroll, don't argue the details."
She gave him a significant jerk of her head, and his eyes
widened in enlightenment; he stepped over to Dirla.

"I had more sleep last night than you did, Mari," said
Dag.

"Dag, I don't know what that was last night after you went down, but it sure wasn't sleep. Sleeping men can be waked up, for one."

"Wait, what's all this?" said Obio.

Utau pushed up on his saddlebow and looked down at Dag a tad ironically. "Malice nearly ripped my ground last night. Dag jumped in and persuaded it to go after him, instead."

"Did it rip you?" Obio asked Dag, eyebrows climbing.

"A little bit," Dag admitted.

"Isn't that something like being a little bit dead?"

"Seemingly."

Obio smiled uncertainly, making Dag wonder just how corpselike he did look at the moment. He was not lovely, that was certain. Would he make Spark's eyes happy all the same? *I bet so.* A bright picture came into his head of the thrill that would flower in her face when he walked into their campsite, when this was all over. Would she drop her handwork and run to his arms? It was the first heartening thought he'd had for hours. Days.

Dag wondered if he'd started to fall asleep standing when a voice broke up this vision, which ran away like water though his hands. He almost cried to have the dream back. Instead, he forced himself to breathe deeply and pay attention.

". . . can send couriers with the news, now," Obio was saying. "I'd like to catch Fairbolt before he sends off the next round of reinforcements."

"Yes, of course," murmured Dag.

Dirla had been talking closely with Mari; at this, she lifted her face, and called, "I'd like to volunteer for that, sir."

You're off duty, Dag started to object, then realized this task would certainly get Dirla home first. Better—she was eyewitness to the malice kill, none closer. If he sent her, Dag wouldn't have to try to pen a report in his present groggy state. She could just *tell* Fairbolt all about it. "You took the malice. You can do any blighted thing you please, Dirla."

She nodded cheerfully. "Then I will."

Obio, his eyes narrowing, said, "In that case, I've a fellow in mind to send with her for partner. His wife was about to have a baby when we left. Absent gods willing, she might still be about to."

Which would cover events from the other part of the company for Fairbolt, too. Good.

"Excellent," agreed Mari. "That's a courier who won't dawdle, eh?"

"You'll need to trade out for fresher horses—" Dag began.

"We'll take care of it, Dag," Razi promised.

"Right. Right." This was all routine. "Dirla. Tell Spark— tell everyone we'll be home soon, eh?"

"Sure thing, Captain."

Obio boosted Mari back on her horse, and she led the rest of the patrol, save Saun and Dirla, off east toward the promised camp. To reassure Obio and Griff, Dag pretended to make an inspection tour of the grove and the bog, for as much good as his eyes could do with his groundsense still clamped down tight.

"There was a dead woman, yesterday," Dag began to Obio.

Obio grunted understanding. "We cut her down and wrapped her, and put her in one of the tents in the village. I'm hoping some of the Bonemarsh folk might come back and identify her before we have to bury her. In this heat, that'll have to be by tomorrow, though."

Dag nodded and trudged on.

The distorting animals trapped in their mud pots were much the same repellent sight as yesterday. The five surviving makers and three patrollers, more inexplicably trapped, were at least physically supported now, as comfortable as they might be made in bedrolls on the ground in the warm summer shade. The other patrollers taking turns to lift them and spoon liquids into them must also be ground-closed and walking blind, Dag realized.

Even apart from the hazard of this peculiar sticky ground-snare, he had the irrational apprehension that opening his ground would be like a man pulling a dressing from a gut wound; that all his insides might spill out. He found that while his back was turned, Saun and Dirla had unsaddled Copperhead and set up Dag's possessions and bedroll in a flat, dry spot raked clear of debris. They'd been awake as long as he had, blight it, why were they so blighted perky? Blighted children . . . The moment his haunches hit his blanket, Dag knew he wasn't getting up again. He sat staring blankly at his bootlaces, transported in memory back to the night after his last malice kill, with Spark on the feather tick in that farmhouse kitchen.

He was still staring when Saun knelt to undo one boot, and Dirla the other. It was surely a measure of . . . something, that he let them.

"Can I bring you anything to eat? Drink?" asked Dirla.

Dag shook his head. While riding he had gnawed down a number of leathery strips of dried plunkin, on the theory that he might so dispose of two tedious chores at the same time. He wasn't hungry. He wasn't anything.

Saun set his boots aside and squinted out into the afternoon light upon the silent, wasted marsh. "How long do you suppose till this place recovers? Centuries?"

"It looks bad now," said Dag, "but the malice was only here a few days, and the blight's not deep. Decades at most. Maybe not in my life, but in yours, I'd say."

Saun's eyes pinched, and he traded an unreadable look with Dirla. "Can I get—do you want anything at all, Captain?"

I want Spark. A mistake to allow himself the thought, because it bloomed instantly into a near-physical ache. In his heart, yes—as if there were any part of him not hurting already. Instead, he said, "Why am I *captain* all at once, here? You call me *Dag*, I call you *Hey, you, boy.* It's always worked before."

Saun grinned sheepishly, but didn't answer. He and Dirla scrambled up; Dag was asleep before the pair left the grove.

Fawn, who hadn't been able to fall to sleep till nearly dawn, woke in the midmorning feeling as though she had been beaten with sticks. Mint tea and plunkin did little to revive her. She turned to her next hand task, plaiting string from her spun plunkin flax to make wicks for a batch of beeswax candles Sarri was planning. An hour into it her eyes were blurring, and the throbbing in her left hand and arm was a maddening distraction that matched the throbbing in her head. Was it her heartbeat or Dag's that kept the time? *At least his heart's still beating.* She set down her work, walked up the road to where the path to Dar's bone shack led off, and stood in doubt.

Dag's his brother. Dar has to care. Fawn considered this proposition in light of her own brothers. No matter how furious she might be with them, would she drop her gripe if they were hurt and needed help? *Yes.* Because that's what family was all about, in her experience. They pulled together in a crisis; it was just too bad about the rest of the time. She set her shoulders and walked down the path into the green shade.

She hesitated again at the edge of the sun-dappled glade. If she was truly parading about ground-naked, as Cumbia accused, Dar must know she was here. Voices carried around the corner of the shack. He wasn't, then, deep in concentration upon some necromantic spell. She continued around to find Dar sitting on the top porch step with an older woman dressed in the usual summer shift, her hair in a knot. Dar was holding a sharing knife. He drew a peeved breath and looked up, reluctantly acknowledging Fawn.

Fawn clenched her left wrist protectively to her breast. "Mornin', Dar. I had a question for you."

Dar grunted and rose; the woman, with a curious glance at Fawn, rose too.

"So what is it?" Dar asked.

"It's kind of private. I can come back."

"We were just finishing. Wait, then." He turned to the woman and hefted the knife. "I can deconsecrate this in the afternoon. Do you want to come back tonight?"

"Could. Or tomorrow morning."

"I have another binding tomorrow morning."

"I'll make it tonight, then. After supper?"

"That would do."

The woman nodded briskly and started away, then paused by Fawn, looking her up and down. Her brows rose. "So you're the famous farmer bride, eh?"

Fawn, unable to figure her tone, gave a safe little knee-dip.

She shook her head. "Well, Dar. Your brother." With this opaque pronouncement, she strode off up the path.

By the bitter twisting of Dar's lips, he drew more information from this than Fawn could. Fawn let it go; she had much more urgent worries right now. She approached Dar cautiously, as if he might bite. He set the knife on the porch boards and eyed her ironically.

Too nervous to plunge straight in, Fawn said instead, "What was that woman here for?"

"Her grandfather died unexpectedly in his sleep a few weeks ago, without getting the chance to share. She brought his knife back to be rededicated."

"Oh." Yes, that had to happen now and then. She wondered how Dar did that, took an old knife and bound it to the heart of someone new. She wished he and she could have been friends—*or even relatives*—then she could have asked.

Never mind that now. She gulped and stuck out her left arm. "Before Dag rode off to Raintree, I asked him if he couldn't fix it so's I could feel him through my marriage cord the way he feels me. And he did." She prayed Dar would not ask how. "Last night about two hours after midnight, I woke up—there was this hurting all up my arm. Sarri, she woke up about the same time, but all she said was that Razi and Utau were still alive. Mari, too, Cattagus says. It didn't do this before—I was afraid that—I think Dag's hurt. Can you tell? Anything more?"

Dar's face was not especially revealing, but Fawn thought a flash of alarm did flicker through his eyes. In any case, he did not snipe at her, but merely took her arm and let his fingers drift up and down it. His lips moved, tightened. He shook his head, not, seemingly, in defeat, but in a kind of exasperation. "Gods, Dag," he murmured. "Can you do worse?"

"Well?" said Fawn apprehensively.

Dar dropped her arm; she clutched it to herself again. "Well . . . yes, I think Dag has probably taken some injury. No, I can't be sure how much."

Offended by his level tone, Fawn said, "Don't you care?"

Dar turned his hands out. "If it's so, it won't be the first time he's been brought home on a plank. I've been down this road with Dag too many times. I admit, the fact that he's company captain is a bit . . ."

"Worrisome?"

"If you like. I can't figure what Fairbolt . . . eh. But you say the others are all right, so they must be taking care of him. The patrol looks after its own."

"If he's not lost or separated or something." Fawn could imagine a hundred somethings, each more dire than the last. "He's my husband. If he's hurt, I should be lookin' after him."

"What are you going to do? Jump on your horse and ride off into a war zone? To lose yourself in the woods, drown in a bog or a river, be eaten by the first wolf—or malice— whose path you cross? Come to think, maybe I should have Omba saddle up your horse and put you on it. It would certainly solve my brother's problems for him."

And it was *extremely* aggravating that just such panicked thoughts had been galloping through her mind all morning. She scowled. "Maybe I wouldn't be as lost as all that. When Dag fixed my cord, he fixed it so's I can tell where he is. Generally, anyhow," she added scrupulously.

Dar squinted down at her for a long, silent, unnerving moment; his frown deepened. "It has nothing to do with your marriage cord. Dag has enslaved some of your ground to his." He seemed about to say more, but then fell silent, his face drawn in doubt. He added after a moment, "I had no idea that he . . . it's potent groundwork, I admit, but it's not a good kind."

"I don't understand."

"Naturally not."

Fawn clenched her teeth. "That means, you have to explain more."

"Do I?" The ironic look returned.

"Yes," said Fawn, very definitely.

A little to her surprise, he shrugged acquiescence. "It's malice magic. Forbidden to Lakewalkers for very good reasons. Malices mind-enslave farmers through their grounds. It's part of what makes farmers as useless on patrol as dogs—a powerful enough malice can take them away and use them against us."

"So why doesn't that happen to Lakewalkers?" she shot back.

"Because we can close our grounds against the attack."

Reluctantly, she decided Dar was telling the truth. So would the Glassforge malice have stolen her mind and will from her if it had been given a bit more time? Or would it simply have ripped out her ground on the spot as it had her child's? No telling now. It did cast a disturbing new light on what she had assumed to be farmer slander against Lakewalkers and their beguilements. But if—

Cattagus's oblique warning about the camp council returned to her mind with a jerk. "How, forbidden?" *How fiercely forbidden, with what penalties?* Had she just handed Dag's brotherly enemy another weapon against him? *Oh, gods, I can't do anything right with these people!*

"Well, it's discouraged, certainly. A Lakewalker couldn't use the technique on another Lakewalker, but farmers are wide-open, to a sufficiently powerful"—he hesitated—"maker," he finished, puzzlement suddenly tingeing his voice. He shook it off. His eyes narrowed; Fawn suddenly did not like his sly smile. "It does rather explain how Dag has you following him around like a motherless puppy, eh?"

Dismay shook her, but she narrowed her eyes right back. "What does *that* mean?" she demanded.

"I should think it was obvious. If not, alas, to my brother's credit."

She strove to quell her temper. "If you're tryin' to say you think your brother put some kind of love spell on me, well, it won't wash. Dag didn't fix my cord, or my ground, or whatever, till the night before he left with his company."

Dar tilted his head, and asked dryly, "How would you know?"

It was a *horrible* question. Was he reading her ground the way Cumbia had, to so narrowly target her most appalling possible fears? Doubt swept through her like a torrent, to smack to a sudden stop against another memory—Sunny Sawman, and his vile threats to slander her about that night at his sister's wedding. That ploy had worked admirably well to stampede Fawn. Once. *I may be just a little farmer girl, but blight it, I do learn. Dag says so.* She raised her face to meet Dar's eye square, and suddenly the look of doubt was reversed from her to him.

She drew a long breath. "I don't know which of you is using malice magic. I do know which of you is the most *malicious*."

His head jerked back.

Yeah, that stings, doesn't it, Dar? Fawn tossed her head,

whirled, and stalked out of the clearing. She didn't give him the satisfaction of looking back, either.

Out on the road again, Fawn first turned right, then, in sudden decision, left. In the time it took her to walk the mile down the shore to patroller headquarters, her courage chilled. The building appeared quiet, although there was a deal of activity across the road at the stables and in the paddocks, some patrol either coming in or going out, or maybe folks getting ready to send the next company west to the war. *Maybe Fairbolt won't be here,* she told herself, and climbed the porch.

A strange patroller at the writing table pointed with his free hand without looking up from his scratching quill. "If the door's open, anyone can go in."

Fawn swallowed her rehearsed greetings, nodded, and scuttled past. *Blight* this naked-ground business. She peeked around the doorjamb to the inner chamber.

Fairbolt was sitting across from his pegboard with his feet up on another chair and a shallow wooden box in his lap, stirrings its contents with one thick finger and frowning. A couple more chairs pulled up beside him held more such trays. He squinted up at his board, sighed, and said, "Come in, Fawn."

Emboldened, she stepped to his side. The trays, unsurprisingly, held pegs. He looked, she thought, very much like a man trying to figure out how to fill eight hundred holes with four hundred pegs. "I don't mean to interrupt."

"You're not interrupting much." He looked up at last and gave her a grimace that was possibly intended to be a smile.

"I had a question."

"There's a surprise." He caught her faint wince and shook his head in apology. "Sorry. To answer you: no, I've had no

courier from Dag since his company left. I wouldn't expect
one yet. It's still early days for any news."

"I figured that. I have a different question."

She didn't think she'd let her voice quaver, but his brows
went up, and his feet came down. "Oh?"

"Married Lakewalkers feel each other through their wedding cords—if they're alive, anyhow. Stands to reason you'd
be listenin' out for any such news from your patrollers—if
any strings went dead—and folks would know to pass it on
to you right quick."

He looked at her in some bemusement. "That's true. Dag
tell you this?"

"No, I figured it. What I want to know is, couriers or no
couriers, have you gotten any such mortal news from Dag's
company?"

"No." His gaze sharpened. "Why do you ask?"

This was where it got scary. Fairbolt *was* the camp council, in a way. *But I think he's patrol first.* "Before he left, Dag
did some groundwork on my cord, or on me, so's I could feel
if he was alive. Same as any other married Lakewalker, just
a little different route, I guess." Almost as briefly as she had
for Dar, she described waking up hurting last night, and her
moonlit talk with Sarri and Cattagus. "So just now I took
my cord to Dar, because he's the strongest maker I know of.
And he allowed as how I was right, my cord spoke true, Dag
was hurt somehow last night." She hardly needed to add, she
thought, that for Dar to grant his brother's farmer bride to be
right about anything, it had to be pretty inarguable.

All the intent, controlled alarm she'd missed from Dar
shone now in Fairbolt's eyes. His hand shot out; he jerked it
to a stop. "Excuse me. May I touch?"

Fawn mustered her nerve and held out her left arm.
"Yes."

Fairbolt's warm fingers slid up and down her skin and
traced her cord. His face tensed in doubt and dismay. "Well,
something's there, yes, but . . ." Abruptly, he rose, strode

to the doorway, and stuck his head through. His voice had an edge Fawn had not heard before. "Vion. Run over to the medicine tent, see if Hoharie's there. If she's not doing groundwork, ask her to step down here. There's something I need her to see. Right now."

The scrape of a chair, some mumble of assent; the outer door banged before Fairbolt turned back. He said to Fawn, somewhat apologetically, "There's reasons I went for patroller and not maker. Hoharie will be able to tell a lot more than I can. Maybe even more than Dar could."

Fawn nodded.

Fairbolt drummed his fingers on his chair back. "Sarri and Cattagus said their spouses were all right, yes?"

"Yes. Well, Sarri wasn't quite sure about Utau, I thought. But all alive."

Fairbolt walked over to the larger table and stared down; Fawn followed. A map of north Raintree was laid out atop an untidy stack of other charts. Fairbolt's finger traced a loop across it. "Dag planned to circle Bonemarsh and drop down on it from the north. My guess was that the earliest they could arrive there was today. I don't know how much that storm might have slowed them. Really, they could be anywhere within fifty miles of Bonemarsh right now."

Fawn let her left hand follow his tracing. The directional urge of her cord, alas, did not seem to respond to marks on maps, only to the live Dag. But she stared down with sudden new interest.

Maps. Maps could keep you from getting lost even in places you'd never been before. This one was thick with a veining of roads, trails, rivers, and streams, and cluttered with jotted remarks about landmarks, fords, and more rarely, bridges. Dar might be right that if she just jumped on her horse and rode west, she would likely plunge into disaster. But if she jumped on her horse with an aid like this . . . she would still be running headlong into a war zone. A mere pair of bandits had been enough to overcome her, before. *I would be more wary, now.* The map was something to think hard about, though.

"What could have happened to Dag, do you think?" she asked Fairbolt. "Dag alone, and no one else?"

He shrugged. "If you want to start with most likely chances, maybe that fool horse of his finally managed to bash him into a tree. The possibilities for freak accidents after that are endless. But they can't have closed in for the malice kill yet."

"Why not?"

His voice went strangely soft. "Because there would be more dead. Dag and I figured, based on Wolf Ridge, to lose up to half the company in this. That's how I expect to know, when . . ." He trailed off, shaking his head. "Obio Grayheron will take command. He's good, even if he doesn't have that edge that . . . ah, gods, I hate this helpless waiting."

"You, too?" said Fawn, her eyes widening.

He nodded simply.

A knock sounded on the doorjamb, and a quiet voice. "Problems, Fairbolt?"

Fairbolt looked up in relief. "Hoharie! Thank you for stopping over. Come on in."

The medicine maker entered, giving Fairbolt a vague wave and Fawn a curious look. Fawn had been introduced to her by Dag and shown the medicine tent, which to Fawn's mind nearly qualified as a building, but they had barely spoken then. Hoharie was an indeterminate age to Fawn's eyes, not as tall as most Lakewalker women. Her summer shift did not flatter a figure like a board, but the protuberant eyes in her bony face were shrewd and not unkind. Like Dag's eyes, they shifted colors in the light, from silver-gilt in the sun to, now, a fine gray.

Fairbolt hastened to set her a chair by the map table, and moved boxes of pegs to free two more. Fawn directed an uncertain knee-dip at her and sat where Fairbolt pointed, just around the table's corner.

"Tell your tale, Fawn," said Fairbolt, settling on her other side.

Fawn gulped. "Sir. Ma'am." Fighting an urge to gabble, Fawn repeated her story, her right hand kneading her left as she spoke. She finished, "Dar accused Dag of making malice magic, but I swear it isn't so! It wasn't Dag's fault—I *asked* him to fix my cord. Dar puts it in the worst possible light on purpose, and it makes me so mad I could spit."

Hoharie had listened to the spate with her head cocked, not interrupting. She said mildly, "Well, let's have a look then, Fawn."

At her encouraging nod, Fawn laid her left arm out on the table for Hoharie's inspection. The medicine maker's lips twisted thoughtfully as she gazed down at it. Her fingers were thin and dry and hardly seemed to press the skin, but Fawn's arm twinged deep inside as they drifted along. Fairbolt watched closely, occasionally remembering to breathe. Hoharie sat back at last with a hard-to-read expression.

"Well. That's a right powerful piece of groundwork for a patroller. You been hoarding talent over here, Fairbolt?"

Fairbolt scratched his head. "If it's so, Dag's been hoarding himself."

"Did he mention that thing about the glass bowl and the ghost hand to you?"

Fairbolt's eyebrows shot up. "No . . . ?"

"Huh."

"*Is* it"—Fawn swallowed—"what Dar said? Bad magic?"

Hoharie shook her head, not so much in negation as caution. "Now, mind you, I've never seen a malice's mind-slave up close. I've just heard about them. Though I have dissected mud-men, and *there's* a tale. This almost reminds me more of matching grounds for healing, truth to tell. Which is like a dance between two grounds that push on each other. As contrasted with a shaped or unshaped ground reinforcement, where the medicine maker actually gives ground away. Could be when a malice matches ground, it's just so powerful it compels rather than dances, pushing the other right over. Though there is a disparity in this as well . . . I wouldn't be able to tell how much unless I had Dag right here."

Fawn sighed wistfully at the notion of having Dag right here, safe.

Fairbolt said in a somewhat choked voice, "Isn't a hundred miles away a bit far for matching grounds, Hoharie? It's usually done skin to skin, in my experience."

"That's where the *almost* comes in. This has both, mixed. Dag's put a bit of worked—rather delicately worked—ground reinforcement into Fawn's left arm and hand, which is what she feels dancing with his ground in the cord. It's all very, um . . . impulsive."

Perhaps taking in the confusion in Fawn's face, Hoharie went on: "It's like this, child. What you farmers call magic, Lakewalker *or* malice, it's all just groundwork of some kind. A maker draws the ground he works with out of himself, and has to recover by growing it back at the speed of life, no more. A malice steals ground from the world around it, insatiably, and puts nothing back. Think of a rivulet and a river in flood. The one'll give you a nice drink on a hot day. The other will wash away your house and drown you. They're both water. But no one sane has any trouble telling one from the other. See?"

Fawn nodded, if a bit uncertainly, to show willing.

"So is my company captain hurt or not?" said Fairbolt, shifting in impatience. "What's going on over there in Raintree, Hoharie?"

Hoharie shook her head again. "You're asking me to tell you what something looks like from a glimpse in a piece of broken mirror held around a corner. In the dark. Am I looking at all of it, or just a fragment? Does it correspond to anything?" She turned to Fawn. "What hurts, exactly?"

Fawn stretched and clenched her fingers. "My left hand, mostly. Up the arm it fades. Except I feel a little shivery all over."

Fairbolt muttered, "But Dag hasn't got a . . ." His face screwed up, and he scowled in a confusion briefly greater than Fawn's.

"It's . . . how shall I put this," said Hoharie in some reluctance. "If the rest of his ground is as stressed as the bit I feel, his body must be in a pretty bad way."

"How bad, *how*?" snapped Fairbolt. Which made Fawn rather glad, because she was much too frightened to yell at the medicine maker herself.

Hoharie opened her hands in a wide, frustrated shrug. "Well, not quite enough to kill him, evidently."

Fairbolt bared his teeth at her, but then sat back in a glum slump. "If I get any sleep at all tonight, Hoharie, it won't be your doing."

Fawn leaned forward and stared at her hand. "I was kind of hoping you would tell me I was a stupid little farmer girl imagining things. Everybody else used to, but now that I want it . . ." She looked up, and added uneasily, "Dag's not going to get in some kind of trouble for this making, is he?"

"Well, if—when he gets back I guarantee *I'll* be asking him a few questions," said Hoharie fervently. "But they won't have anything to do with this argument before the camp council."

"It was all my fault, truly," said Fawn. "Dar made me afraid to tell. But I thought—I thought Fairbolt had a need and a right to know, on account of the company."

Fairbolt pulled himself together, and said gravely, "Thank you, Fawn. You did the right thing. If you feel any changes in this, please tell me or Hoharie, will you?"

Fawn nodded earnestly. "So what do we do now?"

"What we generally have to do, farmer girl," Fairbolt sighed. "We wait."

13

Dag woke well after dark, to roll his aching body up, pull on his boots without lacing them, and stagger to the slit trench. The night air was chill and dank, but the two patrollers on duty had kept the campfire burning with a cheery orange glow. One waved to Dag as he wandered past, and Dag returned the silent salute. The scene looked deceptively peaceful, as though they watched over comrades merely sleeping.

After relieving himself, Dag considered more sleep. His bone-deep grinding fatigue of earlier seemed scarcely improved. The marsh remained silent—this hour should have been raucous with frogs, insects, and night birds—and eerily odorless. Either the reek of its normal life or the stench of death should have saturated this foggy air. Well, the rot would come in time, a week or a month or six or next spring. Which, while it would doubtless smell repulsive enough to gag anyone for a mile downwind, would be a first sign of life beginning its repair of the blight—rot had a lively ground of its own.

Dag stared at the grove, the campfire seeming like a lantern among the trees, remembering his patrol's first approach . . . only yesterday? If this was after midnight—he glanced at the wheel of the stars—he could call it two days ago, though that seemed scarcely more reasonable. Frowning thoughtfully, he counted a careful two hundred paces away from the grove and found a stump to sit upon. He stretched out his aching legs. If he had opened his groundsense at this distance before without triggering the trap, presumably he might do it again.

He hissed in surprise as he eased his veil apart for the first time in days. *Cramping*, Mari had described his closure, and that seemed barely adequate to describe this shaking agony. Normally, he paid as little attention to his own ground as he did to his body, the two conflating seamlessly. Meaning to examine the groundlocked makers, Dag instead found his inner senses wrenched onto himself.

In the ground of his right arm a faint heat lingered, last vestiges of the healing reinforcement snatched from, or gifted by, Hoharie's apprentice. Over time such a reinforcement was slowly absorbed, converted from the donor's ground into that of the recipient's, not unlike the way his food became Dag. Even this trace would be gone altogether in a few more weeks. In the ground of his left arm . . .

His ghost hand was not there at the moment. The ground of his arm was spattered with a dozen dark spots, black craters seeming like holes burned in a cloth from scattered sparks. A few more throbbed on his neck and down his left side. Surrounding them in gray rings were minute patches of blight. This wasn't just fading reverberation from a malice-handling like Utau's, though that echoed in him too. The spots were the residue, he realized, of the ground he'd ripped from the malice in that desperate night-fight. It was like nothing he'd ever seen before, yet immediately recognizable. *Strangely familiar* seemed the perfect summation, actually.

But then, he'd never before met up with anyone crazed enough to try to ground-rip a malice. Maybe he was seeing why it was not a recommended technique? Injury or healing to a living body injured or healed its ground in turn; ground-ripping or prolonged exposure to blight killed a body through its ravaged ground. What was this peculiar infestation doing to his body now? Nothing good, he suspected. With this map to guide him, he could trace deep aches in his flesh that centered over the splotches, if barely distinguishable from his present general malaise. Pain marked damage, normally. What kind of damage?

So . . . was the pulsating grayness slowly being absorbed by Dag's ground, or . . . or was the blight spreading? He swallowed and stared, but could sense no discernible change.

Stands to reason, he could almost hear Spark say. How would a smart little farmer girl analyze this? What were the possibilities?

Well, his ground could be slowly repairing itself, as in any other wound. Or his ground might be unable to repair itself until the sources of injury were removed, the way an arrow had to be extracted before the flesh around it could start to knit. Sometimes, if more rarely, flesh knitted around a fragment that could not be removed. Sometimes it closed but festered. Or . . . was the blight spreading out faster than his ground could repair it? In which case . . .

In which case, I'm looking at my death wound. A mortality flowing as slowly as honey in winter, as inexorably as time.

Spark, no, how long do we—?

In a spasm of inspiration, he tried to call up his ghost hand to grip a splotch, tear it out, dump it in the soil, anywhere—was it possible to ground-rip *yourself*?—but his odd power remained elusive. He then massaged around a spot on his left ribs with his right hand, willing its ground to reach in, but found it as impossible as to will flesh to penetrate flesh. The effort made his side twinge, however.

An even more horrific possibility occurred to him then. The fragments of the first great malice-king, it was said, grew into the plague of the world. What if each of these fragments had the same potential? *Could I turn into a malice?* Or malice food?

Dag bent his head and huffed through his open mouth, his hand clutching his hair. *Oh, absent gods, do you hate me that much?* Or he might split into a dozen malices—or—no, a dominant one would no doubt conquer and subsume the others, then emerge the lone victor of . . . what? Once the miniature malice had consumed all the ground and the life of the body it lived in, it, too, presumably must die. Unless it could escape . . .

Dag panted for breath in his panic, then swallowed and sat up. *Let's go back to the death-wound idea, please?* What if this was not a spew of malice seed, but more like a spatter of malice blood, carrying the toxic ground but not capable of independent life for long. Indeed—gingerly, he turned his senses inward again—there was not that sense of nascent personality that even the lowliest sessile malice exuded. Poison, yes. He could live with—well, be happy with—well . . .

He sat for several shaken minutes in the silent dark, then peeked again. No change. It seemed he was not dissolving into gray dust on the spot. Which meant he was doomed to wake up to his responsibilities in the morning all the same. So. He'd had a reason for coming out here. What was it . . . ?

He inhaled and, very cautiously, extended his ground-sense outward once more. The lingering blight all around nibbled at him, but it was ignorable. He found the dead trees in the grove, the trapped mud-men beyond, the live patrollers on night watch. He steered away from the groundlocked makers, barely letting his senses graze them. Before, he had found a gradient of ground moving through the soil, sucked into the making of the mud-man nursery. Did such a draw sustain it still?

No. The death of the malice had done that much good, at least.

Or . . . maybe not. The mud-men were still alive, even if they'd stopped growing. Therefore, they must still be drawing ground, if slowly. The only source of ground in the system was the locked makers and, now, the three fresh patrollers. And he did not think their depleted bodies could

produce new ground fast enough to keep up. What must be
the end of it, if this accursed lock could not be broken?

The weakest makers would likely die first. With them
gone, increased stress would be thrown onto the survivors,
who would not last long, Dag suspected. Death would cas-
cade; the remainder must die very quickly. At which point
the mud-men would also die. Would that be the end of it, the
problem collapsing into itself and gone? Or were there other
elements, hidden elements at work inside the lock?

No one could find out without opening their ground to the
lock. No one could open their ground to the lock without
being sucked into it, it seemed. Impasse.

My head hurts. My ground *hurts.* But no such collapse
was happening now. Dag clutched the thought to himself
as if it were hope. Perhaps the morning would bring better
counsel, or even better counselors than one battered old patroller so frighteningly out of his depth. Dag sighed, levered
himself up, and stumbled back to his bedroll.

What the morning brought was distractions, mainly. A
pair of scouts returned from the south to report much the
sort of chaos Dag expected—farmer and Lakewalker refugees scattered all over, improvised defenses in disarray—but
also encouraging signs of people beginning to sort themselves out with the news of the death of the malice. About
midday, some two dozen Bonemarsh exiles cautiously approached. Dag assigned his patrol of cleanup volunteers the
initial task of helping them to identify and bury their dead,
including the woman maker, and scavenge the village for
still-usable supplies that might be carried off to the other
north Raintree camps that would be taking in the nearly two
thousand homeless. The Raintree Lakewalkers were likely
in for a straitened winter, coming up. Bonemarsh casualties,
he was glad to learn, had been relatively low. No one seemed

to know yet if the same had been the case for that farmer town the malice had taken first.

Three of the Bonemarsh folks agreed to stay and help nurse their groundlocked makers and the hapless would-be rescuers. The makers all had names, now, and life stories that the returned refugees had determinedly pressed on Dag. He wasn't sure if that helped. In any case, he sent the first batch of locals off with a patroller escort and an earnest request to send him back any spare medicine makers or other experts who might be able to get a grip on his lethal puzzle. But he didn't expect much help from that quarter, as every medicine maker in Raintree had to be up to the ears in nearer troubles right now.

He had slightly more hope of the full patrol of twenty-five he sent home that afternoon, carrying both a warning to Hickory Lake of their neighbor's impending winter shortages, and a much more urgently worded plea for Hoharie or some equally adept maker to come to his aid. To stay at Bonemarsh, Dag selected the best medicine makers—for patrollers—his company had, including several veteran mothers or grandmothers, whom he figured for already knowing how to keep alive people who couldn't talk or walk or feed themselves. Small ones, anyway. *They can work up.*

He hadn't expected them to work up to him, however. "Dag," said Mari, with her usual directness, "the bags under your eyes are so black you look like a blighted raccoon. Have you had anybody look *you* over yet?"

He'd been thinking of quietly hauling one of the better field medicine fellows out of range of the grove to examine him. Mari, he realized glumly, was not only at the top of that list by experience and groundsense skill, but would corner any substitute and have the story ripped out of him in minutes anyway. Might as well save steps.

"Come on," he sighed. She nodded in stern satisfaction.

He led off to his stump of last night, or one like it, sat, and cautiously opened himself. It took a couple of minutes, and he ended with his head bent nearly to his knees. *Still hurts.*

He heard a long, slow hiss through her teeth that for Mari was as scary as swearing. In a tone of cool understatement, she observed, "Well, that don't look so good. What *is* that black crap?"

"Some sort of ground contamination. It happened when I . . ." he started to say, *ground-ripped the malice,* but changed it to, "when I tried to draw the malice off from Utau, and it turned on me. It was like bits of it stuck to me, and burned. I couldn't get rid of it. Then I closed up and passed out."

"You sure did. I thought you were just ground-ripped— hah, listen to me, *just* ground-ripped—like Utau. Does that, um . . . hurt? Looks like it ought to."

"Yeah." Dag turned his groundsense on himself, closing his eyes for an instant to feel more clearly. Two of the gray patches on his left arm, separate last night, seemed to have grown together since like two water droplets joining. *I'm losing ground.*

Mari said hesitantly, "You want me to try anything? Think a bit of ground reinforcement might help, or a match?"

"Not sure. I wouldn't want to get this crud stuck to you. I suspect it's"—*lethal*—"not good. Better wait. It's not like I'm falling over."

"It's not like you're dancing a jig, either. This isn't like . . . Utau's ground, it's like it's scraped raw, shivering and won't stop, but you can see it'll come right in its own time. This . . . yeah, this is outside my ken. You need a real medicine maker."

"That's what I figured. Hope one shows up soon. Meantime, well, I can still walk, it seems. If not jig." Dag hesitated. "If you can refrain from gossiping about this all over camp, I'd take it kindly."

Mari snorted. "So if this had happened to any other patroller, how fast would you have slapped him onto the sick list?"

"Privileges of captaincy," Dag said vaguely. "You know that road, patrol leader."

"Yeah? Would that be the privilege to be stupid? Funny, I don't seem to recall that one."

"Look, if anybody with more skill shows up here to hand this mess on to, you bet I'll be on my horse headed east in an hour." Except that he could not ride away from what he carried inside, now, could he? "I have no idea who the Raintree folks can spare or when, but I figure the soonest we could get help from home is six days." He stared around; the afternoon was growing hazy, with a brassy heat in the air that foreboded evening thundershowers.

Mari glanced toward the grove, and said quietly, "Think those folks will last six more days?"

Dag let out a long breath and heaved himself to his feet. "I don't know, Mari. Does look like we need to rustle up some kind of tent covering to gather them under, though. Rain tonight, you think?"

"Looks like," she agreed.

They strolled silently back to the dead grove.

He wasn't sure how much Mari talked, or didn't, but a lot of people in the grove camp that evening seemed to take it as their mission to tell him to go lie down. He was persuadable, except that with nothing to do but sit cross-legged on his bedroll and stare at the groundlocked makers, he found himself drifting into hating them. Without this tangle, he could have gone home with today's patrol. In three days' time, held Spark hard and not let go even for breathing. His earlier weariness of this long war was as nothing to his present choked surfeit. He slept poorly.

By late the following afternoon, two of the older makers had lost the ability to swallow, and one was having trouble breathing. As Carro, one of Mari's cronies from Obio's

patrol, held the man up in her lap in an effort to ease him,
Dag knelt beside the bedroll and studied his labored gasps.
Breathing this bad in a dying man was normally a signal to
share, and soon. But was this fellow dying? Need he be? His
thinning hair was streaked with gray, but he was hardly el-
derly; before this horror had fallen on him, Dag judged him
to have been hale, lean and wiry. Artin was his name, Dag
didn't want to know, an excellent smith and something of a
weapons-master. Under his own tracing fingers, Dag could
read a lifetime of accumulated knowledge in the subtle calluses of Artin's hands.

Mari blotted the face and hair of the nearby woman she
had just spent several fruitless minutes trying to get water
down, while the woman had writhed and choked. "If we
can't get more drink into them in this heat, they aren't going
to last anything like five more days, Dag."

Carro nodded to the man in her lap. "This one, less."

"I see that," murmured Dag.

Saun paced about. Dag had guessed he would volunteer
for the patrol lingering in Raintree to assist the refugees, and
indeed he'd scorned an offer to ride back to Hickory Lake
yesterday; but, taking his partnership with Dag seriously,
he'd instead requested assignment to this duty. He slept in
the now-reduced camp to the east off the blight, but lived at
Dag's left elbow in the daytime. Which would be a fine thing
if only Saun acted less like a flea on a griddle in the face of
these frustrations.

Now he declared, "We have to try *something*. Dag,
you say you think these makers are still supporting the
mud-men. If that's so, doesn't it make sense to cut off the
load?"

"Obio and Griff said they tried that," said Dag patiently.
"The results were pretty alarming, I gathered."

"But no one *died*. It could be like one of Hoharie's cuttings,
hurting to heal."

It was a shrewd argument, and it attracted Dag more than

the prospect of just sitting here watching while these people suffered and failed. *My company.* He wasn't quite sure how these Raintree makers had become honorary members of it in his mind, but they had. His three unconscious patrollers were the least depleted, so far, but Dag could see that wasn't going to last.

"I admit," Dag said slowly, "I'd like to see what happens for myself." Although how much telling detail he was likely to observe with his groundsense closed was a bitter question. "Maybe . . . do one. And then we'll see."

Saun gave him a quick nod of understanding and went to fetch his sword. It was the same weapon that had put Saun in harm's way back at Glassforge; Dag had heroically refrained from pointing out how useless the deadweight had been to Saun on this trip, too. But for dispatching mud-men in their pots, it would do nearly as well as a spear, and better than a knife.

Sword over his shoulder, Saun trod determinedly back through the grove and out toward the boggy patch, his boots squelching in the mud from last night's rain. He slowed, trying to pick his way more cleanly upon clumps of dead grasses, and peered down into the mud pots with a look of curious revulsion.

The unformed monsters therein were in a revolting enough state, distorted past any hope of returning to their animal lives, and equally far from transformation to their mock-human forms. Innocent but doomed. Dag's brow furrowed. So—if their transformation could somehow be completed, with the malice dead would they switch their slavish allegiance to the Lakewalker makers? It was a disturbing idea, as if Dag's brain didn't teem with enough of those already. The more disturbing for being seductive. Powerful subhuman servants might be used for a multitude of desperately needed tasks. Had the mage-lords of old made something like them? All malices seemed to hatch with the knowledge, not to mention the compulsion, of such makings, which suggested it was an old, old skill. But the mud-slaves presumably would require a continuous supply of ground reinforcement to live, making them lethally expensive to maintain.

Dag was glad to give over this line of thought as Saun called, "Which should I start with? The biggest?"

Mari, her face screwed up in doubt as she stared down at the damp woman maker, said, "The smallest?"

"I'm not sure it matters," Dag called back. "Just pick one."

Saun stepped toward a mud pot, gripped his sword in both hands, braced his shoulders, squinted, and struck. Squalling and splashing rose from the hole, and flying mud; Saun grimaced, pulled back, and struck hastily again.

"What was it?" Mari called.

"Beaver. I think. Or maybe woodchuck." Saun jumped back, looking sick, as the splashing died away.

Carro's cry wrenched Dag's attention around. The makers—all the groundlocked folk—were writhing and moaning in their bedrolls, as if in pain—deep, inarticulate animal sounds. The other two on-duty patrollers hurried to their sides, alarmed. The makers did not seem to be actually convulsing, so Dag stifled a wild look around for something to shove between teeth besides his hook, bad idea, or his fingers.

Artin's breathing passed from labored to choked. Carro pulled down his blanket and pressed her ear to his chest. "Dag, this isn't good."

"No more, Saun!" Dag called urgently over his shoulder, and bent to Artin's other side. The smith's lips were turning a leaden hue, and his eyelids fluttered.

"His heartbeat's going all wrong," said Carro. "Sounds like partridge wings."

Just before the archer shoots the bird out of the air? Dag continued the unspoken thought. *His heart is failing. Blight it, blight it . . .*

Saun hurried back; Dag raised his glance from Saun's

muddy boots to his suddenly drained face. Saun's lips parted, but no sound came out. Dag needed no words to interpret that particular appalled look, of a heart going hollow with fear and guilt. *You should not shoulder such a burden, boy. No one should.* But someone had to.

Not today, blight it.

Help might be coming, if the makers could be kept alive till then. *Somehow.* He remembered, for some reason, his impulsive attack on the malice's cave back in Glassforge. *Any way that works, old patroller.*

"I'm going to try a ground match," Dag said abruptly, moving to get a better grip on Artin's shuddering body. "Dance his heart back to the right beat, if I can." As he had once done for Saun.

Mari's voice called sharply, "Dag, no!"

He was already opening his ground. Finding his way into the other's body through his ground. Pain on pain, clashing rhythms, but Dag's dance was the stronger one. The true world rushed back into his awareness, blight and glory and all, and he became aware of how keenly he'd missed his groundsense, as if he'd been walking around for days with the best part of himself bloodily amputated. *Dance with me, Artin.*

Dag breathed satisfaction as he felt the smith's heart and lungs take up a steadier, stronger cadence once more. Dag did not share in such shocking pain as Saun's injuries, but he could feel the fragility in the maker's ground, how close it was to the edge of another such fall into disorder and death. Were the others as weakened? Dag's perceptions widened in increasing fascination.

All the Lakewalkers' grounds were wound about and penetrated by a subtle gray structure like ten thousand tangled threads. The threads combined and darkened, running out like strands of smoke to the mud-men's pots. The mud-men's grounds were the strangest of all: turned black, strong, compellingly human in shape. The fleshly bodies of the animals labored in vain, straining to match that impulse. Starving in their arrested growth.

The malice spatters on Dag's ground seemed to be shivering in time with the complex ground structure imprisoning the makers, and Dag had a sudden terror that somehow the still-living malice bits lodged within him were what was keeping this thing intact. Would he have to die for it to be broken . . . ? Ah. *No.* Affinity both had with each other, no question, but his spatters were as formless as a ground reinforcement, if an inverted one that was negative and destructive rather than positive and healing.

Dag struggled to understand what he was sensing. In normal persuasive making, the maker pushed and reinforced ground found within the object, striving to make things more themselves, as in Dag's old arrowproof coat where the protection of skin became leather became a shield. In healing, ground was gifted freely, unformed, to be turned into the recipient's ground without resistance. A ground match, such as he had just done for Artin, was a dance in time. The malices' enslavement of farmer minds, Dag realized suddenly, must also be such a ground dance, if enormously powerful to work so compulsively and at such distances. But it had to be continuously maintained, as he had glimpsed from the inside during this last kill, and the match died when the malice did. *It has a limited range, too*, he realized, which was why the malice had been forced to move along with its army.

This groundwork, though . . . had a range of only a hundred paces, but it had most certainly survived its malice maker. Contained, powerful, horrific . . . familiar. Familiar? *So where have I seen anything like this before?* What groundwork both survived its maker's death and retained the nature of its maker, not melding with its recipient, even after it had been released?

Sharing knives do. On a smaller scale, to be sure, but . . . scarcely less complex. The ground of the consecrated knife was shaped by its maker into an involuted container for the donor's future death, and that dissolving ground, once received, was held tight. Altered, if with and not against the donor's will, to something lethal to malices.

Dar must be giving something of himself away with each knife he made, Dag reflected. On some level, folks knew this, which was why they treated their knife makers with such care. How draining was such a making? Again and again and again? *Very.* No wonder Dar had so little left of himself for any other purpose.

Dag turned his inner eye back upon the malice's groundwork. This huge, horrific making was involuted and powerful beyond any scope he would ever have. But—beyond his understanding, as well?

The intuitive leap was effortless, like flying in a dream. *I see how this may be broken!* He grinned and opened his eyes.

Tried to grin. Tried to open his eyes.

Face, eyes, body were gone from him; his mind seemed one with his ground, floating cut off from the outer world. Gray threads wound into him like little searching mouths, like worms, sucking and consuming.

I'm trapped—

Fawn carefully tucked the dozen new beeswax candles that were her share of the afternoon's making into Dag's trunk, closed the lid, drifted out under her tent awning, and stared through the trees at the leaden gleam of the lake under the humid sky. She scratched absently at one of the mosquito bites speckling her bare arms, and pawed at a whine near her ear. Yet another reason to miss Dag, silly and selfish though it seemed. She sighed . . . then tensed.

The heartthrob echo of pain in her left arm and down her side, her constant companion for three days, changed into

something racing. A wave of terror swept through her, and
she could not tell if the first breath of it was Dag's or her
own, though the panting that followed seemed all hers. The
rhythm broke up into something chaotic and uneven; then it
muted. *No, don't die—*

It didn't, but neither did it return to its former definition.
Absent gods forfend, what was that? She gulped, flipped
down her tent flap behind her, and started walking quickly
up the shore road, breaking into a trot till she grew winded,
then walking again. She did not want to draw stares by running like a frightened deer.

She passed patroller headquarters, where one of Omba's
horse girls was leading off two spent mounts, heads down,
lathered, and muddy. Only couriers in a hurry would ride
horses in wet like that, but Fawn quelled hope, or fear, of
word from Dag's company; Fairbolt had said today would
still be too soon. Considering the deathly signals he was
waiting for, she could not wish for more speed.

She popped up the steps to Hoharie's medicine cabin—
medicine tent, she corrected the thought—and stood for a
moment trying to catch her breath, then pushed inside.

Hoharie's apprentice, what was his name, Othan, came
out of the herb room and frowned at her. "What do *you* want,
farmer girl?"

Fawn ignored his tone. "Hoharie. Said I should come see
her. If anything changed in my marriage cord. Something
just did."

Othan glanced at the closed door to the inner room. "She's
doing some groundwork. You'll have to wait." Reluctantly,
he jerked his head toward the empty chair by the writing
table, then went back into the herb room. Something pungent was cooking over its small fireplace, making the hot
chambers hotter.

Fawn sat and jittered, rubbing her left arm, though her
probing fingers made no difference to the sensations. The
former throbbing had been a source of fear to her for days,

but now she wished for it back. And why should her throat feel as though she was choking?

After what seemed forever, the door to the inner chamber opened, and a buxom woman came out with a boy of maybe three in her arms. He was frowning and feverish, eyes glazed, his head resting against her shoulder and his thumb stuck in his mouth. Hoharie followed, gave Fawn a nod of acknowledgment, and went with them into the herb room. A murmur of low voices, instructions to Othan, then Hoharie returned and gestured Fawn before her into the inner room, closing the door behind them.

Fawn turned and mutely thrust out her arm.

"Sit, girl," Hoharie sighed, pointing to a table in the corner with a pair of chairs. Hoharie winced as she settled across from Fawn, stretching her back, and Fawn wondered what she had just done for that little boy, and how much it had cost her in her ground. Would she even be able to help Fawn just now?

While Hoharie, her eyes half-closed, felt up and down Fawn's arm, Fawn stammered out a description of what had just happened. Her words sounded confused and inadequate in her own ears, and she was afraid they conveyed nothing to the medicine maker except maybe the idea that she was going crazy. But Hoharie listened without comment.

Hoharie at last sat up and shook her head. "Well, this was odd before, and it's odder now, but without any other information I'm blighted if I can guess what's really going on."

"*That's* no help!" It came out something between a bark and a wail, and Fawn bit her lip in fear she had offended the maker, but Hoharie merely shook her head again in something between exasperation and agreement.

Hoharie opened her mouth to say more, but then paused, arrested, her head turning toward the door. In a moment, boot steps sounded on the porch outside, and the squeak of the door opening. "Fairbolt," Hoharie muttered, "and . . . ?"

A rap at the inner door, and Fairbolt's voice: "Hoharie? It's urgent."

"Come in."

Fairbolt shouldered through, followed by—tall Dirla. Fawn gasped and sat up. Dirla was as mud-spattered as the horse she must have ridden in on, braids awry, shirt reeking of dried and new sweat, her face lined with fatigue under sunburn. Her eyes, though, were bright.

"They got the malice," Fairbolt announced, and Hoharie let out her breath with a triumphant hoot that made Dirla smile. Fairbolt cast Fawn a curious look. "About two hours after midnight, three nights back."

Fawn's hand went to her cord. "But that was when . . . *What happened to Dag? How bad was he hurt?*"

Dirla gave her a surprised nod, but replied, "It's, um, hard to say."

"Why?"

Fairbolt, his eyes on Hoharie, pulled the patroller forward, and said, "Tell your tale again, Dirla."

As Dirla began a description of the company's hard ride west, Fawn realized the pair must have come to find Hoharie, not her. Why? *Get to the part about Dag, blight you, Dirla!*

". . . we came up on Bonemarsh about noon, but the malice had moved—south twenty miles, we found out later, launching a big attack toward Farmer's Flats. Dag wouldn't let us stop for anything, even those poor makers. I'd never seen anything like it. The malice had enslaved the *grounds* of these Bonemarsh folk, somehow making them cook up a new batch of mud-men for it, or so Dag claimed. It left them tied to trees. The patrol was pretty upset when Dag ordered us to leave them in place, but Mari and Codo came in on his side, and Dag had this look on his face that made us afraid to press him, so we rode on."

Fawn gnawed her knuckles through Dirla's excited description of the veiled patrol slipping through an enemy-occupied farm at night, the breathless scramble up a hill, the rush upon a bizarre crude tower. "My partner Mari had almost made it to the top when the malice jumped down— must have been over twenty feet. Like it was flying. I never knew a malice could look so beautiful . . . Utau went for it. I had my ground shut tight, but later Utau said the malice just peeled his open like popping the husk off a hickory nut. He thought he was done for, but then Dag, who didn't even *have* a sharing knife, went for the thing barehanded. Bare-hooked, anyway. It left Utau and turned on him. Mari shouted for me and threw me down her knife, and I didn't quite see what happened then. Anyway, I drove Mari's knife into the thing, and all its bright flesh . . . burst. Horrible. And I thought it was over, and we were all home alive, and it was a miracle. Utau staggered over and draped himself on me till Razi could get to him—and then we saw Dag."

Fawn rocked, hunched tight with her arms wrapping her waist to keep from interrupting. Or screaming.

Dirla went on, "He was passed out in the dirt, stiff as a corpse, with his ground wrapped up so tight it was stranglin' him, and no one could get through to try to make a match or a reinforcement, though Mari and Codo and Hann all tried. For the next few hours, we all thought he was dying. Half-ground-ripped, like Utau, but worse."

"Wait," said Hoharie. "Wasn't he physically injured at all?"

Dirla shook her head. "Maybe knocked around a bit, but nothing much. But then, around dawn, he just woke up. And got up. He didn't look any too good, mind you, but he made it onto his horse somehow and pushed us all back to Bone-marsh. Seems he was fretting over those makers we'd left, as well he might.

"When we arrived, the rest of the company had made it in, but those makers—their groundlock didn't break when the malice died, and no one could figure out why not. Worse, anyone who tries to open grounds to them gets drawn into their lock, too. Obio lost three patrollers finding that one out. Dag believes they're all dying. Mari couldn't get him to leave them, though she thinks he should be on the sick list—it's like he's obsessed. Though by the time us couriers left that evening, we'd at least got him to sleep for a while. Utau and Mari, they don't like any of it one little bit. So"— Dirla turned her gaze on the medicine maker, her hands clutching each other in unaccustomed plea—"Dag said he wished he had you there, Hoharie, because he needs someone who knows folks' grounds down deep. So I'm asking for you for him, because Dag—he got *us* through. He got us *all* through."

Fairbolt cleared his throat. "Would you be willing to ride to Raintree, Hoharie?"

An appalled look came over the medicine maker's face as she stared wildly around at her workplace. Fawn thought she could just about see the crowded roster of tasks here racing through Hoharie's mind.

"—in an hour?" Fairbolt continued relentlessly.

"Fairbolt!" Hoharie huffed dismay. After a long, long moment she added, "Could you make it two hours?"

Fairbolt returned a short, satisfied nod. "I'll have two patrollers ready to escort you, and whoever you need to take with you."

Fawn blurted, "Can I come with you? Because I think I'm part of Dag's puzzle, too." She nearly held out her left arm in evidence.

The three Lakewalkers stared down at her in uncomplimentary surprise.

Fawn hurried on, "It's not a war zone anymore, and if I went with you, I couldn't get lost, so I wouldn't be being stupid at all. *I* could be ready in an hour. Less."

Dirla said, not scornfully but in a tone of kindness that was somehow even more annoying, "That fat little plow horse of yours couldn't keep up, Fawn."

"Grace is not fat!" said Fawn indignantly. *At least, not*

very. "And she may not be a racehorse, but she's *persistent.*"
She added after a moment, as her wits caught up with her
mouth, "Anyhow, couldn't you put me up on a patrol horse
just like Hoharie?"

Fairbolt smiled a little, but shook his head. "No, Fawn.
The malice may be gone, but north Raintree is going to be
disrupted for weeks yet, in the aftermath of all this. I made
a promise to Dag to see you came to no harm while he was
gone, and I mean to keep it."

"But—"

Fairbolt's voice firmed in a way that made Fawn think of
her father at his most maddening. "Farmer child, you are one
more worry I don't need to have right now. Others have to
wait for their husbands and wives to return as well."

And what was the counterargument to that? *I am not a
child?* Oh, sure, that one had always worked *so well.* "Funny,
I ran around out there in the wide world for eighteen years
without your protection, and survived." *Barely*, she was de-
pressingly reminded.

A bitter smile bent Fairbolt's lips, and he murmured, "No,
farmer child . . . you've always had our protection." Fawn
flushed. As she dropped her eyes in shame, he gave a satisfied nod, and went on more kindly, "I imagine Cattagus
and Sarri would be glad to learn the news about the malice.
Maybe you could run and let them know."

It was a clear dismissal. *Run along.* Fawn looked around
and found no allies, not Dirla, and not even Hoharie, despite the curious look in her eyes; the medicine tent might
be her realm, but it was plain the road was Fairbolt's, and she
would yield to his judgment in the matter.

Fawn swallowed, nodded, and took herself out, as chairs
scraped and the conference continued more intently. Without her. Not being a Lakewalker and all.

She stumped up the path between the medicine tent
and Fairbolt's headquarters, fuming and rubbing her arm.
Its thrumming echoed in her heart and head and gut until

she was in a fair way to screaming from it. So was she a Lakewalker bride or a farmer bride? Because if the first was under Lakewalker disciplines, the other could not be. People couldn't just switch her label back and forth at their convenience. Fair was fair, if not, *hah*, Fairbolt.

In one thing she was surely expert, and that was running away from home. Of which the first well-tested rule was, don't give folks a chance to *argue* with you. How had she forgotten that one? She set her teeth and turned aside at patroller headquarters.

A pair of patrollers conferring over a logbook looked up as she entered. "Fairbolt's not here," said one.

"I know," Fawn replied breezily. "I just talked with him up at Hoharie's." Which was perfectly true, right? No one, later, could say she'd lied. "I need to borrow one of his maps for a bit. I'll bring it back as soon as I can."

The patroller shrugged and nodded, and Fawn whipped into Fairbolt's pegboard chamber, hastily rolled up the map of north Raintree still out on top of the center table, tucked it under her arm, and left, smiling and waving thanks.

She dogtrotted to Mare Island, let herself through the bridge gate, and found one of Omba's girls in the work shed.

"I need my horse," said Fawn. "I want to take her out for some exercise." *A hundred or so miles worth.*

"She could use some," the girl conceded. Then, after a moment, "Oh, that's right. You need *help* summoning her." The girl sniffed, grabbed a halter and line off a nail, and wandered out into the pastures.

While she was gone, Fawn hastily found an old sack and filled it with what she judged to be a three-day supply of oats. Was it stealing, to take the equivalent of what her mare would have eaten anyhow? She decided not to pursue the moral fine point, as the lush grass here grew free and the grain had to be painstakingly brought in from off island. She considered hiding the sack under her skirts, decided it would involve walking funny, then, remembering that sneak thief down in Lumpton Market, just cast it over her shoulder as if she'd a right. The horse girl, when she led Grace in, didn't even ask about it.

Back at Tent Bluefield, Fawn tied Grace to a tree while she went inside, skinned into her riding clothes, and swiftly packed her saddlebags. She pulled her sharing knife from its place in Dag's trunk and slung it around her neck under her shirt, then fastened the steel knife Dag had given her to her belt. Last, she plopped plunkins into her saddlebags opposite the grain sack till they balanced, and fastened the buckles. Food and to spare for one little farmer girl for a three-day ride, and no stopping.

Finally, she fished Dag's spare quill and ink bottle from the bottom of his trunk and knelt beside it, penning a short note on a scrap of cloth. *Dear Cattagus and Sarri. Dag's company killed the malice, but he's hurt, so I'm going to Raintree to meet up with him, because he's my husband, and I have a right. Ask Dirla about the rest. Back soon. Love, Fawn.* She worked it into the tent-flap ties, where it fluttered discreetly but visibly. Then she stood on a stump to saddle Grace, heaved up and tied on her saddlebags, and climbed aboard. She was over the bridge in ten minutes more.

14

By sunset, Fawn guessed she had covered about twenty-five miles from Hickory Lake. The hours of interspersed trotting and walking, nursing her mare along in what she hoped was the best balance between speed and endurance, had given her plenty of time to think. Unfortunately, by now her thoughts were mainly variations on *Have I taken a wrong turn yet?* Fairbolt's map was not as reassuring as she'd hoped. The Lakewalker notion of roads seemed more Fawn's idea of trails; their trails, paths; and their paths, wilderness. So she wasn't altogether sorry when she heard the hoofbeats coming up behind her.

She turned in her saddle. Rounding the dense greenery of the last curve, a husky patroller rode, followed by Hoharie, her apprentice Othan towing a packhorse and a spare mount in a string, and another patroller. Fawn didn't bother trying to race ahead, but she didn't halt, either. In a moment, the others cantered up to surround her, and she let Grace drop back to a walk.

"Fawn!" cried Hoharie. "What are you doing out here?"

"Riding my fat horse," said Fawn shortly. "They told me she needed exercise."

"Fairbolt didn't give you permission to come with us."

"I'm not with you. I'm by myself."

As Hoharie sucked on her lower lip, eyes narrowed in thought, Othan chimed in. "You have to turn around and go back, farmer girl. You can't follow us."

"I'm ahead of you," Fawn pointed out. She added, "Though you're welcome to pass. Go on, run along."

Hoharie glanced back at her two patrollers, now riding side by side at the rear and watching dubiously. "I really can't spare a man to see you home."

"Nobody's asking you to."

Hoharie drew a deeper breath. "But I will, if you make me."

Fawn halted her mare and glanced back at the two big, earnest fellows. They would do their duty; that was a bit of a mania, with patrollers. If she let herself get cumbered with either one of that grim pair, he would see her back to Hickory Lake, sure enough, and in no good mood about it, likely. Patrollers had objections to leaving their partners.

Fawn tried one more time. "Hoharie, please let me come with you. I won't slow you down, I promise."

"That's not the problem, Fawn. It's your own safety. You don't belong out here."

I know where I belong, thank you very much. By Dag's side. Fawn rubbed her left arm and frowned. "I don't want to cost you your escort. If it's that unsafe, you might need them yourself." She let her shoulders slump, her head droop. "All right, Hoharie. I'm sorry. I'll turn around." She bit her tongue on any further artistic embellishments. *Keep it simple. And short.* Lakewalkers read grounds, not thoughts, Dag claimed, and Fawn's ground had plenty of other reasons to be in a roil besides duplicity.

Hoharie stared at her for a long, uncertain moment, and Fawn held her breath, lest the medicine maker be inspired to detach a guard anyhow. But finally Hoharie nodded. "You've come out a long way. If your horse can't make it back tonight, it should still be safe enough to stop if you get within ten miles of the lake."

"Grace is doing all right," Fawn said distantly, and turned away. Although she had to kick the mare back into a walk, as she was much inclined to turn and follow the other horses.

Dag's groundsense range was a mile; Fawn didn't think any of Hoharie's party had a better range, but she let Grace go on for a mile and a bit before halting, just to be safe. She slid down and let her mare browse for a few minutes before leading her back onto the road. In the summer-damp earth, the hoofprints of the Lakewalker horses showed plain even in the failing light. *No wrong turns now.* Fawn grinned and trailed after them till she could barely see in the shadows, then dismounted again and led Grace off the road to outwait the hours of darkness.

Fawn watered the mare in a nearby stream, then rubbed her down and fed her oats. She washed up herself, swatted mosquitoes, gnawed a plunkin slice, squashed a crawling tick with her knife haft, and rolled up in her blanket. The songs of the small night creatures only made the underlying stillness more profound. It weighed in upon her just how different this desolate darkness was from that of her seemingly equally lonesome trudge through the settled country south of Lumpton Market. These vasty woods did harbor wolves, and bears, and catamounts; she'd seen the skins of all three in the stores back at Hickory Lake. In the aftermath of the malice, mindless mud-men like the one Dag had slain so deftly at the Horsefords' could also be wandering around out here. She'd hardly given such hazards a thought when she'd camped during the after-wedding trip up to the lake, in woodlands not so very different. But then she'd had Dag by her side. Curling up in his arms each night had seemed like settling into her own private magical fortress. She touched the steel knife he had given her, sheathed at her belt, and sighed.

But by the first gray light of morning, neither she nor Grace had been eaten by catamounts yet. Heartened, Fawn returned to the trail and found Hoharie's tracks once more.

An hour into the ride, she was given pause when the tracks seemed to part from her map, turning off onto a path. But a closer dismounted searching found them coming back and continuing; likely the party had just diverted to a campsite for the night. A pile of recent horse droppings reassured Fawn that she remained the right distance behind. She kicked Grace along, glumly confident that she risked no chance of overtaking Hoharie prematurely. On the other hand, Grace was carrying barely half the weight of those big patrollers' mounts. Over time that might add up to more of an edge than anyone thought.

Late in the morning Hoharie's tracks were suddenly confused by those of a much larger cavalcade, going the other way. A patrol, Fawn guessed—Raintree Lakewalkers, or part of Dag's company heading home? The heavy prints turned off on another trail, and Fawn, frowning, unrolled her map and studied it. They could be diverting to visit a small Lakewalker camp marked a few miles to the south, or they could be patrolling, or who knew? Their passage rendered the trail they'd come down unmistakable, but also left Hoharie's overlying signs harder to make out in the deeply pocked muddy patches. But at midday, Fawn came to one of the rare timber bridges over a deep-flowing brown river, and was assured of her place on the map once more. From time to time she passed spots where recent deadfalls had been roughly cleared from the road, and she wondered if that was a task patrols undertook as well, when they weren't in a tearing hurry.

By late afternoon, Grace's steps were shortening and stiffening, and Fawn's backside was numb. How did couriers and their horses ever manage such distances at such speed? She dismounted and led the mare up a few of the steeper slopes, insofar as there were any in these parts, fell into resentment at the loss of precious daylight, then finally considered Dirla and ruthlessly cut a switch. This activated Grace again, making Fawn feel equally justified and guilty.

At a close-grown place where the road mud seemed wildly churned, she paused, spooking a couple of turkey vultures and some crows. The former grunted and hissed, reluctantly retreating, and the latter flapped off, yammering complaint. She peeked over the rim of a shallow ravine where the vegetation was trampled down and caught her breath at the sight of half a dozen naked, rotting corpses piled below. She ventured just close enough to be certain they were mud-men and not Lakewalkers, then hastily remounted. She wasn't sure if the patrol had slain them sometime back, or if Hoharie's guards had done for them just recently; the stench was no certain clue. The absence of visible catamounts was suddenly not enough to make her feel safe anymore. She pushed along well past sunset mainly because she was now terrified to stop.

In the deep dark that night she rolled up small and scared, sniveling miserable, stupid tears for the lack of Dag. She buried her face in her blanket edge. With none to see her, she supposed she might bawl to her heart's content, but she really didn't want to make unnecessary noise. She hoped any predator within ten miles would be too replete with scavenged mud-men to hunt farmer girls and plump, tired horses. She slept badly despite her exhaustion.

She'd figured the last morning would be the worst, and truly, she woke hurting just as much as she'd suspected she would. But it would be a much shorter leg than yesterday, and at the end of it, she would find Dag. Her cord still assured her of this; if anything, her arm throbbed more clearly, if more worrisomely, with each passing mile. Barely an hour into the morning's ride she found Hoharie's campsite just off the track, the dirt cast over the campfire ashes still warm. Only the level terrain and Fawn's switch kept Grace plodding forward into the long afternoon.

As the light flattened toward the west, Fawn rode abruptly out of the humid green of the endless woods into an open landscape metallic with heat. *We're here.*

The woods gave way to water meadows, their grasses gone yellow and limp. The sorry shrubs scattered about bore drooping brown leaves, or none. It all looked very sodden and strange. But ahead, she could see a trickle of cook-fire smoke from a stand of skeletal trees along a leaden shoreline. She didn't need her stolen map anymore, hadn't for the past two hours; her aching body bleated to her, *There, there, he's over there.* Hoharie and her little troop were just dismounting.

As Fawn rode up, Mari came striding out of the trees, waving her arms and crying urgently, "Close your grounds! Close your grounds!"

Hoharie looked startled, but waved acknowledgment and turned to check Othan and the patrollers, who apparently also obeyed. She saw Fawn, who brought Grace to a weary halt just a few paces away, and her face set, but before she could say anything, Mari, coming to her stirrup, continued.

"You're here sooner than I dared hope! Dirla fetch you?"

"Yes," said Hoharie.

"Praise the girl. Did you run across the patrol we sent back home?"

"Yes, about a day out of Hickory Lake."

"Ah, good." Mari's eye fell on Fawn, hunched over her saddlebow. "Why'd you bring her?" The tone of the question was not dismissive, but genuinely curious, as though there might be some very good, if obscure, Lakewalkerish reason for Fawn's presence in Hoharie's train.

Hoharie grimaced. "I didn't. She brought herself."

Fawn tossed her head.

Othan leaned over and hissed at her, "You lied, farmer girl! You promised to turn around!"

"I did," said Fawn defiantly. "Twice."

Hoharie looked not-best-pleased, but the shrewd and curious look on Mari's face scarcely changed.

"Did you get a look at Utau, when you passed the patrol?" asked Mari. "We sent him home in Razi's care."

"Oh, yes," said Hoharie. She dismounted and stretched her back. Really, all her party looked as hot and tired and dirty as Fawn felt. So much for Lakewalker conceit about their stamina. "Strangest ground damage I ever saw. I told Utau, six months on the sick list."

"That long?" Mari looked dismayed.

"Likely less, but that'll hold Fairbolt off for three, which should be about right."

They exchanged short laughs of mutual understanding.

Fawn slid off sweaty Grace, who stood head down and flop-eared, liquid eyes reproachful, legs as stiff as Fawn's own. Saun came out of the grove to Mari's shoulder, trailed by a couple of other patrollers, both older women. As the women began to confer with Hoharie and Mari, he strode up to Fawn, looking astonished.

"You shouldn't be out here! Dag would have a fit."

"Where *is* Dag?" She craned past him toward the grove. *So close.* "What's happened to him?"

Saun ran a hand over his head in a harried swipe. "Which time?"

Not a reassuring answer. "Day before yesterday, about the time Dirla rode in to Hickory Lake. Something happened to Dag then, I know it. I *felt* it." *Something terrible?*

His brows drew down in wonder, but he caught her by the arm as she tried to push past him. "Wait! You can't close your ground. I don't know if you'd be drawn in, too—wait!" She wrenched out of his grip and broke into a stumbling run. He pelted after, crying in exasperation, "Blight it, you're as bad as him!"

Among the trees, a number of people seemed to be collected together in bedrolls under makeshift awnings of blankets and hides, four women under one and four men under another. They lay too still for sleep; not still enough for death. A little way off, another bedroll was partly shaded under a blanket hitched to an ash tree's limbs. Fawn fell to her knees beside it and stared in shock.

Dag lay faceup under a light blanket. Someone had removed his arm harness and set it atop his saddlebags at the head of the bedroll. Fawn had watched his beloved face in sleep, and knew its shape in all its subtle movements. This was like no sleep she'd ever seen. The copper of his skin seemed tarnished and dull, and his flesh stretched too tightly over his bones. His sunken eyes were ringed with dark half circles. But his bare chest rose and fell; he breathed, he lived.

Saun slid to his knees beside her and grabbed her hands as she reached for Dag. "No!"

"Why not?" said Fawn furiously, yanking futilely against his strong grip. "What's *happened* to him?"

Saun began to give her a garbled and guilty-sounding account of his trying to help by slaying mud-men in pots— Fawn gazed in bewilderment toward the boggy shoreline where he pointed—that she could only follow at all because of the prior descriptions of the groundlock she'd heard from Dirla. Of Dag, leaping into the eerie danger to save somebody named Artin, which sounded just like Dag, truly. Of Dag being sucked into the lock, or spell, or whatever this was. Of Dag lying unarousable all these three days gone. Fawn stopped fighting, and Saun, with a stern look at her, let her wrists go; she rubbed them and scowled.

"But I'm not a Lakewalker. I'm a farmer," said Fawn. "Maybe it wouldn't work on me."

"Mari says no more experiments," said Saun grimly. "They've already cost us three patrollers and the captain."

"But if you don't . . ." *If you don't poke at things, how can you find anything out?* She sat back on her heels, lips tight. All right: look around first, poke later. Dag's breathing didn't seem to be getting worse right away, anyhow.

Mari, meanwhile, had led Hoharie and Othan out to the mud pots, then back through the grove to examine the other captives. Mari was finishing what sounded to Fawn like a more coherent account of events than Saun's as they came over and knelt on the other side of Dag. Her tale of Dag's ground match with Artin's failing heart had the medicine maker letting out her breath in a faint whistle. Even more frightening to Fawn was Mari's description of the strange blight left on Dag's ground from his fight with the malice.

"Huh." Hoharie scrubbed at her heat-flushed face, smearing road dirt in sweaty streaks, and stared around. "For the love of reason, Mari, what did you drag me here for? In one breath you beg me to break this unholy groundlock, and in the next you insist I don't dare even open my ground to examine it. You can't have it both ways."

"If Dag went into that thing and couldn't get himself out, I know I couldn't. I don't know about you. Hoped you'd have more tricks, Hoharie." Mari's voice fell quiet. "I've been picking at this knot for days, now, till I'm near cross-eyed crazy. I'm starting to wonder when it will be time to cut our losses. Except . . . all of those makers' own bonded knives went missing during the time they were prisoners of the malice. Of the nine people down, only Bryn is carrying an unprimed knife right now. That's not much to salvage, for the price. And I'm not real sure what would happen to someone locked up like that trying to share, or to her knife—or to the others. We had ill luck with those mud-puppies, that's certain."

Saun, now leaning against the barren ash tree with his arms folded, grimaced agreement.

Fawn's belly shuddered as it finally dawned on her what Mari was talking about. The picture of Mari, or Saun, or Hoharie—likely Mari, it seemed her idea of a leader's duty— taking those bone knives and methodically driving them through the hearts of her comrades, going down the rows of bedrolls one after another . . . *No, not Dag!* Fawn touched the knife beneath her shirt, suddenly fiercely glad that her accident with it back at Glassforge had at least blocked this ghastly possibility.

Hoharie was frowning, but it seemed to Fawn more in sorrow than dissent.

"I will say," said Mari, "Dag falling into this lock seemed to give everyone in it new strength—for a little while. But the weaker ones are failing again. If we were to add a new patroller every three days, I don't rightly know how long we could keep them alive—except, of course, the problem would just get bigger and bigger as we strung it out. I'm not volunteerin', note. And I'm not volunteerin' you either, Hoharie, so don't go getting ideas."

Hoharie rubbed the back of her neck. "I'm going to have to get ideas of some sort. But I'm not going to attempt anything at all tonight. Fatigue distorts judgment."

Mari nodded approval, and described the camp off the blight to the east where everyone not tending the enspelled apparently retreated to sleep. When she paused, Fawn motioned at Dag and broke in, "Mari—is it really true I can't touch him?"

Mari said, "It may be. The finding out could be costly."

Or not, thought Fawn. "I rode all this way."

Hoharie said, in a sort of weary sympathy, "We told you to stay home, child. There's nothing for you to do here but grieve."

"And get in the way," muttered Othan, almost inaudibly.

"But I can *feel* Dag. Still!"

Hoharie did not look hopeful, but she rose to her knees, reached across Dag, and took up Fawn's left arm anyway, probing along it. "Has it changed any lately?"

"The ache feels stronger for being closer, but no clearer," Fawn admitted. "It's funny. Dag gave me this for reassurance, but instead it's made me frantic."

"Is that you or him that's frantic?"

"I can't hardly tell the difference."

"Huh." Hoharie let her go and sat back. "This gets us no further that I can see. Yet." With a pained grunt, she rose to her feet, and everyone else did too.

Fawn held out her hands, palms open, to Mari. "Surely there's something I can do!"

Mari looked at her and sighed, but at least it was a sigh of understanding. "There's bedding and catch-rags to be washed."

Fawn's hands clenched. "I can do that, sure." Better: it was a task that would keep her here in the grove, and not exiled a mile away.

"Oh, *that's* important. You rode a long way to do laundry, farmer girl," said Othan, and missed the cool look that the Lakewalker women turned on him. It was no stretch to Fawn to guess who had been doing the washing so far.

Mari said more firmly, "Not that there's a pile. It's so hard to get anything into these people, there's not much coming out. In any case, not tonight, Fawn. You look bushed."

Fawn admitted it with a short nod. When it was all sorted out, the party's horses, including Grace, were led off to the east camp by the patrollers, but Fawn managed to keep her bedroll and saddlebags in the grove by Dag. It was driving her half-mad not to be allowed to touch him, but she set about finding other tasks for her hands, helping with the fire and the batches of broths and thin gruel that these experienced women had cooking.

Hoharie commenced a second, more thorough physical examination of all the silent groundlocked folk, an expression of extreme frustration on her face. "I might as well be some farmer bonesetter," Fawn heard her mutter as she knelt by Dag. The tart thought came to Fawn that really, they might all be better off with one; farmer bonesetters and midwives always had to work by guess and by golly, with indirect clues. They likely grew good at it, over time.

Resolutely, Fawn took on the laundry the following morning as soon as she could rise and move. At least the work

abused different muscles than the ones she'd overtaxed the
past three days. Riding trousers rolled above her knees, she
waded out into the cool water of the marsh towing a makeshift raft of lashed-together deadwood holding the soiled
blankets and catch-rags. The water seemed peculiarly clear
and odorless, for a marsh, but it was fine for washing. And
she could keep an eye on the long lumpy shadow beneath the
ash tree that was Dag, and see the silhouettes of the ground-
closed helpers moving about the grove.

To her surprise one of the Lakewalker men, not a patroller
but a survivor from the ruined village down the shore, came
out and joined her in the task, silently taking up the rubbing
and scrubbing by her side. He said only, "You're Dag Redwing's farmer bride," not a question but a statement; Fawn
could only nod. He had a funny look on his face, drawn and
distant, that made Fawn shy of speaking to him, though she
murmured thanks as they passed clouts back and forth. He
took the main burden of lugging the heavy, wet cloths back
to the blighted trees, and, being much taller, of hanging them
up on the bare branches after she shook them out. The only
other thing he said, rather abruptly as they finished and he
turned away, was, "Artin the smith is my father, see."

Hoharie paced around the grove and squinted, or walked
out to a distance and stared, or sat on a stump and drew
formless lines on the ground with a stick, scowling. She
went methodically through an array of more startling
actions, yelling at or slapping the sleepers, pricking them
with a pin, stirring up the half-formed mud-men in their
pots. Mari and Saun, with difficulty, dissuaded her from
killing another one by way of a test. Flushed after her futile
exertions, she came and sat cross-legged by Dag's bedroll,
scowling some more.

Fawn sat across from her nibbling on a raw plunkin slice.
She wished she could feed Dag—would the taste of genuine
Hickory Lake plunkin be like home cooking to him? But
even if she could touch him, he could not chew—he could

barely swallow water. She supposed she might try cooking
and mashing up some of the root and thinning it down for a
gruel, disgusting as that sounded. She asked Hoharie quietly,
"What do you figure?"

Hoharie shook her head. "This isn't just a lovers' groundlock enlarged. Something of the malice must linger in it. Has
to be an involuted ground reinforcement of some sort, to survive the malice's death; what it's living *on* is a puzzle. Well,
not much of a puzzle; it has to be ground, the mud-men's or
the people's or both. People's, most likely."

"Like . . . like a tick? Or a belly-worm? Made of ground,"
Fawn added, to show she wasn't confused about that.

Hoharie gave a vague wave that seemed to allow the comparison without exactly approving it. "It has to be worked
ground. Malice-worked. Could be—well, it obviously is—
quite complex. I still don't understand the part about it being
so anchored in place. Question is, how long can it last? Will
it be absorbed like a healing reinforcement? And if so, will
it strengthen or slay? Is it just their groundlock paralysis that
is weakening these folks, or is there something more eating
away at them, inside?"

At Fawn's faint gasp Hoharie's eyes flicked up; she glanced
from Dag to Fawn, and murmured, "Oh, sorry. Talking to
myself, I'm afraid."

"It's all right. I want to know everything."

"So do I, child," Hoharie sighed. She levered to her feet
and wandered off again.

Saun having gone off to the east camp to sleep after
taking a night watch, it was Othan who came at noon to
feed Dag broth. Fawn watched enviously and critically as he
raised Dag's head into his lap, wincing at every harsh *click*
of spoon on teeth or muffled choke or dribble lost down over
Dag's chin. At least Dag's face wasn't rough with stubble;
Saun had shaved it just this morning. Fawn had wondered
at the effort, since Dag couldn't feel it—but somehow it did
make him look less sick. So maybe the use of it was not for

Dag, but for the people who looked so anxiously after him. She had smiled gratefully at Saun, anyhow.

Othan, on the other hand, glowered at her as he worked.

"What?" she finally demanded.

"You're hovering. Back off, can't you? Half a mile would do."

"I've a right. He's my husband."

"That hasn't been decided yet."

Fawn touched her marriage cord. "Dag and I decided it. Quite a ways back down the road."

"You'll find out, farmer." Othan coaxed the last spoonful of broth down his patient's throat, which moved just enough to swallow, and laid Dag's head back down on the folded blanket that substituted, poorly, for a pillow. Fawn considered collecting dry grass to stuff it with, later. Othan added, "He was a good patroller. Hoharie says he could be even more. They say you've seduced him from his duty and will be the ruination of his life if the camp council doesn't fix things."

Fawn sat up indignantly. *"They say?* So let *them say* it to my face, if they're not cowards." *And anyhow, I think we sort of seduced each other.*

"My uncle who's a patroller says it, and he's no coward!"

Fawn gritted her teeth as Othan—safely ground-closed Othan—stroked a strand of sweat-dampened hair back from Dag's forehead. How dare he act as if he owned Dag, just because he was Lakewalker-born and she wasn't! The, the *stupid* boy was just a wet-behind-the-ears apprentice no older than she was. Younger, likely. Her longing to shut Othan up, make him look nohow, was quelled by her sudden realization that he might be a lead into just the sort of camp gossip Dag had so carefully shielded her from. Also—this was half an argument. Just what all had Dag been saying back to Hickory Lake Camp? She recalled the day he'd made that poor plunkin into a porcupine with his bow and her arrows. Her spinning mind settled on, "I'm not a patch on your malices, for ruination."

"They're not *our* malices."

Fawn smiled blackly. "Oh, yes, they are." She added after a fuming moment, "And there isn't any *was* about it, unless you want to say he *was* a good patroller, and he now *is* a really good captain! He took his company right through that awful Raintree malice like a knife through butter, to hear Dirla tell it. Despite being married to a farmer, so there!"

"Despite, yeah," Othan growled.

Fawn took a grip on her shredding temper as Mari and Hoharie came up. Othan scrambled to his feet, giving over glaring at Fawn in order to look anxiously at the medicine maker. Hoharie looked grim, and Mari grimmer.

"Which one, then?" said Mari.

"Dag," said Hoharie. "I've worked on his ground enough to be most familiar with it, and he's also the most recent to fall into the lock. If that counts for anything. Othan, good, you're here," she continued without a pause. "I'm going to enter this groundlock, and I want you to try to anchor me."

Othan looked alarmed. "Are you sure, Hoharie?"

"No, but I've tried everything else I can think of. And I won't walk away from this."

"No, you're leaving that dirty job to me," muttered Mari irritably. Hoharie returned her the sort of sharp shrug that indicated a lengthy argument concluded.

Hoharie went on, "I'll set up a light link to you, Othan, and try for a glimpse inside the groundlock, then pull back. If I can't disengage, you are to break with me instantly and *not* try to enter in after me, do you hear?" She caught her apprentice's gaze and held it sternly. Othan gulped and nodded.

Fawn scrunched back in the litter of dry grass and dead leaves on Dag's far side, wrapping her arms around her knees and trying to make herself small, so they wouldn't notice and exclude her.

Hoharie paused, then said, "My knife is in my saddlebags, Mari, if it comes to that."

"When should it come to it, Hoharie? Don't leave me with that decision, too."

"When the weakest start to die, I believe it will throw more strain on the rest. So it will go faster toward the end. That poor maker who died before Dag's patrol arrived showed that such deaths won't break the lock; if anything, it may grow more concentrated. I think . . . once two or more of the nine—no, ten—are down, then start the sharing. And you'll just have to see what happens next." She added after a moment, "Start with me, of course."

"That," said Mari distantly, "will be my turn to pick."

Hoharie's lips thinned. "Mm."

"I don't recommend this, Hoharie."

"I hear you."

Evidently not, because the medicine maker lowered herself cross-legged by the head of Dag's bedroll, motioning Othan down beside her. He sat up on his knees. She straightened her spine and shut her eyes for a moment, seeming to center herself. She then took Othan's hand with her left hand; there apparently followed another moment of invisible-to-Fawn ground adjustments. Without further hesitation, Hoharie's right hand reached out and touched Dag's forehead. Fawn thought she saw him grimace in his trance, but it was hard to be sure.

Then Hoharie's eyes opened wide; with a yank, she pulled her hand from Othan's and slammed the heel of it into his chest, pushing him over backward. Her eyes rolled up, her face drained of color and expression, and she slumped across Dag.

With a muted wail, Othan scrambled up and dove for her. Mari cursed and caught Othan from behind, wrapping her arms around his torso and trapping his hands. "No!" she yelled in his ear. "Obey her! Close up! Close up, blight you, boy!"

Othan strained against her briefly, then, with a choke of despair, sprawled back in her grip.

"Ten," snarled Mari. "That's it, that's all we're doing here.
Not eleven, you hear?" She shook him.

Othan nodded dully, and she let him free. He leaned on
his hands, staring at his unconscious mentor in horror.

"What did you feel?" Mari demanded of him. "Anything?"

He shook his head. "I—nothing useful, I don't think. It
was like I could feel her ground being pulled away from
me, into the dark . . . !" He turned a distraught face to the
patrol leader. "I didn't let go, Mari, I didn't! She pushed me
away!"

"I saw, boy," sighed Mari. "You did what you could."
Slowly, she stood up, and braced her legs apart and her hands
on her hips, staring down at the two enspelled in their heap.
"We'll lay her out with the rest. She's in there with them
now; maybe she can do something different. If this thing
was weakening with age, could we tell? If nothing else, she
may have bought three more days of time." Her voice fell to
a savage mutter. "Except I don't want more time. I want this
to be *over*."

Hoharie's bedroll was placed under the ash tree close to
Dag's. Othan took up a cross-legged station of guard, or
grief, on the opposite side to Fawn, who sat similarly beyond
Dag. They didn't much look at each other.

Toward sunset, Mari came and sat down between the two
bedrolls.

"Blight you two," she said conversationally to the unconscious pair, "for leaving this on me. This is company captain
work, not patrol leader work. No fair slithering out of it, Dag
my boy." She looked up and caught Fawn's eye from where
she lay on her side near Dag. Fawn sat up and returned an
inquiring look.

"Bryn"—Mari hooked a thumb over her shoulder toward

the rank of female sleepers beneath their awning—"will be all of twenty-two next week. If she has a next week. She's young. Good groundsense range. She might yet grow up to have a passel of youngsters. Hoharie, I've known her longer. A medicine maker has valuable skills. She might yet save the lives of a dozen girls like Bryn. So how shall I decide which first? Some choice. Maybe," she sighed, "maybe it won't make any difference. I hardly know which way to wish for.

"Agh! Pay no attention to my maunderings, girl," Mari continued, as Fawn's stare widened. "I think I'm getting too old. I'm going to go sleep off this blight tonight. It drains your wits as well as your strength, blight does. All despair and death. You get into this mood." She clambered back to her feet and gazed blearily down over Dag's supine form at Fawn. "I know you can't feel the blight direct, but it's working on you, too. You should take a break off this deathly ground as well."

Fawn shook her head. "I want to stay here. By Dag." *For whatever time we have left*.

Mari shrugged. "Suit yourself, then." She wandered away into the softening twilight.

Fawn awoke to moonlight filtering down through the ash tree's bare branches. She lay a moment in her bedroll trying to recapture her dreams, hoping for something usefully prophetic. In ballads, people often had dreams that told them what to do; you were supposed to follow instructions precisely, too, or risk coming to several stanzas of grief. But she remembered no dreams. She doubted they'd reveal anything even if she did.

Farmer dreams. Perhaps if she'd been Lakewalker-born . . . she scowled at Othan, asleep and snoring faintly on the other side of Hoharie. If anyone were to have any useful uncanny visions, it would more likely be him, blight him.

No, not "blight him." That wasn't fair. Reluctantly, she allowed he had courage, as he'd shown this afternoon, and Hoharie would not have favored him out of her other apprentices and brought him along if he didn't have promise as well. It was merely that Fawn would feel better if he were completely stupid, and not just stupid about farmers. Then he wouldn't be able to make her doubt herself so much. She sighed and rose to pick her way out to the slit trench at the far edge of the grove.

Returning, she sat up on her blanket and studied Dag. The stippled moonlight made his unmoving face look disturbingly corpse-colored. The dark night-glitter of his eyes, smiling at her, would have redeemed it all, but they remained sunken and shut. He might die, she thought, without her ever seeing their bright daylight gold again. She swallowed the scared lump in her throat. Would they let her touch him after he was dead? *I could touch him now.* But there was little she could do for him physically that wasn't already being done more safely by others. *Wait on that, then.*

Involuted ground reinforcement. She rolled the phrase over in her mind as if tasting it. It clearly meant something quite specific to Hoharie, and doubtless to Dag and Mari as well. And Othan. A ground reinforcement curling up on itself, which didn't gradually become part of its new owner? She rubbed her arm, and wondered if the ground reinforcement Dag had done on her was involuted or not. If she followed Hoharie's explanation, it seemed that the *involution* was a cut-off bit of malice, like her own was a cut-off bit of Dag. Remembering the Glassforge malice, she was glad she and Dag had stopped it before it had developed such far-flung powers.

Her brows bent. Had Hoharie ever seen a malice up as close as Fawn had? Makers seemed to stay back in camp, mostly. So maybe not. Sharing knives might be complicated to make, but they were so simple to use, a farmer child might do so—as Fawn had proven. She smiled now to remember Dag's wild cry: *Sharp end first!*

Her thoughts fell like water drops into a still pool.

Sharing knives kill malices.

There's a bit of leftover malice in Dag and Artin and these other people.

Maybe it just needs an extra dose of mortality to finish cleaning it out.

. . . I have a sharing knife.

She inhaled, shuddering. It wasn't possible for her to think of something to try that Dag and Mari and Hoharie hadn't, and already dismissed for some good reason that Fawn was simply too ignorant to know. Was it?

There was a lot of Lakewalker emotion and habit tied up in sharing knives. Sacrificial in every sense, *sacred*. Not seen as a fit subject for idle fooling around with. She hunched over, wide-awake now.

It didn't have to be through the heart, did it? That was only for unprimed knives, first collecting their dose of mortality. For discharging the death, anywhere in the malice's groundworked body would apparently do. She might have stabbed the Glassforge malice in the foot, to the same stunning effect. So where were the, the malice bits lodged in the enspelled Lakewalkers? Pooled or diffuse, they all had to be connected, because to touch any of them triggered the same trap.

Her knife, Dar had said, was of dubious potency and value. No affinity. *But it's the only one I have a right to.*

Her eyes turned to Dag. *And he's the only one I have a right to. So.*

Swiftly, before her nerve failed her, she rose and, careful not to touch his skin, delicately drew down his blanket. She lifted it past his ribbed chest, his loose breechclout, his long legs, letting it fall again in folds at his feet. His body was all sculpted shadows in the moonlight, too thin. She'd thought she'd started to put some meat on his bones, but it

was all used up again by the past weeks of dire strain, and
then some.

Not the heart, not the eye—*eew!*—not the gut. For nonlethal flesh wounds, one was pretty much limited to arms and
legs, carefully away from where those big veins and nerves
ran down. Under the arm would be bad, she was pretty sure,
likewise the back of the knee and the inner thigh. Better
the outer thigh, or the arm just below the shoulder. Dag's
strappy arm muscles didn't seem all that thick, compared
to the length of the bone blade hanging around her neck.
Thigh, then. She crouched down.

If Hoharie had been conscious, Fawn could have asked
her. But then Fawn would still be waiting for the Lakewalker
expert to fix things, and likely would not have conceived
this desperate notion at all. Now the medicine maker lay
entranced with the rest, leaving only Othan in charge. Fawn
wouldn't have asked Othan for a drink in a downpour, nor
have expected him to give her one. Still . . .

Am I about to be stupid again?

Think it through.

This might do nothing, in which case she would have to
clean the blood off her knife and explain the ugly hole in
her husband tomorrow morning. Envisioning which, she
scrambled back to her saddlebags and dug out one of her
spare clean ragbags stuffed with cattail fluff, and some cord.
There, a good bandage.

This might do what she hoped.

This might do something awful. But something awful was
going to happen anyhow. She could not make things worse.

Right, then.

She laid out the makeshift swab, dragged her pouch from
around her neck, and pulled out the pale knife. The little
delay had sapped her courage. She hunkered by Dag's left
hip a moment, trying to gather it again. She wished she could
pray, but the gods, they said, were absent. She had nothing to
trust in now but her own wits.

She swallowed a whimper. *Dag says you're smart. If you can't trust you, trust him.*

Sharp end first. Anywhere. She drew back her hand, took careful aim at what she hoped was all nice thick muscle, then plunged the bone knife in till the tip nicked against Dag's own bone. Still without ever touching him. Dag grunted and jerked in his sleep. She whipped her shaking hand away from the hilt, which stood out from his lean thigh, all indigo blue and ivory in the silver light.

From over her shoulder, Othan's voice screamed, "What are you *doing*, you crazy farmer?"

He reached to clamp her shoulders and drag her roughly back from Dag. But not before she saw Dag's left arm jolt up from his bedroll as though its invisible hand was wrapping itself around the sharing knife's hilt, and heard the faint, familiar *snap* of splintering bone blade.

15

He had floated in an increasingly timeless gray fog, all distinctions fading. It seemed a just consolation that with them faded all fear, want, and pain. But then, inexplicably, something bright and warm troubled his shredding perceptions, as if the north star had torn herself loose from the sky and ventured too near him in naive, luminous, fatal curiosity. *Don't fall, no . . . stay away, Spark!* Longing and horror wrenched him, for to grasp that joy would slay it. *Is it my fate to blight all that I love?*

But the star fire didn't touch him. Later, a bolt of new strength shot through him, and for a short time, coherent thought came back. Some other light had fallen into this prison, also known to him . . . He recognized Hoharie's intense ground in all its ever-astonishing vigor—so strange that such a spring of strength should dwell in such a slight and unassuming body. But the hope it should have brought him turned to ashes as he took in her anger, horror, and frustration.

I thought sure you'd figure the trick of it from out there, as I could not—I'm the blinder one, I had to look to see it.

And the wailing answer, *I had to look to be sure . . . I had to be certain . . . oh, Dag, I am so sorry . . .* before the fog blurred all to voiceless sorrow once more.

He raced to make his watch rounds in this brief, stolen respite, to count his company as every captain should. Artin, yes, barely holding on, his ground so drained as to be translucent at the edges; Bryn and Ornig; Mallora; the other

Bonemarsh makers. And now Hoharie. He remembered to count himself. Ten, all dying in place. Again he led those who had trusted in him into the boundless dark. *At least this time I can't desert them.*

More timelessness. Gray mouths leeched him.

The star fire moved too close again, and he breathed dread like cold mist. But the sky-spark held something else, a faint, familiar chime; her fair light and its wordless song wound together. Their intertwined beauty overthrew his heart. *This is surely the magic of the whole wide green world; Lakewalker groundwork has nothing to compare with it . . .*

And then pain and the song pierced him.

He could feel every detail of the roiling ground that stabbed into his thigh: Kauneo's bone, his own blood of old, the involuted and shaped vessel for mortality that was the gift of the Luthlian knife maker. Spark's daughter's death, death without birth, self-making and self-dissolution intermingled in their purest forms.

Too pure. It lay self-contained within the involution, innocent of all taint of desire, motion, and time. *It lacks affinity* seemed too flat a statement to sum up its aloof stillness. Free of all attachment. Free of all pain.

We give best from abundance. I can share pain.

Flying as never before, he raised his arm by its ground, and his ghost hand—pure ground, piebald with blight and malice spatter—wrapped the hilt and the ground of the hilt. His own old blood gave him entry into the involution; he let his blackened ground trace up its ancient, dried path; catch; hold; and he remembered the night Fawn had woven his wedding cord with bloody fingers, and so drawn her own ground into it. And her wide-open eyes and unguarded offer, later, on another night of ground-weaving, *Need blood?* As if she would gladly have opened her veins on the spot and poured all that vivid flood into his cupped hands, sparing nothing. *As she does now.*

Do not waste her gift, old patroller.

His blackened touch seemed a violation, but he twisted the mortal ground between his ghost fingers the way Fawn spun thread. He grinned somewhere inside himself to imagine Dar's outraged voice, *You used a* wedding-cord *technique on a* sharing knife . . . *?* The involution uncoiled, giving up its long burden into his hand. Kauneo's bone cracked joyfully, a sound beneath sound heard not with his ears but in his groundsense, and he knew in that moment that Dar's theory of how the farmer babe's death had entered his knife was entirely wrong-headed, but he had no time now to examine it. He held mortality in his hand, and it would not wait.

Within his hand, not upon it; the two were as inextricable as two fibers spun into one strong thread. *Affinity.* Now, at last, he closed his hand upon the malice's dark construction.

His ghost hand twisted, stretched, and tore apart as the mortality flowed from him into the gray mouths, along the lines of draining hunger, and he howled without sound in the agony of that wrenching. The malice spatters on his body were ripped out from their patches of blight as if dragged along on a towline, gashing through his ground and out his arm. The dazzling fire raced, consuming its dark path as it traveled. The gray fog-threads of the malice's involution blazed up in fire all over the grove, leaving a web of red sparks hanging for a moment as if suspended in air. When it reached the mud-men's dense impelling ground-shapes, they exploded in fiery pinwheels, their aching afterimages spinning in Dag's groundsense, weighty as whirlpools peeling off a paddle's trailing edge.

Then—quiet.

Dag had not known that silence could reverberate so; or maybe that was just him. When a long strain was released, the recoil itself could become a new source of pain . . . No, actually, that was just his body. He'd thought he'd missed his body, back when his mind had been set adrift from it in that ground-fog; now he was not so sure. Its pangs were all suddenly very distinctive indeed. Head, neck, back, arm, haunches all cried out, and his bladder definitely clamored for attention. His body was noisy, cranky, and insistent. But he sought something more urgent.

He pried his eyes open, blinking away the glue and sand that seemed to cement his lids together. He was staring up at bare silvered branches and a night sky washed with moonlight strong enough to cast interlaced shadows. Across the grove, voices were moaning in surprise or crying out in shock. Shouts of alarm transmuted to triumph.

In the blue moonlight and red flare of new wood thrown on a nearby fire, a baffling sight met his gaze. Fawn and Hoharie's apprentice Othan seemed to be dancing. Or perhaps wrestling. It was hard to be sure. Othan was breathing hard through his nose; Fawn had both hands wrapped around one of his wrists and was swinging from it, dragging his arm down. His boots stamped in an unbalanced circle as he tried to shake her off, cursing.

Dag cleared his throat and said mildly, albeit in a voice as rusty and plaintive as an old gate hinge, "Othan, quit manhandling my wife. Get your own farmer girl."

The two sprang apart, and Othan gasped, "Sir! I wasn't—"

What he wasn't, Dag didn't hear, because with a sob of joy Fawn threw herself down across his chest and kissed him. He thought his mouth tasted as foul as an old bird's nest, but strangely, she didn't seem to mind. His left arm, deadened, wasn't working. His right weighed far too much, but he hoisted it into the air somehow and, after an uncertain wobble, let it fall across her, fingers clutching contentedly.

He had no idea why or how she was here. It was likely a Fawn-fluke. Her solid wriggling warmth suggested hopefully that she was not a hallucination, not that he was in the best shape to distinguish, just now.

She stopped kissing him long enough to gasp, "Dag, I'm so sorry I had to stab you! I couldn't think of any other way. Does it hurt bad?"

"Mm?" he said vaguely. He was more numb than in pain, but he became aware of a shivering ache in his left thigh. He tried to raise his head, failed, and stirred his leg instead. An utterly familiar knife haft drifted past his focus. He blinked in bemusement. "A foot higher and I'd have thought you were mad at me, Spark."

Her helpless laughter wavered into weeping. The drops fell warm across his chest, and he stroked her shuddering shoulder and murmured wordlessly.

After a moment she gulped and raised her face. "You have to let me go."

"No, I don't," he said amiably.

"We have to get those bone fragments dug out of your leg. I didn't know how far to stick it in, so I pushed it all the way, I'm afraid."

"Thorough as ever, I see."

She shrugged out of his weak grip and escaped, but grinned through her tears, so that was likely all right. He eased open his groundsense a fraction, aware of something deeply awry in his own body's ground just below his perceptions, but managed a head count of the people in the grove before he tightened up again. All alive. Some very weak, but *all* alive. Someone had flung himself onto a horse bareback and was galloping for the east camp. Othan was diverted from his farmer-wrestling to tend on Hoharie, struggling up out of her bedroll. Dag gave up captaining, lay back with a sigh of boundless fatigue, and let them all do whatever they wanted.

In due course Othan came back with Hoharie's kit and some lights and commenced some pretty unpleasant fiddling about down by Dag's side. Weary Hoharie directed, and Fawn hovered. That the blade should hurt worse coming out than going in made some sense, but not that it should do so more *often*. Voices muttered, rose and fell. "It's bleeding so much!" "That's all right. It'll wash the wound out a bit. Now the swab." "Hoharie, do you know what that swab *is*?" "Othan, think. Of course I do. Very clever, Fawn. Now tie the strips down tight. No peeking under it, unless it soaks through." "Did he get it all?" "Yes, look—fit the pieces together like a puzzle, and check for missing chips or fragments. All smooth, see?" "Oh, yes!" "Hoharie, it's like his ground is *shredded*. Hanging off him in strips. I've never felt anything like!" "I saw when it happened. It was spectacular. Get the bleeding stopped, get everyone off this blight and over to the east camp. Get me some *food*. Then we'll tackle it."

The evacuation resembled a torchlight parade, organized by the folks who came pelting over from the east camp, all dressed by guess and riotous with relief. Those freed from the groundlock who could sit a horse were led off two to a mount, holding each other upright, and the rest were carried. Dag was carted eastward feetfirst on a plank; Saun's face, grinning loonlike, drifted past his gaze in the flickering shadows. Mari's voice complained loudly about missing the most exciting part. Dag gripped Fawn's hand for the whole mile and refused to let go.

The east camp didn't settle down till dawn. Fawn woke again near noon, trapped underneath Dag's outflung arm. She just lay there for a while, relishing the lovely weight of it and the slow breath ruffling her curls. Eventually, she gently eased out from under, sat up, and looked around. She thought it a measure of Dag's exhaustion that her motions didn't wake him the way they usually did.

Their bedroll was sheltered under a sort of half tent of bent saplings splinted together supporting a blanket roof. Half-private. The camp extended along the high side of a little creek, well shaded by green, unblighted trees; maybe twenty or twenty-five patrollers seemed to be moving about, some going for water or out to the horse lines, some tending cook fires, several clustered around bedrolls feeding tired-looking folks who nevertheless were doggedly sitting up.

At length, Dag woke too, then it was her turn to help him prop up his shoulders against his saddlebags. Happily, she fed him. He could both chew and swallow, and not choke; halfway through, he revived enough to start capturing the bits of plunkin or roast deer from her with his right hand and feed himself. His hand still trembled too much to manage his water cup without spilling, though. His left arm, more disturbingly, didn't move at all, and she suspected the bandage wrapping his left leg disguised even deeper ills than the knife wound. His eyes were bloodshot and squinty, more glazed than bright, but she reveled in their gold glints nonetheless, and the way they smiled at her as though they'd never quit.

In all, Fawn was glad when Hoharie came by, even if she was trailed by Othan. She was accompanied and supported by Mari, whose general air of relief clouded when her eye fell on Dag. The medicine maker looked fatigued, but not nearly as ravaged as Dag, perhaps because her time in the lock had been the shortest. She had all her formidable wits back about her, anyhow.

Othan unwrapped the leg, and Hoharie pronounced his neat stitches that closed the vertical slit to be good tight work, and the redness only to be expected and not a sign of infection yet, and they would do some groundwork later to prevent adhesions. Othan seemed even more relieved at the chance to rewrap the wound with more usual sorts of patroller bandages.

While this was going on, Mari reported: "Before you ask three times, Dag—everyone made it out of the groundlock alive."

Dag's eyes squeezed shut in thankfulness. "I was pretty sure. Is Artin going to hold on? His heart took hurt, there, I thought."

"Yes, but his son has him well in hand. All the Raintree

folks could be carried off by their kin as early as tomorrow, at least as far as the next camp. They'll recover better there than out here in the woods."

Dag nodded.

"Once they're away our folks will be getting anxious to see home again, too. Bryn and Ornig are up already, and I don't think Mallora will be much behind. Young, y'know. I don't know about you, but I'm right tired of this place. With that hole in your leg it's plain you're not walking anywhere. It's up to Hoharie to say how soon you can ride."

"Ask me tomorrow," said Hoharie. "The leg's not really the worst of it."

"So what about the arm, Hoharie?" Dag asked hesitantly. His voice still sounded like something down in a swamp, croaking. "It's a bit worryin', not moving like that. Kind of takes me back to some memories I don't much care to revisit."

Hoharie grimaced understanding. "I can see why." As Othan tied off the new dressing and sat back, she added quietly, "Time to give me a look. You have to open yourself, Dag."

"Yeah," he sighed. He didn't sound at all enthusiastic, Fawn thought. But he lay back against his saddle prop with a faraway look on his face; his lips moved in something deeper than a wince. Mari hissed, Hoharie's lips pursed, and Othan, who had sewn up bleeding flesh without a visible qualm, looked suddenly ill.

"Well, that's a bigger mess than Utau, and I thought he was impressive," allowed Hoharie. "Let me see what I can do with this."

"You can't do a ground reinforcement after all you just went through!" Dag objected.

"I have enough oomph left for one," she replied, her face going intent. "I was saving it for you. Figured . . ."

Fawn tugged at Mari and whispered urgently, "What's going on? What do you all sense?" *That I can't.*

"The ground down his left side's all marked up with blight, like big deep bruises," Mari whispered back. "But those nasty black malice spatters that I felt before seem to be gone now—that's a real good sign, I reckon. The ground of his left arm, though, is hanging in tatters. Hoharie's wrapping it all up with a shaped ground reinforcement—ooh, clever—I think she means to help it grow back together easier as it heals."

Hoharie let out her breath in a long sigh; her back bent. Dag, his expression very inward, stared down at his left arm as it moved in a short jerk. "Better!" he murmured in pleased surprise.

"Time," said Hoharie, and now she sounded down in that swamp, too. Dag gave her a dry look as if to say, *Now who's overdoing?* She ignored it, and continued, "It'll all come back in time as your ground slowly heals. *Slowly*, got that, Dag?"

Dag sighed in regret. "Yeah . . ." His voice fell further. "The ghost hand. It's gone, isn't it? For good. Like the other."

Hoharie said somewhat impatiently, "Gone for *a* good, to be sure, but not necessarily forever. I know it perturbed you, Dag, but I wish you'd stop thinking of that hand as some morbid magic! It was a ground projection, a simple . . . well, it was a ground projection, anyway. As your ground heals up from all this blight, it should come back with the rest of it. Last, I imagine, so don't go fuming and fretting."

"Oh," said Dag, looking brighter. Fawn could have hit him for winking at her like *that* just then, because it almost made her laugh out loud, and she'd never dare explain why to all these stern Lakewalkers.

"Now," said Hoharie, sitting up and rubbing her forehead with the back of her wrist—Othan, watching her closely, handed her a clean rag, and she repeated the gesture with it and nodded thanks. "It's my chance to ask a few questions. What I need to know is if a similar act would solve a similar problem. Because I need to write this out for the lore-tent if it does, and maybe pass it along to the other hinterlands, too."

"I hope there never is a similar problem," said Mari, "because that would mean another runaway malice like this one, and this one got way too close to being unstoppable. But write it out all the same, sure. You never know."

"No one can know till it's tried," said Dag, "but my own impression was that any primed knife, placed in any of the groundlocked people, would have worked to clean out the malice's involution. It only needed someone to think of it— and dare."

"It seems a strange way to spend a sacrifice," agreed Hoharie. "Still . . . ten for one." All the Lakewalkers looked equally pensive, contemplating this mortal arithmetic. "When did you think of it?"

"Pretty nearly as soon as I was trapped in the groundlock. I could see it, then."

Hoharie's gaze flicked to Fawn's left wrist. Fawn, by now inured to being talked past, almost flinched under the suddenly intent stare. "That was also about the time you felt a change in that peculiar ground reinforcement Dag gave you, wasn't it, Fawn? Did it seem to come with, say, a compulsion?"

Othan sat up straight. "Oh, of course! That would explain how she knew what to do!"

Did it? Fawn's brows drew down in doubt. "It didn't seem anything like so clear. I wish it had been."

"So how did you know?" asked Hoharie patiently. "To use your sharing knife like that?"

"I . . ." She hesitated, casting her mind back to last night's desperation. "I figured it."

"How?"

She struggled to express her complex thoughts simply. A lot of it hadn't even been in words, just in pictures. "Well, you said. That there were cut-off bits of malice in that groundlock. Sharing knives kill malices. I thought it might just need an extra dose to finish the job."

"But your knife had no affinity."

"What?" Fawn stared in confusion.

Dag cleared his throat. His voice went gentle. "Dar was right—about that, anyway. The mortality in your knife was too pure to hold affinity with malices, but I was able to break into its involution and add some. A little extra last-minute making, would you say, Hoharie?"

Hoharie eyed him. "Making? I'm not sure that wasn't *magery*, Dag."

Fawn's brow wrinkled in distress. "Is that what tore up your ghost hand? Oh, if I had known—!"

"Sh," soothed Dag. "If you had known, what?"

She stared down at her hands, clutching each other in her lap. After a long pause, she said, "I'd have done it all the same."

"Good," he whispered.

"So," said Othan, clearly struggling with this, "you didn't really *know*. You were just guessing." He nodded in apparent relief. "A real stab in the dark. And in fact, except for Dag saving it all at the last, you were wrong!"

Fawn took a long breath, considering this painful thought. "Sometimes," she said distantly, with all the dignity she could gather, "it isn't about having the right answers. It's about asking the right questions."

Dag gave a slow blink; his face went curiously still. But then he smiled at her again, in a way that made the knot in her heart unwind, and gave her a considering nod. "Yeah—it was what we in Tent Bluefield call a fluke, Othan," he murmured, and the warm look he gave Fawn with *that* made the knot unwind all the way down to her toes.

⁂

Later in the afternoon, Saun came back from the woods with a peeled-sapling staff—hickory, he claimed; with that and Saun's shoulder for support, Dag was able to hobble back and forth to the slit trench. That cured Dag of ambition for any further movement. He was quite content to lie propped in his bedroll, occasionally with Fawn tucked up under his arm, and watch the camp go by, and not talk. He was especially content not to talk. A few inquiring noises were enough to persuade Fawn to ripple on about how she'd arrived so astonishingly here. He felt a trifle guilty about giving her so little tale in return, but she had Saun and Mari to cull for more details, and she did.

The next day the last of the company's scouts returned, having hooked up with another gaggle of Bonemarsh refugees returning to check on their quick and their dead. With the extra hands on offer, it was decided to move the recovering makers to better shelter that day, and the Raintree cavalcade moved off in midafternoon. The camp fell quiet. At this point, Dag's remaining patrol realized that the only barrier between them and a ride for home was their convalescent captain. The half dozen patrollers who were capable of giving minor ground reinforcements either volunteered or were volunteered to contribute to his speedier recovery. Dag blithely accepted them all, until his left foot began to twitch, his speech slurred, and he started seeing faint lavender halos around everything, and Hoharie, with some dire muttering about *absorption time, blight it,* cut off the anxious suppliers.

The miasma of homesickness and restlessness that permeated the air was like a fog; by evening, Dag found it easy to persuade Mari and Codo to split the patrol and send most of them home tomorrow with Hoharie, leaving Dag a suitable smaller group of bodyguards, or nursemaids, to follow on as soon as he was cleared to mount a horse again.

Mari, after a consultation with Hoharie out of Dag's earshot, appointed herself chief of their number. "Somebody's got to stand up to you when you get bored and decide to advance Hoharie's timetable by three days," she told Dag bluntly, when he offered a reminder of Cattagus. "If we leave you nothing but the children, you'll ride right over 'em."

Despite his pains and exhaustion, Dag was wholly satisfied to lie with Fawn that night in their little shelter, as if he'd entered some place of perfect balance where all needs were met and no motion was required. He wasn't homesick. On the whole, he had no desire at all to think about Hickory Lake and what awaited him there . . . *no.* He stopped that slide of thought. *Be here. With her.*

He petted her, letting her dark hair wind and slide through his fingers, silky delight. In her saddlebags she had brought candles, of all things, of her own making, and had stuck one upright in a holder made from a smooth dented stone she'd found in the stream. He was unaroused and, in his current condition, likely unarousable, but looking at her in this gilded light he was pierced with a pure desire, as if he were gazing at a running foal, or a wheeling hawk, or a radiant, melting sunset. Wonder caught up in flight that no man could possess, except in the eye and impalpable memory. Where time was the final foe, but the long defeat was not *now, now, now . . .*

Fawn seemed content to cuddle atop the bedroll and trade kisses, but at length she wriggled up to do off her boots and belt. They would sleep in their clothes like patrollers, but she drew the line at unnecessary lumps. With a thoughtful frown, she pulled her sharing knife cord over her head.

"I reckon I can put this away in my saddlebags, now." She slid the haft out of its sheath and spilled the three long shards of the broken blade out on the bedroll, lining them up with her finger.

Dag rolled over and up on his elbow to look. "Huh. So, that explains what Othan was doing down there, fishing all those out of me. I wondered."

"So . . . now what do we do with it?" Fawn asked.

"A spent knife, if it's recovered, is usually given back to the kin of the bone's donor, or if that can't be done, burned on a little pyre. It's been twenty years, but . . . Kauneo should have kin up in Luthlia who remember her. I still have her uncle Kaunear's bone, too, back home in my trunk—hadn't quite got round to arranging for it when this Raintree storm blew in on us. I should send them both up to Luthlia in a courier pouch, with a proper letter telling everyone what their sacrifices have bought. That would be best, I think."

She nodded gravely and extended a finger to gently roll a shard over. "In the end, this *did* do more than just bring us together, despite what Dar said about the farmer ground being worthless. Because of your making that redeemed it. I'm—not glad, exactly, there's not much glad about this— satisfied, I think. Dar said—"

He hoisted himself up and stopped her lips with a kiss. "Don't worry about what Dar says. I don't."

"Don't you?" She frowned. "But—wasn't he right, about the affinity?"

Dag shrugged. "Well . . . it would have been strange if he weren't. Knives are his calling. I'm not at all sure he was right about the other, though."

"Other?"

"About how your babe's ground got into my knife."

Her black eyebrows curved up farther.

He lay back again, raising his hand to hover across from his stump as a man would hold his two hands some judicious distance apart. "It was just a quick impression, you understand, when I was unmaking the knife's involution and releasing the mortal ground. I couldn't prove it. It was all gone in the instant, and only I saw. But . . . there was more than one knife stuck in that malice at that moment back at Glassforge. And there is more than one sort of ground affinity. There was a link, a channel . . . because the one knife was Kauneo's marrowbone, see, and the other was her heart's death. Knives don't take up souls, if there is such a thing, but each one has a, a *flavor* of its donor. I expect she died wanting and regretting, well, a lot of things, but I know a child was one. I wouldn't dare say this to anyone else, but I'll swear it to you. It wasn't the malice pushed that ground into Kauneo's bone. I think it was given *shelter.*"

Fawn sat back, her lips parting in wonder. Her eyes were huge and dark, winking liquid that reflected the candlelight in shimmers.

He added very quietly, "If it was a gift from the grave, it's the strangest I ever heard tell of, but . . . she liked youngsters. She would have saved 'em all, if she could."

Fawn whispered, "She's not the only one, seemingly." And rolled over into his arms, and hugged him tight. Then sat up on her elbow, and said, most seriously, "Tell me more about her."

And, to his own profound astonishment, he did.

It came in a spate, when it came. To speak easily of Kauneo at last, to repossess such a wealth of memory from the far side of pain, was as beyond all expectation as claiming a stolen treasure returned after years. As miraculous as getting back a missing limb. And his tears, when they fell, seemed not sorrow, but grace.

16

For the next couple of days Dag seemed willing to rest as instructed, to Fawn's approval, although she noticed he seemed less fidgety and fretful when she sat by him. Saun had stayed on, with Griff for his partner; Varleen replaced Dirla as Mari's partner. There were not too many camp chores for Fawn's hands, everyone having pretty much caught up with their cleaning and mending in the prior days, though she did spend some time out with the younger patrollers working on, or playing with, the horses. Grace hadn't gone lame, though Fawn thought it had been a near thing. The mare was certainly recovering faster than Dag. Fawn suspected Lakewalkers used their healing magic on their horses; if not officially, certainly on the sly.

On the third day, the heavy heat was pushed on east by a cracking thunderstorm. The tree branches bent and groaned menacingly overhead, and leaves turned inside out and flashed silver. The patrollers ended up combining their tent covers—except for the one hide that blew off into the woods like a mad bat—on Dag and Fawn's sapling frame, and clustering underneath. The nearby creek rose and ran mud-brown and foam-yellow as the blow subsided into a steady vertical downpour. By unspoken mutual assent, they all eased back and just watched it, passing around odd bits of cold food while their cook-fire pit turned into an opaque gray puddle.

Griff produced a wooden flute and instructed Saun on it for a time. Fawn recognized maybe half of the sprightly tunes. In due course Griff took it back and played a long, eerie duet with the rain, Varleen and Saun supplying muted percussion with sticks and whatever pots they had to hand. Dag and Mari seemed satisfied to listen.

Everyone went back to nibbling. Dag, who had been lying slumped against his saddlebags with his eyes closed, pushed himself slightly more upright, adjusted his left leg, and asked Saun suddenly, "You know the name of that farmer town the malice was supposed to have come up under?"

"Greenspring," Saun replied absently, craning his neck through the open, leeward side of their shelter to look, in vain, for a break in the clouds.

"Do you know where it is? Ever been there?"

"Yeah, couple of times. It's about twenty-five miles northwest of Bonemarsh." He sat back on his saddlecloth and gestured vaguely at the opposite shelter wall.

Dag pursed his lips. "That must be, what, pretty nearly fifty miles above the old cleared line?"

"Nearly."

"How was it ever let get started, up so far? It wasn't there in my day."

Saun shrugged. "Some settlement's been there for as long as I've been alive. Three roads meet, and a river. There were a couple of mills, if I remember rightly. Sawmill first. Later, when there got to be more farms around it, they built one for grain. Blacksmith, forge, more. We'd stopped in at the blacksmith a few times, though they weren't too friendly to patrollers."

"Why not?" asked Fawn, willing to be indignant on Saun's behalf.

"Old history. First few times farmers tried to settle up there, the Raintree patrollers ran them off, but they snuck back. Worse than pulling stumps, to try and get farmers off cleared land. On account of all the stumps they had to pull to clear it, I guess. There finally got to be so many of them, and so stubborn, it would have taken bloodshed to shift 'em, and folks gave up and let 'em stay on."

Dag frowned.

Saun pulled his knees up and wrapped his arms around them in the damp chill. "Fellow up there once told me Lakewalkers were just greedy, to keep such prime farming country for a hunting reserve. That his people could win more food from it with a plow than we ever could with bows and traps."

"What we hunt, they could not eat," growled Mari.

"That's the same fellow who told me blight bogles were a fright story made up by Lakewalkers to keep farmers off," Saun added a bit grimly. "You wonder where he is now."

Griff and Varleen shook their heads. Fawn bit her lip.

Dag wound a finger in his hair, pulling gently on a strand. He was overdue for another cut, Fawn thought, unless he meant to grow it out like his comrades. "I want to look at the place before we head home."

Griff's brow furrowed. "That'd be a good three days out of our way, Dag."

"Maybe only two, if we jog up and catch the northern road again." He added after a moment, "We could leave here two days early and be home on schedule all the same."

Mari gave him a fishy look. "Thought it was about time for you to start gettin' resty. Hoharie said, seven days off it for that leg. We all heard her."

"Come on, you know she padded that."

Mari did not exactly deny this, but she did say, "And why would you want to, anyway? You know what blight looks like, without having to go look at more. It's all the same. That's what makes it blight."

"Company captain's duty. Fairbolt will want a report on how this all got started."

"Not his territory, Dag. It's some Raintree camp captain's job to look into it."

Dag's eyelids lowered and rose, in that peculiar I-am-not-arguing-about-this look; his gaze met Fawn's curious one. "Nonetheless, I need to see whatever can be seen. I'm not calling for a debate on this, in case any of you were confused." A faint, rare tinge of iron entered his voice. Not arguing, apparently, but not giving way, either.

Mari's face screwed up. "Why? I could likely give you a tolerably accurate description of it all from right where I sit, and so could you. Depressing, but accurate. What answers are you lookin' for?"

"If I knew, I wouldn't have to go look." More hair-twisting. "I don't think I'm even looking for answers. I'm think I'm looking for new questions." He gave Fawn a slow nod.

The next morning dawned bright blue, and everyone spent it getting their gear spread out in the sun or up on branches to dry out. By noon, Dag judged this task well along, and floated the notion of starting out today—in gentle, easy stages, to counter Mari's exasperated look and mutter of *Told you so.* But since Mari was as sick of this place as everyone else, Dag soon had his way.

With the promise of home dangling in the distance, however roundaboutly, the youngsters had the camp broken down and bundled up in an hour, and Saun led their six mounts and the packhorse northwest. They skirted wide around the dead marsh, flat and dun in a crystalline light that still could not make it sparkle, for all that a shortcut across the blight would have saved several miles.

Halfway around, Mari drew her horse to a halt and turned her face to a vagrant moist breeze.

"What?" Saun called back, alert.

"Smell that?" said Mari.

"Right whiffy," said Varleen, wrinkling her nose.

"Something's starting to rot," Dag explained to Fawn, who rode up beside him and looked anxiously inquiring. "That's good."

She shook her head. "You people."

"Hope is where you find it." He smiled down at her, then pushed Copperhead along. He could feel his weary patrol's mood lighten just a shade.

As he'd promised Mari, they weaved through the woodlands of Raintree at a sedate walk. They rode with ground-senses open, like people trailing their hands through the weeds as they strolled, not formally patrolling, but as routine precaution. You never knew. Dag himself had once found and done for a very early sessile that way, when he was riding courier all alone in the far northeast hinterland of Seagate. Still, their amble put a good twelve miles between them and the Bonemarsh blight by the time they stopped in the early evening. Dag thought everyone slept a bit better that night; even he did, despite the throbbing ache in his healing thigh.

They started off the next day earlier, but no faster. Varleen spotted two mud-man corpses off the trail that appeared to have died naturally, running down at the end of the stolen strength the malice had given them, suggesting the hazard from the rest of their cohort was now much reduced. Even at this slow pace, the little patrol came up on the first noxious pinching of the blight around Greenspring by midafternoon.

In the shade of the last live trees before the trail opened out into cleared fields, Dag held up his hook, and everyone pulled their mounts to a halt.

"We don't all have to go in. We could set up a camp here. You could stay with Varleen and Griff, Fawn. Blight this deep will be draining, even if you can't feel it. Bad for you. And . . . it could be ugly." *Will be ugly.*

Fawn leaned on her pommel and gave him a sharp look. "If it's bad for me, won't it be worse for you? Convalescing as you aren't—at least not any too fast, that I can see."

Mari vented a sour chuckle. "She's got you there."

Fawn took a breath and sat up. "This place—it's something like West Blue, right?"

"Maybe," Dag allowed.

"Then—I need to see it, too." She gave a firm little nod.

They exchanged a long look; her resolve rang true. *Should I be surprised?* "Soonest begun, soonest done, then. We won't linger long." Dag braced himself and waved Saun onward.

They rode first past deserted farms: sickly, then dying, then dead, then dead with a peculiar gray tinge that was quite distinctive. Dag knew it well and furled his groundsense in tight around him, as did the other patrollers. It didn't help quite enough.

"What are we looking for?" asked Griff, as the first buildings of a little town hove into view past a screen of bare and broken buckthorn bushes, someone's scraggly attempt at a hedge.

"I'd like to find the lair, to start," said Dag. "See where the malice started out, try to figure why it wasn't spotted."

It wasn't that hard; they just followed the gradient of blight deeper and deeper. It felt like riding into a dark hollow, for all that the land here was as level as the rest of Raintree. The flattened vegetation grew grayer, and even the clapboard houses, with their fences leaning drunkenly, seemed drained of all color. It all smelled as dry and odorless as cave dust. The town was maybe twice the size of West Blue, Dag gauged. It had three or four streets. A sturdy wharf jutted into a river worthy of the name and not just a jumped-up creek, which seemed to flow deeply enough to float small keelboats up from the Grace, and certainly rafts and flatboats down. A square for a day market; alehouse and smithy and forge; perhaps two hundred houses. A thousand people, formerly. None now.

The pit of the blight seemed to lie in a woodlot at the edge of the town. The horses snorted uneasily as their riders forced them forward. A shallow, shale-lined ravine with a small creek running through it shadowed a near cave partway up one side, not unlike the one they'd seen near Glassforge, if much smaller. It was quite empty now, the shale slumping in a slide to half block the water. Alongside the creek the earth was pocked with man-wide, man-deep pits, so thickly clustered in places as to seem like a wasp nest broken open. The malice's first mud-man nursery, likely.

"With all these people around," said Griff, "it's hard to believe that no one spotted any of the early malice signs."

"Maybe someone did," said Fawn, "and no one paid them any mind. Being too young and short. The woodlot is common for the whole town. You bet the youngsters here played in that creek all the time, and in these woods."

Dag hunched over his saddlebow and inhaled carefully, steadying his shuddering stomach. *Yes.* Malice food indeed, of the richest sort. Delivered up. This was how the malice had started so fast. He remembered its beauty in the silver light. How many molts . . . ? *As many as it liked.*

"Did no one know to run?" asked Varleen. "Or did it just come up too quick?"

"It came up fast, sure, but not that fast," opined Mari. She frowned at Dag's huddle. "Some were killed by ill luck, but I expect more were killed by ignorance."

"Why were—" Fawn began, and stopped.

Dag turned his head and raised his brows at her.

"I was going to say, why were they so ignorant," she said in a lower voice. "But I was just as ignorant myself, not long back. So I guess I know why."

Dag, still wordless with the nightmare images running through his mind, just shook his head and turned Copperhead around. They rode up from the ravine on the widest beaten path.

As they returned down the main street near the wharf, Saun's head suddenly came up. "I swear I hear voices."

Dag eased his groundsense open slightly, snapping it back again almost at once, cringing at the searing sensation. But he'd caught the life-sparks. "Over that way."

They rode on, turning down a side street lined with bare trees and empty houses, some new clapboard, the older ones log-sided. A few had broken glass windows; most still made do with old-fashioned parchment and summer netting, though also split or ripped. The street became a rutted lane, beyond which lay a broad field, its trampled grass and weeds gray-dun. A score or so of human figures milled about on its far end along what used to be a tree line. A few carts with dispirited horses hitched to them stood by.

"They can't be back trying to farm this!" said Saun in dismay.

"No," said Dag, rising in his stirrups and squinting, "it's no crop they're planting today."

"They're digging graves," said Mari quietly. "Must be some refugees who've come back to try and find their kin, same as at Bonemarsh."

Griff shook his head in regret.

Dag hitched his reins into his hook, for all that his left arm was still very weak, to free his hand. He waved the patrol forward, but with a cautioning gesture brought them to a halt again at a little distance from the Greenspring survivors.

The townsmen formed up in a ragged rank, clutching shovels and mattocks in a way that reminded Dag a lot of the Horsefords' first fearful approach to him, sitting so meekly on their porch. If the Horsefords had suffered reason to be nervy, these folks had cause to be half-crazed. Or maybe all-the-way crazed.

After an exchange of looks and low mutters, a single spokesman stepped out of the pack and moved cautiously toward the patrol, stopping a few prudent paces off, but within reasonable hearing distance. Good. Reassurances might work better delivered in a soothing tone, rather than bellowed. Dag touched his temple. "How de'."

The man returned a short, grudging nod. He was middle-aged, careworn, dressed in work clothes due for mending that hadn't been washed for weeks, an almost welcome whiff of something human in this odorless place. His face was so gray with fatigue as to look blighted while alive. Dag thought, unwillingly, of Sorrel Bluefield again.

"You folks shouldn't be on this sick ground," Dag began.

"It's our ground," the man returned, his stare distant.

"It's been poisoned by the blight bogle. It'll go on poisoning you if you linger on it."

The man snorted. "I don't need some Lakewalker corpse-eater to tell me that."

Dag tried a brief, acknowledging nod. "You can bury your dead here if you like, though I wouldn't advise it, but you should not camp here at night, leastways."

"There's shelter still standing." The townsman raised his chin and scowled, and added in a tone of warning, "We'll be guarding this ground tonight. In case you all were thinking of sneaking back."

What did the fellow imagine? That Dag's patrol had come around to try to steal the bodies of their dead? Infuriated protests rose in his mind: *We would not do such a foul thing. We have plenty of corpses of our own just now, thank you all the same. Farmer bones are of no use to us, ground-ripped bones are no use to us, and as for ground-ripped farmer bones . . . !* Teeth tight, he let nothing escape but a flat, "You do that."

Perhaps uneasily realizing he'd given offense, the townsman did not apologize, but at least slid sideways: "And how else will we find each other, if any more come back? The bogle cursed us and marched us off all over the place . . ."

Had he been one of the bewildered mind-slaves? It seemed so. "Did no one know to run for help, when the bogle first came up? To spread a warning?"

"What help?" The man huffed again. "You Lakewalkers

on your high horses rode us down. I was there." His voice
fell. "We were all mad with the bogle spells, yes, but . . ."

"They had to defend—" Dag began, and stopped. The
cluster of nervous townsmen had not put down their tool-
weapons, nor dispersed back to their forlorn task. He glanced
aside at Fawn, watching in concern from atop Grace, and
rubbed his aching forehead. He said instead, abruptly, "How
about if I get down from this high horse? Will you step away
and talk with me?"

A pause, a stare. A nod.

Dag steeled himself to dismount. Varleen, watching
closely, slid down and went to Copperhead's bridle, and
Saun dropped from his own mount, unshipped the hickory
staff that he'd carted along slotted under his saddle flap, and
stepped to Dag's stirrup. Dag's leg did not quite turn under
him as he landed on it, and he exchanged an almost-smile
with Saun as the youth carefully unhanded his arm, both,
he thought, thrown back in memory to their night attack on
the bandit camp, ages ago. He gripped the staff and turned
to the townsman, who was blinking as if he was just now
taking in the details of his interrogator's ragged condition.

Dag pointed to a lone dead tree, blown or fallen down in
the field, and the townsman nodded again. As Dag swung
the staff and limped toward it, he found Fawn at his left
side. Her hand slipped around his arm, not yet in support,
but ready if his leg folded again. He wondered if he should
chase her back to Grace, spare her what promised to be some
grim details. He dismissed his doubts—*too late anyway*—
as they arrived at the thick trunk. *She speaks farmer.* With
that thought, Dag guided Fawn around to sit between them.
Both men could see over her head better than she could see
around Dag, and . . . if this fellow's most recent view of a
Lakewalker patroller had been looking up the wrong end of
a spear, he could likely use a spacer. *We both could.*

Dag breathed a little easier as the mob of townsmen went
back to their digging. Now it was the Lakewalkers' turn to

stand in a tight cluster, holding their horses and watching Dag uneasily.

"This bogle was bad for everyone," Dag began again. "Raintree Lakewalkers lost folks, too, and homes. Bonemarsh Camp's been blighted—it'll have to be abandoned for the next thirty or more years, I reckon. This place, longer."

The man grunted, whether in agreement or disagreement was hard to tell. Maybe just in pain.

"Have very many people come back? To find each other?" Fawn put in.

The man shrugged. "Some. Most of us here knew we'd be coming as a burial party, but . . . some. I found my wife," he added after a moment.

"That's good, then," said Fawn in a tone of encouragement.

"She's buried over there," the townsman added, pointing to a long mound of turned earth along the tree line. *Mass grave*, Dag thought.

"Oh," said Fawn, more quietly.

"They waited for us to come back," the man continued. "All the wives and daughters. All the boys. The old folks. It was like there was something strange and holy happened to their bodies, because they didn't rot, not even in the heat. It's like they were waiting for us to come back and find them."

Dag swallowed, and decided this was not the moment to explain the more arcane features of deep blight.

"I'm so sorry," said Fawn softly.

The man shrugged. "Could have been worse. Daisy and Cooper over there, they found each other alive just an hour ago." He nodded toward a man and one of the few women, who were both sitting on the tail of a wagon. Staring blankly, with their backs to each other.

Fawn's little hand touched the man's knee; he flinched. "And . . . why worse?" Fawn could ask such things; Dag would not have dared. He was glad she was here.

"Daisy, she'd thought Coop had their youngsters with

him. Coop, he thought she'd had them with her. They'd had four." He added after a moment, "We're saving the children for last, see, in case more folks show up. To look." Dag followed his glance to a line of stiff forms lying half-hidden in the distant weeds. Behind it, the men were starting to dig a trench. It was longer than the finished mound.

"Are the orphans being sheltered somewhere off the blight?" Fawn asked. Thinking absent-gods-knew-what; about someone brokering some bright arrangement to hook up the lost half families with one another, if he knew her.

The man glanced down at her. Likely she looked as young to him as she did to Dag, for he said more gently, "No orphans here, miss."

"But . . ." She sucked on her lower lip, obviously thinking through the implication.

"We've found none alive here under twelve. Nor many over."

Dag said quietly, as she looked up at him as if he could somehow fix this, "Next to pregnant women, children have the richest grounds for a malice building up to a molt. It goes for them first, preferentially. When Bonemarsh was evacuated, the young women would have grabbed up all the youngsters and run at once. The others following as they could, with what animals and supplies they could get at fast, with the off-duty patrollers as rear guard. The children would have been got out in the first quarter hour, and the whole camp in as little more. They did lose folks beyond the range of warning—some of those makers we freed from the groundlock had stayed to try and reach a party of youngsters who'd gone out gathering that day."

Fawn frowned. "I hadn't heard that part of the tale. Did they find them in time?"

Dag sighed. "No. Some of the Bonemarsh folk who came back later recovered the bodies, finally. For a burial not so different than this." He nodded toward the mounds; the townsman, listening, stared down and dug his boot heel into the dry soil, brows pinching in wonder. *Yes*, thought Dag. *Witness her. Farmers can ask, and be answered. Won't you try us?*

"Did they take their—" Fawn shut up abruptly, remembering not to ask about knife-bones in front of farmers, Dag guessed. She just shook her head.

The townsman gave Dag a sidelong look. "You're not from Bonemarsh. Are you."

"No. My company rode over from Oleana to help out. We're on our way home now."

"Dag's patrol killed your blight bogle," Fawn put in, a little proudly. "When the malice's—bogle's curse lifted from your mind, that was when."

"Huh," said the man. And then, after a bleak silence, "Could have been sooner."

Stung to brusqueness, Dag said, "If any of you had owned the wits to run and give warning at the first, it could have been a *lot* sooner. We did all we could with what we had, as soon as we knew."

A stubborn silence stretched between them. There was too much grief and strain here, thick as mire, for argument or apology today. Dag had pretty much pieced together the picture he'd come for. It was maybe time to go.

A trio of townsmen came out of the barren woods, back from some errand there—pissing, searching?—and stopped to gape at the newcomers. One grizzled head came up sharply; staring, the man began to walk toward the fallen tree, faster and faster. His stride turned into a jog, then a run; his face grew wild, and he waved frantically, crying, "Sassy! Sassy!"

Dag stiffened, his hand drifting to his knife haft. The townsman beside Fawn straightened up with a moan and held out his palm in a gesture of negation, shaking his head. The runner slowed as he neared, gasping for breath, rubbing his red-rimmed eyes and peering at Fawn. In a voice gone gray, he said, "You aren't my Sassy."

"No, sir," said Fawn, looking up apologetically. "I'm Dag's Fawn."

He continued to peer. "Are you one of ours? Did those patrollers bring you back?" He waved toward the Lakewalkers still standing warily with their horses. "We can try and find your folks . . ."

"No, sir, I'm from Oleana."

"Why are you with them?"

"I'm married to one."

Taken aback, the man turned his head to squint; his gaze narrowed on Saun, who was standing holding Copperhead's reins, watching them alertly. The man's mouth turned down in a scowl. "If that's what that boy told you, missie, I'm afraid he was lying."

"*He's* not—" She broke off as Dag covered and squeezed her hand in warning.

The grizzled man took a breath. "If you want to stay here, missie, we could find you, find you . . ." He trailed off, looking around dolefully.

"Shelter?" muttered his comrade. "Not hardly." He stood up and squeezed his friend's shoulder. "Give it over. She's not our business. Not today."

With a disappointed glance over his shoulder, the grizzled man dragged off.

"I hope he finds his Sassy," said Fawn. "Who was—is she? His daughter?"

"Granddaughter," replied the townsman.

"Ah."

"We need to get off this blight, Fawn," said Dag, wondering if, had it been some other day, the townsmen would have made Fawn their business. Disquieting thought, but the dangerous moment, if that had been one, was past.

"Oh, of course." She jumped up at once. "You've got to be feeling it. How's your leg doing?"

"It'll be well enough once I'm in the saddle again." He grounded the butt of the hickory stick and levered himself up. He was starting to ache all over, like a fever. The towns-man trailed along after them as Dag hobbled back to his horse.

It took Saun and Varleen both to heave Dag aboard Cop-perhead, this time. He settled with a sigh, and even let Saun find his left stirrup for him and take away his stick. Varleen gave Fawn a neat boost up on Grace, and Fawn smiled thanks.

"You ready, Dag?" Saun asked, patting the leg.

"As I'll ever be," Dag responded.

As Saun went around to his horse, the townsman's eye-brows rose. "*You're* her Dag?" Surprise and deep disap-proval edged his voice.

"Yes," said Dag. They stared mutely at each other. Dag started to add, "Next time, don't—" but then broke off. This was not the hour, the place, or the man. *So when, where, and who will be?*

The townsman's lips tightened. "I doubt you and I have anything much to say to each other, patroller."

"Likely not." Dag raised his hand to his temple and clucked to urge Copperhead forward.

Fawn wheeled Grace around. Dag was afraid she'd caught the darker undercurrents after all, because the struggle was plain in her face between respect for bereavement and a goaded anger. She leaned down, and growled at the towns-man, "You might try *thank you*. Somebody should say it, at least once before the end of the world."

Disconcerted, the townsman dropped his eyes before her hot frown, then looked after her with an unsettled expression on his face.

As they left the blighted town and struck east up a wagon road alongside the river, Mari asked dryly, "Satisfied with your look-see, Dag?"

He grunted in response.

Her voice softened. "You can't fix everything in the whole wide green world by yourself, you know."

"Evidently not." And, after a moment, more quietly, "Maybe no one can."

Fawn eyed him with worry as he slumped in his saddle, but he did not suggest stopping. He wanted a lot more miles between him and what lay behind him. Greenspring. Should it be renamed Deadspring on the charts, now? Mari had been right; he'd had no need for a new crop of nightmares, let alone to have gone looking for them. He was justly served. Even Fawn had grown quiet. No answers, no questions, just silence.

He rode in it as they turned north across the river, looking for the road home.

17

Some six days after striking the north road, the little patrol clopped across the increasingly familiar wooden span to Two Bridge Island. Fawn turned in her saddle, watching Dag. His head came up, but unlike everyone else, he didn't break into whoops, and his lopsided smile at their cheers somehow just made him look wearier than ever. Mari had decreed easy stages on the ride home to spare their mounts, though everyone knew it had been to spare Dag. That Mari fretted for him troubled Fawn almost more than this strange un-Dag-like fatigue that gripped him so hard. The last day or two the *easy* part had silently dropped out, as the patrol pressed on more like horses headed for the barn than the horses themselves.

They paused at the split in the island road, and Mari gave a farewell wave to Saun, Griff, and Varleen. She jerked her head at Dag. "I'll be taking this one straight home, I think."

"Right," said Saun. "Need a helper?"

"Razi and Utau should be there. And Cattagus." Her austere face softened in an inward look, then she added, "Yep." Fawn wondered if she'd just bumped grounds with her husband to alert him to her homecoming.

Dag roused himself. "I should see Fairbolt, first."

"Fairbolt's heard all about it by now from Hoharie and the rest," said Mari sternly. "*I* should see Cattagus."

Saun glanced at his two impatient comrades, both with families waiting, and said, "I'll stop in and see Fairbolt on my way down island. Let him know we're back and all."

Dag squinted. "That'd do, I guess."

"Consider it done. Go rest, Dag. You look awful."

"Thankee', Saun," said Dag, the slight dryness in his voice suggesting it was for the latter and not the former statement, though it covered both. Saun grinned back, and the younger patrollers departed at a trot that became a lope before the first curve.

Dag, Mari, and Fawn took the shore branch, and while no one suggested a trot, Mari did kick her horse into a brisker walk. She was standing up in her stirrups peering ahead by the time they turned into her campsite.

Everyone had come out into the clearing. Razi and Utau held a child each, and Sarri waved. Cattagus waved and wheezed, striding forward. In addition there was a mob of new faces—a tall middle-aged woman and a fellow who had to be her spouse, and a stair-step rank of six gangling children ranging from Fawn's age downward to a leaping little girl of eight. The woman was Mari's eldest daughter, obviously, back from the other side of the lake with her family and her new boat. They all surged for Mari, although they stepped aside to give Cattagus first crack as she slid from her saddle. " 'Bout time you got back, old woman," he breathed into her hair, and, "You're still here. Good. Saves thumpin' you," she muttered sternly into his ear as they folded each other in.

Razi dumped his wriggling son off on Sarri, who cocked her hip to receive him, Utau let Tesy loose with admonishments about keeping clear of Copperhead, and the pair of men came to help Dag and Fawn dismount. Utau looked tired but hale enough, Fawn thought. Mari's son-in-law and Razi had all three horses unsaddled and bags off in a blink, and the two volunteered to lead the mounts back to Mare Island, preferably before the snorting Copperhead bit or kicked some bouncing child.

Tent Bluefield was still standing foursquare under the apple tree, and Sarri, smiling, rolled up and tied the tent flaps. Everything inside looked very neat and tidy and welcoming, and Fawn had Utau drop their grubby saddlebags under the outside awning. There would be serious laundry, she decided, before their travel-stained and reeking garments were allowed to consort again with their stay-at-home kin.

Dag eyed their bedroll atop its thick cushion of dried grass rather as a starving dog would contemplate a steak, muttered, "Boots off, leastways," and dropped to a seat on an upended log to tug at his laces. He looked up to add, "Any problems while we were away?"

"Well," said Sarri, sounding a trifle reluctant, "there was that go-round with the girls from Stores."

"They tried to steal your tent, the little—!" said Utau, abruptly indignant. Sarri shushed him in a way that made Fawn think this was an exchange much-repeated.

"What?" said Dag, squinting in bewilderment.

"Not stealing, exactly," said Sarri.

"Yes, it was," muttered Utau. "Blighted sneakery."

"They told me they'd been ordered to bring it back to Stores," Sarri went on, overriding him. "They had it halfway down when I caught them. They wouldn't listen to me, but Cattagus came out and wheezed at them and frightened them off."

"Razi and I were out collecting elderberries for Cattagus," said Utau, "or I'd have been willing to frighten them off myself. The nerve, to make away with a patroller's tent while he was out on patrol!"

Fawn frowned, imagining the startling—shocking— effect it would have had, with her and Dag both so travel-weary, to come back and find everything gone. Dag looked as though he was imagining this, too.

"Uncle Cattagus puffing in outrage was likely more effective," Sarri allowed. "He turns this alarming purple color, and chokes, and you think he's going to collapse onto your feet. The girls were impressed, anyway, and left off."

"Ran, Cattagus tells it," said Utau, brightening.

"When Razi and Utau came back they put your tent up again, and then went down and had some words with the folks in Stores. They claimed it was all a misunderstanding."

Utau snorted. "In a pig's eye it was. It was some crony of Cumbia's down there, with a notion for petty aggravation. Anyway, I spoke to Fairbolt, who spoke with Massape, who spoke with someone, and it didn't happen again." He nodded firmly.

Dag rubbed the back of his neck, looking pinch-browed and abstracted. If he'd had more energy, Fawn thought he might have been as angry as Utau, but just now it merely came out saddened. "I see," was all he said. "Thank you." He nodded up to Sarri as well.

"Fawn, not to tell you your job, but I think you need to get your husband horizontal," said Sarri.

"I'm for it," said Fawn. Together, she and Utau pulled Dag upright and aimed him into the tent.

Utau, releasing Dag's arm from over his shoulder as he sank down onto his bedroll, grunted, "Dag, I swear you're worse off than when I left you in Raintree. That groundlock do this to you? Your leg hasn't turned bad, has it? From what Hoharie said, I'd thought she'd patched you up better 'n this before she left you."

"He was better," said Fawn, "but then we went and visited Greenspring on the way home. It was all really deep-blighted. I think it gave him a relapse of some sort." Except she wasn't so sure it was the blight that had drained him of the ease he'd gained after their triumph over the groundlock. She remembered the look on his face, or rather the absence of any look on his face, when they'd ridden out of the townsmen's burying field past the line of small uncorrupted corpses. He'd *counted* them.

"That was a fool thing to do for a ground-ripped man, to go and expose yourself to more blight," Utau scolded. "You should know better, Dag."

"Yeah," sighed Dag, dutifully lying flat. "Well, we're all home now."

Sarri and Utau took themselves out with an offer of dinner later, which Fawn gratefully accepted. She fussed briefly over Dag, kissed him on the forehead, and left him not so much dozing as glazed while she went to deal with unpacking their gear. She glanced up at the lately contested awning of little Tent Bluefield as she began sorting.

Home again.

Was it?

Fawn brought Dag breakfast in bed the next morning. So it was only plunkin, tea, and concern; the concern, at least, he thought delicious. Though he had no appetite, he let her coax him into eating, and then bustle about getting him propped up comfortably with a nice view out the tent flap at the lakeshore. As the sun climbed he could watch her down on the dock scrubbing their clothes. From time to time she waved up at him, and he waved back. In due course, she shouldered the wet load and climbed up out of sight somewhere, likely to hang it all out to dry.

He was still staring out in benign lassitude when a brisk hand slapped the tent side, and Hoharie ducked in. "There you are. Saun told me you'd made it back," she greeted him.

"Ah, Hoharie. Yeah, yesterday afternoon."

"I also heard you weren't doing so well."

"I've been worse."

Hoharie was back in her summer shift, out of riding gear; indeed, she'd made a questionable-looking patroller. She settled down on her knees and folded her legs under herself, looking Dag over critically.

"How's the leg, after all that abuse?"

"Still healing. Slowly. No sign of infection."

"That's a blessing in a deep puncture, although after all

that ground reinforcement I wouldn't expect infection. And the arm?"

He shifted it. "Still very weak." He hadn't even bothered with his arm harness yet this morning, though Fawn had cajoled him into clean trousers and shirt. "No worse."

"Should be better by now. Come on, open up."

Dag sighed and eased open his ground. It no longer gave him sensations akin to pain to do so; the discomfort was more subtle now, diffuse and lingering.

Horarie frowned. "What did you do with all that ground reinforcement you took on last week over in Raintree? It's barely there."

"It helped. But we crossed some more blight on the way back."

"Not smart." Her eyes narrowed. "What's your ground-sense range right now?"

"Good question. I haven't . . ." He spread his senses. He hardly needed groundsense to detect Mari's noisy grandchildren, shouting all over the campsite. The half-closed adults were subtler smudges. Fawn was a bright spark in the walnut grove, a hundred paces off. Beyond that . . . nothing. "Very limited." Shockingly so. "Haven't been this weak since I lost my real hand."

"Well, if you want an answer to, *How am I recovering?* there's your test. No patrolling for you for a while, Captain. Not till your range is back to its usual."

Dag waved this away. "I'm not arguin'."

"That tells a tale right there." Hoharie's fingers touched his thigh, his arm, his side; he could feel her keen regard as a passing pressure through his aches. "After my story and Saun's, Fairbolt reckoned he'd be putting your peg back in the sick box. He wanted me to tell him for how long."

"So? How long?"

"Longer than Utau, anyway."

"Fairbolt won't be happy about that."

"Well, we've talked about that. About you. You did rather

more in that Bonemarsh groundlock than just take hurt, you know."

Something in her tone brought him up, if not to full alertness, which eluded him still, then to less vague attention. He let his ground ease closed again. Hoharie sat back on the woven mat beside the bedroll and wrapped her arms around her knees, regarding him coolly.

"You've been patrolling for a long time," she observed.

"Upwards of forty years. So? Cattagus walked for almost seventy. My grandfather, longer than that. It's a life."

"Ever think of another? Something more settled?"

"Not lately." Or at least, not until this summer. He wasn't about to try to describe how confused he'd become about his life since Glassforge.

"Anyone ever suggest medicine maker?"

"Yes, you, but you weren't thinking it through."

"I remember you complained about being too old to be an apprentice. May I point out, yours could be about the shortest apprenticeship on record? You already know all the herblore, from decades of patrol gathering. You know field aid on the practical side—possibly even more than I do. Your ground-matching skills are astonishing, as Saun has lived to testify to anyone who will listen."

"Saun, you may have noticed, is a bit of an enthusiast. I wouldn't take him too seriously, Hoharie."

She shook her head. "I *saw* you do things with ground projection and manipulation, inside that groundlock, that I can still barely wrap my mind around. I examined Artin, after it was all over. You not only could do it, you could be good, Dag. A lot of people can patrol. Not near as many can do this level of making, fewer still such direct groundwork. I know—I scout for apprentices every year."

"Be reasonable, Hoharie. Groundsense or no, a medicine maker needs two clever hands for, well, all sorts of tasks. You wouldn't want me sewing up your torn trousers, let alone your torn skin. And the list goes on."

"Indeed it does." She smiled and leaned forward. "But—patrollers work in partnered pairs all the time. You're used to it. And I get, from time to time, a youngster mad for medicine-making, and with clever hands, but a bit lacking on the groundsense side. You get along well with youngsters, even if you do scare them at first. I'm thinking—what about pairing you up with someone like that?"

Dag blinked. Then blinked again. *Spark?* She had the cleverest hands of anyone he'd ever met, and, absent gods knew, the wits and nerve for the task. His imagination and heart were both suddenly racing, tossing up pictures of the possibilities. They could work together right here at Hickory Lake, or at Bearsford Camp. Honorable, necessary, respected work, to win her a place here in her own right. He could be by her side every day. And every night. And once she was trained, they might do more . . . would Fawn like the notion? He would ask her at once. He grinned at Hoharie, and she brightened.

"I see you get the idea," she said in a tone of satisfaction. "I'm so glad! As you might guess, I have someone in mind."

"Yes."

"Oh, did Othan talk to you?"

"Beg pardon?"

"It's his younger brother, Osho. He's not quite ready for it yet, mind, but neither are you. But if I knew he'd be pairing with you, I could admit him to training pretty soon."

"Wait, what? No! I was thinking of Fawn."

It was Hoharie's turn to rock back, blinking. "But Dag—even if she's still—she has no groundsense at all! A farmer can't be a medicine maker. Or any kind of a maker."

"Farmers are, in their own way, all the time. Midwives, bonesetters."

"Certainly, but they can't use our ways. I'm sure their skills are valuable, and of course better than nothing, but they just can't."

"I'd do that part. You said."

"Dag . . . the sick and the hurt are vulnerable and touchy. I'm afraid a lot of folks wouldn't trust or accept her. It would be one strange thing too many. There's also the problem of her ground. I like Fawn, but having her ground always open around delicate groundwork, maybe distracting or interfering . . . no."

It wouldn't distract me, he thought of arguing. He settled his shoulders back on his cushion, his little burst of excitement draining away again, leaving his fatigue feeling worse by contrast. Instead, he asked, more slowly, "So why don't we do more for farmers? No, I don't mean the strong makers like you, you're rare and needed here, but all of us. The patrols are out there all the time. We know and use a dozen little tricks amongst ourselves, that we could find ways to share. More than just selling plants and preparations. We could build up goodwill, over time." He remembered Aunt Nattie's tale of her twisted ankle. Just such a good deed had borne some fair fruit, even decades afterwards.

"Oh, Dag." Hoharie shook her head. "Do you think no one's tried it, tempted through pity? Or even friendship? It sounds so fine, but it only works as long as nothing goes wrong, as it inevitably must. That goodwill can turn to bad will in a heartbeat. Lakewalkers who let themselves get in over their heads trying to share such help have been beaten to death, or worse."

"If it were . . ." His voice faltered. He didn't have a counterargument for this one, as it was perfectly true. *There has to be a better way* was easy to say. It was a lot harder to picture exactly how.

Returning to her subject, Hoharie said, "Fairbolt doesn't much want to give you up, but he would for this. He can see a lot of the same things I do. He's watched you for a long time."

"I owe Fairbolt"—Dag lifted his left arm—"everything, pretty much. My arm harness was his doing. He'd spotted

something like it in Tripoint, see. A farmer artificer and a
farmer bonesetter over there had got together to fix things
like it for some folks who'd lost limbs in mining and forge
accidents. Neither of them had a speck of groundsense, but
they had *ideas*."

Hoharie began to speak, but then turned her head; in a
moment, Fawn popped around the tent's open side, looking
equally pleased and anxious. "Hoharie! I'm so glad you're
here. How is he doing? Mari was worried."

As if Fawn didn't expect her own worry to count with the
medicine maker? *And is she so wrong in that?*

Hoharie smiled reassuringly. "He mostly needs time and
rest and not to do fool things."

Dag said plaintively, not to mention horizontally, "How
can I do fool things when I can't do anything?"

Hoharie gave his query the quelling eyebrow twitch it deserved, and went on to give Fawn a set of sensible instructions and suggestions, which added up to *food*, *sleep*, and
mild camp chores when ready. Fawn listened earnestly, nodding. Dag was sure she'd remember every word. And be able
to quote them back at him, likely.

Hoharie rose. "I'll send Othan down in a couple of days to
pull those stitches out."

"I can do that myself," said Dag.

"Well, *don't*," she returned. She glanced down at him.
"Think about what I said, Dag. If your feet—or your heart—
ache too much to walk another mile, you could do a world
of good right here."

"I will," he said, unsettled. Hoharie waved and took herself out.

Frowning, Fawn flopped down on her knees beside him
and ran a small hand over his brow. "Your eyebrows are all
scrunched up. Are you in pain?" She smoothed away the
furrows.

"No." He caught the hand and kissed it. "Just tired, I
guess." He hesitated. "Thinkin'."

"Is that the sort of thinkin' where you sit like a bump for hours, and then jump sideways like a frog?"

He smiled despite himself. "Do I do that?"

"You do." ·

"Well, I'm not jumping anywhere today."

"Good." She rewarded this resolve with a kiss, and then several more. It unlocked muscles in him that he hadn't known were taut. One muscle, at least, remained limp, which would have disturbed him a lot more if he hadn't been through such convalescences before. *Must rest faster.*

Dag spent the next three days mired in much the same glazed lassitude. He was driven from his bedroll at last not by a return of energy, but by a buildup of boredom. Out and about, he found unexpectedly intense competition for the sitting-down camp chores among the ailing—Utau, Cattagus, and himself. He watched Cattagus, moving at about the same rate he did, and wondered if this was what it was going to feel like to be old.

There being no hides to scrape at the moment, and Utau and Razi having shrewdly been first in line to help Cattagus with his elderberries, Dag defaulted to nut-cracking; he had, after all, a built-in tool for it. He was awkward at first with the fiddly aspects, but grew less so. Fawn, who plainly thought the task the most tedious in the world, wrinkled her nose, but it exactly suited Dag's mood, not requiring any thought beyond a vague philosophical contemplation of the subtle shapes of nuts and their shells. Walnuts. And hickory shells. Over and over, very reliably. They might resist him, but only rarely did they counterattack, the hickory being the more innately vicious.

Fawn kept him company, first spinning, then working on two pairs of new riding trousers, one for him and one for her, made of cloth shared by Sarri. Sitting with him in the shade of their awning one afternoon, she remarked, "I'd make you more arrows, but everyone's quivers are full up."

Dag poked at a particularly intractable nutshell. "Do you like making arrows better than making trousers?"

She shrugged. "It just feels more important. Patrollers *need* arrows."

He sat back and contemplated this. "And we don't need trousers? I think you have that the wrong way round, Spark. It's poison ivy country out there, you know. Not to mention the nettles, thistles, burrs, thorns, and bitey bugs."

She pursed her lips as she poked her needle slowly through the sturdy cloth. "For going into a fight, though. When it counts."

"I still don't agree. I'd want my trousers. In fact, if I were waked up out of my bedroll in a night attack, I think I'd go for them before my boots *or* my bow."

"But patrollers sleep in their trousers, in camp," she objected. "Although not in hotels," she allowed in a tone of pleasurable reminiscence.

"That gives you a measure of importance, then, doesn't it?" He batted his eyes at her. "I can just picture it, a whole patrol riding out armed to the teeth, all bare-assed. Do you have any idea what the jouncing in those saddles would do to all our tender bits? We'd never make it to the malice."

"Agh! Now *I'm* picturing it!' She bent over, laughing. "Stop! I'll allow you the trousers."

"And I'll thank you with all my heart," he assured her. "And with my tender bits." Which made her dissolve into giggles again.

He could not remember when she'd last laughed like this, which sobered him. But he still smiled as he watched her take up her sewing once more. He decided he would very much like to thank her with his tender bits, if only they would get around to reporting for duty again. He sighed and took aim at another hickory shell.

Fortunately, or unfortunately, while he was still recuperating, Fawn's monthly came on—a bad one, it seemed, alarmingly bloody. Dag, concerned, dragged Mari over to Tent Bluefield for a consultation; she was reassuringly unimpressed, and rattled off a gruesome string of what Dag decided were the female equivalent of old-patroller stories, about Much Worse Things She Had Seen.

"I don't recall the young women on patrol having this much trouble," he said nervously, hovering.

Mari eyed him. "That's because girls with these sorts of troubles gener'lly don't choose to become patrollers."

"Oh. Makes sense, I guess . . ."

Softening, Mari allowed as how Fawn was likely still healing up inside, which from the state of the scars on her neck Dag guessed to be exactly the case, and that the problems should improve over the next months, and even unbent enough to give Fawn a tiny ground reinforcement in the afflicted area.

Dag thought back to his too-few years with Kauneo, how a married man's life got all wound about in these intimate rhythms, and how they had sometimes annoyed him—till he'd been left to wish for them back. He dealt serenely, wrapping hot stones, and coaxing some of Cattagus's best elderberry wine out of him and into Fawn, and her pains eased.

At last, one bright, quiet morning, Dag hauled his trunk out under the canopy for a writing desk and took on the task of his letter to Luthlia. At first he thought he would keep it painlessly short, a sentence or two simply locating each bone's malice kill. He was so much in the habit of concealing the complications of the unintended priming; it seemed so impossible to set it out clearly; and the tale of Fawn and her lost babe seemed too inward a hurt to put before strangers' eyes. Silence was easier. And yet . . . silence would seem to deny that a farmer girl had ever had any place in all this.

He weighed the smooth shards of Kauneo's bone in his hand one last time before wrapping them up in a square of good cloth that Fawn had hemmed, and changed his mind.

Instead he wrote out as complete an account of the chain of events, focusing on the knives, as he could manage, most especially not leaving out his belief of how the babe's ground had found refuge from the malice. It was still so compressed he wasn't sure but what it sounded incoherent or insane, but it was all the truth as he knew it. When he was done he let Fawn read it before he sealed it with some of Sarri's beeswax. Her face grew solemn; she handed it back with a brief nod. "That'll do for my part."

She helped him wrap up the packet carefully, with an outer cover of deer leather secured by rawhide strings for protection, and he addressed it to Kauneo's kin, ready for Razi to take up to the courier at patroller headquarters. He fingered the finished bundle, and said slowly, "So many memories . . . If souls exist, maybe they lie in the track of time we leave behind us. And not out ahead, and that's why we can't find them, not even with groundsense. We're lookin' in the wrong direction."

Fawn smiled wryly into his eyes, leaned up, and kissed him soft. "Or maybe they're right here," she said.

Fairbolt turned up the next day. Dag had been half-expecting him. They found seats on a pair of stumps out in the walnut grove, out of earshot from the busy campsite.

"Razi says you're feeling better," Fairbolt remarked, looking Dag over keenly.

"My body's moving again, leastways," Dag allowed. "My groundsense range still isn't doing too well. I don't think Hoharie's notion that it has to come all the way back before I patrol again is right, though. Halfway would be good as most."

"It's not about you going back on patrol, for which judgment I'll be relying on Hoharie and not you, thanks. It's about your camp council summons. I've been holding 'em off on the word that you're still too injured and ill after Raintree, which is harder to make stick when it's seen you are up and about. So you can expect it as soon as that Heron Island dredging fracas is sorted out."

Dag hissed through his teeth. "After Raintree—after all Fawn and I did—they're *still* after a camp council ruling against us? Hoharie, and I, and Bryn and Mallora and Ornig would all be dead and buried right now in blighted Bonemarsh if not for Fawn! Not to mention five good makers lost. This, on top of the Glassforge malice—what more could they possibly want from a farmer girl to prove herself worthy?" His outrage was chilled by a ripple of cold reflection—in forty years he had never been able to prove *himself* worthy, in certain eyes. He'd concluded sometime back that the problem was not in him, it was in those eyes, and no doing of his could ever fix it. Why should any doing of Fawn's be different?

Fairbolt scratched his ear. "Yeah, I didn't figure that news would sit too well with you." He hesitated. "I owe an apology to Fawn, for trying to stop her here when you were calling her from out of that groundlock. It seems right cruel, in hindsight. I had no idea it was you behind her restiness that day."

Dag's brows drew down. "You been talking to Othan about the Bonemarsh groundlock?"

"I've been talking to everyone who was there, as I had the chance, trying to piece it all together."

"Well, just for the scribe, it wasn't me who told Fawn to put that knife in my leg, like, like some *malice* riding a farmer slave. She figured it out by her own wits!"

Fairbolt held up both palms in a gesture of surrender. "Be that as it may, how are you planning to handle this council challenge? I've discouraged and delayed it about as much as I can without being bounced off your hearing myself for conflict of interest. And since I don't mean to let myself get excluded from this one, the next move has to fall on you. Which is where it belongs anyway, I might point out."

Dag bent, venting a weary sigh. "I don't know, Fairbolt. My mind's been working pretty slow since I got back. It feels like a bug stuck in honey, truth to tell."

Fairbolt frowned curiously. "An effect of that peculiar blight you took on, do you think?"

"I . . . don't know. It's an effect of something." Accumulation, maybe. He could feel it, building up in him, but he could not put a name to it.

"It wouldn't hurt for you to tell more of your tale around, you know," said Fairbolt. "I don't think everyone rightly understands how much would be lost to this camp, and to Oleana, if you were banished."

"What, brag and boast?" Dag made a face. "I should be let to keep Fawn because I'm special?"

"If you're not willing to say it to your friends, how are you going to stand up in council and say it to your enemies?"

"Not my style, and an insult to boot to everyone who walks their miles all the same, without fanfare or thanks. Now, if you want me to argue that I should be let to keep Fawn because *she's* special, I'm for it."

"Mm," said Fairbolt. If he was picturing this, the vision didn't seem to bring him much joy.

Dag looked down, rubbing his sandal in the dirt. "There is this. If the continued existence of Hickory Lake Camp— or Oleana—or the wide green world—depends on just one man, we've already lost this long war."

"Yet every malice kill comes, at the end, down to one man's hand," Fairbolt said, watching him.

"Not true. There's a world balanced on that knife-edge. The hand of the patroller, yes. But held in it, the bone's donor, and the heart's donor, and the hand and eye and ground of the knife maker. And all the patrol backing up behind who got the patroller to that place. Patrollers, we hunt in packs. Then all the camp and kin behind them, who gave them the horses and the gear and the food to get there. And on and on. Not one man, Fairbolt. One man or another, yes."

Fairbolt gave a slow, conceding nod. He added after a moment, "*Has* anyone said *thank you* for Raintree, company captain?"

"Not as I recollect," Dag said dryly, then was a little sorry for the tone when he caught Fairbolt's wince. He added more wistfully, "Though I do hope Dirla got her bow-down."

"Yes, they had a great party for her over on Beaver Sigh, I heard from the survivors."

Dag's smile tweaked. "Good."

Fairbolt stretched his back, which creaked faintly in the cool silence of the shade. Between the dark tree boles, the lake surface glittered in a passing breeze. "I like Fawn, yet . . . I can't help imagining how much simpler all our lives could be right now if you were to take that nice farmer girl back to her family down in West Blue and tell them to keep the bride-gifts and her."

"Pretty insulting, Fairbolt," Dag observed. He didn't say who to. It would take a list, he decided.

"You could say you'd made a mistake."

"But I didn't."

Fairbolt grimaced. "I didn't think that notion would take. Had to try, though."

Dag's nod of understanding was reserved. Fairbolt spoke as if this was all about Fawn, and indeed, it had all begun with her. Dag wasn't so sure his farmer bride was all it was about now. The *all* part seemed to have grown much larger and more complex, for one. Since Raintree? Since West Blue? Since Glassforge? Or even before that, piling up unnoticed?

"Fairbolt . . ."

"Mm?"

"This was a bad year for the patrol. Did we have more emergences, all told, or just worse ones?"

Fairbolt counted silently on his fingers, then his eyebrows went up. "Actually, fewer than last year or the year before. But Glassforge and Raintree were so much worse, they put us behind, which makes it seem like more."

"Both bad outbreaks were in farmer country."

"Yes?"

"There *is* more farmer country now. More cleared land, and it's spreading. We're bound to see more emergences like those. And not just in Oleana. You're *from* Tripoint, Fairbolt, you know more about farmer artificers than anyone around here. The ones I watched this summer in Glassforge, they're more of that sort"—Dag raised his arm in its harness—"doing more things, more cleverly, better and better. You've heard all about what happened at Greenspring. What if it had been a big town like Tripoint, the way Glassforge is growing to be?"

Fairbolt went still, listening. Listening hard, Dag thought, but what he was thinking didn't show in his face.

Dag pushed on: "Malice takes a town like that, it doesn't just get slaves and ripped grounds, it gets know-how, tools, weapons, boats, forges and mills already built—power, as sure as any stolen groundsense. And the more such towns farmers build, and they will, the more that ill chance becomes a certainty."

Fairbolt's grim headshake did not deny this. "We can't push farmers back south to safety by force. We haven't got it to spare."

"Then they're here to stay, eh? I'm not suggesting force. But what if we had their help, that power, instead of feeding it to the malices?"

"We cannot let ourselves depend. We *must not* become lords again. That was our fathers' sin that near-slew the world."

"Isn't there any other way for Lakewalkers and farmers to

be with each other than as lords and servants, malices and slaves?"

"Yes. Live apart. Thus we avert lordship." Fairbolt made a slicing gesture.

Dag fell silent, his throat thick.

"So," said Fairbolt at length. "What *is* your plan for dealing with the camp council?"

Dag shook his head.

Fairbolt sat back in some exasperation, then continued, "It's like this. When I see a good tactician—and I know you are one—sit and wait, instead of moving, as his enemy advances on him, I figure there could be two possible reasons. Either he doesn't know what to do—or his enemy is coming into his hand exactly the way he wants. I've known you for a good long time . . . and looking at you right now, I still don't know which it is you're doing."

Dag looked away. "Maybe I don't either."

After another silence, Fairbolt sighed and rose. "Reasonable enough. I've done what I can. Take care of yourself, Dag. See you at council, I suppose."

"Likely." Dag touched his temple and watched Fairbolt trudge wearily away through the walnut grove.

The next day dawned clear, promising the best kind of dry heat. The lake was glassy. Dag lay up under the awning of Tent Bluefield and watched Fawn finish weaving hats, the result of her finding a batch of reeds of a texture she'd declared comparable to more farmerly straw. She took her scissors and, tongue caught fetchingly between her teeth, carefully trimmed the fringe of reeds sticking out around the brim to an even finger length. "There!" she said, holding it up. "That's yours."

He glanced at its mate lying beside her. "Why isn't it braided up all neat around the rim like the other?"

"Silly, that's a *girl's* hat. This is a *boy's* hat. So's you can tell the difference."

"Not to question your people, but that's not how *I* tell the difference between boys and girls."

This won a giggle, as he'd hoped. "It just *is*, for straw hats, all right? So now I can go out in the sun without my nose coming all over freckles."

"I think your nose looks cute with freckles." *Or without . . .*

"Well, I don't." She gave a decisive nod.

He leaned back, his eyes half-closing. His bone-deep exhaustion was creeping up on him, again. Maybe Hoharie had been right about that appalling recovery time after all. . . .

"That's it." Fawn jumped to her feet.

He opened his eyes to find her frowning down at him.

"We're going on a picnic," she declared roundly.

"What?"

"Just you wait and see. No, don't get up. It's a surprise, so don't look."

He watched anyway, as she bustled about putting a great deal of food and two stone jugs into a basket, bundled up a couple of blankets, then vanished around behind Cattagus and Mari's tent to emerge toting a paddle for the narrow boat. Bemused, he found himself herded down to the dock and instructed to get in and have a nice lie-down, padded and propped in the bottom of the boat facing her.

"You know how to steer this craft?" he inquired mildly, settling.

"Er . . ." She hesitated. "It looked pretty easy when you did it." And then, after a moment, "You'll tell me, won't you?"

"It's a deal, Spark."

The lesson took maybe ten minutes, once they'd pushed off from the dock. Their somewhat-wandering path evened out as she settled into her stroke, and then all he had to do was coax her to slow down and find the rhythm that would last. She found her way to that, too. He pushed back his boy's hat and smiled from under the fringe at her. Her face was made luminous even beneath the shadow of her own neat brim by the light reflecting off the water, all framed against the deep blue sky.

He felt amazingly content not to move. "If your folks could see us now," he remarked, "they really would believe all those tales about the idleness of Lakewalker men."

He'd almost forgotten the blinding charm of her dimple when she smirked. She kept paddling.

They rounded Walnut Island, pausing for a glimpse of some of the stallions prancing elegantly in pasture, then glided up through the elderberry channels. Several boats were out gathering there today; Dag and Fawn mainly received startled stares in return for their waves, except from Razi and Utau, working again on Cattagus's behalf and indirectly their own. Cattagus fermented his wines in large stone crocks buried in the cool soil of the island's woods, which he had inherited from another man before him, and him from another; Dag had no idea how far back the tradition went, but he bet it matched plunkins. They stopped to chat briefly with the pair. A certain hilarity about Dag's hat only made him pull it on more firmly, and Fawn paddle onward, tossing her head but still dimpling.

At length, to no surprise but a deal of pleasure on Dag's part, they slipped into the clear sheltered waters of the lily marsh. He then had the amusement, carefully concealed under his useful hat fringe, of watching Fawn paddle around realizing that her planning had missed an element, namely, where to spread blankets when all the thick grassy hillocks like tiny private islands turned out to be growing from at least two inches of standing water. He listened to as much of her foiled muttering as he thought he would get away with, then surrendered to his better self and pointed out how they might have a nice picnic on board the boat, wedged for stability up into a willow-shaded wrack of old logs. Fawn took aim and, with only a slightly alarming scraping noise, brought them upright into this makeshift dock.

She sat in the bottom of the boat facing him, their legs interlaced, and shared food and wine till she'd succeeded in fulfilling several of Hoharie's recommendations at once by driving him into a dozy nap. He woke at length more overheated than even farmer hats and the flickering yellow-green willow shade could contend with, and hoisted himself up to strip off his shirt and arm harness.

Fawn opened one eye from her own replete slump, then sat up in some alarm as he lifted his hips to slip off his trousers. "I don't think we can do *that* in a narrow boat!"

"Actually, you can," he assured her absently, "but I'm not attempting it now. I'm going into the water to cool off."

"Aren't you supposed to get cramps if you swim too soon after a heavy meal?"

"I'm not going swimming. I'm going floating. I may not move any muscles at all."

He selected a dry log about three feet long from the top of the wrack, wriggled it loose, and slipped into the water after it. The surface of the water was as warm as a bath, but his legs found the chill they sought farther down, flowing over his skin like silk. He hung his arms over his makeshift float, propped his chin in the middle, kicked up some billowing coolness, and relaxed utterly.

In a little while, to his—alas, still purely aesthetic—pleasure, Fawn yanked her shift over her flushed face, unwedged a log of her own, and splashed in after him. He floated on blissfully while she ottered around him with more youthful vigor, daring to wet her hair, then her face, then duck under altogether.

"Hey!" she said in a tone of discovery, partway through this proceeding. "I can't sink!"

"Now you know," he crooned.

She splashed him, got no rise, then eventually settled down beside him. He opened his eyes just far enough to enjoy the sight of her pale bare body, seemingly made liquid by the water-waver, caressed by the long, fringed water weeds as she idly kicked and turned. He looked down meditatively at the yellow willow leaves floating past his nose, harbinger of more soon to come. "The light is changing. And the sounds in the air. I always notice it, when the summer passes its peak and starts down, and the cicadas come on. Makes me . . . not sad, exactly. There should be a word." As though time was sliding away, and not even his ghost hand could catch it.

"Noisy things, cicadas," Fawn murmured, chinned on her own log. "I heard 'em just starting up when I was riding to Raintree."

They were both quiet for a very long time, listening to the chaining counterpoint of bug songs. The brown wedge of a muskrat's head trailed a widening vee across the limpid water, then vanished with a plop as the shy animal sensed their regard. The blue heron floated in, but then just stood folded as though sleeping on one leg. The green-headed ducks, drowsing in the shade across the marsh, didn't move either. The clear light lay breathing like a live thing.

"This place is like the opposite of blight," murmured Fawn after a while. "Thick, dense . . . if you opened up, would its ground just flow in and replenish you?"

"I opened up two hours ago. And yes, I think it may," he sighed.

"That explains something about places like this, then," she muttered in satisfaction.

A much longer time later, they regretfully pulled their wrinkled selves up onto the wrack and back into the boat, dressed, and pushed back to start for home. The sun was sliding behind the western trees as they crossed the wide part of the lake, and had turned into an orange glint by the time they climbed the bank to Tent Bluefield. Dag slept that night better than he had for weeks.

18

Fawn woke late the next morning, she judged by the bright lines of light leaking around the edges of their easterly tent flaps. The air inside was still cool from the night, but would grow hot and stuffy soon. Wrapped around her, Dag sighed and stirred, then hugged her in tighter. Something firm nudged the back of her thigh, and she realized with a slow smirk that it wasn't his hand. *I thought that picnic would be good for him.*

He made a purring noise into her hair, indicating the same satisfying realization, and she wriggled around to turn her face to his. His eyes gleamed from under his half-closed eyelids, and she sank into his sleepy smile as if it were a pillow. He kissed her temple and lips, and bent his head to nuzzle her neck. She let her hand begin to roam and stroke, giving and taking free pleasure from his warm skin for the first time since he'd been called out to Raintree. He pulled her closer still, seeming to revel in her softness pressing tight to him, skin to skin for the length of her body. This needed no words now, no instruction. No questions.

A hand slapped loudly three times against the leather of the tent flap, and a raspy female voice called, "Dag Redwing Hickory?"

Dag's body stiffened, and he swore under his breath. He held Fawn's face close to his chest as if to muffle her, and didn't answer.

The slaps were repeated. "Dag Redwing Hickory! Come on, I know you're in there."

A frustrated hiss leaked between his teeth. All his stiffening, alas, slackened. "No one in here by that name," he called back gruffly.

The voice outside grew exasperated. "Dag, don't fool with me, I'm not in the mood. I dislike this as much as you do, I daresay."

"Not possible," he muttered, but sighed and sat up. He ran his hand through his sleep-bent hair, rolled over, and groped for his short trousers.

"What is it?" Fawn asked apprehensively.

"Dowie Grayheron. She's the alternate for Two Bridge Island on camp council this season."

"Is it the summons?"

"Likely."

Fawn scrambled into her shift and trailed after Dag as he shoved through their tent flap and stood squinting in the bright sun.

An older woman, with streaked hair like Omba's braided up around her head, stood drumming her fingers on her thigh. She eyed Dag's bed-rumpled look in bemusement, Fawn more curiously. "The camp council hearing for you is at noon," she announced.

Dag started. "Today? Short notice!"

"I came around twice yesterday, but you were out. And I know Fairbolt warned you, so don't pretend this is a surprise. Here, let me get through this." She spread her legs a trifle, pulled back her shoulders, and recited, "Dag Redwing Hickory, I summon you to hear and speak to grave complaints brought before the Hickory Lake Camp Summer Council by Dar Redwing Hickory, on behalf of Tent Redwing, noon today in Council Grove. Do you hear and understand?"

"Yes," Dag growled.

"*Thank* you," she said. "That's done."

"But I'm not Dag Redwing," Dag put in. "That fellow no longer exists."

"Save it for the grove. That's where the argumentation

belongs." She hesitated, glancing briefly at Fawn and back to Dag. "I will point out, you've been summoned but your child-bride has not. There's no place for a farmer in our councils."

Dag's jaw set. "Is she explicitly excluded? Because if she has been, we have a sticking point before we start."

"No," Dowie admitted reluctantly. "But take it from me, she won't help your cause, Dag. Anyone who believed before that you've let your crotch do your thinking won't be persuaded otherwise by seeing her."

"Thank you," said Dag in a voice of honeyed acid. "I think my wife is pretty, too."

Dowie just shook her head. "I'm going to be so glad when this day is over." Her sandals slapped against her heels as she turned and strode off.

"There's a woman sure knows how to blight a mood," Dag murmured, his jaw unclenching.

Fawn crept to Dag's side; his arm went around her shoulders. She swallowed, and asked, "Is she any relation to Obio Grayheron?"

"He'd be her cousin by marriage. She's head of Tent Grayheron on this island."

"And she has a vote on the council? That's . . . not too encouraging."

"Actually, she's one I count as friendly. I patrolled for a year or so with her back when I was a young man, before I left to exchange and she quit to start her family."

If that was friendly, Fawn wondered what hostile was going to be like. Well, she'd soon find out. Was this all as sudden as it seemed? Maybe not. The camp council question had been a silence in the center of things that Dag had been skirting since they'd returned from Raintree, and she'd let him lead her in that circuit. True, he'd plainly been too ill to be troubled with it those first few days. But after?

He doesn't know what he wants to do, she realized, cold knotting in her belly. *Even now, he does not know.* Because

what he wanted was impossible, and always had been, and so
was the alternative? What was a man supposed to do then?

They dressed, washed up, ate. Dag did not return to cracking nuts, nor Fawn to spinning. He did get up and walk rest-
lessly around the campsite or into the walnut grove, wherever
he might temporarily avoid the other residents moving about
their own early chores. When the dock cleared out from the
morning swimmers, he went down and sat on it for a time,
knees bent under his chin, staring down into the water. Fawn
wondered if he was playing at that old child's amusement
he'd showed her, of persuading the inedible little sunfish that
clustered in the dock's shade to rise up and swim about in
simple patterns. The sun crept.

As the shadows narrowed, Dag came up under their
awning and sat beside her on his log seat. He propped his
right elbow on his knee, neck bent, staring down at his
sandals. At length he looked up toward the lake, face far
away—Fawn couldn't tell if he was trying to memorize the
view or not seeing it at all. She thought of their visits to the
lily marsh. *This place nourishes him.* Would he starve in his
spirit, exiled? A man might die without a mark on him, from
having his ground ripped in half.

She took a breath, sat straight. Began, "Beloved."

His face turned sideways to her in a fleeting smile. He
looked tired.

"What are you going to do?"

"I don't know." He seemed for an instant if he wanted to
amend that bluntness in some reassuring fashion, but then
just let it stand.

She angled her face away. "I wasn't going to tell you this
story, but now I think I will. When you were first gone to
Raintree, I knitted up another pair of socks like those you'd
been so pleased with, and took them to your mother for a
present. A peace offering, like."

"Didn't work." It wasn't a guess, nor a chiding; more of a
commiseration.

Fawn nodded. "She said—well, we said several things to each other that don't matter now. But one thing she said sticks. She said, once a patroller sees a malice, he or she doesn't ever put another thing—or person—ahead of patrolling."

"I do wonder sometimes how she was betrayed, and who the patroller was. My father, I suspect."

"Did sound like," Fawn conceded. "But not with another woman, I don't guess."

"Me, either. Something Aunt Mari once let slip—Dar and I once may have had a sister who died as an infant in some tragic way. He says he doesn't remember any such thing, so she would have had to be either before or within a few years after he was born. If so, she was buried in a deep, deep silence, because Father never mentioned her, either."

"Huh." Fawn considered this. "Could be . . . Well." She bit her lip. "I'm no patroller, but I *have* seen a malice, and if there's anything your mama was right about, it's that. She said if you didn't love me enough, you'd choose the patrol." She held up a hand to stem his beginning protest. "And that if you loved me beyond all sense—you'd choose the patrol. Because you couldn't protect me for real and true any other way."

He subsided, silenced. She raised her face to meet his beautiful eyes square, and went on, "So I just want you to know, if you have to choose the patrol—I won't die of it. Nor be worse off for having known and loved you for a space. I'll still be richer going down the road than when you met me, by far, if only for the horse and the gear and the knowing. I never knew there was as much knowing as this to be had in the whole world. Maybe, looking back, I'll remember this summer as a dream of wonders . . . even the nightmare parts. If I didn't get to keep you for always, *leastways* I had you for a time. Which ought to be magic enough for any farmer girl."

He listened gravely, not attempting, after his first protest, to interrupt. Trying to sort it out, maybe, for he said, "Are you saying you're too tired to keep up this struggle any-more?"

She eyed him. "No, that's you, I think."

He gave a little self-derisive snort. "Could be."

"Keep it straight. I love you, and I'll walk with you down any path you choose, but . . . this one isn't my choice to make. It's yours."

"True. And wise." He sighed. "I thought we both chose in that scary little parlor back in West Blue. And yet your choice will be honored or betrayed by mine in turn. They don't come separately."

"No. They don't. But they do come in order. And West Blue, well—that was before either you or I saw Greenspring. That town could've been West Blue, those people me and mine. I watched your lips move, counting down that line of dead . . . To keep you, there's a lot of things I'd fight tooth and toenail. Your kin, my kin, another woman, sickness, farmer stupidity, you name it. Can't fight Greenspring. *Won't.*"

He blinked rapidly, and for a moment the gold in his eyes looked molten. He swiped the shiny water tracks from his cheekbones with the back of his hand, leaned forward, and kissed her on the forehead, that terrifying kiss of blessing again. "Thank you," he whispered. "You have no idea how that helps."

She nodded shortly, swallowing down the hot lump in her own throat.

They went into their tent to change, him out of his short trousers and sandals, her out of her somewhat grubby shift. When, on her knees sorting through his trunk, she tried to hand him up his cleanest shirt, he surprised her by saying, "No—my *best* shirt. The good one your Aunt Nattie wove."

He hadn't worn his wedding shirt since their wedding. Wondering, she shook it out, its folds wrapped in other clothes to keep it from creasing—her green cotton dress, as it happened.

"Oh, yes, wear that one," he said, looking over his shoulder. "It's so pretty on you."

"I don't know, Dag. It's awfully farmer-girl. Shouldn't I dress more Lakewalker for this?"

He smiled crookedly down at her. "No."

It was disquieting, in this context, to be all gussied up in their wedding-day clothes again. She adjusted the hang of the cord on her left wrist, and the gold beads knocked cool against her skin. Were they to be unmarried in this new noon hour, as if tracing back over some exact path after they had gotten lost? Maybe they *had* gone astray, somewhere along the way. But fingering the links of events back one by one in her memory, she couldn't see where.

Dag had picked up his hickory stick, so she guessed they were in for a longish walk to this grove, since he'd stopped using it around the campsite a few days back. She brushed her skirts straight, slipped her shoes on, and followed him out of the tent.

Dag realized he'd walked for a mile without seeing a single thing that had passed his eyes, and it wasn't because the route was so familiar. His mind seemed to have come to some still place, but he wasn't sure if it was poised or simply numb. They were passing patroller headquarters when Fawn, uncharacteristically silent till then, asked her first question: "Where is this council grove, anyhow?"

He glanced down at her. The rosy flush from their walk in the noon warmth kept her from being pale, but her face was set. "Not much farther. Just past Hoharie's medicine tent."

She nodded. "Will there be very many people there? Is it like a town council?"

"I don't know town councils. There are nearly eight thousand folks around Hickory Lake; the whole point of having a camp council is so they don't have to all show up for these arguments. Anyone can come listen who's interested, though. It depends on how many people or families or tents are involved in a dispute. It's only Tent Redwing—and Tent Bluefield—today. There'll be Dar and Mama, but not too many friends of theirs, because they wouldn't care to have them watch this. My friends are mostly out on patrol this season. So I don't expect a crowd." He hesitated, swinging his staff along, then shrugged his left shoulder. "Depends on how they take our marriage cords. *That* affects most everyone, and could grow much wider."

"How long will it take?"

"At the start of a session, the council leader lights a session candle. Session lasts as long as it takes to burn down, which is about three hours. They say of a dispute that it's a one-candle or two-candle or ten-candle argument. They can spread over several days, see." He added after a few more paces, "But this one won't." *Not if I can help it.*

"How do you know?" she asked, but then it was time to turn off into the grove.

Grove was a misnomer; it was more of a clearing, a wide circular space at the edge of the woods weeded of poison ivy and other noxious plant life and bordered by huge, flowering bushes people had planted over the years—elderberry, forsythia, lilac—some so old their trunks were thick as trees. Upended log seats were scattered about on grass that a couple of placid sheep were at work nibbling short. To one side rose an open frame nearly the size of patrol headquarters under a shingled roof, for bad weather, but today a small circle of seats was set up in the shade at the clearing's edge. A few more folks were walking in as Dag and Fawn arrived, so apparently they were not late.

Fairbolt Crow, talking head down with Mari, arrived last. They split off from each other, Fairbolt taking the remaining unoccupied log seat at the end of a close-set row of seven backed up to some venerable elderberry bushes, branches hanging heavy with fruit. Mari strode over to the gaggle of patrollers seated to Dag's right. Dag was not surprised to see Saun, Razi, and Utau already there; Saun jumped to his feet and rolled up a log for her. He was a little more surprised to see Dirla—had she paddled all the way over from Beaver Sigh for this?—and Griff from Obio's patrol.

Clustered to the left of the councilor's row were only Dar, Cumbia, and Omba, the latter plainly not too happy to be there. His mother looked up from a bit of cord she was working in her lap for habit or comfort, shot Dag one glance of grim triumph, which he scarcely knew how to interpret— *See what you made me do?* maybe—then looked away. The *looked away* part he had no trouble understanding, since he did the same, like not watching a medicine maker rummage in one's wound. Dar merely appeared as if he had a stomachache, and blamed Dag for it, hardly unusual for Dar.

One log seat waited directly across from the councilors. Utau muttered something to Razi, who hurried to collect another from nearby and set it beside the first. Not ten feet of open space was left in the middle. No one was going to have to bellow . . . at least, not merely to be heard.

Fawn, looking every bit as wary as a young deer, stopped Dag just out of earshot by clutching his arm; he bent his head to her urgent whisper, "Quick! Who are all those new people?"

Fairbolt was seated, perhaps not accidentally, closest to the patrollers, and Dowie Grayheron beside him. Dag whispered back, "Left from Fairbolt and Dowie is Pakona Pike. She's council leader this season. Head of Tent Pike." A woman of ninety or so, as straight-backed as Cumbia and one of her closer friends—Dag did not expect benign neutrality from her, but he didn't say it to Fawn.

"Next to her are Laski Beaver and Rigni Hawk, councilor and alternate from Beaver Sigh." Laski, a woman in her eighties, was head of Tent Beaver on Beaver Sigh, and a leather maker—it was her sister who made the coats that turned arrows. No one would ever have pulled *her* from her making for council duty. Rigni, closer to Dag's age, came from a tent of makers specializing in boats and buildings, though she herself was just emerging from raising a brood of children. She was also one of Dirla's aunts; she might have heard some good of Dag and Fawn.

"Next down from them, Tioca Cattail and her alternate Ogit Muskrat, from Heron Island. I don't know them all that well." Only that Tioca was a medicine maker, and since the recent death of her mother head of Tent Cattail on Heron. Ogit was a retired patroller of about Cumbia's age, curmudgeonly as Cattagus but without the charm; of no special making skills, he liked being on council, Dag had heard. While he was not close friends with Cumbia, the two had certainly known each other for decades. Despite Ogit's patrol connections Dag did not hold much hope for an ally in him.

Fawn blinked and nodded, and Dag wondered if she would remember all this and keep it straight. In any case, she now let him lead her forward. He seated her on his right, to the patroller side of things, and settled himself, laying his hickory staff at his feet and sitting up with a polite nod to the councilors across from him.

On a shorter sawed-off log in front of Pakona sat a beeswax candle. She nodded back grimly, lit the wick, and lowered a square parchment windbreak around it, lanternlike. From beside it she picked up a peeled wooden rod, the speaker's stick, and tapped it three times against the makeshift table. Everyone fell silent and regarded her attentively.

"There's been a deal of talk and gossip about this," she began, "so I don't think anyone here needs more explaining-to. The complaint in the matter comes from Tent Redwing against its member Dag Redwing. Who's speaking for Tent Redwing?"

Dag stirred at his naming, but voiced no protest. *Let that one go for now. You'll find your chance.*

"I do," said Dar, holding up one hand; behind him, Cumbia nodded. Cumbia, as head of Tent Redwing, was more than capable of speaking for herself and everyone else, and Dag wondered at this trade-off. An extension of Dag's shunning? Didn't trust herself to keep her voice and argument steady? She looked like old iron, today. But mostly, she looked old.

"Pass this down to Dar, then," said Pakona. The stick went from hand to hand. "Speak your tent's complaint, Dar."

He took the stick, inhaled, cast Dag a level stare, and began. "It won't take long. As we all know, Dag returned late from a patrol this summer with a farmer paramour in tow that he named his wife, on the basis of a pair of wedding cords that no one had witnessed them make. We say that the cords are counterfeit, produced by trickery. Dag is in simple violation of the long-standing rule against bringing such . . . self-indulgences within the bounds of camp. Tent Redwing requests the camp and the patrol enforce the usual penalties, returning the girl to her people by whatever means required and fining Dag Redwing for his transgression."

Dag, rigid with surprise, exhaled carefully. How *interestingly* clever of Dar—yes, this had to be Dar's idea. He had entirely shifted his argument from the one threatened before Dag had departed for Raintree, of forced string-cutting or banishment. A glance at Fairbolt's rising eyebrows told Dag the camp captain, too, had been taken by surprise; he cast Dag an apologetic glance. Dag wasn't sure how long ago Dar had rethought his attack, but he had been shrewd enough to keep it from Fairbolt.

Dag opened his ground just enough to catch the councilors' sevenfold flicker of ground examination upon him and Fawn. Tioca Cattail tilted her head, and said, "Pardon, but they appear to be perfectly usual cords to me. Can't that girl shut down her—no, I suppose not. How do you think they are false?"

"They were falsified in the making," said Dar. "The exchange of grounds in the cords marks a true marriage, yes, but the making also acts—normally—as a barrier against anyone not bearing Lakewalker bloodlines from contaminating our kinships. It's not a great making, true. It's more like the lowest boundary. We tend to think *everyone can do it*, but that is itself the sign of the value of this custom in the past.

"I say the farmer girl did *not* make her own cord, but that Dag made it for her, with a trick he stole from my knife-making techniques, of using blood to lead live ground into an object. It represents nothing but cunning."

"How do you know this, Dar?" asked Fairbolt, frowning.

Dar said, a trifle reluctantly, "Dag told me himself."

"That's not what I said!" Dag said sharply.

Pakona held up a quelling hand. "Wait for the stick, Dag."

"Hold on," said Rigni Hawk, her nose wrinkling. "We're taking hearsay testimony on a matter when we have two eye-witnesses sitting right in the circle?"

"*Thank* you, Rigni," huffed Fairbolt in relief. "Quite right. Pakona, I think the stick should go to Dag for this tale."

"He has reason to lie," said Dar, looking sullen.

"That'll be for us to sort out," said Rigni firmly.

Pakona waved, and Dar reluctantly handed the stick around via Omba to Dag.

"So how did you make those cords?" asked Tioca in curiosity.

"Fawn and I made both cords together," Dag said tightly. "As *some* of you may remember, my right arm was broken at the time"—he made the old sling-gesture—"and the other is, well, as you see. Lakewalker blood or no, I was quite incapable of weaving any cord at all. Fawn wove the cord she now wears, I sat behind her on the bench with my arms along hers, and I cast my ground into it in the usual way. I don't see how anyone in his right mind can maintain *that* cord is invalid!"

Pakona waved to quell him again, but murmured, "So, go on. What about the other?"

"I admit, I attempted to aid her in catching up her ground

to weave into the second cord. We were having no luck at all when suddenly, all on her own, she cut open both her index fingers and wove while bleeding. Her ground welled right up and into the cord. I didn't help her any more than she helped me; less, I'd say."

"You instructed her to do this, then," said Tioca.

"No, she came up with it—"

"A few nights earlier, Dag and I had been talking about ground," Fawn put in breathlessly, "and he'd told me blood held ground after it left the body, because it was, like, alive separately from the person. Which I thought was a right disturbing idea, so I remembered it."

"You've not been given leave to speak here, girl," said Pakona sharply.

Fawn sat back and clapped her hand over her mouth in apology and alarm. Dag set his jaw, but added, "Fawn is exactly right. I recognized it as a technique that any of us here who have been bonded to sharing knives have likewise seen, but I didn't suggest it. Fawn thought of it herself."

"They used a *knife-making* technique on *wedding cords*," Dar said in a voice of outrage.

"Groundwork is groundwork, Hoharie says," Dag shot back. "I defy you to find a rule anywhere says you can't."

Tioca's eyes narrowed in considerable intrigue. "Medicine-making does have to be a little more . . . adaptable than some other kinds of making," she allowed. *Such as knife-work* hung implied. In a kindly sort of tone. Dag allowed himself an instant of enjoyment, watching Dar's teeth grit.

"One brother's word against t'other's," rumbled Ogit Muskrat from his end of the row. "One's a maker, one's not. Given the matter is making, I know which I'd trust."

Fawn, her lips pressed tight, cast a look up at Dag: *But you're a maker, too!* He gave her a small headshake. He was letting himself get distracted, wound up in side issues. This wasn't about their cords.

Very canny of Dar to try to make it so, though. It dropped

the whole smoldering issue of threatened banishment against a, what was that word Fairbolt had used, *notable patroller*, into the lake. Was that part Cumbia's doing—shaken by doubt of her son's allegiance despite her harsh words to Fawn? A reaction to whatever reputation Dag had won in Raintree? It certainly avoided complicated and possibly ferocious campwide debates over the council's right to force a string-cutting. If Dar could make it stick, it made everything simple and the problem go away, without anyone having to change anything.

And if Dar couldn't make it stick, there was still the other strategy to fall back on. But Dag doubted there was a person on council who wouldn't prefer the simpler version, Fairbolt not excepted.

"But if you rule the girl's cord is invalid," said Laski Beaver, scratching her head, "yet Dag's is not, does that mean he's married to her but she's not married to him? Makes no sense."

"Both are invalid," snapped Dar. Pakona, with admirable even-handedness, gave him the same quelling glower and headshake she'd given Dag, and he subsided.

Pakona turned back, and said, "Bring those things up here, Dag. We need a closer look." She added reluctantly, "The girl, too."

Dag had Fawn roll up the soft fine fabric of his left sleeve and dutifully rose to walk slowly down the row of councilors. Fawn followed, silent and scared. The touches, both with fingers and groundsense, were for the most part brief enough to be courteous, although a couple of the women's hands strayed curiously to the fabric of his shirt. Tioca, Dag was almost certain, detected his fading ground reinforcement being slowly absorbed in Fawn's left arm, but she said nothing about it to the others. Fairbolt, at the end of the line, waved them both away: "I've seen 'em. Repeatedly."

Dag and Fawn recrossed the circle and sat once more.

He watched her head bend as she straightened her skirts. In the green dress, she looked like some lone flower found in a woodland pool, in a spring-come-late. *Very late. She is not your prize, old patroller, not to be won nor earned. She's her own gift. Lilies always are.* His only-fingers traced her cord on his arm, and fell back, gripping his knee.

"There's our vote, then," said Pakona. "Is this unusual cord-making to be taken as valid, or not?"

"There's this," said Laski, slowly. "Once word gets out, I'd think others could repeat this trick. Acceptance would open the door to more of these mismatches."

"But they're good ground constructions," said Tioca. "As solid as, well, mine." She wriggled her left wrist and the cord circling it. "Are cords not to be proof of marriage anymore?"

"Maybe all cord-makings will have to be witnessed, hereafter," said Laski.

A general, unenthusiastic *hm* as everyone envisioned this.

"I suggest," said Pakona, "that we set the future actions of future folks beyond the scope of this council, or we'll still be arguing as the hundredth candle burns down. We only have to rule on this couple, this day. We've seen all there is to see, heard from the only ones who were there. Whether the idea for the thing was Dag's or the farmer girl's seems to me not to make a great deal of difference. The outcome was the same. A *no* vote will see it finished right now. A *yes* vote will . . . well, it won't. Dar, is this agreeable to Tent Redwing?"

Dar leaned back for a low-voiced exchange with their frowning mother. Cumbia had run out of cord to play with; her hands now kneaded the fabric of her shift along her thin thighs. A grimace, a short nod. Dar turned back. "Yes, we accept," he replied.

"Dag, you?"

"Yes . . . ," said Dag slowly. He glanced aside at Fawn, watching him in trusting bewilderment, and gave her a little nod of reassurance. "Go ahead."

Dar, expecting more argument, looked at him in sharp surprise. Dag remembered Fairbolt's word picture of the sitting tactician. Wise man, Fairbolt. He settled back to watch the candle burn down as Pakona started down the row.

"Ogit?"

"No! No farmer spouses!" Well, that was clear.

"Tioca?"

A slight hesitation. "Yes. I can't reconcile it with my maker's conscience to say that's not a good making."

Rigni, called upon, looked plaintively at Tioca and at last said, "Yes."

Laski, after a bit of a struggle, said, "No."

Pakona herself said, "No," without hesitation, and added, "if we let this in, it's going to be every kind of mess, and it will go on and on. Dowie?"

Dowie looked down the row and made a careful count on her fingers, and looked appalled. A *no* from her would finish the matter. A *yes* would create a tie and throw it onto Fairbolt. After a long, long pause, she cleared her throat, and said, "Yes?"

Fairbolt gave her palpable cowardice a slow, blistering, and ungrateful glare. Then he sighed, sat up, and stared around. A longer silence stretched.

You know they're good cords, Fairbolt, Dag thought. Dag watched the struggle in the captain's face between integrity and practicality, and admired how long it was taking the latter to triumph. In a way, Dag wished the integrity would pull ahead. It wasn't going to make a bit of difference in the end, after all, and Fairbolt would feel better about himself later.

"Fairbolt?" said Pakona, cautiously. "Camp captain always goes last to break the tie votes. It's a duty."

Fairbolt waved this away in a *Yeah, yeah, I know* gesture. He cleared his throat. "Dag? You got anything more to say?"

"A certain amount, yes. It will seem roundabout, but it will go to the center in the end. Makes no never mind to me whether it's before or after you have your say, though."

Fairbolt gave him a little nod. "Go ahead, then. You have the stick."

Pakona looked as though she wanted to override this, but thought better of annoying Fairbolt while his vote hung in the breeze. She crossed her arms and settled back. Dar and Cumbia were frowning in alarm, but Dag certainly had all their attention.

Dag's mind was heavy, his head ached, but his heart felt light, as if it were flying. *Might just be falling. We'll know when we hit the ground.* He set the speaking stick aside, reached down, gripped his hickory staff, and stood up. Full height.

"Excepting the patrollers who just came back from Raintree with me, how many folks here have heard the name of a farmer town called Greenspring?"

An array of blank looks from the center and left, although Dirla's aunt Rigni, after a glance at her patroller niece, hesitantly raised her hand for a moment. Dag returned her a nod.

"I'm not surprised there are so few. It was the town in Raintree where that last malice started up, unchecked. No one told me the name either, when I was called out to ride west. Now, partly that was due to the confusion that always goes with such a scramble, but you know—partly, it wasn't. No one knew, or said, because it didn't seem important to them.

"So how many here—not my patrollers—know the numbers of dead at Bonemarsh?"

Ogit Muskrat said gruffly, "We've all heard them. 'Bout fifty grown-ups and near twenty youngsters."

"Such a horror," sighed Tioca.

Dag nodded. "Nineteen. That's right." Fairbolt was watching him curiously. *No, I'm not taking your advice about boasting, Fairbolt. Maybe the reverse. Just wait.* "So who knows how many died at Greenspring?"

The patrollers to his right looked tight-lipped, holding back the answer. The majority of the councilors just looked baffled. After a stretch, Pakona finally said, "Lots, I imagine. What has this to do with your counterfeit wedding cords, Dag?"

He let that *counterfeit* slide unchallenged, too. "I said it was roundabout. Of a thousand townsfolk—roughly half the population of Bonemarsh—Greenspring lost about three hundred grown-ups and *all*—or nearly all—of their youngsters. I counted not less than one hundred sixty-two such bodies at the Greenspring burying field, and I know there were the bones of at least three more at the Bonemarsh mudmen feast we cleaned up after. Didn't mention those three to the townsmen doing the burying. It wouldn't have helped, at the time."

He glanced down at Fawn, glancing up at him, and knew they were both wondering if some of those scattered bones might have been the missing Sassy. Dag hoped not. He shook his head at Fawn, to say, *no knowing*, and she nodded and hunkered on her seat.

"Does anyone but me see something terribly wrong with those two sets of numbers?"

The return stares held discomfort, more than a twinge of sympathy, even pity, but no enlightenment. Dag sighed and plowed on. "All right, try this.

"Bonemarsh died—people slain, animals slaughtered, that beautiful country blighted for a generation—*because we failed at Greenspring.* If the malice had been recognized and stopped there, it would never have marched as far as Bonemarsh.

"It wasn't lack of patrollers or patrolling that slew Greenspring. Raintree patrol is as stretched as anyone else's, but there would have been enough, if only. It was a lack of . . . something else. Talking. Knowing. Friendships, even. A whole lot of simple things that could have been different, that one man or another might have changed, but didn't."

"Are you blamin' the Raintree patrol?" burst out Mari, unable to contain herself any longer. "Because that isn't the way I saw it. Seems the farmers were told not to settle there, but they didn't *listen*." Pakona made her hand-wave again, though not with any great conviction.

"I'm not blaming either side more than the other," said Dag, "and *I don't know the answers.* And I know I don't know. And it's stopped me, right cold.

"But you see—once upon a time, I didn't know dirt about patrolling, either. And half of what I thought I did know was wrong. There's a cure for ignorant young patrollers, though—we send 'em for a walk around the lake. Turns 'em into much smarter old patrollers, pretty reliably. Good system. It's worked for generations.

"So I'm thinkin'—maybe it's not enough anymore just to walk around the lake. Maybe we, or some of us, or *one* of us, needs to walk around the world."

The circle had grown very quiet.

Dag took a last breath. "And maybe that fellow is me. Sometimes, when you don't know how to start, you just have to start anyway, and find out movin' what you'd never learn sittin' still. I'm not going to argue and I'm not going to defend, because that's like asking me to tell you the ending before I've begun. There may not even be an ending. So Fairbolt, you can cast that last vote any way you please. But tomorrow, my wife and I are going to be down that road and gone. That's all." He gave a short, sharp nod, and sat back down.

19

Fawn let out her breath as Dag settled again beside her. Her heart was pounding as though she'd been running. She wrapped her arms around herself and rocked, looking around the circle of formidable Lakewalkers.

From the restive pack of patrollers to her right, she heard Utau mutter, "You all were asking me what it felt like to be ground-ripped? Now you know."

To which Mari returned a low-voiced, "Shut up, Utau. You don't have the stick."

Razi said under his breath, "No, I think we've just been hit with it." She motioned him, too, to shush.

Both Pakona and Fairbolt glanced aside, not friendly-like, and the patrollers subsided. Fairbolt sat back with his arms folded and glowered at his boots.

Dag murmured to Fawn, "Give this back to Pakona, will you, Spark? I won't be needing it again." He handed her the little length of wood they'd called the speaking stick.

She nodded, took it carefully, and trod across the circle to the scary old woman who looked even more like Cumbia's sister than Cumbia's sister Mari did. Maybe it was the closer age match. Or maybe they were near-related; these Lakewalkers all seemed to be. Neither of them wishing to get as close to the other as to pass it from hand to hand, Fawn laid the stick down next to the candle-lantern and skittered back to the shelter of Dag. Despite the prohibition on her speaking here, she swallowed, cupped her hand to his ear, and whispered, "Back at the firefly tree, I thought if I loved you any harder, I wouldn't be able to breathe. I was right." Gulping, she sat back down.

His crooked smile was so tender it pierced her like some sweet, sharp blade, saying better than words, *It's all right*. All wrong and all right, mixed together so confusingly. He hugged her once around the shoulders, fiercely, and they both looked up to watch Fairbolt, as did everyone else.

Fairbolt grimaced, scratched his head, sat up. Smiled a little Fairboltish smile that wasn't the sort of thing anybody would want to smile along with. And said, "I abstain."

A ripple of dismay ran along the line of his fellow councilors, punctuated at the end by an outraged cry from Dar, "*What?*"

"You can't do that!" said Dowie. She swiveled to Pakona, beside her. "Can he do that?" And less audibly, "Can I do that?" which made Fairbolt rub his forehead and sigh.

But he answered her, "I can and do, but not often. I generally prefer to see things settled and done. But if Dag is taking his farmer bride away regardless, I fail to see the emergency in this."

"What about Tent Redwing?" demanded Dar. "Where's our redress?"

Fairbolt tilted his head, appearing to be considering this. "Tent Redwing can do as any other disputant can in the event of a locked council decision. Bring the complaint again to the new council next season. It's only two months now to Bearsford Camp."

"But he'll be gone!" wailed Cumbia. It was a measure of her distress, Fawn thought, that she didn't even grab for the stick before this outburst. But for once, Pakona didn't wave her down; she was too busy gripping her own knees, maybe.

Fairbolt shook his head. "This marriage-cord redefinition is too big and complicated a thing for one man to decide, even in an emergency. It's a matter for a campwide meet, separate from the emotions of a particular case. Folks need time to talk and think about this, more careful-like."

Fawn could see that this argument was working on the camp council. And it was plain enough that to some, it didn't matter how Fawn went away, as long as she went. The mob of patrollers was looking downright mulish, though—if not as mulish as Dar.

Dar turned around for a rapid, low-voiced consultation with Cumbia. She shook her head, once in anger, once in something like despair, then finally shrugged.

Dar turned back. "Tent Redwing requests the speaking stick."

Pakona nodded, picked it up, and hesitated. "You can't ask for another vote on the same matter till Bearsford, you know."

"I know. This is . . . different but urgently related."

"That string-cutting idea, that's for a camp meet as well. And as I've told you before, I don't think you'll get it. Especially not if *she's*"—a head jerk toward Fawn—"already gone."

"It's neither," said Dar. She shrugged acceptance and passed the stick along to him.

Dar began, "Tent Redwing has no choice but to accept this delay." He glowered at Fairbolt. "But as is obvious to everyone, by Bearsford season Dag plans to be long gone. Our complaint, if sustained, involves a stiff fine owed to the camp. We ask that Dag Redwing's camp credit be held against that new hearing, lest the camp be left with no recourse if the fine is ordered. Also to assure he'll show up to face the council."

Pakona and Ogit looked instantly approving. Laski and Rigni looked considering, Tioca and Dowie dismayed. Fairbolt had hardly any expression at all.

Pakona said, in a tone of relief, "Well, that at least has plenty of precedent."

Dag was smiling in a weird dry way. Fawn dared to push up on one knee and whisper in his ear again, "What does that mean? Can they make you come back?"

"No," he murmured to her. "See, once in a while, some angry loser receives a council order to make restitution and tries to resist by drawing out his camp credit and hiding it. This stops up that hole, till the settlement is paid. But since Dar will never be able to bring the complaint to Bearsford Council—or anywhere else, since I won't be there to answer it—this would tie up my camp credit indefinitely. Stripping me like a banishment, without actually having to push through a banishment. May work, too, since no one likes to see the camp lose resources. Right clever, except that I was ready to walk away stark naked if I had to. I won't be rising to this bait, Spark."

"Brothers," she muttered, subsiding back to her hard seat.

His lips twitched. "Indeed."

Pakona said, "Tent Redwing's request seems to me reasonable, especially in light of what Dag Redwing said about his intention to leave camp."

"Leave?" said Ogit. "Is that what you call it? I'd call it plain desertion, wrapped up in fancy nonsense! And what are you going to do about *that*, Fairbolt?" He leaned forward to glare around the council at the camp captain on the other end.

"*That* will be a matter internal to the patrol," Fairbolt stated. And the iron finality in his voice was enough to daunt even Ogit, who sat back, puffing but not daring to say more.

Breaking his intent to speak no further, Dag gave Fairbolt a short nod. "I'll like to see you after this, sir. It's owed."

Fairbolt returned the nod. "At headquarters. It's on your way."

"Aye."

Pakona knocked her knuckles on the log candle table. "That's our vote, then. Should Dag Redwing's camp credit be held till the Bearsford council? *Yes* will hold it, *no* will release it." It was plain that she struggled not to add something like, *To be taken off and frittered away on farmer paramours,* but her leader's discipline won. Barely, Fawn sensed. "Ogit?"

"Yes." No surprise there. The string of three more yesses, variously firm or reluctant, were more of a disappointment; the vote was lost before it even came to Pakona's firm *Yes*. Dowie looked down the row, seemed to do some mental arithmetic, and murmured a safely useless, "No."

Fairbolt grimaced, and grumbled, "No," as well.

Pakona stated, "Tent Redwing's request is upheld. Camp council rules Dag Redwing's camp credit is held aside until the Bearsford rehearing."

A little silence fell, as it all sank in. Until broken by Saun, surging up to yell, "You blighted *thieves* . . . !" Razi and Griff both tackled him and wrestled him back into his seat. "After Raintree! After *Raintree!*" Mari turned and scowled at him, but seemingly could not force herself to actually *chide*. As she turned back, the look she shot at her nephew Dar would have burned bacon, Fawn thought.

Omba's jaw had been working for quite some time. Now she snatched the speaking stick out of her surprised husband's hand, waved it, and cried out, "*Make him take his horse!* Copperhead is a blighted menace. The beast has bitten three of my girls, kicked two, and torn more hide off his pasturemates than I ever want to sew up again. I don't care if Dag walks out bare to the skin, but I *demand* his horse go with him!" Which all sounded plenty irate, except that her eye away from Dar and toward Dag shivered in a wink.

"*There's* a mental picture for you, Spark," Dag said out of the corner of his mouth at her. "Me and Copperhead, bareback to bare-backside . . ."

She could have shaken him till his teeth rattled for making her almost laugh aloud in the midst of this mess. As it was, she had to clap her hand over her mouth and look down into her lap until she regained control. "Happy eyes!" she whispered back, and had the sweet revenge of watching him choke back a surprised guffaw.

Dar glowered at them both, furiously impotent against their private jokes. Which was also pretty tasty, amongst the ashes.

"Wherever did you come by that horse, anyhow?" Fawn asked under her breath.

Dag murmured back, "Lost a game of chance with a keelboat man at Silver Shoals, once."

"Lost. Ah. That explains it."

Pakona considered Dag, not in a friendly way. "That does bring up the question of where camp credit leaves off and personal effects begin." And if she was picturing Dag walking out naked, it wasn't with the same emotions Fawn did, by a long shot.

Fairbolt rumbled, "No, it doesn't, Pakona. Unless you want to start a revolt in the patrol."

Saun, still squirming in his seat with Utau's hand heavy on his shoulder, looked as if he was ready to begin an uprising right now. And if steam wasn't billowing from Dirla, Razi, and Griff, it was only because they weren't wet.

Pakona raised an eyebrow at Fairbolt. "Can't you keep your rowdy youngsters under control, Fairbolt?"

"Pakona, I'd be *leading* them."

Her mouth thinned in lack of appreciation of his humor, or whatever that was—black and sincere, anyhow. But she veered off, nonetheless. "Very well. Till the Bearsford rehearing, the . . . *former* patroller can take away his horse Copperhead, its gear, and whatever personal effects it can carry. The farmer girl can leave with whatever she came with; it's no business of ours."

"What about all those bride-gifts he sent off?" said Dar suddenly.

Dag stirred, his eyes narrowing dangerously.

Mari looked up at this one. "Dar, *don't even start.*" Fawn wasn't sure if that was her patrol leader voice or her aunt voice, or some alloy of the two, but Dar subsided, and even Pakona didn't reprimand her.

Pakona straightened her spine and looked around the circle. "Tent Redwing, do you have anything more to say before I close this session?"

Dar choked out through flat lips, "No, ma'am." The camp-credit ruling had left him looking bitterly satisfied, but Cumbia, behind him, was drawn and quiet.

"Dag Redwing?"

Dag shook his head in silence.

Pakona held out her hand, and the speaking stick was passed back to her. She tapped it three times on the log table, leaned forward, and blew out the session candle.

At the door to his pegboard chamber, Fairbolt excluded Dag's outraged escort of fellow patrollers and their increasingly imaginative and urgent offers to wreak vengeance on Dar. Dag was just as glad. Fairbolt gestured him and Fawn to seats, but Dag shook his head and simply stood, hanging wearily on his hickory stick. *Not fellow patrollers anymore, I suppose.* What was he now, if not Fawn's patroller? He hardly knew. Fawn's Dag, leastways. *Always.* She leaned up under his left arm, looking anxiously at Fairbolt, and Dag let some of his weight rest on her slim shoulders.

"I'm sorry about how that came out back there," said Fairbolt, jerking his head in the general direction of the council grove. "I didn't expect Dar to blindside me. Twice."

"I always said my family was impossible. I never said they were stupid," sighed Dag. "I thought it was a draw between the two of you, myself. I'd made up my mind to it when I walked into that circle that I was going to walk out banished for real, and if they didn't offer it, I was going to take it myself." He added, "You have my resignation, of course. I should have stopped in here before the session and not blind-sided you with that, too, but I wasn't just sure how things were going to play out. If you want to call it desertion, I won't argue."

Fairbolt leaned down and plucked Dag's peg from the painted square on the wall labeled *Sick List*. He straightened up and weighed it thoughtfully in his palm. "So what are you going to do out there, walking around farmer country? I just can't picture you plowing dirt."

"Leastways it would involve movin', though right now sitting looks pretty good. That mood'll pass, it always does. I wasn't joking when I said *I do not know*." He had once traveled great distances. For all he knew, the next great journey would be all in one place, but walked the long way, through time, a passage he could barely envision, let alone explain. "No plan I ever made has been of the least use to me, and sometimes—plans keep you from seeing other paths. I want to keep my eyes clear for a space. Find out if you really can teach an old patroller new tricks."

"You've learned quite a few lately, from what Hoharie says."

"Well . . . yes." Dag added, "Give my regrets and thanks to Hoharie, will you? She almost tempted me away from you. But . . . it would have been the wrong road. I don't know much right now, but I know that much."

"No lordship," said Fairbolt, watching him.

"No," Dag concurred. "I mean to find some other road, wide enough for everyone. Someone has to survey it. Could be the new way won't be mine to make, but mine to be given, out there. From someone smarter than me. If I keep my ground open, watch and listen hard enough."

Fairbolt said meditatively, "Not much point for a man to learn new things if he doesn't come back to teach 'em. Pass 'em on."

Dag shook his head. "Change needs to happen. But it

won't happen today, here, with these people. Camp council proved that."

Fairbolt held his hand out, palm down, in a judicious rocking gesture. "It wasn't unanimous."

"There's a hope," Dag conceded. "Even if it was mainly due to Dowie Grayheron having a spine of pure custard." Fairbolt barked a laugh, shaking his head in reluctant agreement.

Dag said, "This wasn't my first plan. I'd have stayed here with Spark if they'd have let me. Be getting myself ready for the next patrol even now."

"No, you'd still be on the sick list, I assure you," said Fairbolt. He glanced down. "How's the leg? You were favoring it, walking back, I noticed."

"It's coming along. It still twinges when I'm tired. I'm glad I'll be riding Copperhead instead of walking, bless Omba's wits. I'll miss that woman."

Fairbolt stared out the hooked-open window at the glimmer of the lake. "So . . . if you could have your first plan back—sorry, Fawn, not even what you call Lakewalker magic could make that happen now, but *if*—would you take it?"

It was a testing question, and a good one. Dag tilted his head in the silence, his eyelids lowering, rising; then said simply, "No." As Fawn looked solemnly up at him, he gave her a squeeze around the shoulders. "Go on and chuck my peg in the fireplace. I'm done with it."

Fairbolt gave him a short nod. "Well, if you ever change your mind—or if the world bucks you off again—you know where to find us. I'll still be here."

"You don't ever give up, do you?"

Fairbolt chuckled. "Massape wouldn't let me. Very dangerous woman, Massape. The day I met her, forty-one years gone, all my fine and fancy plans for my life fell into Hickory Lake and never came up again. Hang on to your dangerous woman too, Dag. They're rare, and not easy to come by."

Dag smiled. "I've noticed that."

Fairbolt tossed the peg in his palm once more, then, abruptly, held it out to Fawn. "Here. I think this is yours, now. Don't lose it."

Fawn glanced up at them both, her eyebrows climbing in surprise, then smiled and folded the peg in her firm little grip. "You bet I won't, sir."

Dag made plans to leave in the gray light of dawn, in part to get a start on a day that promised to turn cool and rainy later, but mostly to avoid any more farewells, or worse, folks who still wanted to argue with him. He and Fawn had packed their saddlebags the night before, and Dag had given away what wouldn't fit: his trunk to Sarri, his good ash spear to Razi, and his father's sword to Utau, because he sure wasn't passing it back to Dar. His winter gear in storage at Bearsford he supposed he must abandon with his camp credit. Tent Bluefield he left standing for Stores to struggle with, since they'd been so anxious for it.

Dag was surprised when Omba herself, and not one of her girls, appeared out of the mists hanging above the road leading Copperhead and Grace. She gave him a hug.

"Sneaking in a good-bye out of sight of the kin?" he inquired, hugging her back.

"Well, that, and, um . . . I have to offer an apology to Fawn."

Fawn, taking Grace's reins from her, said, "You never did me any harm that I know of, Omba. I'm glad to have met you."

Omba cleared her throat. "Not harm, exactly. More of an . . . accident." She was a bit flushed in the face, Dag was bemused to note, not at all like her usual dry briskness. "Fawn, I'm very sorry, but I'm afraid your horse is pregnant."

"What?" cried Fawn. She looked at Grace, who looked back with a mild and unrepentant eye, and snuffled her soft muzzle into Fawn's hand in search of treats. "Grace! You bad girl, what have you been up to?" She gave her reins a little shake, laughing and amazed.

"Omba," said Dag, leaning against Copperhead's shoulder and grinning despite himself, "who have you gone and let ravish my wife's mare?"

Omba sighed hugely. "Rig Crow's stallion Shadow got loose and swam over from Walnut about five nights ago. Had himself a fine old time before we caught up with him. You're not the only mares' owners I'm going to have to apologize to today, though you're the first in line. I'm not looking forward to it."

"Will they be angry?" asked Fawn. "Were they planning other mates? Was he not a good horse?"

"Oh, Shadow is a fine horse," Dag assured her. "You would not believe how many furs Rig asks for, and gets, as a stud fee for that snorty horse of his. I know. I paid through the nose last year to have him cover Swallow, for Darkling."

"And therefore," said Omba, pulling on her black-and-white braid, "everyone will *say* they are very upset, and carry on as convincingly as possible. While Rig tries to collect. It could go to the camp council."

"You'll forgive me, I trust, for wishing them all a long, tedious dispute, burning many candles," said Dag. "If Rig asks, my wife and I are just *furious* about it all." He vented an evil laugh that made even Fawn raise an eyebrow at him.

"I wasn't even going to mention Grace," Omba assured him. "I'll be having troubles enough over this."

Utau and Razi came out to help them saddle up, followed by Sarri, and Mari and Cattagus together. Dag mostly exchanged sober nods, except with his aunt Mari, whom he embraced; Fawn hugged everybody.

"Think you'll be back?" asked Utau gruffly. "For that Bearsford Council, maybe?"

"Not for that. For the rest, who can say? I've left home for good at least four times that I recall, as Mari can testify."

"I remember a spectacular one, 'bout eight years back," she allowed. "There was a lot of shouting. You managed to be gone for seventeen months."

"Maybe I'll get better at it with practice."

"Could be," she said. Then added, "But I sort of hope not."

And then it was time to mount up. Razi gave Dag a leg up and sprang away, Copperhead put in his usual tricks and was duly chastised, and Utau boosted Fawn onto Grace. On the road, Dag and Fawn both turned and gave silent waves, as silently returned. As the blurring forms left behind parted to their different tents, the mist swallowed them all.

Dag and Fawn didn't speak again till the horses had clopped over the long wooden span from the island. She watched him lean his hand on his cantle and stare over his shoulder.

She said quietly, "I didn't mean, when I fell in love with you, to burn your life to the ground."

He turned back, giving her a pensive smile. "I was dry, dry timber when you met me, Spark. It'll be well." He set his face ahead and didn't look around again.

He added after a while, "Though I'm sorry I lost all my camp credit. I really thought, when I promised your folks I would care for you, to have in hand whatever you'd need for your comfort, come this winter and on for a lot of winters more. All the plunkins in the Bearsford cold cellars won't do us much good now."

"As I understand it, your goods aren't lost, exactly. More like, held. Like my dowry."

His brows rose. "There's a way of looking at it I hadn't thought of."

"I don't know how we'd manage traveling anyhow, with a string of, what did you say—eight horses?"

He considered this picture. "I was thinking more of con-

verting it into Tripoint gold tridens or Silver Shoals silver
mussels. Their monies are good all up and down the Grace
and the Gray. But if all my camp credit for the past eighteen
years were converted into horses—average horses, not Cop-
perheads or Shadows . . . hm. Let me see." He did some
mental estimating, for the curiosity of it. "That would be
about forty horses, roughly. Way too many for us to trail in
a string, it's true."

"Forty horses!" said Fawn, sounding quite taken aback.
"You could buy a farm for the price of forty horses!"

"But I wouldn't know what to do with it once I had it."

"But *I* would—oh, never mind." She added, "I'm glad I
didn't know this yesterday. I'd have been a lot more upset."

"Offends your notions of economy, does it?"

"Well, yes! Or my notions of *something*."

He gave her a wink. "You're worth it at twice the price,
Spark. Trust me."

"Huh." But she settled again, thumping her heels gently
against Grace's wide-sprung sides to urge her to keep up,
looking meditative.

They pulled their horses to a halt at the place, a mile
from the bridge, where the road split in three. "So," he said.
"Which way?"

"Don't you know?"

"No. Well, not north. Not this late in the season." In the
meadows, the cicadas were growing noisier as the morning
warmed, but the first frosts would silence them soon enough.
"Whichever way we go, we'll need to travel in easy stages,
see, on account of Grace's delicate condition." He suspected
he could get a lot of use out of Grace's condition if he played
it right.

Not fooled a bit, Fawn looked narrowly at him, and
said, "Couldn't agree more." She swiveled her head. "But
still . . . which road?" Her eye was caught by something,
and she twisted in her saddle. "What's this?"

Dag followed her gaze, and his stomach knotted coldly

at the sight of Saun and Dirla, galloping madly from the
bridge and waving at them. *Please, please, not some other
malice outbreak . . . I don't want to have to do all this leaving over again.* But their flushed faces, when they pulled up
and sat panting on their fidgeting mounts, weren't that sort
of anxious.

"I was afraid we'd missed you," gasped Dirla.

"Kindly," said Dag, touching his temple. "But I thought
we'd all said good-bye yesterday?" And, while not enough . . .
it had been enough.

Saun, catching his breath, waved this away. "It's not that.
It's this." He stuck a hand in his vest and pulled out a leather
bag, which clinked. "A lot of folks from our company, and in
the patrol, weren't too pleased with how things went yesterday in the camp council. So Dirla and Griff and I took up a
little collection. It's nothing compared to what Dar stripped
you of, I know, but it's *something.*" He thrust out the bag
toward Dag, who let Copperhead shy away a step.

"I thank you kindly, Saun, but I can't take that."

"Not as many chipped in as I thought should," said Dirla,
looking irate. "But at least the blighted camp council has
nothing to do with this."

Dag was both touched and embarrassed. "Look, you children, I can't—"

"*Fairbolt* put in three gold tridens," Saun interrupted him.
"And told us not to tell Massape."

"And *Massape* put in ten silver mussels," Dirla added, "and
told us not to tell Fairbolt." She paused in reflection. "You do
wonder what they'll say if they catch up with each other."

"Are you telling?" Saun asked her, interested.

"Nope."

Well . . . the Crow clan was rich. Dag sighed, looking at
those earnest, eager faces. He could see he wasn't getting out
of this one. "I suppose the patrol will be wearing out some of
those horses I left behind."

"Likely," said Saun.

Dag smiled in defeat and held out his hand.

Saun passed the bag across, grinning. "I'll try and remember all you taught me. No more swordplay in the woods, right."

"That's a start," Dag agreed. "*Duck faster* is another good one, 'cept you learned that one all by yourself. It'll stick better that way, I do allow. Take care of each other, you two."

"The patrol looks after its own," said Dirla firmly.

Dag gave her a warm nod. "The patrol looks after everybody, Dirla."

Her return smirk was quite Spark-like. "Then you're still some kind of patroller. Aren't you. Take care—Captain."

They waved and turned away.

Dag waited till they'd stopped craning around and looking back, then hefted the bag and peeked in. "Huh. Not bad. Well, this gives us a direction."

"How so?" Fawn asked.

"South," he said definitely.

"I've been south," she objected. "All the way to Glassforge."

"Spark, south doesn't even start till you get to Silver Shoals. I'm thinkin' . . . this season, passage on a flatboat going down the river isn't too expensive. We could ride slow down as far as Silver Shoals, pick out a boat . . . load Grace and Copperhead in too. I could see a lot of farmer country *and* sit still at the same time. Very enticin', that notion. I've always wanted to do that. Follow fall all the way down to the sea, and show you the sea. Ride back easy, come spring— you can make spring last a long time, riding north at the right pace. Bet my ground will be healed by then. What do you think?"

Her mouth had fallen open at this sudden spate of what were to her, he guessed, quite fantastical visions. She shut it and swallowed. "When you say travel," she said, "you don't think small."

"Oh, that's just a jaunt, by old patroller standards," he assured her. He twisted in his saddle to tuck the leather purse away in his saddlebag, then frowned when his fingers, pushing through a fold of blanket cloth, encountered an unidentifiable lump. He traded off and pulled out the lump to hold up to the light, and gazed in some astonishment at a plunkin ear. "What's this? Did you pack this?" he asked Fawn.

She blushed. "Them. Yes. I thought you should have your food, wherever we end up."

"We don't eat the ears, love."

"*I* know that." She tossed her head. "They're for planting. Sarri told me the ears'll keep good for two or three years, dry. I snuck round last night after you fell asleep and filched some out of the feed bin on Mare Island. Not the best, maybe, but I picked out the nicest-looking that were there."

"What were you thinking, farmer girl?"

"I was thinking . . . we might have a pond, someday." And at his look, "Well, we might!"

He couldn't deny it. He threw back his head and laughed. "Smuggling plunkins! And horses! No, no, Spark, it's all clear to me now. The only future for us is going to be as road bandits!"

She grinned in exasperation and shook her head. "Just ride, Dag."

As they chirped their horses into a walk, a patrol of some two dozen wild geese flew overhead, calling hauntingly, and they both turned their faces upward to mark the beating wonder of those wings.

"A bit early," Fawn commented.

"Maybe they're out for a jaunt."

"Or lost."

"Not those fellows. It looks like a pointer to me, Spark. I say, let's follow 'em."

Stirrup to stirrup, they did.

Turn the page for a sample of

THE SHARING KNIFE, VOLUME THREE PASSAGE

the next part of the *New York Times* bestselling romantic fantasy

"[A] saga of daring deeds and unlikely romance . . . Unforgettable characters [and] a world filled with unique monsters and an original approach to magic."
Library Journal

Dag was riding up the lane thinking only of the chances of a Bluefield farm lunch, and his likelihood of needing a nap afterward, when the arrow hissed past his face.

Panic washing through him, he reached out his right arm and snatched his wife from her saddle. He fell left, dragging them both off and behind the shield of their horses, snapping his sputtering groundsense open wide—range still barely a hundred paces, *blight* it—torn between thoughts of Fawn, of the knife at his belt, of the unstrung bow at his back, of *how many, where*? All of it was blotted out in the lightning flash of pain as he landed with both their weights on his healing left leg. His cry of "Spark, get behind me!" transmuted to "Agh! Blight it!" as his leg folded under him. Fawn's mare bolted. His horse Copperhead shied and jerked at the reins still wrapped around the hook that served in place of Dag's left hand; only that, and Fawn's support under his arm as she found her feet, kept him upright.

"Dag!" Fawn yelped as his weight bent her.

Dag straightened, abandoning his twisting reach for his bow, as he at last identified the source of the attack—not with his groundsense, but with his eyes and ears. His brother-in-law Whit Bluefield came running across the yard below the old barn, waving a bow in the air and calling, "Oh, sorry! Sorry!"

Only then did Dag's eye take in the rag target tacked to a red oak tree on the other side of the lane. Well . . . he assumed it was a target, though the only arrow nearby was stuck in the bark about two feet below it. Other spent arrows lay loose on the ground well beyond. The one that had nearly clipped off his nose had plowed into the soil a good twenty paces downslope. Dag let out his pent breath in exasperation, then inhaled deeply, willing his hammering heart to slow.

"Whit, you ham-fisted fool!" cried Fawn, rising on tiptoe to peer over her restive horse-fort. "You nearly shot my husband!"

Whit arrived breathless, repeating, "Sorry! I was so surprised to see you, my hand slipped."

Fawn's mare Grace, who had skittered only a few steps before getting over her alarm at this unusual dismount, put her head down and began tearing at the grass clumps. Whit, familiar with Copperhead's unsociable character, made a wide circle around the horse to his sister's side. Dag let the reins unwrap from his hook and allowed Copperhead to go join Grace, which the chestnut gelding did after a few desultory bucks and cow-kicks, just to register his opinion of the proceedings. Dag sympathized.

"I wasn't aiming at you!" Whit declared anxiously.

"I'm right glad to hear that," drawled Dag. "I know I annoyed a few people around here when I married your sister, but I didn't think you were one of 'em." His lips compressed in a grimmer line. Whit might well have hit *Fawn*.

Whit flushed. A head shorter than Dag, he was still a head taller than Fawn, whom, after an awkward hesitation, he now embraced. Fawn grimaced, but hugged him back. Both Bluefield heads were crowned with loosely curling black hair, both faces fair-skinned, but while Fawn was nicely rounded, with a captivating sometimes-dimple when she smirked, Whit was skinny and angular, his hands and feet a trifle too big for his body. Still growing into himself even past age twenty, as the length of wrist sticking from the sleeve of his homespun shirt testified. Or perhaps, with no younger brother to hand them down to, he was just condemned to wear out his older clothes.

Dag took a step forward, then hissed, hook-hand clapping to his buckling left thigh. He straightened again with an effort. "Maybe I want my stick after all, Spark."

"Of course," said Fawn, and darted across the lane to retrieve the hickory staff from under Copperhead's saddle flap.

"Are you all right? I know I didn't hit you," Whit protested. His mouth bent down. "I don't hit anything, much."

Dag smiled tightly. "I'm fine. Don't worry about it."

"He is not fine," Fawn amended sternly, returning with the stick. "He got knocked around something fearsome last month when his company rode to put down that awful malice over in Raintree. He hasn't nearly healed up yet."

"Oh, was that your folks, Dag? Was it really a blight bogle—malice," Whit corrected himself to the Lakewalker term, with a duck of his head at Dag. "We heard some pretty wild rumors about a ruckus up by Farmer's Flats—"

Fawn overrode this in concern. "That scar didn't break open when you landed so hard, did it, Dag?"

Dag glanced down at the tan fabric of his riding trousers. No blood leaked through, and the flashes of pain were fading out. "No." He took the stick and leaned on it gratefully. "It'll be fine," he added to allay Whit's wide-eyed look. He squinted in new curiosity at the bow still clutched in Whit's left hand. "What's this? I didn't think you were an archer."

Whit shrugged. "I'm not, yet. But you said you would teach me when—if—you came back. So I was getting ready, getting in some practice and all. Just in case." He held out his bow as if in evidence.

Dag blinked. He had quite forgotten that casual comment from his first visit to West Blue, and was astonished that the boy had apparently taken it so to heart. Dag stared closely, but not a trace of Whit's usual annoying foolery appeared in his face. *Huh. Guess I made more of an impression on him than I'd thought.*

Whit shook off his embarrassment over his straying shaft, and asked cheerfully, "So, why are you two back so soon? Is your patrol nearby? They could all come up too, you know. Papa wouldn't mind. Or are you on a mission for your Lakewalkers, like that courier fellow who brought your letters and the horses and presents?"

"My bride-gifts made it? Oh, good," said Dag.

"Yep, they sure did. Surprised us all. Mama wanted to write a letter back to you, but the courier had gone off already, and we didn't know how to get in touch with your people to send it on."

"Ah," said Dag. *There's a problem.* There was *the* problem, or one aspect of it: farmers and Lakewalkers who couldn't talk to each other. *Like now?* For all his mental rehearsal, Dag found it suddenly difficult to spit out the tale of his exile, just off the cuff like this.

Fortunately, Fawn filled in. "We're just visitin'. Dag's sort of off-duty for a time, till his hurts heal up."

True in a sense—well, no, not really. But there would be time to explain further—maybe when everyone was together, so he wouldn't have to repeat it all over and over, a prospect that made him wince even more than the vision of explaining it to a crowd.

They strolled to recapture the horses, and Whit waved toward the old barn. "The stalls you used before are empty. You still got that man-eating red nag, I see." He skirted Copperhead to gather up Grace's reins; from the way the bay mare resisted his tugging to snatch a few last mouthfuls of grass, one would take her for starved, clearly not the case.

"Yep," said Dag, stooping with a grunt to scoop up the gelding's reins in turn. "I still haven't met anyone I disliked enough to give him to."

"And he's been ridin' Copperhead for eight straight years. It's a wonder, that." Fawn dimpled. "Admit it, Dag, you like that dreadful horse." She went on to her brother, in a tone of bright diversion, "So, what's been happening here at West Blue since I left?"

"Well, Fletch and Clover was married a good six weeks ago. Mama was sorry you two couldn't be here for the wedding." Whit cast a nod at the solid stone farmhouse, sited on the ridge overlooking the wooded valley of the rocky river. The newlyweds' addition of two rooms off the near end, still in progress when Dag had last seen it, seemed entirely complete, with glass windows, a wood-shingle roof, and even some early autumn flowers planted around the foundation, softening the fresh scars in the soil. "Clover's all moved in, now. Ha! It didn't take *her* long to shift the twins. They lit out about twenty miles west to break land with a friend of theirs, only last week. You just missed 'em."

Dag couldn't help reflecting that of all his Bluefield in-laws, the inimical twins Reed and Rush were probably the ones he'd miss the least; judging from the sudden smile on Fawn's face, she shared the sentiment. He said affably, "I know they'd been talking about it for a long time."

"Yeah, Papa and Mama wasn't too pleased that they picked just before harvest to finally take themselves off, but everyone was so glad of it they didn't hardly complain. Fletch came in on Clover's side whenever they clashed, naturally, which was pretty much every day, and they didn't take any better to him telling them what to do than to her. So it's a lot more peaceable in the house, now." He added after a reflective moment, "Dull, really."

Whit continued an amiable account of the small doings of various cousins, uncles, and aunts as they unsaddled the horses and turned them into the box stalls in the cool old barn. With a glance at Dag's stick, Whit actually helped them put up their gear without being asked, and hoisted Dag's saddlebags over his shoulder. Feeling that such an apologetic impulse should be encouraged, Dag let him take them. As they made their way back out to climb the hill to the house, Fawn refused to give up her own bags to Dag, telling him to *mind himself*, and thumped along under the weight with her usual air of determination. Despite their late difficulties she seemed far less troubled than at her previous homecoming, judging from the smile she cast over her shoulder at him, and he couldn't help smiling back. *Yeah, we'll get through this somehow, Spark. Together.*